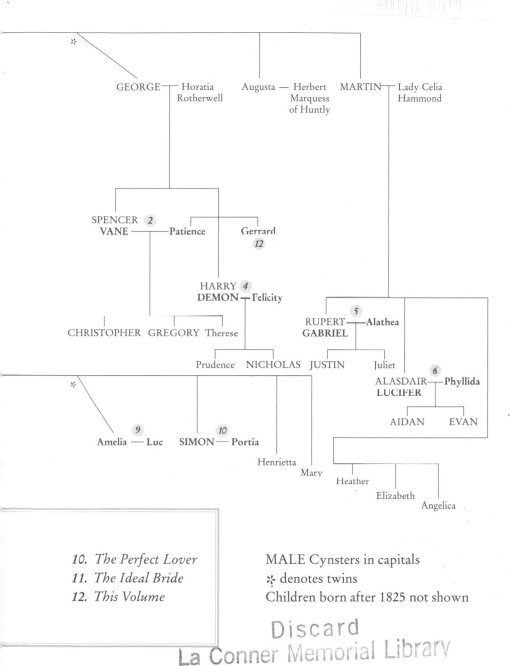

MALE Cynsters in capitals
✣ denotes twins
Children born after 1825 not shown

The Truth About Love

ALSO BY STEPHANIE LAURENS

Cynster Novels

The Ideal Bride
The Perfect Lover
On a Wicked Dawn
On a Wild Night
The Promise in a Kiss
All About Passion
All About Love
A Secret Love
A Rogue's Proposal
Scandal's Bride
A Rake's Vow
Devil's Bride

Bastion Club Novels

A Lady of His Own
A Gentleman's Honor
The Lady Chosen
Captain Jack's Woman

STEPHANIE LAURENS

William Morrow
An Imprint of HarperCollins*Publishers*

The Truth About Love

THE TRUTH ABOUT LOVE. Copyright © 2005 by Savdek Management Proprietory Ltd. All rights reserved. Printed in the United States of America. No part of this book may be used or reproduced in any manner whatsoever without written permission except in the case of brief quotations embodied in critical articles and reviews. For information address HarperCollins Publishers Inc., 10 East 53rd Street, New York, NY 10022.

HarperCollins books may be purchased for educational, business, or sales promotional use. For information please write: Special Markets Department, HarperCollins Publishers Inc., 10 East 53rd Street, New York, NY 10022.

FIRST EDITION

Designed by Renato Stanisic
Map illustrated by Jeffrey L. Ward

Printed on acid-free paper

Library of Congress Cataloging-in-Publication Data has been applied for.

ISBN 0-06-050575-3

05 06 07 08 09 COM/RRD 10 9 8 7 6 5 4 3 2 1

To Merilyn Bourke,
longtime friend, fellow author and romance critic extraordinaire

—with thanks and much love

SL

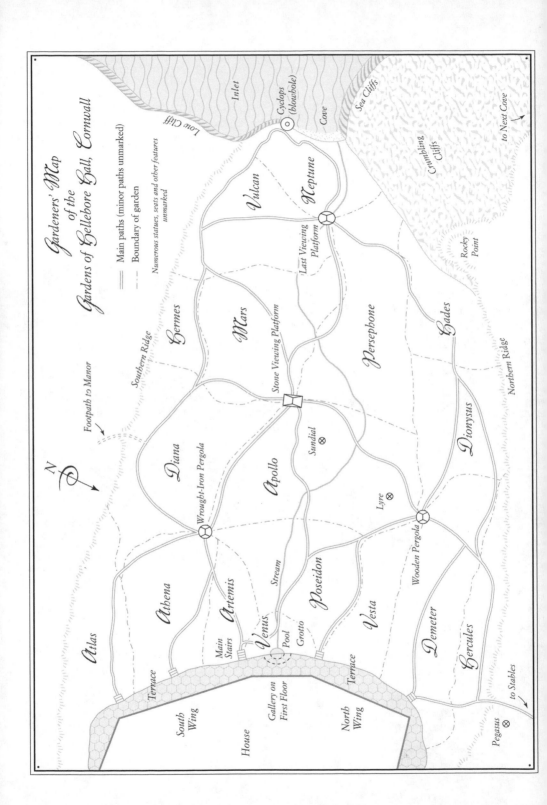

1

London, Early June 1831

"Mr. Cunningham, as I've already made clear, I have no interest whatever in painting a portrait of Lord Tregonning's daughter." Gerrard Reginald Debbington lounged elegantly in an armchair in the smoking room of his select gentleman's club. Concealing his mounting frustration, he held Lord Tregonning's agent's gaze. "I agreed to this meeting in the hope that Lord Tregonning, having been informed of my refusal of the commission to paint the portrait, had agreed to allow me access to the Hellebore Hall gardens."

He was, after all, the ton's foremost landscape painter; Lord Tregonning's famous gardens were long overdue a visit from such as he.

Cunningham blanched. Clearing his throat, he glanced down at the papers spread on the small table between them.

Around them, a discreet hum held sway; Gerrard was peripherally aware of occasional glances thrown their way. Other members saw him, but on noticing Cunningham, they checked; recognizing that business was being conducted, they refrained from intruding.

Cunningham was in his mid-twenties, some years younger than Gerrard's twenty-nine. Attired in sober, rusty black over serviceable linen and a biscuit-colored waistcoat, his round face, faint frown, and the intent attention he gave to his papers marked him clearly as someone's business agent.

By the time Cunningham deigned to speak, Gerrard had a sketch assembled in his head, titled "Business Agent at Work."

"Lord Tregonning has instructed me to convey that while he appreciates your reservations over committing to a portrait of a subject you haven't yet seen, such reservations only strengthen his conviction that you are indeed the painter he needs for this work. His lordship fully comprehends that you will paint his daughter as you see her, without any obfuscation. That is precisely what he wishes—he wants the portrait to be a faithful rendition, to accurately portray Miss Tregonning as she truly is."

Gerrard's lips thinned; this was going nowhere.

Without looking up, Cunningham went on, "In addition to the fee offered, you may take as many months short of a year as you deem necessary to complete the portrait, and over that time you will have unfettered access and unrestricted permission to sketch and paint the gardens of Hellebore Hall. Should you wish, you may bring a friend or companion; you would both be accommodated at Hellebore Hall for the duration of your stay."

Gerrard stifled his exasperation. He hadn't needed to hear that offer again, no matter how sweetly laced; he'd turned it down two weeks ago, when Cunningham had first sought him out.

Stirring, he caught Cunningham's eye. "Your employer misunderstands—I do not, indeed, have never painted on commission. Painting is an abiding interest, one I'm wealthy enough to indulge. Painting portraits, however, is no more than an incidental pastime, successful perhaps, but not in the main of serious attraction to me, to my painterly soul if you will."

Not strictly true, but in the present circumstance, apt enough. "While I would be delighted to have the opportunity to paint the Hellebore Hall gardens, not even that is sufficient incentive to tempt me to agree to a portrait I have no inclination, or need, to paint."

Cunningham held his gaze. He drew in a tight breath, glanced briefly down, then looked up again, his gaze fixing over Gerrard's left shoulder. "His lordship instructed me to inform you that this will be his final offer . . . and that should you refuse it, he will be forced to find some other painter to undertake the portrait, and that other painter will be accorded the same license in respect of the gardens as was offered to you. Subsequently, Lord Tregonning will ensure that during his lifetime and that of his immediate heirs, no other artist will be allowed access to the gardens of Hellebore Hall."

Suppressing his reaction, remaining seated, took all Gerrard's considerable willpower. What the *devil* was Tregonning about, resorting to what amounted to extortion . . . ?

He looked away, unseeing.

One thing was clear. Lord Tregonning was bound and determined to have him paint his daughter.

Leaning his elbow on the chair arm, his clenched jaw on his fist, fixing his gaze across the room, he searched for some acceptable way out of the well-baited trap. None immediately leapt to mind; his violent antipathy to allowing some portrait panderer to be the only artist to gain access to the fabulous landscapes said to surround Hellebore Hall was clouding his perception.

He looked at Cunningham. "I need to consider his lordship's proposal more carefully."

Given the clipped accents that had infected his speech, he wasn't surprised that Cunningham kept his expression carefully neutral. The agent nodded once. "Yes, of course. How long . . . ?"

"Twenty-four hours." If he let such a subject torture him for any longer, unresolved, he'd go insane. He rose and extended his hand. "You're at the Cumberland, I believe?"

Hurriedly gathering his papers, Cunningham stood and grasped his hand. "Yes. Ah . . . I'll wait to hear from you."

Gerrard nodded curtly. He remained by the chair until Cunningham had left, then stirred and followed him out.

He walked the parks of the capital—St. James, Green Park, then into Hyde Park. A poor choice; his boots had barely touched the lawn when he was hailed by Lady Swaledale, eager to introduce him to her daughter and her niece. A bevy of matrons with bright-eyed damsels in tow leaned from their carriages, hoping to catch his attention; others hovered, parading along the grassed verge.

Spotting his aunt Minnie, Lady Bellamy, in her carriage drawn up by the side of the Avenue, he excused himself to a particularly clinging fond mama on the grounds of paying his respects. The instant he reached the carriage, he grasped Minnie's hand and with an extravagant gesture, kissed it. "I'm throwing myself on your mercy—save me," he implored.

Minnie chortled. She patted his hand and leaned down to offer her lined cheek, which he dutifully bussed. "If you'd just make your choice, dear, they'd go off and hunt someone else."

"Not, of course, that we want you to rush your choice." Timms, Minnie's companion, leaned forward to give Gerrard her hand. "But while you remain unattached, you must expect to be pursued."

Gerrard assumed an expression of mock-dismay. "*Et tu,* Timms?"

Timms snorted. She'd grown more gaunt with the years, but there was nothing wrong with her mind.

Or with Minnie's; she regarded him shrewdly, if affectionately. "Endowed as you are with an excellent estate, and the business interests the Cynsters have sponsored you into, let alone being my principal heir, there's no getting away from it, m'boy—if you'd been as ugly as sin you might have given them pause, but as you are, celebrated gentleman painter that you've become, you're in a fair way to being a matchmaking mama's fondest dream."

Gerrard looked his disgust. "I'm not at all sure marriage, at least in the near future, is in my best interests."

That was his current stance, although not one he'd to date shared with anyone else.

"Oh?" Minnie opened her eyes wide. Serious for a moment, she searched his face, then her soft smile returned. "I wouldn't worry your head with such considerations, dear." She patted his hand. "When the right lady appears, it'll all be very plain."

Timms nodded sagely. "Indeed. No sense imagining it'll be up to you to decide."

Far from reassuring him, their words elicited a twinge of alarm. He hid it behind a smile. Sighting a group of friends, he seized the opportunity to retreat; farewelling Minnie and Timms, he strolled across the lawn.

The four gentlemen hailed him. All were known to him; all, like him, were of marriageable age and condition. They were standing a little apart, surveying the field.

"The Curtiss chit's quite fetching, ain't she?" Philip Montgomery raised his glass the better to observe the beauty parading with her two sisters.

"If you can stand the giggling," Elmore Standish replied. "For my money, the Etherington girl's more the ticket."

Gerrard half listened to their commentary; he was one of them in the social sense, yet his unconventional hobby set him apart. It had opened his eyes to a truth his peers had yet to see.

He exchanged a few comments, wryly cynical, then walked on, into the relative safety of Kensington Gardens. At that hour, the gravel walks were busy with nannies and nursemaids watching over their charges as they romped on the lawns. Few gentlemen strolled there; ladies of the ton rarely ventured that way.

He'd intended refocusing on Lord Tregonning's outrageous proposition; instead, the gay shrieks of the youngsters distracted him, sending his mind down a quite different track.

Family. Children. The next generation. A wife. A successful marriage.

All were elements he assumed one day he'd have; they still spoke to something in him, still meant something to him. They were things he still desired. Yet ironically, while his painting, especially his portraits, had elevated him to a position where he could have his pick of the unattached ladies, the very talent that enabled him to create such striking art had opened his eyes, and left him wary.

Of taking a wife. Of marriage. Most especially of love.

It wasn't a matter he was comfortable discussing; even thinking of love made him uneasy, as if doing so was somehow tempting fate. Yet what he'd seen and grappled with while painting his sister Patience and her husband, Vane Cynster, and later the other couples who'd sat for him, what he'd reacted to and striven to portray on canvas was so inherently powerful he'd have had to be blind not to comprehend the ability of that power to impact on his life. To affect him, to distract him. Perhaps to sap the creative energy he needed to give his works life.

If he surrendered to it.

If he ever fell in love, would he still be able to paint? Would falling in love, marrying for love, as his sister and so many others in his wider family had, be a wellspring of joy, or a creative disaster?

When painting, he poured all he was into the act, all his energies, all his passions; if he succumbed to love, would it drain him and impair his ability to paint? Was there even a connection—was the passion that fired love the same as that which fired his creative talent, or were the two totally separate?

He'd thought long and hard, but had found little comfort. Painting was an intrinsic part of him; every instinct he possessed violently recoiled from any act that might reduce his ability to paint.

So he'd recoiled from marriage. Stepped back. Regardless of Timms's view, he'd made the decision that for him, at least for the next several years, love was an emotion he'd do well to avoid; marriage, therefore, did not presently feature on his horizon.

That decision ought to have settled his mind. Instead, he remained restless, dissatisfied. Not yet at peace with his direction.

Regardless, he couldn't see any other sensible course.

Refocusing, he discovered he'd stopped; he stood staring at a group of children playing about the pond. His fingers itched, a familiar symptom of the craving for a pencil and sketch pad. He remained for several minutes, letting the vignettes of children at play sink into his visual memory, then moved on.

This time, he succeeded in turning his mind to Lord Tregonning's offer. To considering its pros and cons. Desires, instincts, and the consequent impulses left him twisting in the wind, swinging first this way, then that. Returning to the bridge over the Serpentine, he halted and took stock.

In three hours he'd accomplished precisely nothing, beyond confirming how accurately Tregonning had read him. He couldn't discuss such a proposal with any fellow artist; his nonartist friends wouldn't comprehend how tempted yet torn he felt.

He needed to talk to someone who understood.

It was nearly five o'clock when he climbed the steps of Vane and Patience Cynster's house in Curzon Street. Patience was his older sister. His parents had died when he was young; Patience had been his surrogate parent for years. When she'd married Vane, Gerrard had found himself welcomed into the Cynster fold, treated as one of the family, as Vane's protégé. In becoming the man he now was, the influence of the Cynsters had been critical, a fact for which he was deeply grateful.

His father, Reggie, had been no satisfactory model; to the Cynsters, Gerrard owed not just his financial success, but also his elegance, his unshakable confidence, and that touch of hard-edged arrogance that among tonnish gentlemen set them, and him, apart.

In reply to his knock, Bradshaw, Vane's butler, opened the door;

beaming, he assured him that Vane and Patience were indeed in and presently to be found in the back parlor.

Gerrard knew what that meant. Handing over his cane, he smiled and waved Bradshaw back. "I'll announce myself."

"Indeed, sir." Fighting a grin, Bradshaw bowed.

Gerrard heard the shrieks before he opened the parlor door. The instant he did, silence fell. Three heads jerked up, pinning him with accusatory stares—then his nephews and niece realized who'd dared to interrupt their playtime.

They came to life like demons. Uttering ear-splitting cries of "Uncle Gerrard!" they hurled themselves at him.

Laughing, he caught the eldest, Christopher, and dangled him upside down. Christopher shrieked with joy; laughing, Gregory jumped up and down, peering into his brother's upturned face. Therese joined in. After shaking Christopher thoroughly, Gerrard set him down and, growling like an ogre, spread his arms and swept the younger two up.

Juggling them, he walked to the chaise facing the fireplace.

From the armchair angled before the hearth, with her youngest son, Martin, bobbing on her knees, Patience smiled indulgently up at him.

His broad shoulders propped against the side of Patience's chair, Vane grinned; he'd been wrestling with the three older children when Gerrard had walked in. "What brings you our way? Surely not the chance to have your hair pulled by our resident monsters."

Disengaging Gregory's and Therese's death grips on his previously neat locks, Gerrard fleetingly returned the grin. "Oh, I don't know." Setting the pair on the chaise, he dropped down to sit between them. He looked from one to the other. "There's a certain something about them, don't you think?"

The children crowed, and seized the opening to bombard him with tales of their recent exploits. He listened, as always drawn in by their innocent, untarnished view of mundane events. Eventually, they tired. The boys slumped on either side of him; Therese yawned, slipped from the chaise and crawled into her father's lap.

Vane dropped a kiss on her soft curls and settled her, then looked at Gerrard. "So what is it? There's obviously something."

Leaning back, Gerrard told them of Lord Tregonning's offer.

"So you see, I'm trapped. I absolutely definitely don't want to do the portrait. His daughter will doubtless prove to be a typical, spoilt featherbrain, worse, one who's used to ruling as queen in her rustic territory. There'll be nothing there for me to paint beyond vacuous self-interest."

"She might not be that bad," Patience said.

"There's every likelihood she'll be even worse." He sighed deeply. "I rue the day I allowed those portraits of the twins to be shown."

From his earliest years, he'd been a landscape artist. He still was—it was his first and deepest calling—but ten years ago, purely out of curiosity, he'd tried his hand at painting portraits of couples. Vane and Patience had been the first he'd asked to sit for him; that painting hung above the drawing room fireplace in their house in Kent, safely private. He'd subsequently painted other couples, all family or connections, but the resulting paintings had always graced private rooms. Yet his hankering for challenge had lured him on; after painting portraits of each couple, he'd decided to paint matching portraits of the Cynster twins, Amanda, now Countess of Dexter, and Amelia, Viscountess Calverton, each holding their firstborn sons.

The portraits were intended to be hung in their country homes, but those of the ton who saw the portraits while they'd still been in London had set up such a clamor the custodians of the Royal Academy had begged, literally *begged* him to allow the works to be shown in the annual portrait exhibition. The attention had been sweet; he'd allowed himself to be persuaded.

And had lived to regret it.

Vane regarded him with amused affection. "So hard to be such a success."

Gerrard snorted. "I should appoint you my agent and let you deal with the horde of matrons, each of them ineradicably convinced that their daughter is the perfect subject for my next great portrait."

Patience jigged Martin on her knee. "It is just one portrait."

Gerrard shook his head. "That's not how it works. It's one of those great risks—choosing a subject. At present, my reputation is solid and intact. One truly ghastly portrait could incalculably damage it. Regardless, I refuse to pander to the expectations of my subjects, or their parents. I paint what I see, which means Lord Tregonning and his darling daughter are very likely to be disappointed."

The children were growing restless. Patience rose as their nurse looked in; she beckoned to the matronly woman and glanced at the children. "It's time for your tea. Bread pudding tonight, don't forget."

Gerrard hid a wry smile as the allure of bread pudding trumped the attraction of remaining with him. Both boys slid to the ground, reciting polite farewells. Therese, helped up out of her father's lap, blew him a kiss, then ran to beat her brothers out of the door.

Patience handed the baby over, then shut the door on her departing brood and returned to her chair. "So why are you so agonized? Simply decline his lordship's invitation."

"That's just *it*." Gerrard raked his fingers through his hair. "If I decline, I not only lose all chance of painting the famous Garden of Night myself, but ensure that the only painter who'll get the chance in the next fifty years will be some portrait dabbler who probably won't even recognize what he's looking at."

"Which will be what?" Vane rose, stretched, then moved to another chair. "What is it about these gardens that makes them so special?"

"The gardens of Hellebore Hall in Cornwall were originally designed in 1710." Gerrard had searched out the details after Cunningham had first called on him. "The area's unique—a narrow protected valley angled southwest that captures the weather in such a way that the most fantastic plants and trees that grow nowhere else in England thrive there.

"The house is situated at the head of the valley which runs all the way to the sea. The proposed designs were seen by many, and generated much excitement at the time. Subsequently, the gardens were created over some thirty-odd years, but the family turned reclusive. Very few people have seen the gardens complete." He glanced at Patience. "The few who did were enraptured.

"Landscape artists have been itching to paint the gardens of Hellebore Hall for decades. None have succeeded in gaining permission." His lips quirked. He glanced at Vane. "The valley and its gardens lie within a large private estate, and the cove is rocky and dangerous, so slipping in and sketching on the sly has never been a viable option."

"So every landscape painter in England—"

"And the Continent and even the Americas."

"—would jump at the opportunity to paint these gardens." Vane cocked his head. "Are you sure you want to pass up the chance?"

Gerrard let out an explosive breath. "*No.* That's my problem. Especially given the Garden of Night."

"Which is?" Patience asked.

"The gardens comprise multiple areas, each named for an ancient god or mythical being. There's a Garden of Hercules, which stands along one ridge and has lots of big, tall trees, and a Garden of Artemis, with topiary animals, and so on.

"One of the areas is the Garden of Venus. It contains a large number of aphrodisiacs and heavily perfumed species, many of which are night-blooming, and incorporates a grotto and a pool fed by the stream that runs through the valley. It's located at the valley's head, just below the house. Due to some quirk of nature, that particular area grew rampant. One lucky soul who saw it only a decade or so after planting described it as a gothic heaven—a dark landscape to eclipse all others. It became known as the Garden of Night."

He paused, then added, "In landscape artist's terms, painting the Garden of Night is akin to attaining the Holy Grail. It's there, but has for generations remained out of reach."

Vane grimaced. "Difficult choice."

Gerrard nodded. "Very much a 'damned if I do, and damned if I don't' decision."

Patience looked from one to the other. "Actually, the decision's quite simple." She caught Gerrard's eye. "All you have to decide is whether you're willing to risk that your talent is up to the task of painting a *reasonable* portrait of this young lady, against the certainty of being able to paint your Holy Grail."

She tilted her head. "Put it another way—how much do you want to paint the Garden of Night? Enough to challenge yourself to creating a decent portrait of one young lady?"

Gerrard met her gray eyes, held her direct gaze. After a moment, he glanced at Vane. "Sisters."

Vane laughed.

E ven after Patience's succinct reduction of the decision facing him, he might have refused, if it hadn't been for the dream. He spent the evening with Patience and Vane, idly chatting about other things; when he parted from Patience in the hall, she kissed his cheek and whispered, "You know what you want to do, so do it. Take the risk."

He'd smiled, patted her shoulder, then ambled home, wondering, examining the possibilities, but increasingly along the lines of how he might pull off a portrait of a vain flibbertigibbet without being overtly insulting.

Reaching his rooms in Duke Street, he climbed the stairs to his bedchamber. Compton, his gentleman's gentleman, came hurrying up to divest him of his coat and bear it away to be brushed and accorded all proper respect. Gerrard grinned, undressed and fell into bed.

And dreamed of the Garden of Night.

He'd never seen it, yet it appeared so vivid, so enticing, so mesmerizingly dark. So full of that dramatic energy that as a painter he was most attuned to. There was danger and excitement, a hint of menace, and something even more profound, more elementally sinister lurking in its shadows.

It called to him. Whispered seductively.

He woke in the morning with the summons still fresh in his mind.

He didn't believe in portents.

Rising, donning a velvet robe over trousers and shirt, he went downstairs. Making major decisions on an empty stomach was never wise.

He'd barely made a start on ham and eggs when a rat-a-tat-tat knock fell on the front door. Recognizing the signal, he reached for the coffeepot and filled his cup—before the Honorable Barnaby Adair could drain the pot dry.

The parlor door flew open. "My heavens!" Barnaby, a tall, elegant, golden-haired figure sporting a dramatically hunted look, swept in. "May the saints preserve me from all doting mamas!" His gaze fell on the coffeepot. "Any left?"

Smiling, Gerrard waved at both pot and platters as Compton hurried in with an additional place setting. "Help yourself."

"Thank you—you're a savior." Barnaby sank into the chair beside Gerrard.

Gerrard eyed him with affectionate amusement. "And good morning to you. What's put you out? Did Lady Harrington's ball prove too exercising?"

"Not Harrington." Barnaby closed his eyes, savoring the coffee. "She's a decent enough sort." Opening his eyes, he considered the platters. "It was Lady Oglethorpe and her daughter Melissa."

"Ah!" Gerrard recalled the connection. "The old friend of your dear mama's who was hoping you'd oblige and escort her darling about town?"

"The same." Barnaby took a bite of toast. "You remember the story of the ugly duckling? Well, Melissa is that in reverse."

Gerrard laughed.

Barnaby and he were much of an age, of similar temperament and background, had similar likes and dislikes, and both favored an eccentric pastime. He couldn't remember how they'd first come to knock around town together, but over the last five years, they'd seen each other through various adventures, growing ever more comfortable in each other's company, and now unhesitatingly called on the other for any and all support.

"Nothing for it," Barnaby declared. "I shall have to flee the capital."

Gerrard grinned. "It can't be that bad."

"Yes it can. I tell you, Lady Oglethorpe isn't looking to me just for escort duties. She has a gleam in her eye I mistrust, and if that wasn't bad enough, the dreadful Melissa clasped her hands to her bosom—not a bad bosom, but the rest is hopeless—and fervently stated that yours truly was her ideal, and that no gentleman in the ton could hold a candle to my magnificence." Barnaby grimaced horrendously. "Coming it a great deal too strong, as the pater would say—made me feel quite ill. And it's *June*—don't they know the hunting season's over?"

Gerrard regarded his friend thoughtfully. Barnaby was the third son of an earl, and had inherited a substantial estate from a maternal aunt; like Gerrard, he was a prime target for matrons with daughters to establish. While Gerrard could and did use his painting as an excuse to avoid the worst of the invitations, Barnaby's hobby of studying crime was a far less acceptable diversion.

"I suppose," Barnaby mused, "I could go to m'sister's, but I'm no longer sure she's not dangerous, too." His eyes narrowed. "If she invited the Oglethorpes to visit over summer . . ." He shuddered.

Gerrard leaned back and reached for his coffee cup. "If you're set on escaping the dreadful Melissa, you could come with me to Cornwall."

"Cornwall?" Barnaby blinked his blue eyes wide. "What's in Cornwall?"

Gerrard told him.

Barnaby perked up.

"Mind you," Gerrard warned, "there'll be at least one unmarried young lady present, and where there's one—"

"There's usually a pack." Barnaby nodded. "Nevertheless, I've handled all comers to now—it's just Melissa, her mother, and the family connection that have so demoralized me."

Said demoralization had clearly been transient; Barnaby fell to demolishing the last sausage, then he looked at Gerrard. "So, when do we leave?"

Gerrard met his eyes. Patience had been right, not that he'd ever tell her. "I'll write to Tregonning's agent today. I'll need to get in extra supplies, and make sure all else is in order here . . . shall we say the end of next week?"

"Excellent!" Barnaby raised his cup in a toast, drained it, then reached for the coffeepot. "I'm sure I can lie low until then."

Twelve days later, Gerrard tooled his curricle between a pair of worn stone gateposts bearing plaques proclaiming them the entrance to Hellebore Hall.

"It's certainly a long way from London." Relaxed on the seat beside him, Barnaby looked around, curious and mildly intrigued.

They'd set out from the capital four mornings before, and spelled Gerrard's matched grays over the distance, stopping at inns that caught their fancy each lunchtime and each evening.

The driveway, a continuation of the lane they'd taken off the road to St. Just and St. Mawes, was lined with old, large-boled, thickly canopied trees. The fields on either side were screened by dense hedgerows. A sense of being enclosed in a living corridor, a shifting collage of browns and greens, was pervasive. Between the tops of the hedges and the overhanging branches, they caught tantalizing glimpses of the sea, sparkling silver under a cerulean sky. Ahead and to

the right, the strip of sea was bounded by distant headlands, a medley
of olive, purple and smoky gray in the early afternoon light.

Gerrard squinted against the glare. "By my reckoning, that
stretch of water must be Carrick Roads. Falmouth ought to lie directly ahead."

Barnaby looked. "It's too far to make out the town, but there are
certainly plenty of sails out there."

The land dipped; the lane followed, curving slowly south and
west. They lost sight of Carrick Roads as the spur leading to St.
Mawes intervened on their right, then the tree sentinels that had lined
the lane abruptly ended. The curricle rattled on, into the sunshine.

They both caught their breath.

Before them lay one of the irregular inlets where an ancient valley
had been drowned by the sea. To their right lay the St. Mawes arm of
the Roseland peninsula, solid protection from any cold north wind; to
their left, the rougher heathland of the southern arm rose, cutting off
any buffets from the south. The horses trotted on and the view
shifted, a new vista opening as they descended yet further.

The lane led them down through sloping fields, then steeply
pitched and gabled roofs appeared ahead, between them and the blue-
green waters of the inlet. Swinging in a wide, descending arc, the lane
went past the house that majestically rose into view, then curved back
to end in a wide sweep of gravel before the front door.

Rounding the final curve, Gerrard slowed his horses; neither he
nor Barnaby uttered a word as they descended the last stretch. The
house was . . . eccentric, fabulous—*wonderful*. There were turrets too
numerous to count, multiple balconies laced with wrought iron, odd-
shaped buttresses aplenty, windows of all descriptions, and segments
of rooms forming fanciful angles in the gray stone walls.

"You didn't say anything about the house," Barnaby said as the
horses neared the forecourt and they were forced to stop staring.

"I didn't *know* about the house," Gerrard replied. "I'd only heard
about the gardens."

Arms of those gardens, the famous gardens of Hellebore Hall,
reached out of the valley above which the house sat and embraced the
fantastical creation, but the major part of the gardens lay hidden behind. Poised sentrylike at the upper end of the valley that ran down to
the inlet's rocky shore, the house blocked all view of the valley itself
and the gardens it contained.

Gerrard let out the breath he hadn't been aware he'd been hold-ing. "No wonder no one ever succeeded in slipping in to paint unde-tected."

Barnaby shot him an amused look, straightening as Gerrard tight-ened the reins, and they entered the shaded forecourt of Hellebore Hall.

Seated in the drawing room of Hellebore Hall, Jacqueline Tre-gonning caught the sound she'd been waiting for—the clop of hooves, the soft scrunch of gravel under a carriage's wheels.

None of the others scattered about the large room heard; they were too busy speculating on aspects of the nature of the visitors who'd just arrived.

Jacqueline preferred not to speculate, not when she could view with her own eyes, and make up her own mind.

Smoothly, quietly, she rose from the armchair beside the chaise on which sat her closest friend, Eleanor Fritham, and Eleanor's mother, Lady Fritham of neighboring Tresdale Manor. Both were engaged in a spirited discussion with Mrs. Elcott, the vicar's wife, over the descrip-tions of the two gentlemen shortly expected that Mrs. Elcott's and Lady Fritham's correspondents in the capital had provided.

"Bound to be arrogant, the pair of them, my cousin said." Mrs. Elcott grimaced disparagingly. "I daresay they'll think themselves a cut above us."

"I don't see why they should," Eleanor returned. "Lady Hum-phries wrote that while both were from excellent families, very much the haut ton, they were perfectly personable and amenable to being entertained." Eleanor appealed to her mother. "Why would they turn their noses up at us? Aside from all else, we're all the society there is around here—they'll lead very quiet lives if they cut us."

"True," Lady Fritham agreed. "But if they're half as well bred as her ladyship makes out, they won't be high in the instep. Mark my words"—Lady Fritham nodded portentously, setting her multiple chins and the ribbons in her cap bobbing—"the mark of a true gentle-man shows in the ease with which he comports himself in any com-pany."

Unobtrusively slipping away, gliding silently up the long room to the window that gave the best view of the front portico, Jacqueline cynically noted the others present; aside from her father's sister, Millicent, who after her mother's death had come to live with them, none had any real reason to be there.

Not unless one deemed rampant curiosity sufficient reason.

Jordan Fritham, Eleanor's brother, stood chatting with Mrs. Myles and her daughters, Clara and Rosa, both as yet unwed. Millicent stood with them, Mitchel Cunningham by her side. The group was engrossed in discussing portraiture, and the singular success of Mitchel and her father in persuading society's foremost artistic lion to grace Hellebore Hall and favor her with his talents.

Calmly, Jacqueline approached the window. Regardless of her father's, Mitchel's, or the artistic lion's belief, *she* would be the one bestowing the favor. She hadn't yet decided whether she would sit for him, and wouldn't, not until she'd evaluated the man, his talents, and, most importantly, his integrity.

She knew why her father had been so insistent this man, and only he, could paint the portrait her father required. Millicent had been nothing short of brilliant in planting the right seeds in her father's mind, and nurturing them to fruition. As the one most intimately involved on all counts, Jacqueline was aware that the man himself would be pivotal; without him, his talents, and his vaunted integrity regarding his work, their plans would come to naught.

And there was no other way to turn.

Halting two paces from the window, she looked out at the occupants of the curricle that had just rocked to a stop before the portico; in the circumstances she felt no compunction in spying on Gerrard Debbington.

First, she had to identify which of the two men he was. The one who wasn't driving? That tawny-haired gentleman stepped lithely down, then paused to throw a laughing comment to the other man, who remained on the box seat, the reins held loosely in his long-fingered hands.

The grays between the curricle's shafts were prime horseflesh, and had been well spelled; Jacqueline registered that in the briefest of glances. The man holding the reins was dark-haired, with strong, chiseled features; the tawny-haired one was prettier, the darker the more handsome.

In the second it took her to blink, she realized how odd it was for her to notice; male beauty rarely impinged on her mind. Then she looked again at the pair in the forecourt, and inwardly admitted that their physical attributes were hard to ignore.

The man on the box seat moved; a groom appeared and he descended from the carriage, handing over the reins.

And she had her answer; *he* was the painter. He was Gerrard Debbington.

A dozen little things confirmed it, from the strength apparent in those very long fingers as he surrendered the ribbons, to the austere perfection of his clothes, and the reined intensity that hung about him, every bit as real as his fashionable coat.

That intensity came as a shock. She'd steeled herself to deal with some fashionable fribble or vain popinjay, but this man was something quite different.

She watched as he answered his friend with a quiet word; the line of his thin lips didn't so much curve as ease—the veriest hint of a smile. Controlled power, intensity harnessed, ruthless determination—those were the impressions that sprang to her mind as he turned.

And looked straight at her.

Her breath caught, suspended, but she didn't move; she was standing too far from the pane for him to see her. Then she heard skirts rustling, footsteps pattering at the far end of the room; glancing sideways, she saw Eleanor, both Myles girls, and their mothers crowding around the far window that was angled to the forecourt. Jordan peered over their heads.

Unlike her, they'd crowded close to the glass.

Looking back at Gerrard Debbington, she saw him studying them, and inwardly smiled. If he sensed someone watching him, he'd think it was them.

Gerrard regarded the cluster of faces blatantly staring from the wide windows facing the forecourt. Raising a supercilious brow, he turned away; avoiding the gaze of the single woman standing back from the window closest to the portico, he looked at Barnaby. "It seems we're expected."

Barnaby could see the goggling crowd, too, but the angle of the nearer window hid the lone woman from him. He gestured to the door. "Shall we make our entrance?"

Gerrard nodded. "Ring the bell."

Strolling to an iron handle dangling by the door, Barnaby gave it a tug.

Turning his head, Gerrard looked once more at the woman. Her stillness confirmed she thought he couldn't see her. Light spilled into the room from windows behind her, diagonally across from where she stood; courtesy of that she was, indeed, primarily a silhouette, barely illuminated. She was intelligent enough, then, to have realized that.

But she'd forgotten, or hadn't known of, the effect of painted woodwork. Gerrard would take an oath the frame surrounding the window was at least eight inches wide, and painted white. It threw back enough light, diffused and soft, true, but light nevertheless, to let him see her face.

Just her face.

He'd already glimpsed three youthful female faces, every bit as uninspiring as he'd expected, in the other group. Doubtless his subject was one of them; God knew how he'd manage.

This lady, however . . . he could paint her. He knew it in an instant; just a glance, that's all it took. Even though her features weren't that clear to him, there was a quality—one of stillness, of depth, of a complexity behind the pale oval of her face—that commanded his attention.

Just like his dream of the Garden of Night, the sight of her face reached for him, touched him, called to the artist that was his soul.

The front door opened and he turned away. Outwardly set himself to the task of greeting and being greeted. Cunningham was there, doing the honors; Gerrard shook his hand, his expression mild, his mind elsewhere.

A governess, or a companion. She was in the drawing room, the doors of which he could now see, so unless she beat a very rapid retreat, he would meet her. Then he'd have to find some way of ensuring she was included along with the gardens in the other subjects he was permitted to paint.

"This is Treadle." Cunningham introduced the butler, who bowed. "And Mrs. Carpenter, our housekeeper."

A stern-faced, competent-looking woman bobbed a curtsy. "Anything you need, sirs, please ask." Mrs. Carpenter straightened.

"I've not yet assigned rooms, not being sure of your requirements. Perhaps, once you've looked around and decided which rooms would best suit, you could let Treadle and me know, and we'll have everything arranged in a blink."

Gerrard smiled. "Thank you. We will." The charm behind his smile worked its usual magic; Mrs. Carpenter's face eased, and Treadle unbent a fraction.

"This is Mr. Adair." Gerrard introduced Barnaby, who with his usual air of genial bonhomie nodded to the two servants and Cunningham.

Gerrard looked at Cunningham.

Who seemed suddenly on edge. "Ah . . . if you'll come this way, I'll introduce you to the ladies, and inform Lord Tregonning that you're here."

Gerrard let his smile grow a fraction more intent. "Thank you."

Cunningham turned and preceded them to the double doors leading into what Gerrard had surmised must be the drawing room.

He was right. They stepped into a room long enough to boast three separate areas for comfortable conversation. At one end, no longer by the window but gathered about the chairs angled before a large fireplace, was the group of ladies and the young man who'd peered out at them, and one other, middle-aged lady he hadn't previously seen.

Directly ahead, on the chaise that faced the doors, were two matrons, one of whom was eyeing Barnaby and him with incipient disapproval.

Although he didn't glance her way, Gerrard was instantly aware of the single lady, standing alone and regarding them levelly from the other end of the room.

Suppressing his impatience, he halted beside Cunningham, who'd paused a yard over the threshold. Barnaby halted just behind his shoulder. Gerrard looked at the bevy of young misses, waiting to see which one came forward—which of the three he was going to hate to have to paint. To his surprise, they all hung back.

The middle-aged lady, a welcoming expression on her face, started toward them.

As did the lone lady on his left.

The middle-aged lady was too old; she couldn't be his subject.

The younger lady drew nearer; he could no longer resist, but looked directly at her.

And saw her, her face, for the first time in good light.

He met her eyes, and realized his error.

Not a governess. Not a companion.

The lady his fingers were already itching to paint was Lord Tregonning's daughter.

2

With a lady approaching from either side, Cunningham dithered over whom to introduce first. The decision was taken out of his hands by the middle-aged lady, who swept up with a smile. "I'm Millicent Tregonning, Lord Tregonning's sister." She held out her hand. "Allow me to welcome you to Hellebore Hall."

Brown haired, well dressed, but severe both in style and expression, Millicent Tregonning was saved from appearing overly hard by the softness of her hazel eyes. Clasping her hand, Gerrard bowed. "Thank you."

He introduced Barnaby; stepping aside so his friend could greet the elder Miss Tregonning brought him closer to the younger lady — Lord Tregonning's daughter, his subject, she who would be one focus of his artistic attention for the next several months.

She'd halted beside her aunt; of average height, clad in a gown of apple-green muslin enticingly displaying generous breasts, and hinting at a slender waist, nicely curved hips, and legs perfectly gauged to satisfy his critical eye, she calmly waited while Barnaby exchanged greetings. Momentarily free, Gerrard studied her.

Turning her head, unruffled, she met his gaze. Her eyes, a medley of gold, amber and green, were large, well spaced under delicately arched brown brows. Her hair was glossy teak with lighter shades streaked through it, neatly confined in a topknot with just a few tendrils flirting about her ears. The pale oval of her face was bisected by a straight nose; her complexion was flawless, ivory tinged with a healthy glow, while her lips had been drawn with a subtle hand, full feminine curves yet exquisitely mobile—elementally expressive. He already knew where to look for hints of her real thoughts, her real feelings.

At present, her eyes were calm pools of quiet confidence; she was observing, assessing, totally contained. Totally unperturbed and unthreatened. Despite his presence, and Barnaby's for that matter, he could detect not the slightest hint of feminine fluster.

She wasn't seeing them as gentlemen—as men—but as something else.

The truth came to him as her gaze deflected to her aunt. She was viewing him solely as a painter.

"And this is my niece, my brother's daughter, Miss Jacqueline Tregonning."

Jacqueline turned to Gerrard Debbington. Smiling, she held out her hand. "Mr. Debbington. I hope your journey down was pleasant—it's such a long way."

He again met her gaze, then took her hand, the long fingers she'd remarked earlier closing, not too tightly yet firm and sure, about her slender bones. He bowed gracefully, his eyes never leaving hers. "Miss Tregonning. I'm grateful your father sought me out. The journey was indeed long, yet, had I not made it, I would certainly have lived to regret it."

She barely registered his words. The tone of his voice, low, masculine, slid over her like a caress; the strength in his fingers, a sense of male power, spread over her skin and set her nerves flickering. His gaze held hers, intent with an interest she couldn't name. Her fingers quivered in his—shocked, she stilled them.

His face, lightly tanned skin stretched over high cheekbones, the angular planes aristocratically austere, remained impassive, his expression politely detached—it was that intentness in his eyes, glowing brown, rich and alive as they held hers, that shook her.

That forced her to look again, and truly see.

She'd dubbed him society's lion and he was unquestionably that, yet his polished elegance wasn't a guise adopted for the world but a reflection of himself; it exuded from him, a tangible shield. His lightly waving hair, a darker brown than her own, was fashionably cut, framing his wide forehead and deep-set eyes; his brows were dark, well arched, his lashes long and thick.

He was tall, almost a head taller than she, broad of shoulder and long of limb; although he was lean rather than heavy, his graceful movements screamed of muscled strength camouflaged by stylish manners. That sense of innate strength was echoed in his face, in the hard lines of brow, nose and chin.

No fop, no self-absorbed popinjay. A lion, albeit a subtle one—in thinking him that she'd been right. He was dangerous, more dangerous than she'd imagined any man might be. Just by holding her hand, meeting her eyes and uttering a few words—what the devil had he said?—he'd made her lungs seize.

The realization rattled her; determinedly, she drew breath and politely inclined her head. "Indeed." She hoped the old standby fitted; it usually did, regardless of what the preceding comment had been.

He smiled—briefly, tantalizingly—a genuine smile of such rampant charm she was distracted all over again. With an effort, she turned to his friend; Gerrard Debbington relinquished her hand, which aided considerably in her battle to focus her wits.

The tawny-haired god smiled at her. "Barnaby Adair, Miss Tregonning. I'm delighted to make your acquaintance."

She managed a smile and gave him her hand—and waited. Yet while Adair appeared cut from the same cloth as Gerrard Debbington, the clasp of his fingers had no discernible secondary effects; his eyes—a merry blue—were simply a pair of laughing eyes, and his voice held no power to make her forget his very words.

Relieved, she welcomed him, then stood back as Mitchel and Millicent made to usher the two gentlemen to the chaise, there to continue the introductions.

Mitchel, Millicent and Adair started off. Gerrard Debbington hesitated; she sensed him looking down at her. She looked up and met his eyes. With the lightest of gestures, the faintest lift of his brows, he indicated he expected her to accompany them. Acquiescing—she wasn't entirely sure why, but quibbling was clearly ineligible—she stepped out in her aunt's wake.

He prowled by her side.

By the simple expedient of not moving until she did, Gerrard kept

Jacqueline Tregonning beside him throughout the introductions. He had no interest whatever in those he met, yet he was adept at the social niceties; part of his mind dealt with them, responding appropriately, placing names with faces, noting the connections. None of those with whom he spoke would have guessed his entire attention was riveted on the woman by his side.

He could barely believe his luck. Far from being a hated and deeply detested chore, painting Lord Tregonning's daughter was going to be . . . precisely the sort of challenge he relished.

She'd captured every last shred of his awareness; there was so much about her to learn. Put simply, she fascinated him.

He was distantly conscious that elements of that fascination were similar to those elicited by ladies who sexually rather than artistically caught his eye, yet given Jacqueline Tregonning was the first lady he'd decided to paint to whom he was not in some way related, he wasn't sure that wasn't to be expected. He saw women as they were, as whole, complete, sexual beings; that was one of the reasons behind his portraits' success.

With Jacqueline Tregonning, he'd struck painter's gold—a subject who had depth, who had layers of emotions and feelings, cares and concerns, all residing behind a face that in itself was intriguing. Just one glance into her beautiful eyes and he'd known what he was looking at—a subject who embodied the vital thing he needed to create a true work of art. She was an enigma.

She was too young to be as she was. Ladies of her years did not normally possess depths, let alone hidden depths; they hadn't lived long enough, hadn't experienced enough of life's tragedies to have acquired them. Yet Jacqueline Tregonning was the epitome of a person of whom it was said: still waters run deep. She was a still, deep pool, calm and glossy smooth on the surface, but with strong currents, strong emotions, running beneath.

Of what those emotions were, of what had caused not just them but her to be as she was, he had as yet no clue, yet he would need to learn the answer to that and all else about her in order to capture all he could see in her eyes, all he could sense behind her controlled expression.

He remained attuned to her as they spoke with those present; with each one, he instinctively catalogued not so much her outward reactions as what he sensed of her true feelings. *Reserve, distance, a keeping apart.* Her attitude was so consistent, so striking, the words resonated in his head. It wasn't shyness; she didn't seem at all shy. She was comfortable and assured, at ease in her own home with people he gathered she'd known most of her life. But she didn't trust them.

Not a single one, with the sole exception of her aunt Millicent.

He was assimilating that when he heard a slow step and the soft thump of a cane. He turned, as did the others, as an older gentleman appeared in the doorway. The man located him, studied him, then came forward. Slowly, yet his movements weren't frail or ponderous so much as measured.

Marcus, Lord Tregonning, was of the old school. Gerrard recognized the signs—the outdated cut of his coat, the knee breeches, the deliberately slow gait, the cane he didn't need, the apparent invisibility of all others beyond the person in his lordship's sights.

Himself. He was glad of the discipline Vane and Gabriel Cynster had taught him, the ability to keep his expression impassive, in this case squelching the urge to smile. Neither he nor Barnaby were likely to be affected by the intimidatory style of their grandsires.

From the corner of his eye, he could see Barnaby fighting a grin—an appreciative one, although his lordship was unlikely to see it so. They were, after all, guests in the man's house, and there they stood, very much like predators, of distinctly different caliber to the other males in the room, bloods in their prime in the old lion's territory.

Lord Tregonning's dark gaze held a sharper, even more critical assessment than his daughter's had. His face was pale, deeply lined, by grief, Gerrard suspected. His hair was still thick and dark, his eyes heavy-lidded and sunk deep; he carried himself erect, spine rigid. The hand wrapped about the head of the cane was aged, the skin mottled, but his grip showed no sign of weakness. The description that sprang to Gerrard's mind was careworn, yet still as proud as bedamned.

His lordship halted no more than two feet distant. Old eyes, agatey brown, bored into his, then Lord Tregonning nodded. "Gerrard Debbington, I presume?"

Gerrard bowed. His lordship extended his hand; Gerrard shook it, calmly returning the old man's steady regard.

"I'm delighted you were able to accept my commission, sir."

Gerrard knew better than to display eagerness over business dealings. "The gardens, as you know, are a draw—the chance to paint them was difficult to pass up."

Tregonning raised his brows. "And the portrait?"

Gerrard glanced at Jacqueline Tregonning; she'd moved a few paces away to chat with the other young ladies. "As to that, I believe my initial reservations, those I understand Mr. Cunningham conveyed to you, have been laid to rest. I'm quite looking forward to commencing the work."

It took effort to keep his drawl even, his tone no more than mildly interested; in reality, he would like nothing better than to consign Tregonning and everyone else to some outer planet so he could haul out his sketch pad, sit Jacqueline Tregonning down, and get started.

Forcing his gaze from her, he turned back to his host in time to glimpse relief fleetingly flit across Tregonning's worn features. "If you'll permit me to introduce the Honorable Barnaby Adair?"

Tregonning shook hands with Barnaby; Gerrard seized the moment to confirm his impression. Yes, Tregonning had fractionally relaxed; the rigid set of his shoulders had eased, the sense of grim resolution had faded somewhat.

Turning from Barnaby, Tregonning eyed him once more, measuringly yet, Gerrard felt, also with a touch of approval. "Perhaps"—Tregonning flicked a glance at the ladies, both young and not so young attempting to appear not to be listening for all they were worth—"we should repair to my study and discuss your requirements."

"Indeed." Gerrard glanced at Jacqueline, now moving further down the room. "It would be wise to establish the procedures I'll follow, and what will be necessary to ensure a portrait of the quality I imagine we both wish to see."

"Good, good." Tregonning gestured to the door. "If you'll come with me . . . ?"

"Marcus? *Marcus,* do wait!"

With Tregonning, Gerrard turned to see the older lady introduced as Lady Fritham, a close neighbor, beckoning.

Brows rising, Tregonning held his ground. "Yes, Maria?"

"I'm holding a dinner party tomorrow evening, and I wished to invite you and Mr. Debbington and Mr. Adair to attend. It'll be the perfect opportunity for them to meet our local set." Her improbably blond curls quivering with eagerness, Lady Fritham opened her blue eyes wide and clasped bejeweled hands to her bosom. "*Do* say you'll come, gentlemen."

Gerrard glanced at Tregonning, deferring to his host.

Tregonning met his gaze briefly, then looked again at Lady Fritham. "I'm sure Mr. Debbington and Mr. Adair will be delighted to accept, Maria. As for myself, I fear you must excuse me."

He bowed with austere grace, then turned away.

"I'll remain here." Barnaby nodded politely and went to join Millicent Tregonning.

Lord Tregonning made for the doors. Gerrard fell in beside him, wondering whether his lordship would summon his daughter—wondering if he should suggest it. They reached the doorway; Tregonning didn't glance back. Inwardly shrugging, Gerrard followed him out.

Tregonning asked about London in the terms of one who hadn't visited in decades; Gerrard replied as they crossed the hall and headed down a long corridor.

In some ways, his host was almost as intriguing as his daughter. There was an aura of weariness about the man; it colored his voice, yet was countered by a strong sense of grim, unquenchable resolve. Tregonning's wasn't a face Gerrard could read; the man kept his emotions too locked away, repressed, concealed, and under too tight a rein to be accurately discerned even by an observer as acute as Gerrard knew himself to be.

He thought again of Jacqueline Tregonning. Perhaps the reserve he sensed in her was a familial trait, but in her case, her exterior hadn't yet ossified. Regardless, that didn't explain how she, a young lady of . . . he wasn't sure of her age . . . came to have tragic secrets.

He looked about him as they walked. He was accustomed to ducal residences, but this house was enormous and more convoluted in design than was usual. The furnishings were of good but not exceptional quality, tending toward the dark, heavy and ornate, with ornamentation approaching the baroque. The overall effect was Gothic, fanciful, but not overwhelming.

At the end of the corridor, Tregonning preceded him up a flight of stairs. Opening a door off the landing, he led the way into a darkly appointed yet luxurious study.

It was a comfortable room, very male in ambience; sinking into the large leather armchair Tregonning indicated, Gerrard suspected his host spent most of his reclusive days there.

Settling into another armchair, Tregonning gestured. "My house and staff are at your disposal. What do you need?"

Gerrard told him. "The studio must have excellent light—old nurseries are often suitable."

Tregonning nodded. "We have a large nursery no longer in use. I'll give orders for it to be cleared and made ready. It has very large windows."

"Excellent. I'll inspect it to confirm it will suit. It would be helpful if my room, and that of my man, Compton, could be located nearby."

Tregonning waved. "I'm sure the inestimable Mrs. Carpenter will be able to arrange matters as you wish."

Gerrard detailed his other requirements—a long table, a double lock on the door, and other sundry items. Tregonning accepted all without quibble, naming those of his staff who would handle each point.

"I've brought all else I need with me—Compton should be arriving shortly with the luggage. While I will at some point have to return to the capital to replenish my supplies, exactly when is impossible to guess."

Tregonning nodded. "Do you have any idea how long the portrait will take?"

"At this stage, I can't say. My previous portraits were executed over a period of months; the longest took eight months. However, in those cases, the subjects were well-known to me. In your daughter's case, I'll need to spend some time simply observing her before I attempt even preliminary sketches.

"Apropos of that, one matter we should discuss is sittings, and what that term encompasses. For a portrait of the nature you wish, I'll need, at least initially, to have first call on your daughter's time. I'll need to observe her in different situations and settings about this house, her home. It's essential I have some understanding of her character and personality before I set pencil to paper." He added, purely as a matter of form, "I assume she understands this and is willing to commit the time necessary for a successful portrait."

Tregonning blinked. It was the first time Gerrard had seen

him anything less than absolutely, unquestioningly confident of all around him.

Jacqueline Tregonning's assessing look flashed into his mind; a sinking feeling assailed him. Had she agreed to let him paint her?

Tregonning frowned. "She indicated she was willing to sit for a portrait, but I didn't then know what you've just explained. She may well not appreciate the necessity . . ." He stirred, lips firming. "I'll speak with her."

"No. With due respect, it might be better if I did. I could then answer any questions she may have, which will ensure there are no subsequent misunderstandings." Gerrard held Tregonning's gaze. "The demands on her time will actually decrease once we commence formal sittings."

Tregonning's face cleared; nodding, he relaxed in his chair. "That might be best. She did say she was agreeable, and I'm sure she won't refuse, but it would be wise for her to know what you need of her."

Gerrard quietly exhaled. He had much greater confidence in his powers of persuasion than he had in Tregonning's. The man seemed distant from everything, and that might well include his daughter; while he hadn't yet gained even an inkling of Jacqueline's attitude to her father, he didn't want to risk any adverse reaction from her.

He was even more determined than Tregonning that his portrait of Jacqueline Tregonning would go ahead, and under the most favorable circumstances. So he'd talk to the lady himself, and ensure he got an agreement he could fall back on if she later turned difficult.

Reviewing all they'd covered, he continued, "As I don't normally accept commissions, I think it wise to be plain about what I'll eventually deliver. The commission is for a final, framed, full-length portrait in oils of your daughter—unless there's some major catastrophe that prevents its execution, that's what I'll deliver to you within the next year. I, however, will retain all sketches and preliminary works. In addition, I never permit any early viewing of my work—the first you'll see of it will be the completed work I present to you. Should you not wish to accept it, I will keep the portrait and no commission will apply."

Tregonning was nodding. "That's entirely acceptable." He caught Gerrard's eye. "You're also keen to paint the gardens."

Gerrard blinked. "Indeed." He glanced at the window; the fabulous gardens that had for decades obsessed him and his peers lay displayed before him. "Whatever sketches and paintings of the gardens I complete will be mine to keep. Should I ever offer any for sale, you will, of course, be given first refusal."

Tregonning humphed. "I suppose," he said, levering himself up from the depths of the armchair, "that you'll want to start exploring the gardens straightaway."

His gaze still locked on the vista beyond the window, Gerrard rose, too, then turned to meet Tregonning's old eyes. "Actually, no. I don't anticipate exploring the gardens, artistically speaking, other than as a backdrop for your daughter, until I've got the portrait under way."

Tregonning was surprised but pleased, indeed, gratified.

Accompanying him back to the drawing room, Gerrard was aware of the irony. He'd come here to paint the gardens of Hellebore Hall, yet despite his obsession with them, ever since he'd laid eyes on Jacqueline Tregonning, he'd been consumed by thoughts of painting her.

Against her allure, not even the Garden of Night could compete.

They returned to the front hall. Lord Tregonning saw him to the drawing room door, but stopped short of entering. "I'll instruct Treadle and Mrs. Carpenter as to your needs—no doubt they'll consult with you."

"Thank you."

With a nod, Tregonning turned away. Gerrard watched him walk back in the direction from which they'd come. Feminine chatter spilled out of the drawing room. Clearly his lordship intended to seek refuge in his study, leaving him and Barnaby to the tender mercies of Lady Fritham, Mrs. Myles and the censorious Mrs. Elcott.

Accepting the inevitable, he turned and strolled back into the fray. Tea had been served in his absence; Millicent Tregonning smiled and poured him a cup. Accepting it, he chatted to her and Mrs. Myles, seated beside her, regarding his first impressions of the area. Mrs. Myles was instantly recognizable as a mother with daughters to establish; her bright eyes and gushing comments explained why Barnaby was on the other side of the room.

Returning his empty cup, Gerrard excused himself and followed.

Of course, neither he nor Barnaby could truly escape. They would remain the cynosure of local attention until the novelty of their presence faded.

Avoiding the chaise on which Lady Fritham sat absorbed in spirited argument with the severe Mrs. Elcott—clad in gray twill that matched her gray hair, the vicar's wife behaved as if holding herself ready to be scandalized at any moment—he walked down the room to where the younger crew was holding court, Barnaby unsurprisingly center stage.

The Misses Myles saw him approaching, and quickly shifted to create a space between them. He smiled his practiced smile, and with an easy nod strolled around the group to Jacqueline Tregonning's side.

Although following Barnaby's tale, she sensed him draw near. She glanced fleetingly up at him, then moved aside to allow him to stand beside her. Detecting exasperation in her brief glance, Gerrard wondered . . . then realized she couldn't study him while he was standing next to her.

His lips eased, curved.

Across the circle, the Misses Myles's eyes brightened. Without appearing to notice, Gerrard gave his attention to Barnaby. The last thing he wished was to raise any hopes in the Misses Myles's young breasts.

The thought had him glancing discreetly down, to his left, to where Jacqueline's breasts rose above the scooped neckline of her gown. Her skin was flawless, creamy white; his fingertips tingled—he would wager that skin was rose-petal soft.

Although of perfectly acceptable style for a young lady some years beyond her first season, Jacqueline's endowments filled out the gown in a manner guaranteed to draw gentlemen's eyes. Retrieving his gaze, Gerrard glanced around the circle; other than Barnaby, who he was aware had noticed, the other two gentlemen seemed oblivious of Jacqueline's charms. Contempt for the familiar, or . . . ?

In between attending Barnaby's story, Mitchel Cunningham ignored the Myles sisters and shot brief, very brief, glances at Eleanor Fritham, Lady Fritham's daughter. Eleanor was indeed a beauty, a touch older than Jacqueline and in very different style. She was taller, reed slender, with alabaster skin and long, pale fair hair. Her eyes were cerulean blue, her lashes and brows brown. She was using them shamelessly on Barnaby, her attention slavishly fixed on him.

Much good would it do her. She might be a beauty, yet Gerrard instinctively knew she was unlikely to be of serious interest to either him or Barnaby.

Noting another of Cunningham's swift glances, Gerrard made a mental note to mention the association to Barnaby, purely in pursuit of a peaceful existence, something Barnaby appreciated as much as he.

The brevity of Cunningham's glances was almost certainly attributable to the other gentleman in the group, Eleanor's older brother, Jordan Fritham. A brown-haired, precociously superior gentleman in his mid-twenties, he stood between his sister and the Myles girls. Taking in Jordan's stance, Gerrard smothered a grin. The sketch that sprang to life in his mind was titled: "Cock of the Local Walk Greatly Displeased by the Appearance of Interlopers on His Patch."

Barnaby and he were the interlopers, yet as far as Gerrard could tell, it wasn't his attention to Jacqueline but Eleanor's to Barnaby that was ruffling Jordan's feathers. He strove to hide his reaction, but there was a hard glint in his eyes, a twist to his thin lips that screamed his irritation.

"So when Monteith came thundering up in his curricle thinking he'd won"—Barnaby struck a dramatic pose—"there was George Bragg, leaning on his whip, waiting to greet him!"

The Myles sisters gasped; Eleanor Fritham's eyes glowed with laughter. With an engaging grin, Barnaby concluded his tale of the latest curricle-racing scandal. "Monteith was furious, of course, but there was nothing he could do but put a good face on it and stump up the blunt."

"Oh, that *must* have hurt." Eleanor lightly clapped her hands.

"Oh, it did," Barnaby assured her. "Monteith took off for his Highland eyrie and hasn't been sighted since."

Gerrard knew the story; he'd been there. Jordan Fritham made some slighting comment about London horseflesh. Gerrard didn't catch Barnaby's reply; Jacqueline had turned to him, considering him. He looked down and met her frankly measuring gaze.

"Are you inclined to such pastimes, Mr. Debbington?"

She'd forgotten he was a man again. He smiled, deliberately charming, and watched her blink. "No," he murmured. "I have better things—more rewarding things—to do with my time."

For an instant, she held his gaze, then the bustling rustle of skirts gave her an excuse to glance away.

And breathe in. Deeply. He was acutely aware—to his fingertips aware—of the rise and fall of her breasts.

The interruption was Lady Fritham, come to summon Eleanor and Jordan away. Mrs. Myles somewhat reluctantly followed, gathering her daughters, and the party broke up.

Millicent, Mitchel and Jacqueline went to see the visitors to their carriages. Following some paces behind, Gerrard and Barnaby halted in the front hall.

"An unthreatening bunch, don't you think?" Barnaby said.

"I've been focusing on Jacqueline Tregonning."

"I noticed." Barnaby's eyes danced. "Artist smitten by subject—not an entirely original plot."

"Not smitten, you idiot, just absorbed. There's a great deal more to her than meets the eye."

"You'll get no argument from me on the latter. As for the former"—Barnaby shot him a sidelong glance he chose to ignore—"we'll see."

Mrs. Carpenter entered the hall. She came forward. "Mr. Debbington, Mr. Adair, we have your rooms ready. If you'll come with me, we can make sure they suit."

Gerrard smiled. "I'm sure they will." With a last glance for Jacqueline, standing, waving, on the front porch, he turned and with Barnaby followed Mrs. Carpenter upstairs.

She and her staff had been as efficient as Lord Tregonning had intimated; the room to which she led Gerrard was just along the first-floor corridor from the stairs that led up to the old nursery.

"Treadle's had the footmen up there moving the heavy pieces. I'll have the maids go up first thing tomorrow, sir. Perhaps if you'll look in after breakfast and let us know how you'd like things set up?"

"My thanks, Mrs. Carpenter, and to Treadle, too. I'll consult with you after breakfast."

Mrs. Carpenter bobbed a curtsy and left. Gerrard turned and surveyed the room. It was large, with a sitting area before a wide fireplace and a huge tester bed set on a dais at the opposite end. A door to one side of the fireplace led to a dressing room from which Compton had looked out, nodded on seeing him, then retreated to finish unpacking his things.

They'd left Barnaby in a similar room, in the same wing but closer to the main stairs. Gerrard ambled to the open dressing room door and looked in. "Everything to our liking?"

"Indeed, sir." Compton had been with him for eight years; a veteran of the Peninsula campaigns, he was now approaching middle age. "A very well-run enterprise, and a pleasant household with it." Compton shot Gerrard a sidelong glance. "Belowstairs, at least."

"As to abovestairs," Gerrard said, answering the unvoiced question, "all seems comfortable enough, but we're still at first glance. Where does Cunningham fit in, do you know?"

"Eats with the family, he does." After a moment, Compton asked, "Want me to ask about?"

"Not about him, but report anything you hear about the younger Miss Tregonning—I need to get to know her better, and quickly."

"Will do. Now, will the brown Bath superfine do for tonight, or do you want to go with the black?"

Gerrard considered. "The black." Leaving Compton to fig out his evening clothes, he turned back into the bedroom and headed for the glass-paned doors that opened onto the balcony.

The private semicircular balcony ran half the length of the room. Because of the odd shape of the house and the angle of the room next door, no other room was visible, and vice versa; both balcony and room were essentially private, and offered a unique and stunning view over the gardens.

Gerrard stepped out, entranced.

Even through the lengthening shadows of approaching dusk, the gardens were magical—fantastical shapes rose out of the twilight, a plethora of fairy-tale landscapes scattered across and down the valley, each opening out from the last, then merging into the next.

On the horizon, the sea shimmered gold in the last light of the dying sun, then melted through shades of gilt and silver laid over blue to become the iridescent surf breaking on the rocks clogging the inlet's narrow beach. He let his gaze slowly travel nearer, noting how the gardens became progressively more structured the closer they got to the house. In the ring of areas adjoining the house, he glimpsed a garden of round boulders on one ridge, a formal Italianate garden nearer at hand, statuary in another section and a towering pinetum on the other ridge.

He could hear the tinkling music of water running over rock. Looking down toward the sound, he saw a terrace below the balcony. The terrace skirted the house on the valley side, giving views and also access to the gardens; he could just make out steps leading down in several places. Toward the middle of the house, a denser, darker patch of thick vegetation ran right up to the terrace, perhaps even extending beneath it.

That, Gerrard guessed, on a mild surge of satisfaction, had to be the famous Garden of Night.

Tomorrow, he'd explore. He tried to focus on the prospect, only to find his mind drifting, insistently, back to Jacqueline Tregonning.

How was he going to gain her trust, gain her confidence enough to learn all he wanted to know?

Considering the best way to approach a young lady he now knew wasn't as conventional as he'd blithely assumed, he wandered back into the room, absentmindedly shutting the door on the darkening gardens.

Dinner was a curious experience. The food was excellent, the conversation beyond subdued. The hour passed in oddly peaceful quiet, with long stretches of silence, yet strangely without any sense of repression. They spoke as necessary, but there was no compulsion to fill the gaps.

Gerrard was fascinated. Both he and Barnaby had been watchful, quick to match their hosts' behavior. Both found the family intriguing, Barnaby because, as a student of crime, he found the vagaries of human nature absorbing, while for Gerrard, Jacqueline's interaction with her family would inevitably form the cornerstone of his mental picture of her, the basis of the understanding he ultimately brought to her portrait.

Regardless of the relative silence, the established procedures were followed; when the covers were drawn, the ladies rose and left the gentlemen to pass the port. Mitchel asked Barnaby about the curricle-racing scandal. Lord Tregonning grasped the moment to inquire whether the room he'd been given met with Gerrard's approval. On being assured it did, his lordship nodded and lapsed once more into comfortable silence.

Gerrard sat back, comfortable, too, and considered his best way forward with Jacqueline. At the end of a restful twenty minutes, they all rose and quit the dining room. Lord Tregonning left them in the hall, heading for his study. Together with Mitchel and Barnaby, Gerrard strolled back to the drawing room.

They crossed the threshold to the gentle strains of a sonata. Gerrard looked at the pianoforte set in one corner, but it was Millicent at the keys. Jacqueline was seated at one end of the central chaise, a lamp on the table beside her, the soft light sheening on her tumbling curls as, head bent, she plied her needle over a piece of embroidery.

He headed her way, eager to learn of her interests, her pastimes— of her.

She looked up, smiled politely, then made to gather up the embroidery; a basket sat by her feet.

"No—I'd like to look." He smiled when, surprised, she blinked up at him. He summoned his charm. "If I may?"

She stared at him for a moment, then made a small gesture. "If you wish." Her tone stated she didn't understand why he would.

Sitting beside her, he cast an inevitably critical eye over the fine linen she spread on her lap so he could see. His gaze raced over it, then slowed. It was his turn to blink. He leaned closer, looked harder.

He'd expected the usual embroidery ladies wasted their time with, some conventional scene done in conventional style. That wasn't what she was creating.

And creating it was.

His painter's eyes drank in the lines, the balance of shapes and colors, the use of varying textures to give the illusion of depth. "This isn't from a pattern."

No question. After a moment, she said, "I make it up as I do it. I have a picture in my head."

He was barely conscious of nodding; he hadn't expected her to have any artistic streak, but this . . . He pointed to a patch above the center. "You'll need a visually strong element there—it's the focal point."

The look she cast him was faintly irritated. "I know." She gathered the linen, tucking the strands of silk she was working with into the folds. "There's a sundial there."

He could see it; that would work. He glanced at her as she bent to tuck the embroidery into the basket. "Do you paint or draw?"

She hesitated, then answered, "I draw a little, but mostly in preparation." She looked back, met his eyes. "I do watercolors."

Not perhaps the easiest of confessions to make to the country's foremost landscape artist; his landscapes were watercolors. "You must show me your works sometime."

Her eyes, currently more green than gold, snapped. "I don't think that'll be necessary."

"I mean it." His tone, clipped and definite, faintly impatient, emphasized that fact. "I want to—will need to—see them."

She held his gaze, faintly puzzled; beyond that, he couldn't read her thoughts. Then she said, "Speaking of painting, are the amenities provided adequate to your needs? If there's anything more you require, please ask."

A clear change of subject, but she'd given him precisely the opening he wanted.

"The amenities are satisfactory, however, there are a number of aspects we need to discuss." He glanced at the pianoforte; Barnaby was turning music for Millicent and chatting with Mitchel. Before dinner, he'd asked Barnaby to keep Millicent and any others occupied to clear his way with Jacqueline. Barnaby had grinned widely, but wisely made no comment beyond assuring him he'd be delighted to oblige.

He returned his gaze to Jacqueline's face. "I find music rather distracting. Perhaps we could walk on the terrace, and I'll explain what will be necessary to create the portrait your father wants."

She hesitated, her gaze on his face yet not, he would swear, seeing him, then she nodded. "That would be helpful."

Rising, he offered his hand. Again she hesitated, yet this time he knew why; he was aware of how she steeled herself before placing her fingers in his. He gripped, and felt a surge of purely male satisfaction at the faint tremor he detected before she suppressed it. He drew her up, then released her; suavely waving her to the French doors open to the terrace, he reminded himself it formed no part of his plan to discompose her, much less make her wary of being in his company.

Side by side they strolled out, into the soft night. Onto the terrace he'd seen from his balcony. Below his room, the terrace was relatively narrow; here it spread wide, an area in which guests from the drawing room and the ballroom next door could gather and admire the view.

Tonight the view was shrouded in shadows, the moon a mere sliver shedding just enough light to limn all it touched in silver, transforming the gardens into a fantastical landscape, yet his attention remained on the creation who walked beside him, not on those spread before him.

She'd walked to the right, away from the area he was increasingly certain contained the Garden of Night. It was said to be best viewed in the evening, yet he felt no urgency over exploring it just yet; he'd see it in daylight first, tomorrow maybe.

He glanced at Jacqueline. Her gown of pale green silk faded to beaten silver in the faint light; her skin appeared translucent; only the rich color of her hair retained its warmth. Her expression was calm, composed, yet he sensed she was thinking rapidly.

It seemed wise to speak before she could distract him. "I mentioned to your father the necessary demands that sitting for a portrait places on the subject—he wasn't sure you were aware of the details."

Strolling slowly beside him, Jacqueline told herself to concentrate on his words, and ignore the voice that uttered them. "What are those demands—in detail?"

Lifting her head, she met his eyes, dark in the night, and marveled again that she was so quiveringly aware of him in a way she'd never been of any other before. She battled to quell a shiver, difficult to excuse given the warmth of the gentle, perfumed breeze wafting about them.

After a moment, he replied, "Initially, I'll demand a great deal of, if not most of, your time, although largely in social settings, much the usual round of your life. I need to gain a strong sense of who you are, how you feel about many subjects." He glanced out at the gardens. "How you react to things, your likes, dislikes, and the reasons behind them. The subjects you're happy to talk of, and those you'd rather avoid."

They walked on for a few paces, then he looked at her. "Basically, I need to get to know you."

She studied his face. The light was good enough for her to make out his expression, but she couldn't read his eyes. His expression he controlled; his eyes were more revealing. What he was suggesting was frankly unnerving. "I thought portraitists paint"—she gestured—"at best what they see."

His lips quirked in wry acknowledgment of the qualification. "Most do. I don't. I paint more."

"How so?"

He didn't immediately answer; as they walked on, she sensed he was considering the question for the first time. Eventually, he said, "I think it's because every person I've painted to date is someone I've known for years, someone I'm connected to, whose background and family I know." He met her gaze. "What I paint goes far deeper than a face and an outward expression. Just as with landscapes I paint not just the detail but the atmosphere as well, so, too, with people. It's the intangibles that are most powerful."

She nodded and looked ahead. "I've heard of your reputation, but I've never seen any of your works."

"All are in private hands."

She glanced at him. "You don't show them?"

"Not the portraits. They were created as gifts." He lightly shrugged. "And to see if I could."

"Do you mean to say my portrait will be the first for which you've received a commission?"

Her tone was even, the question direct if somewhat forward; nevertheless, it struck a nerve. Gerrard halted, and waited until she did the same and faced him. "Miss Tregonning, why do I get the impression you're assessing my abilities as a portraitist?"

She blinked at him, then equally succinctly replied, "Probably because I am." She tilted her head, studying him. "Surely you didn't expect me to simply agree to be painted by"—she gestured—"someone whose talents are unknown to me?"

"Just any old artist" was what she'd meant to say. He narrowed his eyes; she didn't react, her expression remained open. "Your father gave me to understand that you'd agreed to allow me to paint your portrait."

She frowned slightly. Her gaze remained steady on his face. "I agreed to sit for a portrait. Not to sit for any particular painter. Papa chose you—I've yet to decide whether you meet my requirements."

Again he had cause to thank Vane and Gabriel Cynster for teaching him the knack of impassivity in the face of extreme provocation. He let a moment go by—a fraught moment in which he reined in his reaction, and found words in which he could acceptably express it. "Miss Tregonning, do you have any idea how many petitions, if not outright pleas, I've received to do portraits of young ladies of the ton?"

"No, of course not, but that's neither here nor there. This is me, my portrait, not theirs. I'm not one to be ruled by the opinion of the giddy horde." She looked at him with slightly more interest. "Why did you refuse them? I assume you did?"

"Yes. I did." His words were excessively clipped; she didn't seem perturbed in the least. Her eyes remained on his, waiting . . . "I wasn't interested in painting any of them. *Now*, before we go any further"— before she asked the obvious next question— "it seems I should share with you the particulars I made clear to your father. I paint what's there, both in a face *and* behind it. I won't alter, exaggerate or suppress what I see—any portrait I paint will be a faithful representation not just of how the person appears, but also of who they are."

She'd raised her brows at his fervor, but all she said was, "And *what* they are?"

"Indeed. In the final work, what they are will show through."

She held his gaze for a moment—a frankly assessing moment— then she nodded, once, decisively. "Good. That's precisely what I need—what my father needs."

She turned and walked on. Gerrard mentally shook his head, then followed, still grappling with the way the situation had swung around. Apparently his painting her was not, as he'd thought, a case of his con- ferring a boon on her; it seemed there'd been a real question of whether she'd condescend to sit for him!

The possibility of her not doing so forced him to tread carefully. Lengthening his stride, he came up with her. He glanced at her face; her expression was uninformative, her eyes veiled. "So . . ." He felt forced to ask the plain question. "Will you sit for me?"

She halted and faced him. Calmly, she met his gaze. For the first time, he felt he was seeing further—that she was letting him sense something of the woman she was, and the strength she possessed—the reason, surely, for her steadiness, her assurance, so much stronger than usually found in young ladies of her age . . .

"How old are you?"

She blinked. "Why? Does it matter?"

His lips thinned at the faint amusement in her tone. "I need to get to know you, to understand you, and knowing how old you are helps to get an idea of your life, and what questions to ask, what else I need to know."

She hesitated; he sensed her withdrawing, being more careful. "I'm twenty-three." She lifted her chin. "How old are you?"

He recognized the diversion, but calmly replied, "Twenty-nine."

Her brows rose. "You seem older."

It was hard to remain on his high horse when she was so determinedly ignoring convention. "I know." The understated elegance he'd absorbed from Vane always had made him appear more mature.

He continued to hold her gaze. "So do you." Also true.

She smiled fleetingly, a genuine, amused if faintly wry expression. It was the first spontaneous smile he'd seen from her; he immediately determined to see more.

They stood for a moment, each studying the other, then he said, "You haven't answered my question."

She held his gaze for a moment longer, then her lips slowly curved. Swinging around, she started strolling back toward the drawing room. "If you're half the painter you believe yourself to be"—she glanced over her shoulder, caught his eye, then faced forward and strolled on—"then, yes, I'll sit for you." Her words drifted back to him. "Papa chose well, it seems."

He watched her walk away, aware to his bones of her bold yet veiled challenge, and his response to it. Deliberately, he fixed his gaze on her exposed nape, then let it slide caressingly down her back, tracing the line from shoulder to hip, to ankle . . . then he stirred, and followed her.

3

He spent a restless night and was awake and out on his balcony to see the sun rise over the gardens.

And consider Jacqueline Tregonning.

She was so very different from what he'd expected. They were closer in age than he'd anticipated, although in terms of worldly experience, his was far greater. Regardless, there had to be some experience, some incident in her life to account for the steel he sensed in her. It wasn't simply strength of character, latent and unrecognized, but mature inner strength that had been tried, tested and found true; she possessed the inner fortitude of a survivor.

Which begged the question: What had she survived?

Whatever it was, did it also account for the shadows in her eyes? She might be self-confident and strangely assured, yet she wasn't lighthearted; she was definitely not carefree, as by rights she ought to be. It wasn't precisely sorrow he sensed coloring her world, nor yet simple sadness. She wasn't of a maudlin or morose disposition.

Hurt? Perhaps, but something, certainly, had caused her reserve, her distancing from those about her. It wasn't her nature but a deliberate choice—that's why he'd noticed it.

What had happened to her, and when, and why did its effects still linger?

Compton arrived with his washing water; Gerrard quit the balcony to shave and dress. On his way downstairs, he remembered the other nagging question his evening's interlude with Jacqueline had left circling in his brain.

What had she meant by saying she, and her father, needed the portrait to show what, specifically *what*, she was?

Inwardly frowning, he walked into the breakfast parlor. Courtesy of his room being all but at the end of the farthest wing, he was the last to arrive. He inclined his head to Lord Tregonning, at the table's head, nodded to Millicent and Jacqueline, then headed for the sideboard.

Treadle deftly lifted the lids of the chafing dishes. After making his selection, he returned to the table and took the chair next to Barnaby—opposite Jacqueline.

His gaze drifted over her as he sat. She looked ... the word he needed was *ravishing*, no matter he normally recoiled from such flowery language. She was delectable in a gown of ivory muslin sprigged with tiny oak leaves in golds and greens. The scooped neckline again did justice to her charms; the bodice was gathered beneath her lovely breasts with a spring-green ribbon.

Shifting in his chair, he reached for the coffeepot.

Barnaby grinned at him, but said nothing, returning his attention to a plate piled high with ham and kedgeree.

Unlike dinner, breakfast was a relatively mundane affair. Mitchel, seated beside his employer, spoke in an undertone about crops and fields.

Across the table, Millicent caught Gerrard's eye. "I trust your room was comfortable?"

"Perfectly, thank you." Gerrard swallowed a sip of coffee. "I was wondering if you and Miss Tregonning had time this morning to show myself and Mr. Adair about the gardens, at least enough for us to get our bearings."

"Yes, of course." Millicent glanced at the blue skies beyond the windows. "It's a perfect day for it."

A second of silence passed.

Gerrard had learned enough to be careful. "Miss Tregonning?" When she glanced up, plainly at a loss, he politely inquired, "Will you be free?"

She met his eyes, then smiled—another spontaneous expression, this time one of amused appreciation. Gerrard found himself smiling back.

"Yes, of course. The gardens are extensive." She glanced down at her plate. "It's easy to get lost."

Lost in the gardens, or in the web of her distracting personality? Gerrard knew which for him posed the greater danger; he had an excellent sense of direction.

An hour later, after he'd inspected and approved the attic nursery as his studio and explained how he wished things set out, the four of them met on the terrace.

"It's easiest if we start at a spot that has some meaning." With her furled parasol, Jacqueline pointed at the ridge to the immediate right of the house. "The Garden of Hercules is the most northerly of the gardens, and is also the way to the stables, a fact most gentlemen can be relied upon to remember." She turned to them. "Shall we?"

Barnaby flourishingly waved her on. "Lead on, fair damsel—we'll follow."

She laughed and set out. Barnaby fell in beside her.

Gerrard accompanied Millicent. He'd asked Barnaby to initially escort Jacqueline, giving him an opportunity to square matters with her aunt. They strolled the length of the terrace; by then Barnaby and Jacqueline were far enough ahead to permit private conversation.

"Thank you for agreeing to this outing," Gerrard said. "It can't be all that exciting for you—you must know the gardens like the back of your hand."

Millicent smiled. "Actually, I don't. I'm quite glad to have the opportunity to refresh my memory."

Gerrard blinked. "I thought . . . that is, I assumed this was your home."

"It was when I was very young, but our mother vastly preferred life in Bath, and I was the youngest, so I most often went with her. And then Papa died, and she and I stayed in Bath permanently. Over the years, I've only visited briefly. Mama became an invalid years ago, and, truth be told, I agreed with her—life at Hellebore Hall is terribly quiet. But then Miribelle, Jacqueline's mother, died so tragically . . . My older sisters have families of their own, so of course I came to stay."

They'd reached the end of the terrace; Gerrard gave Millicent his arm down a short flight of steps to a gravel path that led to the ridge.

Once they were strolling again, he asked, "How long ago did Jacqueline's mother die?" *And how?*

"Just fourteen months ago. We've only been out of mourning for two months."

Gerrard fought to hide his astonishment. Tregonning had been after him to paint Jacqueline for more than two months. Because he was paranoid he'd lose her, too, and wanted the portrait done before he did? That seemed . . . distinctly odd.

Before he could frame a useful question, Millicent spoke again.

"My brother has explained to me, Mr. Debbington, that your work on Jacqueline's portrait will necessitate your spending considerable time in her company, that you will need to learn about her to lend your work authority. My brother is very keen that the portrait be accurate. I can see that that will inevitably require you to spend time alone with Jacqueline." Millicent turned a severe, rather dauntingly level gaze on him. "You appear to be an estimable gentleman, sir, and your reputation is spotless. Yes, indeed"—she nodded—"I checked."

She looked ahead as they continued strolling. "Consequently, as far as your association with Jacqueline goes, I believe I can trust in your honor. If you will give me your word you will preserve the proprieties to the extent no harm will come to Jacqueline's good name, then I believe that, in these circumstances, I can relax my vigilance regarding the appropriate distance that should be preserved between gentlemen and young ladies such as my niece."

Gerrard blinked. Direct speaking was clearly a family trait; it was distinctly refreshing. "Thank you, ma'am. I give you my word that no harm will come to your niece's good name through any action of mine."

"Very good." Millicent nodded ahead to where Barnaby was regaling Jacqueline with some story, the two bright heads close. "In that case, I suggest you send Mr. Adair back to me. I would dearly love to hear what that scoundrel Monteith has been up to now. I knew his father, and a bigger blackguard I never did meet."

Gerrard couldn't suppress his grin. Bowing, he left Millicent and quickly overtook the pair ahead.

Barnaby was intrigued by Millicent's request; he happily fell back to walk with her, leaving Jacqueline strolling with Gerrard.

A small forest of tall conifers, all shades of dark green, some carrying their canopies high above long boles, others more like thick bushes, appeared before them. The path wound on between the trees, through the still shade; they followed it, their feet crunching on dry needles.

"The stables lie beyond the ridge." Jacqueline waved ahead. "This path takes you to them, but we'll turn off it soon. Each segment of the gardens was designed to represent one of the ancient gods, Roman or Greek, or one of the mythical creatures associated with them." In the cool beneath the trees, her voice carried easily to Millicent and Barnaby behind them. "This"—she gestured about them—"is the Garden of Hercules, the massively strong trunks representing his fabled strength.

"He was, of course, a demigod, but an obvious one to include." She smiled briefly at Gerrard. "My ancestors weren't dogmatic over their choice of subjects, and in that time, there was great interest in the ancient myths."

Gerrard nodded. They reached the ridge line and paused; ahead lay the usual stable buildings, separated from the gardens by a strip of open field through which the path continued. To the left of the path was a fenced paddock in which horses grazed; to the right, out of the center of a ring of tall corn rose an old, worn but still recognizable statue.

"Pegasus." Gerrard smiled.

"They had him shipped from somewhere in Greece." Jacqueline studied the winged horse for a moment. "He's one of my favorites. To get to the stables, you have to pass beneath his eye."

She turned left onto a connecting path that led along the ridge a little way before curving back down into the gardens; brows rising, Gerrard followed. Barnaby and Millicent had paused to exchange comments on Pegasus; they eventually followed some yards behind.

"This next garden," Jacqueline said as the conifers thinned and the path led on into the sunshine, "is the Garden of Demeter. Among other things, she was the goddess of crops and the fruitful earth, so . . ."

They walked out into a large and varied orchard. Some of the trees still held a few blossoms; the scent of growing fruit was tangy and sharp on the air. Bees lazily buzzed as they strolled down the gravel path, descending deeper into the valley. Jacqueline and Millicent unfurled their parasols; the sun was high enough to flood the valley with warmth and light.

The house now lay to their left, rising above them as they descended into the valley. Directly ahead at the junction of four paths—theirs and three others that spread like an open fan into the gardens before them—stood a small wooden pergola, painted white. Roses rambled over it in lazy profusion, spilling yellow blooms over the roof and down the carved pillars.

Jacqueline pointed left to a long strip of garden that ran from the pergola back to the terrace. "The kitchen gardens, otherwise known as the Garden of Vesta, goddess of the hearth."

It didn't look like any kitchen garden Gerrard had ever seen. As if reading his thoughts, Jacqueline said, "What you can see are mostly herbs. There are vegetables planted between, but the rampant growth of the herbs screens them."

" 'Rampant' being a very apt word," Barnaby returned. "Everything seems"—he glanced around them—"extraordinarily healthy."

Pausing under the pergola, Jacqueline nodded. "It's the situation, the shelter, and the soil." She waited while they all looked around, then waved to the three paths diverging before them. "This path"—she pointed to the one to the left, angling back to the house—"leads to the Garden of Poseidon."

"There?" Barnaby blinked. "I thought he would be down by the shore, god of the sea that he is."

"Ah, but Poseidon was the god of *all* water—fresh as well as salt—and it was claimed all springs flowed from where his trident struck." Jacqueline pointed to where, directly ahead, they could see sunlight glinting off the rippling waters of a stream running down the valley. "The stream is fed by a spring that rises in a grotto under the central section of the terrace. Poseidon therefore presides over the point where its waters start to flow freely down the valley, leaving the shoreline to Neptune."

"Aha! Very neat." Barnaby squinted down the valley toward the distant cove, but it was too far away, and there were too many intervening trees, shrubs, and rises and dips in the land to get any real view.

Gerrard decided he'd waited long enough; the Garden of Poseidon seemed to lie just below the area of thick, dark vegetation he'd noted the previous evening. "Where's the famous Garden of Night?"

He was standing beside Jacqueline; she didn't move, yet he was aware she stiffened. Nothing showed in her face, but it had suddenly become a mask. However, when she spoke, her tone was even, albeit devoid of emotion.

"The Garden of Night is reached through the Garden of Poseidon, or directly from the terrace via the main garden stairs. It abuts the terrace—in fact the grotto where the spring rises is part of the Garden of Night, more properly the Garden of Venus, who aside from being the goddess of love was also the first goddess of gardens, hence her preeminence here." Looking down, Jacqueline stepped out of the pergola onto the central of the three paths leading on. "I'm sure you've heard about the various plants that grow in the Garden of Night. As it's closest to the house, we'll leave it for later."

Gerrard held his peace, following her out into the sunshine; the others strolled after him.

Resetting her parasol, Jacqueline waved up the path to their right; it wended up and then along the steeply sloping north ridge. "That path leads through the Garden of Dionysius—it's full of grapevines of various sorts. Beyond it, you can see the cypresses of the Garden of Hades, cypresses being the tree of graveyards. That path rejoins this one farther down the valley, at the last viewing stage."

She gestured about them. "This area, directly below the Garden of Poseidon, is the Garden of Apollo. It's one of the gardens that uses statuary—he's the god of music, hence the once-gilded statue of a lyre."

They came upon the statue, an intricate work in iron, on a pedestal in the center of a small circle of lawn. The path wound its way past. They approached the stream; a small wooden bridge spanned it. "Music," Jacqueline continued, "is also created by the sound of the stream running over the rocks and the small weirs placed along its course."

They halted and listened. Watery music did indeed fill the air, tinkling, burbling, almost singing. It was a pleasant, relaxing sound. Gerrard scanned the area; it was rich with lush lawns and burgeoning flower beds.

Jacqueline stepped onto the bridge. "Apollo was also the god of light, and this area of the gardens has light for the longest time each day. The sundial"—she pointed to it, on the lawn just off the path ahead—"marks the point considered the center of the gardens."

They followed her on. The path steadily descended down a bank of verdant growth. Glancing back, Gerrard noted that while the roofs of the house were still visible high above the head of the valley, areas nearer to hand that they'd already traversed were not. It would indeed be easy to get lost.

"The four viewing stages," Jacqueline said as they reached the next, a rectangular stone platform with a wooden roof, "are placed at the main junctions of paths and also where a number of gardens meet."

There were five paths, including the one they'd just arrived on, radiating from the stone platform.

"We've just left the Garden of Apollo. That path"—Jacqueline pointed to the next path on the higher side of the platform—"leads back to the house via the Gardens of Poseidon and Venus. The next also leads back to the house, but through the Gardens of Diana, Athena and Artemis—we'll go back that way later. The next path"—she pointed to one heading up the southern ridge—"initially goes through a portion of the Garden of Mars, but then forks—you can head back to the house via the Garden of Diana, or go farther down the valley through the Gardens of Hermes and Vulcan. Which brings us to the path we'll take, heading down to the cove."

She led the way; Gerrard followed, taking her elbow to steady her down the steps. She glanced briefly at him, then looked ahead. "Thank you."

Once on the path, he released her. They waited until the others joined them, then Jacqueline turned and walked on. "This is the Garden of Mars. Although everyone knows him as the god of war, most gods have multiple, often contradictory faces, so Mars is also the god of fertility and farming, especially of all things that grow in the spring."

The beds they were passing were full of plants that had flowered and now carried seed pods of every description.

"Your relative, whoever he was, was quite inventive in choosing his gods." Hands in his pockets as he ambled beside her, Gerrard added the questions of how Jacqueline's mother had died, and why Jacqueline disliked the Garden of Night, to his growing list.

"My great-great-great-grandfather started it, my great-great-grandfather completed the design, but the planting wasn't complete until my great-grandfather's time."

They walked on, Jacqueline naming the gardens as they went, describing the association of each with the god for whom the area was named. They descended through the Garden of Persephone, goddess of plenty, lying below the dark mass of the Garden of Hades, her husband, lord of the underworld. The path led them to the lowest of the viewing platforms, a wooden one giving an excellent view of the narrow cove filled with rocks on which the waves crashed, then slowly, sussuratingly, receded.

The platform sat squarely at the intersection of four paths. The one leading to the shore wended through a landscape comprised of plants with unusual leaves or strange shapes. "The Garden of Neptune, god of the sea. The plants were chosen because they look like various seaweeds, or suggest another world."

They all stood at the balustrade, drawn to the view of the sea, gentle today yet the waves still rolled in. Gulls wheeled on the updrafts rising up the cliffs to the right, their screeching a sharp counterpoint to the rumble and whoosh of the waves. To the left, the cove was bound by a rocky outcrop, the extreme seaward section of which consisted of a single, massive boulder.

"Here comes a big wave." Barnaby pointed.

Gerrard looked; from the corner of his eye he saw Jacqueline glance at him, caught the curving of her lips . . . now what?

A sudden roaring sound reached them; before they could react, a spout of water exploded upward from the center of the massive rock.

Gerrard stared.

Barnaby grabbed his arm. "Good Lord! It's a blowhole!"

They both turned to Jacqueline. Smiling, she nodded. "It is indeed a blowhole—known as Cyclops, of course."

"Of course!" Barnaby's face was alight.

"What you just witnessed was a mild eruption. Every day as the tide comes in, there's a time when every fourth wave or so sends up a huge fountain. During king tides, the height and amount of water thrown out is simply amazing."

"Does the path lead down to it?" Gerrard asked.

"Yes, but it doesn't go onto Cyclops, the rock, itself—it's too dangerous. The surface is perennially slippery, and the sea's quite deep just there. The currents are very strong, and, of course, if anyone ever got sucked into the blowhole, they'd be smashed against the rocks inside."

He glanced at her. "Can we go closer?"

Her smile deepened. "I was planning to. Beyond Cyclops, the path curves around and heads back to the house."

Jacqueline started down the steps onto the last path. Gerrard moved to follow her.

"Jacqueline, dear, I'll wait for you here."

With Jacqueline, Gerrard turned to look back at Millicent. She smiled gamely at them. "While I'm certain I have enough stamina to return to the house from here, going down that last stretch might just be too much."

"Oh . . . all right. We'll just go down and come back."

Gerrard glanced at Barnaby, still on the platform beside Millicent.

"Actually," Barnaby said, "I have a better idea. You said that path curves around—does it meet this one?" He pointed to the path to his left.

Jacqueline frowned lightly. "Yes, they converge in the Garden of Vulcan just below the south ridge. From there, the path leads through the Gardens of Hermes and Diana, to the upper viewing platform, the only one we've yet to visit."

Barnaby turned to Millicent. "Why don't we head that way, taking in the sights at our leisure, and these two can go down and view Cyclops, then join us at the upper platform?"

"But don't you wish to view Cyclops from closer range?" Millicent asked.

"I do." Barnaby smiled, distinctly devil-may-care; he lowered his voice to a conspiratorial whisper. "But I would prefer to get closer than Miss Tregonning would probably think wise, and I would be loath to argue with such a charming hostess." He flashed his irrepressible smile at Jacqueline. "I'll come back later."

Jacqueline looked uncertain.

"Go on." Barnaby waved them on. "I'll stroll with Miss Tregonning and enjoy the sylvan delights." So saying, he offered Millicent his arm. Surrendering, she took it and allowed him to lead her up the other path.

Jacqueline stood watching, frowning.

Gerrard waited for a moment, then touched her arm. "Shall we?"

She didn't jump, but when she turned her head and her eyes met his, they were a fraction wide. "Yes, of course."

She sounded a touch breathless. Side by side, they walked down the sloping path. His latest questions burned in his brain, but he decided to ask someone else—possibly Millicent—about Jacqueline's mother rather than put his foot wrong with her. As for her reaction to the Garden of Venus, he wasn't yet sure what that was, but she'd said they would pass it on their way back—time enough to probe then.

They rounded the last bend in the path; the breeze off the waves hit them, and snatched at her parasol. She quickly furled it; he waited while she secured it, then offered his arm. "It'll be safer if you hold on to me."

She drew in a breath, then slid her hand around his elbow, laying her fingers on his sleeve. Sensing her uncertainty, he didn't draw her close, but now they were in the open, the breeze shrieked about them, plastering her dress to her figure, tugging at her skirts. She really would be safer clinging to him, taking refuge in his windshadow.

He wished she would. Most young ladies would unhesitatingly seize the opportunity; instead, she struggled to walk by his side and keep a decorous distance between them. Despite his unwanted sexual awareness of her, still notably high, her caution rankled.

They reached the line of rocks above the sloping shore. At the southern end of the cove, the massive bulk of Cyclops rose from the waves, its seaward faces cloaked in spume and spray.

Gerrard squinted. "Is that a ledge running around it?"

"Yes." Jacqueline raised her voice over the crash of the waves. "It's terribly dangerous, as you can see. At neap tide, you can follow the ledge all the way around and into the blowhole chamber itself, but at most times, the waves are too high, and the footing far too treacherous."

He stepped off the edge of the path to get a better view. Bracing one booted leg against a large rock, he studied the outcrop, noting the proportions. "I'll have to come down at sunset. Or sunrise. Or perhaps we'll have a storm?" He wanted to see more variations of light on Cyclops, and more movement about it, too.

Pushing back from the rock, he straightened and turned.

Only to discover Jacqueline had leaned toward him, fighting to hold back her hair with one hand.

They were suddenly very close, their faces only inches apart. Her eyes widened. Her lips were parted; she'd leaned close to say something.

Their eyes locked. Looking into hers, into the moss-agatey depths, he realized she'd forgotten what she'd been about to say.

Beyond his control, his gaze dropped to her lips. Soft, intensely feminine, shaped for passion, and mere inches away.

As was her body, those delectable breasts and elementally female curves. All he had to do to bring her against him was tip her to him, or take half a step more.

The impulse to do so was nearly overpowering; only the thought that she might panic held him back. Yet the allure of those lips, the desire to taste them, to raise his hands, frame her face and angle it up so his lips could cover hers and he could learn . . .

His gaze lowered to where the pulse beat wildly at the base of her throat, then lowered further, to her breasts, high, full . . . frozen. She wasn't breathing.

Forcing his gaze up, he met her eyes, and read in them how shocked, stunned and uncertain she was—how out of her depth she was.

He couldn't take advantage of such innocence, such clear and open naïveté. She might be twenty-three, but she had no idea what this was.

She'd clearly had no experience with desire, much less lust.

Taking a firm grip on his own, he grasped her arm, and gently moved her back so he could step up onto the path.

"Ah . . ." Jacqueline blinked and looked around; she fixed on Cyclops. "I was going to ask . . ."

She dragged in a huge breath, and grabbed hold of her wayward wits. Keeping her gaze on the huge rock, she battled to steady her giddy head and ignore the man by her side. "I was about to ask about Mr. Adair. He wouldn't be so reckless as to try to explore Cyclops, would he?"

When her companion didn't immediately reply, she glanced briefly at him, ready to be mortified if he said anything about that fraught moment an instant ago.

Instead, he was looking, not at her, but at Cyclops. Retaking her arm, he urged her on; hesitantly, trying not to notice the sensations his touch evoked, she fell into step once more beside him.

"Barnaby's insatiably curious, but not rashly so—not to the point of endangering himself. He might be many things, incorrigible and impossible to restrain at times, but he's not stupid."

"I didn't mean to imply he is," she hurried to say. "But . . . well, you know." She gestured. "Young men and their follies and reckless ways."

He looked at her then. She met his eyes—and realized they were warm, that his lips had eased, fractionally curving—that he was genuinely amused, not trying to be charming.

His natural smile was more potent than he knew.

"Young men," he repeated, then quietly said, "Neither Barnaby nor I are that young."

His eyes held hers for an instant, then his gaze lowered to her lips, then dropped away as he looked ahead.

They walked five paces before she remembered how to breathe.

Foolish, foolish, *foolish*! She had to overcome this ridiculous sensitivity that he, somehow, triggered. She might have led a quiet country life, but she'd attended country assemblies aplenty and she'd never—not ever—responded to a gentleman—to the man, to his presence—as she did to Gerrard Debbington.

It was nonsense—her reaction made no sense at all.

She had to, was determined to, overcome it, and if she couldn't do that, then she'd ignore it, certainly hide it so he got no inkling of her witless sensibility.

After that moment on the shore, ignoring all he made her feel seemed eminently wise.

The path led them around the edge of Cyclops, some distance back from the blowhole itself. Gerrard paused at the point where the path rose; looking down on the rock, they could see the hole clearly. A muffled rumbling reached them, then a small spout of water gushed up through the hole.

"The tide's turning," she said, and moved on.

He followed, his long fingers still wrapped about her elbow; she didn't shake free, didn't want to call attention to her awareness of his touch.

Yet she was aware—to her bones aware—of the latent strength not just in his fingers but in the lean, hard body keeping pace so close beside her.

Once they'd left Cyclops, the delights of the Garden of Vulcan, with its fiery red and orange flowers and bronze foliage, followed in turn by the Gardens of Hermes and Diana, the former dotted with ornamental stone cairns, the latter incorporating a small wood that was home to a herd of deer, gave her fodder enough to distract him. And herself.

By the time they reached the upper viewing stage, a delicate wrought-iron pergola, and rejoined Barnaby and Millicent, she'd managed to press that moment on the shore to the back of her mind.

She indicated the path that left the pergola to wind up the incline of the south ridge. "That leads to the Garden of Atlas, which is a rare example of a rock garden created with nothing but spherical boulders, rocks and stones."

"Reflecting the globe Atlas shouldered?" Shading his eyes, Barnaby looked up at the ridge.

"Indeed. From the upper end of that garden, steps give access to the south end of the terrace." Beckoning, she stepped onto the other path leading toward the house. "This will take us into the Garden of Athena. We could go straight through to the terrace—there's another set of steps—but if we take the fork that goes through the Garden of Artemis, we'll pass by the Garden of Night, too, before climbing the main terrace stairs."

"Lead on." Gerrard smiled easily as he came to pace beside her.

He looked ahead; she grasped the moment to surreptitiously study his profile. He'd asked numerous questions about the gardens as they'd walked. He was a landscape artist; the gardens would be of consuming interest, yet she had a suspicion he'd asked more because she'd expected him to, more to put her at ease, to soothe her leaping nerves . . . he couldn't know how he affected her, could he?

Facing forward, she pushed the disturbing notion out of her conscious mind. "The Garden of Athena, goddess of wisdom, is laid out in formal style, using primarily olive trees, sacred to the goddess." Her knowledge of the gardens was extensive; from childhood, she'd quizzed the gardeners, some of whom were older than her father and remembered the changes the decades had wrought.

They took the fork she indicated and strolled on into the fanciful landscape of the Garden of Artemis, home to a host of topiary animals, lions and tigers among them, the goddess's especial followers.

The sun shone strongly; the temperature was significantly higher than it had been when they'd set out. She slowed her pace; Millicent had to be tiring. She and her aunt had only recently become close, but she'd quickly grown fond of Millicent.

Ahead, the main steps up to the terrace rose in a curving flight of white marble with the same waist-high balustrade that ran the length of the terrace itself. The path they were following led to the bottom of the steps, then curved away into the Garden of Night.

She'd thought she was up to it, to taking them at least a little way into that most famous area of the gardens, but the closer they got to the heavy, large-leaved, dark green foliage that enclosed it, she felt instinctive resistance rise, until it was choking her.

It was broad daylight, she chided herself, yet her mind instantly conjured how dark, almost subterranean, the garden felt regardless of the hour, with its wide still pool into which the spring all but silently flowed, the closeness of the humidity the spectacularly rampant growth held in, the muted quality of the light, so diffused and broken by the thick canopy that even at noon the garden resembled a cavern, and above all else, the claustrophobic stillness and the heavy, suffocating medley of perfumes.

Dragging in a breath past the vise that, with each step, tightened about her lungs, she halted at the foot of the stairs. "I have several matters I must attend to before luncheon, which will be served shortly, so perhaps, Aunt"—she glanced at Millicent—"we should go inside?"

Approaching on Barnaby's arm, Millicent nodded. "I think so." The long walk had clearly wearied her. She furled her parasol. "I must speak with Mrs. Carpenter before luncheon."

Relieved, Jacqueline turned to Gerrard and Barnaby. "If you wish to go on, that path leads through the Garden of Night, and then into the Garden of Poseidon." She managed a light smile. "As Papa has doubtless told you, you should feel free to explore the gardens at will." Glancing at Barnaby, she considered reiterating her warning about venturing onto Cyclops, then remembered Gerrard's words, and thought better of it.

Barnaby had been peering ahead; he flashed her a grin. Reaching for her hand, he bowed over it. "Thank you for a fascinating tour." Straightening, he looked at the Garden of Night. "I'm sure we can manage on our own from here."

She smiled and shifted her gaze to Gerrard, expecting to see a similar eagerness to explore in his face. Instead, he was watching her, studying her.

Her breath caught; her lungs seized.

Millicent, thank heavens, spoke to him, deflecting his attention. By the time his too acute gaze returned to her, she'd recovered and was ready. She inclined her head, her lips lightly curved. "I hope you feel comfortable within the gardens now, sir, enough to go about on your own."

"Indeed." His brown eyes held hers. "If you're sure we can't tempt you to accompany us, and leave those 'several matters' until later?"

Her smile felt tight. "Quite sure. Unfortunately . . ." She broke off before completing the lie. Millicent moved past her, starting up the steps. She reminded herself she owed him no explanation. Drawing a determined breath, she met his eyes. "I'll see you at luncheon, sir. Treadle will ring the bell on the terrace, so you'll be sure to hear it."

His disturbingly intent gaze lingered on her face, but then he bowed. "Until then, Miss Tregonning."

Inclining her head, she turned and followed Millicent up the steps. Her senses pricked, nervously flickering. Gaining the terrace, she paused, then looked back.

Gerrard hadn't moved. He'd remained where she'd left him, watching her . . . as if he knew how tight her lungs were, how tense her nerves . . . how her heart was thudding.

His eyes met hers. For an instant, all about them stilled . . .

She turned and followed Millicent across the terrace and into the house.

4

After luncheon, another quiet meal, Gerrard retreated to his studio while Barnaby hied out to explore Cyclops and the gardens in general.

Earlier, they'd explored the Garden of Night—a curious, dramatic and vaguely disturbing place. The atmosphere had been all Gerrard's dream had promised, not just darkly Gothic but with a sinister undertone carried in the oppressive stillness. The more cheery Garden of Poseidon had lightened their mood before Treadle's gong had summoned them back to the house.

Closing the nursery-cum-studio door, Gerrard got to work. His purpose was defined—to set out all he needed, to unpack the boxes the footmen had left stacked against the walls and lay out paints, pads, pencils and the various paraphernalia with which he habitually surrounded himself—yet while his hands were busy, his mind remained engrossed.

Thinking of Jacqueline Tregonning.

Reliving, reviewing, all the moments he'd thus far shared with her, and trying to make sense of them, trying to wring every last iota of meaning from each, to get some firm concept—some concept he could accept as firm enough—of what she was, of what, with her, he was dealing with.

His initial view of her had been that she had character. That had proved true, yet her character was complex, far more so than he'd expected. He'd labeled her an enigma, and she still was to him.

He hadn't, yet, made any real headway in understanding her. His observations to date had yielded not answers but yet more questions.

And that surprised him.

He would, he felt, have coped with that surprise, with the challenge she posed, well enough, if it hadn't been for the rest of it—the aspects of their interaction he hadn't foreseen, and wasn't sure how to deal with.

Despite his experience, this was one situation he'd never before had to face. Not even when his subjects had been ravishing beauties, the twins for example, had he found himself wondering what their lips would taste like.

He kept telling himself that the sexual attraction he felt would fade, would merge into his customary, curious-yet-detached attitude as he learned more of Jacqueline. Instead, thus far at least, the more he learned, the closer he drew to her, the more powerfully the attraction flared.

Throwing the heavy locks on a case, he laid it open on the floor, then hunkered down to examine the pencils and charcoals neatly arrayed within. He tried to focus on his art, on the practical acts necessary to bring it to life, tried to channel his edginess into that, and didn't succeed.

Selecting two pencils, he closed the case. Straightening, he crossed to where the table he'd requested sat at right angles to one end of the wide windows. Sketch pads lay stacked, the lightly textured paper he favored for first drawings spread ready, virginal white, waiting for his impressions, his first attempts at capturing them.

Such a sight always brought a surge of excitement, of eagerness to plunge into a new work; he felt the expected lift, the sharpening of his senses, yet there was something else, something more compelling, hovering in his mind, distracting him.

Laying down the pencils, he breathed in and closed his eyes—and vividly recalled how her eyes, moss, amber, gold and brown, had appeared in that fraught instant on the shore.

He focused on that moment, one that kept replaying in his brain; he remembered what he'd felt, how the feelings had flowed.

Realized that it wasn't purely his reaction to her, the sexual attraction itself, that was destabilizing his concentration. It was her reaction to him, and his subsequent response to that—all of those elements combined.

Opening his eyes, he blinked. Frowned.

He couldn't recall ever having his attention captured, ensnared, by a woman's reaction to him. Yet every time her fingers trembled in his, he wanted to seize, not just them but her; every time her lovely eyes flared, he was visited by an urge to touch her, caress her, and watch them widen even more.

Beneath his breath, he swore. Every time he thought of her, he ended envisioning making love to her.

A tap fell on the door, light, uncertain.

Not Jacqueline, was his first thought.

He raked his hand through his hair. "Come in." Any distraction was better than the circle his thoughts seemed determined to tread.

The door swung open; Millicent stood in the doorway. Seeing him, she smiled and walked in. She looked around, but that seemed merely a polite action, because she thought she should show interest.

"You seem to be settling in quite nicely—is everything to your liking?"

No—lusting after your niece is driving me deranged. Gerrard smiled. "Thank you. I have all I need."

"Well . . ." Millicent hesitated; clearly there was some purpose behind her visit, one she was reluctant to broach.

Gerrard gestured to the window seat beneath the farther window, the area he'd left for consultation, away from his work. "Won't you sit down?"

Turning, Millicent saw the window seat. "Oh, yes. Thank you."

Following her across the room, Gerrard picked up a straight-backed chair and set it down facing the seat, close enough to see Millicent's eyes, yet not close enough to crowd her.

He waited for her to sit, then sat himself. When she didn't say anything but studied his face, as if wondering whether to speak at all, he prompted, "Was there something you wished to tell me?"

She studied his eyes for a moment longer, then grimaced. "Yes—you're very acute."

He made no reply but waited.

She sighed. "It's about Jacqueline, and, well . . . the reason she no longer goes into the Garden of Night."

He nodded encouragingly. "I noted her hesitation this morning."

"Indeed." Millicent clasped her hands tightly in her lap. "It's because of her mother—or rather, Miribelle's death. She fell to her death, you see. From the terrace, into the Garden of Night."

He felt his expression blank with shock.

Millicent saw; she leaned forward, concerned. "I'm sorry. I see you didn't know, but I wasn't sure whether Marcus would think to mention the details, and, of course, having to learn about Jacqueline in order to paint her properly, you were bound to notice and wonder . . . well, as you did."

He managed to nod; what he desperately needed was to think. "How did it happen?" When Millicent frowned, as if unsure what he meant, he restated the query, "What caused Jacqueline's mother to fall?"

Millicent's eyes widened a fraction; she sat back. He got the impression he'd put a foot wrong, but couldn't imagine how or where.

A hand rising to fiddle with her neckline, Millicent said, her tone now careful, "It was, of course, thought to be an accident. Anything else . . . well, there never was any suggestion of anything else."

She'd grown flustered; to his dismay, she stood. "So now you understand why Jacqueline won't go into that area of the gardens. I don't know that she'll ever grow comfortable enough to venture there again. Please don't press her."

Gerrard rose, too. "No, of course not."

Millicent turned quickly to the door. "Now I really must get on. You will remember that we're dining with the Frithams this evening? The carriage will leave at seven."

"Yes. Thank you." Gerrard followed her to the door.

She didn't wait for him to open it, but did so herself and started down the narrow stairs. "At seven, remember," she called back, then whisked away down the corridor.

Gerrard leaned against the doorjamb, and wondered why Millicent had suddenly decided she'd said too much. What had she told him?

So little. Just enough to show him how much more he'd yet to learn.

G ood Lord! She fell to her death from the terrace?"

"So Millicent said, and I doubt she invented it." Gerrard

lolled on the end of Barnaby's bed, watching while his friend, now distinctly absentmindedly, tied his cravat.

Gently lowering his chin, creasing the folds expertly, Barnaby shot him a sidelong glance. "And there's some question over the death, you say?"

"No, I don't say—I infer." Gerrard altered his voice to an approximation of Millicent's. "Anything else . . . well, there never was any suggestion of anything else." He reverted to his usual tones. "All said with her eyes wide and a look that clearly stated that while no one had ever *suggested* such a thing, it was the question in everyone's mind."

"A mystery!" Barnaby's eyes glowed.

"Possibly." Gerrard wasn't entirely convinced of the wisdom of setting Barnaby loose on the subject, but he had to know more, and his friend was a master at ferreting out such things. "I asked Compton what he'd heard. Apparently, the late Lady Tregonning was well liked, nay, loved by all who knew her. The accepted theory is that she peered over the balustrade to look at something in the Garden of Night, overbalanced and fell. Tragic and regrettable, but nothing else. There's no question but that the fall killed her—her neck was broken. That's the story from the servants' hall."

"They usually know," Barnaby murmured, easing on his coat.

"True." Gerrard sat up. "However, if there's no question over what killed her, then what caused her to go over the balustrade is the only thing that might remain in question—the only aspect that might account for Millicent's reaction."

Engaged in placing his handkerchief, watch and sundry other items into various pockets, Barnaby hmmed. "Suicide? It's always an option in such cases."

Gerrard grimaced and rose. "It could be that. Millicent wanted to explain so I wouldn't press Jacqueline to enter the Garden of Night, then realized she'd revealed too much . . . yes, that might be it."

He headed for the door; it was nearly seven o'clock.

Barnaby joined him. "But . . . ?"

Hand on the knob, Gerrard met his friend's eyes. "I need to know the truth, whatever it is, and for obvious reasons I can't ask Jacqueline."

Barnaby grinned and clapped him on the back. "Leave it to me—I'll see what I can learn this evening. There's sure to be someone attending who'll be eager to swap a bit of gossip and scandal."

Shaking his head, Gerrard led the way out of the room. "Just don't make it sound like we're conducting an investigation."

"Trust me." Barnaby followed him out and shut the door. "I'll be the soul of discretion."

Gerrard started for the stairs, inwardly debating. Eventually, he murmured, "There's one other thing."

"Oh? What?"

"I need to understand why Jacqueline's unmarried. She's twenty-three, attractive, and Tregonning's heiress—even buried out here, she must have, or have had, suitors. Who? And where are they now? No one's suggested there's any gentleman in the wings. Is her mother's death in some way responsible for that?"

"Interesting point." They reached the head of the stairs; Barnaby slanted a cheerfully inquisitive glance Gerrard's way. "Just tell me—is that the way the wind now blows?"

Gerrard snorted. "Spare me." He started down the stairs. "I need to know for the portrait."

"Such things shouldn't be too hard to learn."

"Just remember—discretion is imperative."

"You know me."

"Indeed—that's why I'm reminding you."

It wasn't, in truth, Barnaby's discretion that caused Gerrard concern, but his enthusiasm; once embarked on solving a mystery, Barnaby was apt to forget such niceties as feminine susceptibilities and social strictures. From his position in the circle of which Jacqueline was a member, Gerrard kept an eye on his friend as Barnaby prowled the Frithams' drawing room.

Hunting for information. With his bright eyes, cheery personality and, when he wished it, polished address, it was an undertaking at which he admittedly excelled.

Gerrard was doing his own reconnoitering. Lady Fritham had summoned a good slice of the local gentry. By remaining in the same group as Jacqueline, he was able to gauge her reactions to others as they came up to greet them. In between shaking hands and keeping track of relationships, he viewed again the continuing conundrum of her behavior. Outwardly, she was confident, assured and serene, yet she remained reserved, aloof emotionally as distinct from physically, as if she'd taken a step back from everyone there; while she knew them well, she saw them as people to keep at a distance.

He'd thought it was distrust, and there were certainly traces of that in her stance, yet now, after hearing of her mother's death, he wondered if what he was sensing was instead a form of inner shield, a protection she maintained so others couldn't reach her, couldn't hurt her.

Why would they hurt her?

Had these people hurt her? If so, how?

He started looking more closely, not at Jacqueline but at everyone else, watching, analyzing . . . He felt the shift in his attitude as a sudden honing of his senses, a definite alert that spread through him.

In addition to Lord and Lady Fritham and their son and daughter, the Myles family entire were present, Mr., Mrs., Master Roger and both Misses, Clara and Rosa. The severe Mrs. Elcott and her spouse were absent, perhaps not surprisingly. A Mr. and Mrs. Hancock were there, with two daughters, Cecily and Mary, in train; a local squire, Sir Humphrey Curtis, a widower, was attending with his sister, Miss Amabel Curtis.

Lord Trewarren, a local landowner, his lady and their two sons, Giles and Cedric, were presently part of their circle, along with Mitchel Cunningham and Millicent.

"Mr. Debbington, you really must share your opinion of the Hellebore Hall gardens." Lady Trewarren, head high, peered at him myopically across the circle. "Millicent tells me you viewed them today. Will you paint them?"

"Eventually, yes, but as for my opinion, it's difficult to rate something that's so very unique. It certainly ranks as one of the best sources for landscape art I've seen."

Lady Trewarren turned to Millicent. "Millicent, dear, you really must work on Marcus to open up the gardens on occasion. What is the point of having such wonderful gardens if no one ever sees them?"

Millicent murmured that she quite agreed. "I'm hoping that the interest sure to accrue when Mr. Debbington shows his works will help convince Marcus."

Gerrard returned Millicent's smile, but his attention had deflected to Lady Trewarren, and the sudden distraction he saw in her face. She'd glanced to where her older son Giles was speaking with Jacqueline.

Gerrard could hear their conversation, Giles politely inquiring whether Jacqueline would like to join him, his brother and unspecified others on a ride to St. Just tomorrow.

Giles seemed a likable enough chap; he smiled with pleasure when Jacqueline accepted the simple invitation—throwing Lady Trewarren into a maternal flutter. Gerrard had seen the like before, usually in the context of fond mamas wanting to protect their darling sons from entanglements with encroaching cits. Yet Giles was hardly a babe, and Jacqueline was no cit; regardless, as Lady Trewarren turned back to him and Millicent, conscious of her distraction and, it seemed, wishing to disguise it, her desire to suppress any association between Jacqueline and Giles showed in her eyes.

Millicent hadn't noticed; she'd been discussing the recent spate of fine weather with Lord Trewarren.

Gerrard allowed the conversation to claim him, but he kept an eye on Lady Trewarren. Sure enough, when an opening offered, she claimed, not her husband's but her eldest son's arm and, excusing them from the circle, moved on.

Jacqueline showed no sign of consciousness over having a handsome admirer removed from her side, and indeed, Giles's place was almost immediately filled by Roger Myles.

"Quite," Gerrard said, replying to a query about the capital. "It's sweltering in late summer."

He shifted, scanning the crowd—trying to locate Mrs. Myles, to see if she, too, would react as Lady Trewarren had.

"Ladies and gentlemen." The Frithams' butler stood in the open doorway; when everyone turned to him, he bowed magisterially. "Dinner is served."

The usual mild chaos ensued as Lady Fritham partnered them. Waving to this one, then that, she set Barnaby to escort Clara Myles, then pounced on Gerrard; linking her arm with his, she led him across the room.

Leaning close, she murmured, "Millicent mentioned that you need to spend time with Jacqueline, in pursuit of the portrait, as it were, but tonight is hardly a time for work—I've asked Eleanor to make sure you enjoy yourself."

So saying, she delivered him to her daughter.

Amenable enough, Gerrard smiled and claimed Eleanor's hand, and wondered what opportunities the seating would afford.

When they filed into the long dining room, he found himself in perfect accord with Lady Fritham's organization. Entirely without intending to, indeed, for quite the opposite reason, she'd given him what for him was the perfect place—directly opposite Jacqueline.

That meant he couldn't converse with her, but at the moment, that wasn't his aim. Observing her was, along with Lady Trewarren and Mrs. Myles, both mothers of young gentlemen of Jacqueline's acquaintance.

As it happened, Jacqueline had Roger Myles and Cedric Trewarren flanking her; all three were of much the same age, which, Gerrard judged, made Roger and Cedric too young for Jacqueline. From what he saw of their interactions as, with Mary Hancock, they took their seats, they'd known each other for years; they treated each other as friends, nothing more.

Having seated Eleanor, he drew out the chair beside her and sat. Cecily Hancock was on his left. From the gleam in both young ladies' eyes, they were eager to entertain him.

Charm to the fore, he asked about the local attractions.

Throughout the meal it proved easy enough to deal with Eleanor and Cecily, both of whom openly vied for his attention, while simultaneously watching Lady Trewarren and Mrs. Myles. Both ladies were seated at one end of the table, opposite each other; he had to face Cecily to see Lady Trewarren, but, thanks to Cecily's increasingly blatant attempts to monopolize him, that was easy to disguise.

As the courses came and went, he watched and analyzed. Lady Trewarren, while noting her younger son chatting animatedly to Jacqueline, seemed less concerned than when Giles had sought Jacqueline's attention; presumably her ladyship recognized the nature of Cedric's and Jacqueline's friendship. With Mrs. Myles, however . . . the desserts were on the table before Gerrard glimpsed, just fleetingly, a touch of the same motherhen concern he'd seen in Lady Trewarren.

Mrs. Myles was much more guarded in her expressions, yet Roger was her only son; when, along with Jacqueline and Cedric, Roger laughed at some joke, she leaned forward and looked down the table—not censorious but worried, concerned . . . She saw, then sat back. Absentmindedly she patted her lips with her napkin, her brow faintly creased, her gaze far away, then Lord Fritham spoke to her and she looked his way.

Gerrard let his gaze return to Cecily.

Just in time to see her shoot a smug, spite-filled glance, first at Eleanor, then across the table at Jacqueline, who glanced up just in time to catch it.

Then Cecily looked at him, positively oozing what she no doubt imagined was sultry seductiveness. He'd obviously missed something he ought to have nipped in the bud.

"I'm sure I don't know," Cecily purred, leaning closer, "why it's so important that you paint Jacqueline—why, everyone knows brown hair is entirely out of fashion. But now you're in the area, I daresay you'll be on the lookout for other suitable ladies to paint, to make your stay down here worthwhile." Touching fingertips to her primped blond curls, she smiled and all but batted her lashes at him. "I would be *very* happy to sit for you."

Gerrard decided against telling her she was precisely the sort of young lady he daily prayed he'd never have to paint. Informing her that if he painted her, all her spite and nastiness—from what he'd taken in of her comments she was well endowed with both—would show, also seemed unwise; she'd probably shriek, faint or accuse him of something.

Yet thanks to her indiscreetly modulated voice—he was quite sure she'd intended all around them to hear—everyone was waiting to hear his response. Beside him, Eleanor had angrily tensed; seated beyond Cecily, Mitchel Cunningham had colored painfully, but was avidly listening. Jacqueline had calmly turned to Roger and made some comment, drawing both Cedric and Mary—a quiet girl quite different from her sister—into the conversation, yet although they were ostensibly involved in their discussion, they were all waiting, listening, too.

It took him a mere instant to absorb that; he smiled, gently, at Cecily. "I'm afraid, Miss Hancock, that painters such as I don't follow fashion." His tone was cool, his drawl patronizingly light. He hesitated a heartbeat, holding her gaze, before adding, "We set it."

With that, he turned to Eleanor, smoothly engaging her with a question about St. Just, without compunction leaving Cecily-the-spiteful to come about as best she could.

For a few minutes, she sat in total silence, then he heard Mitchel Cunningham ask her a polite question. After a moment, Cecily quietly replied.

Across the table, Jacqueline caught his eye. Their gazes held for a heartbeat; he sensed she was grateful, yet puzzled, too—why, he had no clue.

A few minutes later, Lady Fritham rose, gathered the ladies and led them from the room. The gentlemen regrouped, congregating in the chairs about the table's head as the brandy and port were set before Lord Fritham. Gerrard was surprised when Jordan Fritham circled the table to claim the chair beside him. They both helped themselves to the port as the decanter was passed around, then settled back.

Lord Fritham appealed to Barnaby, "What's this I hear about Bentinck? Got himself in a spot of bother, so I hear."

Understanding his lordship's request, Barnaby launched into a highly colored recounting of Samuel Bentinck, Lord Mainwarring's latest and possibly last attempt at matrimony. Gerrard sat back, relaxed; he knew the story, had heard Barnaby's version at least twice, yet his friend was an excellent raconteur—it was no hardship to hear the tale again.

Barnaby rattled on; beside Gerrard, Jordan Fritham grew restless.

Eventually, he leaned closer to Gerrard, lowering his voice. "Quite a coup, I understand, that old Tregonning managed to persuade you to travel into our wilds to paint Jacqueline."

Gerrard glanced at Jordan. He'd looked down, studiously examining the wine as he twirled his port glass. Jordan was in his mid to late twenties, yet Gerrard found it difficult to view him as a peer; Jordan's perpetual arrogance, his condescending attitude, his often petulant, if not truculent expression, marked him so clearly as immature.

Barnaby's story had some way to run; Gerrard was curious as to where Jordan intended to lead their conversation. "I rarely paint portraits of anyone."

Jordan nodded, looking up—along the table, not at Gerrard. "Ah, yes—your real interest lies in the gardens, of course." Raising his glass, he sipped, then, still without meeting Gerrard's gaze, murmured, "A very lucky circumstance that Tregonning could offer you access to the gardens as inducement."

Gerrard inwardly frowned. What the devil was Jordan getting at? "Lucky?"

Jordan darted a glance his way, then once more fell to studying his port. "Well, it's common knowledge, at least to those of us who know the family well, why Tregonning wants the portrait done."

He was too experienced to ask the question Jordan wanted him to ask—not yet. "You and your family know the Tregonnings well?"

Looking up, Jordan frowned. "Of course."

"I understood from your father that the family hailed from Surrey."

"Originally, but so did Miribelle, Tregonning's late wife. As girls, she and m'mother were neighbors, bosom bows. Then they both married and Miribelle moved down here. After a few years, Mama and she grew frustrated with talking only through letters, so, as Tregonning wouldn't leave Hellebore Hall, Mama convinced the pater they should buy Tresdale Manor, and"—Jordan gestured, his lip curling, his tone hardening—"here we are."

He drained his port glass.

Gerrard wondered if Jordan knew just how transparent his resentment at being buried in the country, far from all excitement, was. Possibly he did, and didn't care.

"You've been at the Hall for over a day now, long enough to see what a mausoleum it's become. Miribelle was the life of the house; she and Mama constantly held parties and balls, all sorts of revelry. Not so much at the Hall itself, mostly here, but the brightness spilled into the Hall—even Tregonning used to smile occasionally." Jordan set down his glass and reached for the decanter. He wasn't drunk so much as well lit.

Gerrard said nothing, just waited. As he'd hoped, Jordan picked up his tale.

"Then Miribelle died." Jordan paused to sip, then went on, "Suddenly, for no reason, she fell to her death. Ever since, we've barely had a party in the neighborhood." His lip curled again; he glowered darkly across the room, then looked down, into his glass, and more quietly said, "It was given out it was an accident, of course."

And there it was. Gerrard froze, physically, emotionally, as his mind made the mental leap and he saw the connections—the portrait, *why* Tregonning wanted it, Tregonning's insistence that he was the only painter who would do, even to the point of stooping to extortion, Jacqueline's comment that her portrait done by him was what she and her father *needed*, the importance she'd placed on it showing *what* she truly was . . .

Raising his glass, he took a long, slow sip of Lord Fritham's excellent port; he barely tasted it. Yet nothing of his thoughts, of the sudden eruption of feelings churning through him, showed in his face, for which he was grateful—especially before a prat like Jordan Fritham.

"Indeed." Anyone who knew him would have taken warning from his tone. Even Jordan looked up, alert, although not apparently understanding why. Gerrard sipped again, then cocked an eyebrow at Jordan. "Am I to take it that all those round about know of . . . the reason I'm here to paint Jacqueline's portrait?"

He couldn't keep the simmering anger completely from his voice, but while Jordan heard it and faintly frowned, he nevertheless answered with a light shrug. "I suppose all those who know the family well."

"Most of those here, then?"

"Oh, not the younger ones—not the girls or Roger or Cedric."

"I see." Gerrard was suddenly very certain he did.

Lord Fritham chose that moment to push back his chair. Gerrard realized Barnaby had concluded his tale; all the usual exclamations and comments had been made and had died away.

"Very entertaining, Mr. Adair. Now I suspect it's time we rejoined the ladies." Beaming genially, Lord Fritham stood.

Chairs scraped. They all rose. Lord Fritham turned to speak to the butler. Gerrard moved with the others to the door; he hung back and Barnaby joined him.

They fell in at the rear of the group heading along the corridor to the drawing room; Lord Fritham had remained behind, but would no doubt shortly follow. They both slowed.

"What's the matter?" Barnaby asked.

Gerrard shot him a glance; Barnaby was one of the few who would notice his state. "I've just learned something disturbing, too complicated to explain here. Have you learned anything?"

"Not about Lady Tregonning's death, but I did hear about Jacqueline's suitor."

"She had a suitor?"

"*Had* being the operative word. The son of a local landowner, well liked, a good match on all sides. They were apparently fond of each other, everyone expected an announcement any day . . . then he disappeared."

"Disappeared?" Incredulous, Gerrard glanced at Barnaby.

Who nodded grimly. "Just *disappeared.* He visited Jacqueline one afternoon, then he left for the stables, and hasn't been heard of to this day."

Gerrard looked ahead. "Good God."

"Indeed." The drawing room doors were approaching; they both checked and looked back. And saw Lord Fritham coming along, the very picture of a jovial host, in their wake. They both hesitated, then Barnaby murmured, "Do you know what the odds against having two strange, unexplained happenings occurring *innocently* at one house are?"

"Too long," Gerrard replied, and stepped into the drawing room.

Barnaby followed, but then wandered away, no doubt intent on learning more.

Gerrard left him to it; using his height, he scanned the room, searching for the one person he wanted to interrogate himself.

But Mitchel Cunningham was nowhere in sight.

Mrs. Hancock and Miss Curtis, seated on a chaise, had spotted him standing alone. They beckoned; perforce, he went. He chatted with this one, then that; while the Myles sisters and Mary Hancock entertained the company with various airs on the pianoforte, he waited for Mitchel Cunningham to reappear.

Time passed, and the agent didn't return. Eventually, Gerrard paused by the side of the room and took stock. Eleanor Fritham was also absent.

On the thought, draperies further down the long room stirred, and Eleanor appeared, strolling easily back to join the guests. She was visually stunning, with her long, fine blond hair floating about her, her pale skin, long neck and slender, sylphlike figure; she wasn't quite ethereal, yet at the same time, not quite of this world . . . and she, too, was unmarried, apparently unspoken for.

Gerrard inwardly frowned; he watched as Eleanor joined the circle of which Jacqueline was a member, smoothly linking her arm in Jacqueline's in a gesture that screamed of long friendship. Given what he now suspected, Gerrard wondered at that apparent closeness. Jacqueline was facing away; he couldn't gauge her reaction.

Shifting his gaze, he scanned the room again; he was about to move on when, from behind the same set of drifting draperies through which Eleanor had appeared, Mitchel Cunningham stepped into the room.

Gerrard changed direction and strolled his way, intercepting Mitchel before he could join any other guests. "Could I have a word, Cunningham?" When Mitchel blinked, he added, "It's about the portrait."

Cunningham had dealt with him enough to comprehend the significance of his clipped accents. Lips thinning, he nodded. "Yes, of course."

Gerrard turned to the French doors giving onto the terrace. "Perhaps in more private surrounds."

Cunningham went with him. As they stepped onto the flagstones, Gerrard glanced along the terrace; the long window with the billowing draperies did indeed give onto the terrace—at the heavily shadowed end.

Jordan Fritham's dog-in-the-manger attitude over his sister, apparent whenever Cunningham drew close, now made sense; the notion of having a brother-in-law who was a mere gentleman's agent would not sit well with Jordan's sense of self-worth.

Cunningham had noticed him glancing at the far window; returning his gaze to the agent's eyes, Gerrard didn't hide his comprehension, but Cunningham's aspirations were not his concern.

"I've discovered," he said, "that the reason behind Lord Tregonning's insistence that *I* paint his daughter's portrait goes somewhat deeper than mere appreciation of my art."

Cunningham paled; even in the poor light, his increasing nervousness was obvious. "Ah . . ."

"Indeed." Gerrard held his temper on a tight rein. "I see that you're aware of it. I have one question: Why wasn't I informed?"

Cunningham swallowed, but gamely lifted his head and met Gerrard's gaze. "I advised telling you, but Lord Tregonning forbade it."

"Why?"

"Because he was uncertain how you would react to his reason, whether you might decline to do the portrait in such circumstances, and then later, once you'd accepted the commission, he was concerned not to . . . to prejudice your view in any way."

He had to fight to keep the anger building inside him from his face. The situation was beyond outrageous, yet . . . he couldn't, now, simply walk away. "Is Miss Tregonning aware of her father's expectations of the portrait?"

Cunningham looked appalled. "I assume not . . ." He blinked. "But I don't know. Her knowing or not was not discussed with me."

"I see." So many aspects of the situation were fueling his ire, his mind was swinging violently, railing over first one, then the next. That Tregonning would pander to such suspicions of his daughter made him see red; that Jacqueline, knowing of her father's scheme, should so meekly agree made him want to shake her. How could she accept, as she patently had, that such suspicion was even reasonable?

How could she so calmly accept that he, an unknown gentleman, should judge her?

How dared she—they—place such an onus on him?

He was furious, but fought to keep his rage contained. Focusing, grimly, on Cunningham's pale face, he nodded. "Very well. I suggest, since Lord Tregonning does not wish me to know of his expectations, that there's no reason for him to know of this discussion."

Cunningham's Adam's apple bobbed; he nodded. "As you wish."

"Indeed." Gerrard caught the agent's eye. "I suggest you endeavor to forget this conversation took place, and I"—deliberately he glanced toward the end of the terrace—"will do the same."

With another nervous nod, Cunningham turned and walked back into the drawing room. Gerrard waited for a full minute, then followed.

Pausing just inside, he looked across the room at Jacqueline Tregonning.

He couldn't wait to get back to Hellebore Hall.

5

The dinner party drew to a close; along with Millicent, Barnaby and a subdued Mitchel Cunningham, they thanked their hosts and left Tresdale Manor. They traveled back to Hellebore Hall in Lord Tregonning's antiquated coach; the distance wasn't great—the manor was the nearest large house—yet with only two horses pulling the heavy carriage, the journey took nearly half an hour.

Throughout, Gerrard sat in the dark, his shoulder against Barnaby's, with Jacqueline sitting directly opposite, her knees, covered by the fine silk of her gown, courtesy of the country road frequently brushing his.

It wasn't just the contact that unnerved her, but his unwavering regard. He knew she was conscious of it, but was past caring; he wanted answers to many questions, and she was the key to the most important.

That's precisely what I need—what my father needs.

She knew; he wanted to hear it from her lips.

They reached the Hall and trailed into the foyer, there to exchange the customary good-nights. He bowed over Jacqueline's hand, squeezed it, caught her eye as he released her. She couldn't know what he intended, but at least she'd be alert.

The look she cast back at him as she followed Millicent up the wide staircase confirmed that.

With a nod to him and Barnaby, Mitchel Cunningham walked off down a corridor; after dallying a moment to let the ladies go ahead, he and Barnaby started up in their wake.

The gallery at the head of the stairs was long, and presently a collage of moonlight and shadow. The ladies turned right; a few paces behind, Gerrard and Barnaby headed left, toward their rooms. Gerrard put out a hand, halting Barnaby. Glancing back, he confirmed that Jacqueline and Millicent were sweeping on, unaware, and were now out of earshot. He turned to Barnaby. "Did you learn anything more about the suitor?"

"Only that he disappeared between two and three years ago, when Jacqueline was twenty. Although there'd been no formal declaration, she went into half-mourning. Then her mother died fourteen months ago, which in large part fills the time to date and explains why there have been no other suitors."

"Did you hear anything about her mother's death?"

"No, but I didn't have the right opportunities to pursue it. It's the older ladies we need to butter up for that."

Gerrard nodded. Glancing back along the gallery, he saw Jacqueline turn down the corridor at its end, Millicent still by her side. "I'll see you tomorrow."

He turned and, swift and soft-footed, followed Jacqueline.

"Hey!" Barnaby kept his voice down.

"Tomorrow," he flung back sotto voce, and continued on.

He reached the corridor and looked along it. It was empty; another corridor opened to the right at its end. He went quickly down, then peered around the corner into the next wing—and saw Jacqueline pause outside a door. She spoke to Millicent, who nodded, then walked on; Jacqueline opened the door and went in. He hung back, watching Millicent's dark figure recede into the shadows. At last she stopped, opened a door, and went in. He waited until the faint click of the latch reached him, then walked—stalked—down the corridor.

Reaching Jacqueline's door, he knocked—two sharp, preemptory raps, not overly loud.

An instant later, the door opened. A little maid, stunned, stared up at him.

Gerrard looked at the maid, then looked past her.

"Holly? Who is it?"

Holly's eyes grew rounder. "Ah, it's . . ."

Jacqueline came into view, halfway across the room. She'd taken off her jewelry, but had yet to unpin her hair. Her eyes widened, too.

Gerrard ignored the maid and beckoned, imperiously, to Jacqueline. "I need to talk to you."

His tone gave her warning his mood was deadly serious; he wasn't proposing any waltz in the moonlight.

She met his gaze; her expression grew careful. She came to the door.

The little maid ducked back, out of the way. Jacqueline set a hand to the door's edge. "You need to talk to me *now*?"

"Yes. Now." Reaching in, he grasped her hand, wrapping his fingers around hers. He glanced at the maid. "Wait here—your mistress will be back shortly."

He tugged Jacqueline over the threshold. She opened her mouth. He shot her an openly furious glance; she blinked, stunned, and wisely said nothing. Unceremoniously, he towed her back along the corridor, back into the gallery, then down the side stairs that led directly to the terrace.

They emerged beside the drawing room, opposite the main stairs leading down into the gardens, to the path leading into the Garden of Night.

"No!" Jacqueline pulled back against his hold. "Not into the Garden of Night."

He looked at her face. "Was it night when your mother died?"

She blinked; a moment passed before she said, "No. It was sometime in the late afternoon or early evening."

He frowned. "You're not sure when?"

She shook her head. "They found her later in the evening."

He saw pain in her face, saw memories flit across her features, dulling her eyes. He nodded curtly and towed her unrelentingly on—along the terrace away from the main stairs.

She realized, and reluctantly kept pace. "Where are we going?"

"Someplace that's relatively open."

Where they'd be visible to anyone who looked out, but out of earshot of the house—private, yet not hidden, not secluded. Somewhere that would reduce the impropriety of talking with her alone in the middle of the night.

"The Garden of Athena will do." The formal garden, the least conducive to seduction. Seduction was definitely not what he had in mind.

And any lingering influence to wisdom wouldn't go astray.

Resigned, Jacqueline followed him along the terrace, then grabbed up her skirts as he went quickly down the secondary stairs that led to the Garden of Athena. That one look he'd shot her when she'd been about to protest had been enough to assure her humoring him would be wise, no matter what weevil had wormed its way into his brain. Clearly he'd learned about her mother's death; how much he'd heard she'd no doubt soon learn.

Despite the tension humming through him, suppressed temper she had not a doubt, despite his precipitate actions, the abruptness of his growled words—despite the strength in the fingers wrapped about her hand—she felt not the slightest quiver of alarm, not the smallest qualm in allowing him to lead her far from her room, into the depths of the gardens in the dark of the night.

It wasn't, in truth, all that dark. As he stalked along the graveled path through Athena's garden, between the neatly clipped hedges and geometrically laid rows of olive trees, the moon bathed all about them in a steady radiance that cast everything in either silver or smudged black, a moorish enamel.

They reached the center of the formal garden, a circle between the inner points of four long rectangles. Abruptly, Gerrard halted; releasing her hand, he swung to face her.

His eyes, black in the night, raked her face, then locked on her eyes. "You know why your father wanted me—*specifically* me—to paint your portrait, don't you?"

She studied his face, then lifted her chin. "Yes."

"How did you know?"

Because she and Millicent had concocted the plan and Millicent had seeded it into her father's brain. She decided against confessing, not until she knew why he was so angry. "He didn't tell me, but once I heard of your reputation, his . . . *purpose* wasn't hard to guess."

"Not for you, or for any of those others interested in the mystery of your mother's death."

A vise slowly tightened about her chest; she ignored it. "I suspect that's so, although I haven't thought much of it."

"*They've* certainly thought of it."

She hoped so, but his tone sounded vicious. Unsure of his direction, she made no response.

After a long moment of, distinctly grimly, studying her face, he abruptly said, "Let's take off the gloves here."

When she raised her brows in surprise, he clarified, "And speak plainly. For some reason that I've yet to fathom, *you* are suspected of being in some way behind your mother's falling from that terrace"— he stabbed a finger toward the place in question—"to her death. Your father"—his jaw clenched; hands gripping his hips, he swung and paced away—"being one of those who credit portrait painters with an ability to see beyond any superficial façade, has commissioned me to paint a portrait of you, presumably convinced that I will see, and through my painting reveal, your guilt or innocence."

Reined temper—nay, fury—invested every sharp, decisive movement; it resonated in his tone, in the crisply bitten-off words. Swinging around, he stalked back to her. Halting before her, he looked into her face. "Is that correct?"

She held his gaze, replayed all he'd said, then nodded. Once. "Yes."

For one second, she thought he'd explode. Then he swung violently away, hands rising to the sky as if invoking the gods whose gardens surrounded them. "In the name of all Heaven, *why*?"

He swung back; his gaze impaled her. "Why does your father suspect *you*? How *can* he suspect you? You didn't have anything to do with it."

She stared at him, dumbstruck, for one heartbeat quite sure the earth beneath her feet had tilted. Slowly, she blinked, but his expression—the charged conviction she could see in it, limned in silver— didn't change. Softly, she exhaled; the vise about her lungs eased a notch. "How do you know?"

He did know, absolutely; it was written in his face. He'd already seen the truth where others did not.

Impatient, he pulled a face, but the intensity in his expression didn't waver. "I see—I know. Believe me, I know." He moved closer, his gaze razor sharp as he examined her face. "I've seen evil—I've looked into the eyes of more than one man who truly was evil. Some people hide it well, but if I spend sufficient time with them, they'll slip and it'll show—and I'll know."

He paused, then went on, his gaze steadying on her eyes. "I've been watching you carefully, albeit for less than two days. What I've seen is all manner of emotions, complicated and complex feelings, but of the shadow of evil I've seen not a trace."

After a moment, he added, "I would have by now if it was there. What I see is something quite different."

His voice had changed, softened. Enough for her to feel she could ask, "What do you see?"

He looked at her for the space of ten slow heartbeats, then shook his head. "I'm not good with words—I paint things I can't describe."

She wasn't sure that was the truth, but before she could think of how to probe, he asked, "I need to know before I speak with him— why does your father think you were in any way involved with your mother's death?"

Apprehension flared. "Why—what are you going to speak with him about?"

His temper returned; the smile he flashed her was all restrained violence. "Because I have no intention of being his unwitting pawn in judging his daughter."

"No!" She grasped his sleeve. "Please—you *must* do the portrait. You agreed!"

Her desperation rang clearly. He frowned, then he twisted his arm, breaking her grip, catching her hand. She felt his fingers move over hers, then they stilled.

A moment passed, then he sighed. He raked his other hand through his hair, met her eyes again. "I don't understand. Why don't you simply tell him you're innocent? Force him to believe you— surely he will? He's your *father*."

His frown deepened. "You shouldn't have to go through this, to face what amounts to a public examination with me as your inquisitor, laying all you are bare."

Concern, open and sincere, colored his tone—concern for her. It had been so long since she'd been offered such straightforward and unconditional support—and more, defense—she wanted to close her eyes, wrap herself in all the tenor of his voice conveyed, and wallow.

But he was confused, and he had to understand—had to understand and agree to paint her portrait.

She drew in a long breath, felt the cool night air reach her brain. She glanced around; her gaze fell on the bench around the central fountain, presently silent and still. She gestured. "Let's sit, and I'll explain what happened, and you'll see why things are as they are."

Why I need you to paint me as I truly am.

He didn't release her hand, but led her to the bench, waited until she sat, then sat beside her. Leaning forward, one elbow on his knee so he could watch her face, he closed his hand around hers—and waited.

She was supremely conscious of his nearness; ignoring her prickling senses, she cleared her throat. "Papa . . . you must understand he's in an invidious position. He loved my mother dearly—she was literally the light of his life. When she died, that light went out and he lost . . . his connection with the world. He was dependent on her in that sense, so losing her was doubly difficult for him. This is what happened, what he knows."

Pausing, she assembled the facts in her mind. "My mother and I got along well, as well as any mother and daughter. Socially speaking, I'm more like her than Papa—I quite enjoy entertaining, the balls and parties. Mama lived for them—entertaining was a central part of her existence. She and I shared our liking of that part of life, but I'm also my father's daughter, and can manage perfectly well on a diet of peace and quiet that would have driven Mama insane."

A small smile curved her lips as she remembered; she felt it fade as her memories rolled on. "She was thrilled when Thomas Entwhistle started calling—he's the son of Sir Harvey Entwhistle. I suppose you would say he was my suitor. We planned to wed, we talked of announcing our betrothal . . . and then Thomas disappeared.

"Mama was . . . upset. As was I, of course, but after a time she seemed to think that I'd said something to Thomas to send him off, but I hadn't." She frowned, looked down. And saw her hand cradled in Gerrard's strong fingers. She drew breath and went on, "That was the start of a . . ." She paused, then shrugged. "I suppose it was a growing estrangement. No specific break, just a stepping back on her part—I never understood why. Perhaps with time . . . but then . . ."

She drew a huge breath; lifting her head, she looked straight ahead, felt Gerrard's fingers firm about hers. "The day of her death, she came down late to breakfast—Papa had already gone to his study. She passed Mitchel in the doorway as he left. She looked . . . as if she hadn't slept all night."

She glanced at Gerrard. "My mother was beautiful, but even the slightest illness showed in her face. I asked what was wrong, but she denied anything was. She plainly wanted me to ignore her state, so I did. Then she realized I was in my riding habit. I can remember her looking at me—no, at *it* . . . it was so strange. She'd seen the habit any number of times—she'd bought it for me—but that morning she looked at it as if it were . . . oh, greasy kitchen rags. A nauseating sight. She asked where I was going—her voice was odd. I told her I was going riding with the others—she went dead white, and said no.

"I was so taken aback I laughed. But then I realized she was in earnest. I asked why not, but she would only shake her head and say I couldn't go."

She sighed; the deadening feeling that afflicted her whenever she thought of the rest of that day slipped slowly down her veins. "We argued. Increasingly bitterly. The servants heard, of course, and I think Mitchel did, too—his office is just down the hall from the breakfast parlor. She simply kept saying I couldn't go riding—no reason, no explanation of any kind. She got increasingly strident . . . in the end, I simply walked out."

When she didn't go on, Gerrard stroked her hand, gently prompted, "And?"

"I went riding."

He frowned. "And she fell from the terrace?"

She shook her head. "No. That was sometime later. This was the morning. I rode out, and we went into St. Just. I didn't get back until mid-afternoon, and went straight to my room. Despite the ride, I was . . . upset. Unhappy and uncertain. I didn't know what would happen, but I wasn't going to be treated like a child, told I couldn't go here or there with no reason.

"I threw myself on my bed—and fell asleep. Later, I woke, bathed and dressed for dinner, then went down. My father came down—I could tell he knew nothing of the argument. Then Mitchel came in, and we waited for my mother to appear." She lifted her free hand in a small gesture. "She never did."

After a moment, she went on, "Eventually, Papa sent upstairs and Mama's maid came hurrying down, saying Mama hadn't come up to change for dinner. She'd had afternoon tea in the parlor, but when Treadle collected the tray, she wasn't there. He'd assumed she was walking on the terrace, or had gone down into the gardens.

"Everyone thought she must have gone walking and perhaps sprained her ankle. The servants went out to look; they scoured the gardens. They didn't search the Garden of Night until last, because it's so close to the house—you can hear anyone calling from there, and anyone there can hear those on the terrace. But she couldn't, of course, because she was dead."

Gerrard sat, slowly stroking his fingers over her hand, putting all she'd told him in sequence, in context. "I still don't understand why anyone would imagine you had a hand in your mother's death."

She laughed, not humorously; there was pain in the sound. "You could say that came about by default." She looked down at her fingers, locked in his. "Default in the sense that there were no other suspects. Also in the sense that I didn't protest my innocence, not until far too late."

She drew in an unsteady breath. "Immediately after . . . when they found her and later, I was distraught. Despite that odd estrangement, we'd still been very close. I was . . . in anguish, not just over her death and the manner of it, but because of the argument, because she'd gone with that between us, because the last words we'd exchanged were so horrible."

Her voice quavered; she swallowed and shook her head. "I cried for days. I don't remember all I said—all I know is that people view how I behaved then as a sign of my guilt."

Gerrard felt his jaw clench. To honestly and openly grieve for a parent, then have that held against one, used against one . . . he smothered the caustic words that rose to his tongue; her revelations were flowing freely—not a good time to interrupt.

She went on, her voice low but clear, her gaze fixed on their linked hands. "We went into deep mourning—I didn't set foot out of the house for three months and I didn't receive callers. I don't remember much of that time other than that Millicent came for the funeral and stayed. I don't know what I would have done without her.

"Eventually, however, I emerged, and went about again . . . and that was when I realized what people were thinking—that *I'd* pushed Mama to her death. When I first realized, I laughed, it struck me as so nonsensical. I couldn't believe anyone would credit it. I assumed it was one of those silly notions that flare, then fade . . . only it didn't."

Jacqueline heard the strength building in her voice, felt again the upswell of hurt and, even more, the anger that had followed it, that fueled her determination to see her plan through. She looked up. "By the time I realized that, it was too late. I tried to speak with my father, but he refused to discuss the subject. The others were the same—the Frithams, even Mrs. Elcott, who'll normally talk about anything. She was the one who made me understand what was going on—that the reason they all wished the subject of Mama's death closed, deemed an accident and forgotten, was because they all believed that any examination of the facts would point to me."

She drew breath, and more evenly stated, "They think they're protecting me. The only people who believe in my innocence are Millicent, Jordan and Eleanor. The other younger people weren't aware or involved, so they don't have any real opinion, but everyone else . . . we've tried, but none of us can get the subject mentioned, let alone discussed!"

Frustration rang in her tone; Gerrard squeezed her fingers. "So while you were in deep mourning, essentially cut off, you were tried, found guilty—and then absolved, with the incident to be buried."

"Yes!" She thought for a moment, then amended, "Well, no, not quite. Everyone around has known me all my life—they don't *want* to believe I'm guilty. But they fear I am, so they've decided to avoid the question altogether. They don't want to look at who killed Mama because they're afraid they'll find it was me, so they've declared her death an accident, and are determined to leave well enough alone."

"But you don't want it left alone."

"No!" She shot him a glance—wondered, fleetingly, why she felt she could be so open, so direct, so unguarded with him. "Mama's death *wasn't* an accident. But until I can convince them it wasn't *me* who pushed her over the balustrade, they won't look for who did."

She saw in his eyes that he understood. After a moment, she went on, her gaze locked with his, "Jordan and Eleanor gave up, but Millicent and I—we kept thinking. We had to find a way to make people question the notion that's become embedded in their brains—that it was me. We thought of a portrait. If it was good enough to show my innocence clearly . . . it was the only way we could think of to open people's eyes."

His eyes narrowed, steady on hers. "So having me paint you was your idea."

She shook her head. "The idea of the portrait was ours. Millicent took months to seed the notion into my father's head. For him, a portrait was a viable way forward—if it shows me guilty, he'll hide it away; even if someone finds it, it's not proof, not real proof that can convict someone of a crime. To him, a portrait is the only way to end his . . . well, his misery. He loves me, but he loved Mama even more, and he's torn by thinking I killed her—and yet not knowing."

Her voice had thickened; clearing her throat, she went on, "Entirely fortuitously through her correspondents in town, Millicent heard of the Academy's exhibition and your portraits—the information seemed godsent. She suggested your name to Papa." She paused, then added, "You know the rest."

Gerrard held her gaze for a moment longer, then straightened; looking out across the regimented rows of olive trees, he leaned back against the edge of the fountain. The stone was cold across his shoulders; the sensation helped to anchor him, to help him re-form his view of what, precisely, was going on at Hellebore Hall.

So much more than he'd imagined when he'd accepted the commission to paint Lord Tregonning's daughter.

What she'd told him . . . he didn't doubt it was the truth. Not only was he sure she couldn't successfully lie to him, what she'd said explained so much he hadn't understood, like Tregonning's position—invidious indeed—and his choice of the way forward, and the attitude of others toward Jacqueline. And hers to them.

He'd held her hand throughout; the feel of her fingers, slim and slender under his, helped settle his thoughts, and focus his mind in the right direction. Forward. "What are you expecting to happen once the portrait is painted and shown?" He glanced at her, caught her gaze. "Once people start to question the circumstances of your mother's death, won't they think . . ." He paused, then rephrased, "Couldn't the answer be suicide?"

She shook her head vehemently. "No—no one who knew Mama would even suggest it. She loved life, loved living. She wouldn't have suddenly decided she no longer wished to."

"You're sure?"

"Absolutely. No one has ever raised that prospect, not even though, believing me guilty yet not wanting it to be so, they'd grasp at any straw, even that." She straightened, briefly searched his face.

"Until I—we—convince them it wasn't me, that it's all right—safe if you like—to look for Mama's killer, they won't. And the real killer will remain free."

Looking into her eyes, he grasped the point she knew, but had thus far not stated. "Your mother's killer is still here—he's someone you know."

She held his gaze steadily. "He must be. You've seen the estate. It's not easy to slip in undetected, not unless you know the place, and there were no gypsies or suspicious outsiders in the area when she died."

He looked away, across the garden, still, silent and eerily beautiful under the now waning moon. A moment passed, then he felt her fingers tense within his hand, lightly grip. He turned his head, met her gaze, darkly shadowed in the night.

"You will paint my portrait, won't you?"

How could he refuse?

She angled her head, brows arching, faintly challenging. "Can you do it? Paint me that well that my innocence will show?"

"Yes." He had absolutely no doubt he could.

She drew a breath, held it, then quietly said, "I can understand your resistance to being manipulated into being an unwitting judge, but at my request, could you agree to being a witting one?"

He held her gaze, let a moment tick by purely out of habit; he didn't need to think. "If you truly wish it, then yes. I will."

She smiled.

"There will, however, be a price."

Her brows rose, this time in surprise, but, her eyes searching his, she didn't confuse his "price" with his commission. "What?"

He didn't know—he didn't even know what had prompted him to utter the words, but he wasn't about to take them back. "I'm not certain, yet."

She held his gaze, then calmly replied, "Let me know when you are."

Desire lanced through him. From her tone, low and faintly sultry, he couldn't tell whether she was deliberately challenging him, or simply meeting *his* challenge with her usual directness.

She drew breath and evenly continued, "Until then . . . I'll do whatever you ask, tell you anything you wish, sit for however many hours you want—just as long as you paint me as I truly am so that everyone will know I'm not my mother's murderer."

"Done." He held her gaze for an instant longer, then lifted the hand he held to his lips. He brushed a kiss to her knuckles, watched the slight shiver she fought to suppress, then turned her hand and, watching her still, deliberately pressed a much more intimate kiss to her palm.

And had the satisfaction of seeing her lids fall, of sensing her irrepressible response.

She was the quintessential damsel in distress and she'd asked him to be her champion; as such, he was entitled to her favor.

But he'd yet to decide what he wanted from her, and they were in the middle of an open garden. Reining in his impulses, with her unusually strong, unexpectedly definite, he rose, drew her to her feet, and escorted her back into the house.

H
ell's bells—what a coil!" Barnaby paused to study Gerrard's face. "Can you truly do that—paint innocence?"

"Yes, but don't ask how." Sprawled in an armchair, waiting while Barnaby dressed for the day, Gerrard looked out at the sunlit gardens, at the lightly ruffling canopies. "It's not so much a finite quality, as something that shines through in the absence of aspects that dim or tarnish it, like guilt and evil. In this case, given the effect the crime has had on Jacqueline, it'll be a case of painting all she is, of getting the balance of the different elements right so that it's plain what isn't there."

"The evil necessary to commit matricide?"

"Precisely."

Seeing Barnaby loading his pockets with the paraphernalia he always carried—not just the usual gentlemanly things like handkerchief, watch and coin purse, but a pencil and notepad, string, and pocketknife—Gerrard rose. "In the circumstances, I want to get started on the portrait straightaway. The sooner I get to grips with it— get down what I need to show and decide how to pull it off—the better."

The sooner Jacqueline would be free of the haunting of her mother's death. And the sooner he'd be free, too, although what it was that, courtesy of Lord Tregonning bringing him here, now had him in its grip, he wasn't sure.

As they left the room, Barnaby shot him a glance. "So you're committed to this—to doing the portrait and, through that, starting a search for the real killer?"

"Yes." They started down the corridor; Gerrard looked at Barnaby. "Why do you ask?"

Barnaby met his gaze, for once deadly serious. "Because, dear boy, if that's your tack, then you really will need me here to watch your back."

They'd reached the stairs; a noise in the hall below had them both looking down. Jacqueline, unaware of them, crossed the hall, heading for the breakfast parlor. She passed out of sight. In step, they started down.

"And, of course," Barnaby mused, "someone will need to watch the lovely Miss Tregonning's back, too."

Gerrard knew a taunt when he heard one, knew he should resist, yet still he heard himself say, far too definitely to be misconstrued, "That, you may leave to me."

Suppressed laughter rippled beneath Barnaby's words. "I was sure you'd feel that way."

An instant later, however, when they stepped off the stairs and Barnaby glanced at him, all trace of amusement had flown. "All teasing aside, chum, we will need to exercise a degree of alertness. I haven't learned any more to the point yet, but I've heard more than enough to convince me there's something very odd going on down here."

H e wanted to start sketching her immediately, but . . . "I'm terribly sorry." Faint color tinged Jacqueline's cheeks. "Last evening, Giles Trewarren invited me to ride with him and a few of the others to St. Just this morning—I agreed to meet them at the top of the lane."

Gerrard could read in her eyes that their discussion of the previous night—all she'd promised in return for his agreement to paint her—was fresh in her mind; she truly was sorry she'd accepted Giles's invitation.

In light of that, he swallowed the urge to throw a painterly tantrum and insist she spend the day with him, wandering the house and gardens while he drew her out, and captured what showed in quick pencil sketches. The most preliminary of works, there would be many of them before he was satisfied he had the right setting, the right pose, and even more importantly the right expression for the portrait he was determined to create.

His enthusiasm and determination were running high; his commitment was absolute. Despite the success of his portraits of the twins, he was convinced his portrait of Jacqueline would transcend them; it would be the finest thing he'd done to date. His fingers were not just itching, the tips were almost burning with the desire to grip a pencil and wield it.

"I do hope you don't mind?"

Her hazel eyes declared her sincerity. He inwardly sighed. "Perhaps Mr. Adair and I could accompany you—if you don't mind?"

She smiled, genuinely relieved. Perhaps genuinely pleased? "That would be perfect. You haven't seen much of the local area yet, and St. Just is the nearest town."

Barnaby was happy to go jauntering—happy for the opportunity to talk to more locals and see what he could learn of the mysteries. After breakfast, the three of them met on the terrace, then headed for the stables.

Jacqueline was an accomplished rider; Gerrard inferred as much from the spirited bay mare that was waiting for her at the mounting block. Swinging up to the saddle of the chestnut gelding the stableman had chosen for him, he settled the horse, watching as Jacqueline let her mount prance, let her dance, then deftly brought her alongside.

The instant Barnaby had finished getting acquainted with his mount, a young black, they headed out, Jacqueline in the lead. She left the drive almost immediately, turning onto a grassed track between rolling green fields. Gerrard, watching her, caught the laughing glance she threw over her shoulder, then she touched her heels to the mare's flanks—and raced ahead.

He was after her in an instant, instinctively, without thought.

With a startled "Whoop!" Barnaby followed.

They thundered over the turf, the rush of their passage converting the mild breeze to a wild wind whistling past their ears, raking through their hair.

The land rose steadily as they climbed out of the valley in which the Hall stood. When she crested the rise, Jacqueline pulled up, her mare cavorting, eager to fly on.

She looked back.

Gerrard was close behind her, closer than she'd realized; he wheeled the chestnut to a halt beside her. Barnaby, a few seconds behind, slowed; it was he who noticed the view first.

"I say!" His eyes grew round.

Gerrard turned. He said nothing, but when she looked at his face, she smiled. He was speechless. In that instant, the artist in him, the ability of his talent to take control of him utterly, was manifest. He sat mesmerized by the view, the magnificent sweep across Carrick Roads to Falmouth on the shore beyond.

"Well," Barnaby said, "never let it be said that Cornwall has no scenery."

"Indeed not!" She asked about the scenery of his own country; it transpired he'd been born and raised in Suffolk.

"Undramatic views we have aplenty—lots of windmills and flat fields. But"—sitting his horse, he looked again across the water—"nothing like this."

After a moment, he glanced at Gerrard, between them, still staring avidly across the water, then he looked at Jacqueline. "You could try twitting him on the scenery of his county—it might break the spell."

Gerrard murmured, "I can hear, you know."

"Ah, but you can't see. Not anything beyond the landscape, anyway." Barnaby nodded down the rise to where a group ahorse milled at a spot in a lane. "Are they waiting for us?"

Jacqueline looked and waved. "Yes. That's our group." She glanced at Gerrard; he gestured her on.

"I take it that spot's the top of the lane?"

"Yes." She urged her mare into a walk, angling down the rise. "It's where we usually meet. From there, we can follow the lane that way"—she pointed south—"to St. Mawes, or if we go north a little way, we'll come to the lane to St. Just."

Gerrard took stock of the group ahead. Both Trewarrens, Giles and Cedric, were there, both Frithams, and both Hancock girls, Cecily and Mary. He saw Jacqueline regard Cecily with some surprise; given his treatment of Cecily the previous evening, he had to wonder why, if she wasn't a regular member of the riding group, she'd come.

He didn't have to wonder for long. When they joined the others and exchanged greetings, Cecily treated him coolly, then turned her attention entire on Barnaby.

Gerrard stifled a grin. If Cecily had thought him harsh in putting her in her place, she'd be well advised not to corner Barnaby.

Leaving Barnaby to fend for himself, he gave his attention entire to Jacqueline, to observing how she reacted to the others and they to her, not joining in with the group but standing one pace back, neither judging nor encouraging, prepared to be amused, but not making any demands. It was a stance that worked well as they trotted down the lane to St. Just, then walked down the steep streets to an ancient inn, the Jug and Anchor. Leaving their horses in the inn's stables, they set out along a stone-paved path that wended around the steep shoreline, giving glorious views across Carrick Roads.

It should have been a battle not to let the landscape claim him; instead, walking by Jacqueline's side, unable to—with no reason to—take her arm, yet highly conscious of the desire to do so, his attention didn't waver in the least. Indeed, it seemed oddly heightened, more focused on her because of their company, yet when, realizing, he looked more closely, he couldn't understand why some part of him felt as if the younger males—Jordan, Giles and Cedric—posed some threat.

Jacqueline herself remained calm, composed, not as aloof, as carefully shielded as she had been in the company of their elders, yet she appeared perfectly capable of snubbing any pretentious behavior toward her. Not that any of the younger men tried.

Listening to their conversation, mostly led by Jacqueline and Eleanor, walking on her other side, he concluded they were all simply friends, easy in their joint company. Only Jordan occasioned any constraint, and that purely because of his arrogance. His attitude was so staggeringly superior, Gerrard found it hard not to let his amusement show.

At one point, on the heels of a statement from Jordan that "Everyone who's anyone knows that the latest color for coats is light brown—tan to be precise," Jacqueline cast him a glance, almost as if she worried that he might take umbrage; his coat, after all, was deep green. He felt his lips ease; she smiled lightly back, then looked ahead, and with that he felt quite content—content enough to shut his ears to anything Jordan might say.

They turned back to the inn at midday. They'd decided to take

luncheon there; Gerrard gathered it was a routine they'd often followed in younger days. He glanced back to see how Barnaby was far-
ing, and was frankly surprised to see no sign of ennui in his friend's
face. Quite the opposite; Barnaby was being his charming best, and
Cecily was enthralled . . .

Barnaby had found a source of information nearer to hand than
the "older ladies."

Facing forward, Gerrard smiled, and kept pace at Jacqueline's side
as they approached the inn and climbed the steps to its porch.

The inn door opened; a young gentleman stepped out. He
stopped the instant he saw them. His gaze passed over the men, and
locked on Jacqueline. "I saw you riding down earlier—I've booked
the parlor."

There was a fractional hesitation, then Jacqueline smiled and went
forward. "Matthew, how lovely of you to see to it."

Giving the young man her hand, she turned to introduce them.
"Matthew Brisenden—Gerrard Debbington." To Matthew, she said,
"Papa has asked Gerrard to paint my portrait." She looked at Ger-
rard. "Matthew is the son of Mr. Brisenden, the sexton."

Gerrard shook hands; the intensely disapproving look in
Brisenden's face wasn't hard to interpret. To some, painters ranked
only a few rungs higher than opera dancers on the "persons whose
existence should be deplored" scale. However, his elegance, and
the fact he'd been commissioned by Lord Tregonning, was clearly
causing young Brisenden some difficulty. He wasn't sure how he
should treat him.

Gerrard smiled charmingly, and left him to figure it out on his
own.

At least, that was his intention, until Matthew reached for Jacqueline's arm. Beside her, Gerrard sensed her recoil, but they were too
tightly packed into the porch for her to avoid Brisenden's grasping
fingers; he locked them about her elbow.

Gerrard was aware of Barnaby's surprise, then the swift, warning
glance his friend sent him—he was more aware of a sudden surge of
reaction that left him tensed, momentarily deaf, with his vision closed
down, cloudy around the edges, crystal clear in the center, something
that normally would have sent him into a panic, but just now seemed
totally right . . .

What might have transpired he couldn't have said, but he—they—

were saved from it by two men trying to leave the inn. They couldn't get through the door because Brisenden was blocking their way. He had to release Jacqueline and move on to allow the two past.

Gerrard reached for Jacqueline's hand, wound her arm through his and laid her hand on his sleeve. Her fingers fluttered, but then settled and gripped lightly—a tentative touch he felt to his marrow. The departing customers clattered down the steps, and Brisenden reascended; Gerrard waved to the door. "Why don't you lead us in, Brisenden?"

Brisenden noted Jacqueline's hand lying on his sleeve. The young man's expression turned to stone. He raised his eyes and met Gerrard's levelly, but then he inclined his head and led the way in.

From that point on, ably assisted by Barnaby who alternated between acting the distracting fool and deftly engineering both seating and conversation, Gerrard took charge. Enough was enough; Brisenden was banished to the end of the table farthest from Jacqueline, who found herself sitting between Gerrard and Jordan Fritham.

Despite his painful superiority, Jordan had given not the slightest hint of any interest in Jacqueline. In return for Barnaby's keeping Brisenden occupied, Gerrard felt saving his friend from Jordan was the least he could do.

The meal passed smoothly and pleasantly enough. The conversation flowed easily, ranging over the usual elements of country life, the upcoming church fair, the fishing, the expected balls and parties— who had been to London for the Season and would be there to report the latest news . . . Almost in unison, all eyes turned to Barnaby.

He smiled, and happily regaled them with a tale of two sisters intent on taking the ton and its peers by storm. Only Gerrard knew how severely censored Barnaby's account was; he was amused and impressed by how agile his friend's mind could be.

At the end of the meal, they all rose and left, settling with the innkeeper by placing the whole on their respective fathers' slates.

Their horses were waiting. Matthew hovered, transparently expecting to help Jacqueline to mount; he didn't get a chance.

Gerrard escorted her from the inn, down the steps, to her mare's side. With a crisp command to the groom to hold the mare steady, he released Jacqueline, grasped her waist and lifted her to her saddle.

Easily. But then his eyes locked with hers, the feel of her body, lithe and elementally feminine between his hands, registered, the widening of her lovely eyes impinged . . . He realized he'd stopped breathing. He had to battle to force his hands from her, to let her go, and step back.

"Thank you." She sounded even more winded than he felt.

Walking to where another groom held his mount, he flung himself into the saddle. By the time they'd all mounted and were ready to start the steep climb up the lane, he'd managed to unlock his jaw, and was breathing normally again.

He brought his chestnut alongside Jacqueline's mare as they started up the incline. She noticed, but other than a fleeting look, did nothing, said nothing.

He wasn't sure there was anything she could have said. Nothing that would have left either of them less on edge. Less aware.

Matthew Brisenden stood on the inn porch, his hand raised in farewell.

Regardless of his senses' preoccupation with the woman riding by his side, Gerrard felt Brisenden's dark and brooding gaze between his shoulder blades until they reached the upper slope and left the inn behind.

6

I hope you won't read too much into Matthew's behavior."

"Brisenden?" Gerrard caught Jacqueline's eye. It was late afternoon, and they were heading out to the gardens. He had a sketch pad under one arm, and three sharpened pencils in his pocket. "Why do you say that?"

"Oh . . . because he appears so intense, so focused on me, but he isn't, or rather he means nothing by it, not really."

"Not really?" He shot her a sharp glance. "He acted too familiarly, as you—and the others, too—recognized perfectly well."

Her lips formed a small moue. "Perhaps, but he always behaves like that."

"As if he owns you—has some claim on you?"

"He's not usually that bad. He seems to have taken it into his head that it's his personal duty to protect me and keep me from all harm."

"Hmm." Gerrard kept to himself the observation that to Brisenden, him painting her portrait might well constitute "harm."

Reaching the steps leading to the Garden of Athena, Jacqueline led the way down. "His whole family's quite . . . well, *intense,* if you take my meaning. About religion and God and all the rest. And he is their only son."

Gerrard digested that as he followed. Reaching the gravel, he stepped out in her wake. "Be that as it may, Mr. Brisenden needs to keep his hands to himself, at least when their assistance isn't required."

They'd ridden back without further incident. Jordan and Eleanor had cantered with them all the way to the Hall; Tresdale Manor lay farther on—the way through the Hall lands was a shortcut. To Gerrard's relief, the Frithams hadn't lingered, but had left them at the stable arch and ridden on.

Barnaby had parted from them when they'd reached the terrace; by then Gerrard had confirmed that the light in the gardens was perfect, and had declared that Jacqueline had to sit for him, at least until the light died. She'd met his eyes, hesitated, then agreed, but she'd insisted on changing out of her habit. He'd permitted it only because he'd had to go and fetch his pads and pencils.

He glanced at her as she walked beside him. It hadn't occurred to him to specify what she wore, yet the gown she'd chosen was perfect for the late afternoon light, a soft, very pale green that complemented her hair and eyes. He had an excellent memory for color; a few jotted notes in his margins would be enough to bring his sketches alive, vibrant in his mind.

The gardens spread out before them; he glanced around, pulse quickening with the familiar lift of energy, of eagerness, that came with the start of a new project. He pointed to the bench where they'd sat the previous night. "Let's start there."

She sat on the stone bench built out from the square fountain. "You'll have to instruct me in how one sits for an artist."

"At this stage, the requirements are not arduous." He sat at the other end of the bench, swiveling to face her. "Turn to face me and get comfortable." While she did, he placed his ankle on his knee, opened his sketch pad and balanced it on his thigh. Quickly, he laid down a few strokes, just enough to give him setting and perspective.

"Now." Glancing up, he met her gaze, and smiled with his usual easy charm. "Talk to me."

Her brows rose. "About what?"

"Anything—tell me about your childhood. Start as far back as you remember."

Her brows remained high as she considered, then slowly lowered, her gaze growing distant. He waited, his eyes on her, his fingers smoothly moving lead across the paper. She wasn't looking directly at him; he didn't think she would. Like most people relating such things, she'd fasten her gaze to the side of his face, giving him precisely the not-quite-direct angle he wanted. His suggestion of topic hadn't been as idle as he'd intimated; thinking of childhood elicited all sorts of memories, memories that showed in his subjects' faces.

"I suppose," she eventually said, "that the earliest moment I can remember clearly is being set atop my first pony."

"Did you enjoy it?"

"Oh, yes! His name was Cobbler. He was a tan and black cob, and had the sweetest nature. He died years ago, but I can still remember how he loved apples. Cook always gave me one when I went out for my riding lesson."

"Who taught you?"

"Richards, the head stableman. He's still here."

"Did you go walking through the gardens?"

"Of course—Mama and I used to walk every day, rain or shine."

"When you were a child?"

"And later, too."

For a moment, he let silence claim them. She didn't move, either because she was held by her memories, or because she knew how fast his fingers were moving, how rapidly he was re-creating the expressions that had flowed across her face—the simple delight of childhood happiness shadowed by more mature sorrow.

Eventually, he flipped over the page; without looking up, he said, "It must have been quite lonely when you were young—the Frithams weren't here then, were they?"

"No, they weren't—and yes, I was lonely. There weren't even children among the staff or the nearer workers, so I was entirely on my own except for my nanny and later my governess. It was wonderful, the start of a new and exciting life, really, when the Frithams came."

Again, the happiness in her face shone clear; Gerrard worked to get some sense of it down. "How old were you then?"

"Seven. Eleanor was eight and Jordan ten. Their mama, Maria, and mine were childhood friends, which was why they came to live close. Overnight, I had an older brother and sister. Of course, I knew the area much better than they did, especially the gardens, so we were more equal, so to speak. Later ... well, Eleanor is still my closest friend, while Jordan treats me much as he does Eleanor, as an older brother."

He was tempted to ask how she viewed Jordan; instead, he asked about their youthful exploits. She described a number of incidents, the process occasionally bringing a smile to her lips, a laughing glint to her eyes.

After twenty minutes had passed, she glanced at him. "Is this working?"

He added a few more strokes, then lifted his gaze and met her eyes. "You're doing wonderfully. That's all there is to this stage of sitting. Just chatting and letting me get acquainted with your face, your expressions."

Finishing his latest sketch, he flipped back the earlier sheets and critically reviewed them. "During the next days"—he scanned what he'd caught so far, various expressions all from the same angle—"I'll do a lot of these, but as I become more certain what expressions I want to work more deeply with"—and what topics elicited the emotions in her that gave rise to those expressions—"I'll do fewer sketches but they'll be in greater detail, until I have enough practice in re-creating exactly the effect I want to show."

Looking up, he met her gaze. "Until I can draw you as we need to portray you."

Jacqueline held his gaze for a moment, then looked away. "It seems far easier than I'd thought, at least for me."

"This is the easy part—the further we go, the more time I spend on each sketch, the longer you'll have to sit in one place, in one pose." Shutting the pad, he smiled. "But not yet. By the time we get to the final sittings and you need to sit perfectly still for an hour, you'll be trained to it."

She laughed, conscious of a tightening in her chest, of a tension she was coming to recognize as more akin to excitement and anticipation than fear.

He rose; sketch pad in one hand, he held out the other.

She looked up at him, then laid her fingers across his palm. Steeled herself as his long fingers closed over hers.

Felt, for one finite instant, her heart skip, still, then start beating again, more rapidly.

His eyes were locked with hers; he didn't move.

And she suddenly saw, realized, understood that what she was feeling, sensing between them . . . it wasn't just her alone.

He felt it, too.

She saw the truth in the shifting planes of his face, the sudden tightening of his jaw, the almost imperceptible flare of something behind the glowing brown of his eyes.

He drew her up and she rose. He hesitated, then released her hand.

Looking down, she smoothed her skirts; glancing up from beneath her lashes, she saw him look away, saw the rise of his chest as he drew in a breath—one that seemed as tight as hers.

He waved deeper into the gardens. "Let's walk. I want to see you against different backdrops, in different levels of light."

They walked into the Garden of Diana, but after two quick sketches, he shook his head. Dappled shade, he declared, wasn't appropriate. They strolled on into the Garden of Mars, which met with his approval. He had her sit by a burgeoning bed while he sprawled nearby. Again he asked questions and she answered; it was odd for he didn't expect her to meet his eyes. From his sudden silences, filled with the swift scratch of pencil on paper, she realized he wasn't really listening but watching, that it was her expressions he was reading.

A curious communication.

A strange catharsis—she quickly realized she could say almost anything, and he wouldn't react; he wasn't there to judge what she said, but to see how she felt about the subjects he raised, to explore her feelings as she allowed them to show.

It had been a long time since she'd spoken her thoughts freely; the exercise, focusing on her reactions, allowed her to examine them, to know and recognize what she felt and how she felt.

After a while he rose, drew her up briskly and waved her on into the Garden of Apollo. He had her sit before the sundial; this time, he sketched from her other side. "Given we're here," he said, "let's talk about time."

"Time how?" she murmured, cheek on her updrawn knees as he'd requested.

"Time as in, do you feel, living down here, that it's passed you by?"

She thought about that. "Yes, I suppose I do. There's very little to do down here. I'm twenty-three and I feel my life—my adult life—should have started by now, yet it hasn't." She paused, then added, "What with Thomas disappearing, and then Mama's death, I feel as if I've been placed in limbo."

"You need to free yourself before you can move on."

"Yes." She nodded, then remembered and repositioned her head. "That's it exactly. Until Mama's killer is caught, time for me will stand still. I can't go away and leave it—the suspicion—behind; it'll follow me wherever I go. So I have to shatter it, disperse it, eradicate it, before I'll be free to start living again."

He said nothing. She slanted a glance his way. He was rapidly sketching. A small, beguiling smile played at the corner of his lips.

"What are you smiling at?"

He looked up, met her gaze—and she was instantly aware of a sense of communion, a connection of a sort she'd never shared with anyone else.

Looking down, he continued sketching, but the curve of his lips deepened. "I was thinking I ought to call this 'Waiting for Time to Move.'"

She smiled, turning her head fractionally so she could direct that smile at him.

He looked up; his gaze sharpened, his eyes narrowed. "Don't move—stay just like that." His fingers had already whipped the page over and he was furiously sketching anew.

Mentally raising her brows, she did as he asked. "Sitting" was tiring, but also strangely relaxing.

They'd been sitting in perfect peace for ten or more minutes when a firm step on the path approaching the stone viewing stage, not far away, had them both turning to look.

Gerrard got to his feet, closing his sketchbook. "I've got enough of that pose for now."

He crossed to where she sat and reached for her hand; he ignored their mutual sensitivity—that odd, concerted leap of their pulses—and drew her to her feet. Her hand locked in his, he held her beside him and turned to face whoever was marching along the path; it wasn't Barnaby, and no gardener walked with such an assured tread.

"It's Jordan," Jacqueline said, as if sensing his alertness.

Sure enough, brown hair ruffled and nattily dressed—a trifle overdressed for Gerrard's taste—Jordan came into view, stepping onto and then off the stone viewing platform. Straightening, he saw them.

It was instantly apparent he hadn't come looking for them, yet it wasn't just surprise that showed in his face. A petulant expression came into being, but as Jordan approached, Gerrard got the impression it wasn't disapproval of him and Jacqueline being alone, but the fact they were there at all that had irritated.

Jacqueline tugged; unobtrusively, he released her hand.

"Good afternoon, Jordan."

Jordan nodded. "Jacqueline." His gaze moved to Gerrard. "Debbington."

Gerrard returned his nod. "Fritham. Are you looking for Lord Tregonning?" If so, that was odd, for Jordan wasn't coming from the house.

"No, no—just out for a constitutional." Jordan glanced at the gardens around them. "I often walk here—Eleanor and I were made free of the gardens a long time ago."

Turning back to him, Jordan looked at his sketch pad. "Making a start on the portrait?"

"Indeed."

"Good, good." Jordan shifted his gaze to Jacqueline. "The sooner that's done and all can see the result, the better."

The comment—in tone as well as words—was ambiguous. Gerrard glanced at Jacqueline, but could detect nothing in her expression to guide him; her inner shield was up. Whatever Jordan thought wasn't going to be allowed to touch her, yet she'd said Jordan was one of the few who believed in her innocence. Perhaps he was one of those who thought portraits were inherently false, revealing nothing real.

"Well." Jordan shifted; Jacqueline had given him no encouragement to dally, but he didn't seem to wish to. "I'll leave you then. Don't want to delay the great work."

With a nod to them both, he continued on, heading up the garden to the northern viewing stage.

Gerrard turned to look in the direction from which he'd come. "How did he get here?"

Jacqueline's inner reserve melted away. "He walked. The Manor's in the next valley—although it's a considerable way by road, the house is much closer as the crow flies. The ridge"—she nodded toward the southern ridge bordering the gardens—"is only ten minutes' walk from the Manor's side door, and there's a footpath that leads down through the woods to join the gravel walk in the Garden of Diana."

"Does he often just turn up like that?"

"Sometimes. I don't know how often he walks here. The gardens are so large, I doubt anyone would know."

"Hmm." Jordan had gone through the wooden pergola and then disappeared into the Garden of Dionysius. Looking down the long valley to the west, noting the angle of the sinking sun, Gerrard waved Jacqueline on. "Let's try the Garden of Poseidon. Water's an interesting element at sunset."

When the day before he'd set eyes on the spot where the stream flowing out from the Garden of Night emerged into the light, cascading over shallow stone steps to pour into a narrow rectangular pool, he'd suspected he'd found the perfect setting. Now he knew what his painting had to achieve, there wasn't a skerrick of doubt left in his mind. It had to be here. He'd paint her in the studio, but the setting in which, in the final portrait, she stood, would be this.

"I want you over there—sit on the edge of the pool." At the bottom of the stone steps, the water gathered into a channel, then flowed into the pool through a spout.

She went to do as he'd asked. From beneath his lashes, he watched for any sign of unease, and was relieved when he detected none.

"Like this?" She sank gracefully onto the stone coping beside the spout, facing him.

He smiled. "Perfect."

It was; the golden light of the westering sun flowed up the valley to carom off the pool's surface and bathe her in soft gilt. Her skin took on a shimmering glow; her hair came alive, rich and sheening. Even her lips seemed to hold a touch of deeper mystery, and her eyes were full of . . . dreams.

He felt something inside him still; she looked past him, down the valley, into that golden light. The expression on her face . . .

Without further thought, he drew.

Furiously fast, yet exact, precise, he transferred all he could see in that brief, shining moment onto the white page. He knew the instant he had enough, when one more line would ruin it. He stopped, leafed over the page, and looked up, pencil poised.

Her lips curved lightly. "What next?"

"Just stay there." What next was for him to get the first rendering of the setting he wanted. The lower entrance to the Garden of Night, an archway of deep green leaves and vines beyond which dark shadows drifted, lay behind her—ten good paces behind her, but perspective in an artist's hands was a tool, a weapon. When he finally drew her, she would stand framed in that archway; the Garden of Night was the perfect symbol of what held her trapped, of what she wanted to and needed to escape, and from which the portrait would release her. The rectangular pool would lie before her feet, reflecting light up over her, a symbol of her emergence from the darkness into the light.

Perfect.

The essence of the Garden of Night came to life beneath his pencil, created with deft strokes of his fingers.

When he finally paused and truly looked at what he'd done, he was satisfied.

More, he was moved; it was the first time he'd attempted to meld the artistic halves of himself—the lover of Gothic landscapes, and the observer and recorder of people and their emotions. He hadn't consciously realized he would, but he had, and now he knew.

He couldn't wait to dive deeper into the challenge.

Turning over another leaf, he looked at her. "Tell me about your mother."

"Mama?" She'd learned not to look directly at him; she continued to stare down the valley.

A moment passed, then she said, "She was very beautiful, quite vain in fact, but she was always so *alive.* Enthused by life. She truly lived every day—if she woke up and there wasn't something to do, she'd organize some outing, some event however impromptu. She was something of a butterfly, but a gay, giddy one, and there was no unkindness in her, so . . ."

He let her talk, watched, waited until the right moment to ask, "And when she died?"

Her expression changed. He watched the sadness close in, dousing the happy memories, saw not just loss of a loved one, but loss in a wider sense—a loss of innocence, of trust, of security.

She didn't reply, yet his fingers flew.

After a very long moment, she murmured, "When she died, we lost all that—this place and all who lived here lost our wellspring of life."

"And of love?" He hadn't meant to say the words; they just slipped out.

After another long silence, she replied, "More that love became tangled and confused."

He continued sketching, very aware—elementally aware—when she drew in a deep breath, and shifted her gaze to look at him.

For some moments, her expression was unreadable, then she asked, "What do you see?"

A woman trapped through others' love for her. The words rang in his mind as his eyes held hers, but he didn't want to reveal how clearly he saw her, not yet. "I think"—he closed his sketch pad—"that you saw her more clearly than she saw you."

She tilted her head, studying him, examining his words—and, he suspected, his motives. Then she inclined her head. "You're right."

He looked steadily back at her. His comment, he felt sure, was also true for others—like her father, Mitchel, Jordan, even Brisenden. Their view of her was of a weak female; they were the type to assume that females were inherently less able, less strong than themselves on any plane. He'd grown up too close to too many strong women to make such a mistake. Jacqueline was nothing if not strong, and commitment only strengthened her resolve.

If he were the killer, he'd be very wary of her.

The thought came out of nowhere, and chilled him. Suppressing an inner shiver, he looked down at his sketches, flipping through them, rapidly evaluating what he'd done.

Released from his scrutiny, Jacqueline watched him. For this pose, he'd stood to sketch her; he'd fallen into a comfortable wide-legged stance, broad shoulders square, his long-limbed, lean body loose and relaxed. While in the throes, he didn't seem to feel the urge to move, as if all his vitality, all the intensity that was so much a part of him, were concentrated in his fingers and his eyes, and the brain that connected them.

He was fascinating, compelling. To her, yes, but she wouldn't be the only female so affected. Eleanor would find him attractive, too.

He had such a high-handed tendency to command, to order . . . she felt her lips curve; she wasn't even sure he was aware of it, so focused was he on his goals.

It was that focus, intense and powerful, that would draw Eleanor—she'd want to force him to turn it on her. To surrender it to her.

For a moment, Jacqueline wondered—did she feel the same, for the same reason? An instant's reflection returned the answer: no. That's where she and Eleanor differed. Eleanor would delight in using force, yet for her, the conquest would be in his willingly lavishing on her the intensity of devotion she saw in him as he sketched, as he viewed her as his subject.

Not as her.

A ripple of awareness skittered through her as she recalled his "price" and the reckless promise she'd made in the moonlight, that she'd meet it whatever it might be. Had he been viewing her as his subject then, or as her? At the time she'd assumed the former, but now she'd realized there were moments when he was as physically aware of her as she was of him . . .

She'd thought his attentions, the hot kiss he'd pressed to her palm, had been to learn how she responded to such things, that he'd wanted to know as a painter. What if he'd wanted to know as a man?

The idea left her feeling as if she were teetering on the brink of a precipice, unsure whether to step forward or back. Back would be safe, yet forward . . . as fascinating and compelling as she found him, if he beckoned, would she go?

Another shiver, this time one of anticipation, coursed down her spine. She let her gaze slide over him again, felt the compulsion rise.

Closing his sketch pad, he looked up. His eyes fixed on hers.

After a moment, his gaze drifted up. "Your hair . . ."

"What about it?"

"When I paint you, it needs to be different. Can you unpin it? It'll help if I see how we need it to be, then you can wear it that way from now on."

Her hair was secured in a neat chignon; raising her hands, she started removing pins. The chignon unraveled; she set the pins down, shook the long strands free, then threaded her fingers through them, drawing them out, letting them fall across and over her shoulders.

He frowned. "No, that's not right, either."

He closed the space between them in a few long strides. Setting his pad and pencils down, he sat on the coping, facing her.

She felt her lungs constrict, but she was growing used to the effect.

His gaze was locked on her face, gauging. He reached for her chin, turned her face to his, then reached for her hair, long fingers sliding into the unruly mass.

She caught her breath, prayed she wasn't blushing, prayed she'd be able to hide her reaction.

His frown remained as he bunched her hair, shifting it this way, then that, clearly unsatisfied. Then he twisted the tresses and set the bunched curls on the top of her head. Looking into his face, she sensed him still . . .

With his other hand, Gerrard reached for her chin, fought not to notice the delicacy of bones and skin as he gently gripped and turned her face first to the left, then to the right, then to the precise angle he thought was best suited for the portrait, all the while holding her hair atop her head.

There. Angle right, and hair up, a neat knot with a tendril or two trailing down on the right, a subtle highlight to draw attention to the exposed curve of her throat.

That was the line he wanted to capture, vulnerability, grace and strength combined. Youth, yet with intrinsic wisdom, instinctive and true. A pose that had clarity, that resonated with truth.

Again his gaze skimmed the line of her throat, skin white and flawless, tinted by the fading golden light. Raising his gaze, he took in the medley of browns, vibrant and earthy, worldly, too, of her hair; he would capture that and use it.

He lowered his gaze to her face.

Met her eyes, the mossy shade darker, the gold more intense as they widened, darkened.

Her lips were lush, edged with rose gilt.

Time stood still.

He raised his gaze to her eyes, saw a curiosity the counterpart of his own staring at him from the hazel depths.

What would it be like?

Lowering his head, tipping her face up, he touched his lips to hers.

Felt them quiver. And took, seized, albeit gently, with all the expertise he'd learned over the years. He increased the pressure beguilingly, seductively, brushing lightly, tantalizing and tempting.

He wanted to devour, yet it was she who captured him with a tentative response so slight it was like gossamer, a fleeting moment of innocence and pleasure. For one fraught instant he felt completely caught, taken captive—then reality returned, and he realized what he'd done.

Realized he'd gathered her into his arms.

Realized he'd taken the step he hadn't yet made up his mind he would take. He'd been tempted, not solely by his own desires but by hers, too, yet the feel of her in his arms, of her lips beneath his—the feelings those sensations evoked—assured him at some elemental level that this was right.

Yet if he was wise, he'd go slowly.

Lifting his head, he looked down into eyes the color of woodland moss. He drew in a breath, surprised to discover his lungs parched and tight. "I'm sorr—" He broke off, unable as he looked into her eyes to utter the polite lie. He felt his jaw firm. "No. I'm *not* sorry, but I shouldn't have done that."

She blinked up at him. "Why not?"

He searched her eyes; she was asking with her usual candor, an open honesty he'd grown to treasure. "Because it'll make it that much harder not to do it again."

The truth. She heard it; he saw comprehension widen her eyes, followed swiftly by calculation.

"Oh . . ."

He looked into her eyes, was drowning in them . . . With a mental curse, he shut his. "Don't do that."

"What?"

He gritted his teeth, and kept his eyes shut. "Look at me as if you want me to kiss you again."

She didn't reply. Three heartbeats passed.

He was debating whether to open his eyes when her soft whisper reached him.

"I'm not good at lying."

Five words, and she vanquished him. Overthrew that part of his mind that was fighting to maintain control, and cast him adrift. Into the sea of desire that welled in her eyes as they met his when he lifted his lids.

She searched his eyes, hesitated for a heartbeat, then lifted her lips to his. Touched lightly.

He could no more resist the explicit invitation than stop the sun from sinking beneath the sea.

Summoning what restraint he could, he kissed her back, then, unable to deny her or himself, he pressed the caress further, aware that, just as he had expectations of the kiss, so, too, would she. He wondered what they were, why . . . but then he traced her lower lip with the tip of his tongue, her lips parted, and he stopped thinking.

Jacqueline quivered as his tongue slid between her lips, held her breath as he shifted and gathered her deeper into an embrace that, no matter how alien, felt safe. His arms were steel bands, caging her, but protectively, his chest a muscled wall of comforting solidity against her breasts. His lips moved on hers, impressing, engaging. Tentatively she met his questing tongue with hers, lightly stroked—and sensed his encouragement, his appreciation.

She relaxed, secure in his arms, and mirrored his actions. There was heat in the exchange, persuasive and tempting, beguiling yet contained, not overwhelming but tantalizing, a promise of more, later. For now, she was content returning his caresses. Raising one hand, she lightly traced his cheek, the angular planes quite different from her own, cloaked in abrading stubble lacing firm skin.

By subtle degrees, he deepened the kiss and she, knowingly, followed. With growing confidence she kissed him back—and gloried in his response, in the continuing exchange that spun out in delight and mutual pleasure.

The reciprocity, for she knew it was so, caught her, and held her enthralled.

She tasted like summer wine, heady and sweet, potent and warm. Faintly illicit, carrying the promise of dark sultry nights and stirring passion. Now he'd learned, now he'd savored, he should draw back, yet still Gerrard lingered. The question of what she sought from the kiss returned; he now knew she'd shared few kisses, if any, before, not like this.

The reluctance he felt to end the interlude was not solely on his own account.

And that surprised him. Who was leading whom, and was that safe? The question gave him the strength to act, to gradually draw back and lift his head.

He watched as she opened her eyes, as she blinked and refocused on his. He'd kissed many ladies in far more illicit encounters, yet this time his charm didn't come to his aid. No glib words sprang to his tongue, no suave smile to his lips. This time, he didn't want to end the moment, didn't want to let her go; despite his experience, he couldn't pretend he did.

Looking into her eyes, a glorious medley of greens and gold, he could only hold her, and wonder . . .

Jacqueline saw his equivocation, felt it in the arms surrounding her that didn't ease. She comprehended something of what she read in his eyes; she, too, felt . . . distracted. As if she'd just experienced something that was important to explore further, but . . . the moment was already slipping away.

Her hands had come to rest against his chest; she found a half smile and gently pushed back. After an instant's hesitation, his arms eased, and he released her.

"The sun's almost gone." She looked down the valley to where the burning orb of the sun was disappearing below the horizon. Shifting along the coping, she glanced his way. "We should go inside. It'll soon be time to change for dinner."

He nodded and stood. He picked up his sketch pad, stuffed the pencils in his pocket, then he looked at her, and held out his hand.

She met his gaze, then placed her fingers in his and let him help her to her feet.

He released her once she was steady. Together they turned, and, side by side, without words, walked up through the gardens.

With one long, shared glance, they parted on the terrace.

7

Late that night with the moon riding the sky, Gerrard stood in the balcony doorway of his bedroom staring moodily out at the silvered gardens, and considered where fate had led him.

Not by the nose, but by another part of his anatomy, together with a section of his psyche he hadn't previously known existed.

He could hardly claim he hadn't known what he was doing, that he hadn't been cognizant of the dangers, the risks. He'd known, but had acted anyway; he couldn't remember when last he'd been so heedlessly impulsive.

Arms folded, he leaned against the doorjamb; eyes fixed unseeing on the shadows below, he tried to get some mental purchase on what, precisely *what,* was driving him. It wasn't anything he'd experienced before.

He knew what he wanted: Jacqueline. He'd wanted her from the moment he'd seen her watching him through the window when he'd arrived at Hellebore Hall—but what was driving him to it? The compulsion that was growing day by day, pressing him to make her his—from where did that spring?

Lust was certainly there, familiar enough, yet this was lust of a different order, an unusual degree. He'd lusted after ladies before; it didn't feel like this. With Jacqueline, the drive came from deeper within him, from some more primitive, more intense realm of emotion . . . Words, as always, failed him, yet if he painted it, it would glow with myriad shades of red, all the varied hues, not just one.

The vision shone in his mind. After a moment, he shifted his shoulders, then settled back against the frame.

His reaction to her, his fascination with her, was only half his problem. The other half was her fascination with him. He was aware of that to his bones; every little twitch, every instinctive feminine response she made, he felt like a sharpened spur, digging in, heightening his awareness of her, stirring his lust, and the need to slake it.

Never before had he been in the grip of such elemental and reckless desire.

That was what had led to that kiss. Then her curiosity, her directness, had snared him, and drawn him with her into deeper waters.

Unwise. He'd known it at the time, but hadn't called a halt, as he could have done.

Worse, he knew beyond doubt that it would happen again, and it wouldn't end with just a kiss. If he stayed and painted the portrait he was now desperate to paint, met the irresistible challenge fate had laid before him and painted the work she and her father wanted and needed him to paint . . .

For long minutes, he stood gazing out at the night-shrouded gardens, grappling with what he now faced. If he stayed and painted Jacqueline's portrait, he would risk falling in love with her.

Would the passion, the lust, the desire—all that love encompassed—drain the passion he drew on to paint? Or were the two separate? Or complementary?

Those were the questions he hadn't wanted to face, that he'd hoped, at least for the next several years, to leave unbroached.

But they faced him now, and he didn't know the answers.

And could think of only one way to learn them.

Yet if he took that route and the answer to his first question was yes . . . he would have risked and lost all he was.

Resigning Lord Tregonning's commission and leaving Hellebore Hall immediately was the only way to avoid putting those questions to the test. The ultimate test. A good portion of his mind, the logical, cautious side of him, strongly urged leaving as the most sensible course.

The painter in him said no. Emphatically no. The chance to paint the gardens aside, he would never, not ever, find such a challenging portrait, such a challenge to his talent and skills. To walk away without even attempting it smacked of sacrilege, at least to his painter's soul.

The man he was said no, very definitely no, too. Jacqueline trusted him; that was implicit in her behavior, in her invitation to him to be her champion, her "witting judge." She needed him; the situation she faced was perilous, potentially life-threatening. She and her father had been right; with his reputation backed by his ability, he was the only one able to open the doors of others' minds and free her from the peculiar web ensnaring her.

He stood staring into the night for half an hour more. Would he continue, paint her portrait and free her, accept and embrace the likelihood of falling in love with her, and so risk losing the one thing he valued above all else, his ability to paint?

Behind him in the darkened room, the clock on the mantelpiece chimed, a single bell-like note. With a self-deprecating grimace, he pushed away from the door frame and turned into the room. He was racking his brains to no purpose; his decision had already been made, virtually by default; he was here, so was she—he wasn't going anywhere. Certainly not now he'd held her in his arms and felt her lips beneath his.

The die was cast, his direction set.

Closing the balcony door, he reached up to tug the curtain across—a movement in the gardens caught his eye.

He looked, and saw the bright glint again.

A spyglass on a tripod had appeared in the room the day after he'd arrived, courtesy of Lord Tregonning; he'd already set it to scan the gardens. Striding to where it stood, he brought it to bear on the area in question, quickly focused.

On Eleanor Fritham.

She walked down the path out of the wood in the Garden of Diana. Her hair caught the moonlight—the glint he'd seen.

"It's one o'clock. What the devil's she doing—" He broke off as, scanning ahead of Eleanor, he discovered someone else. Someone in a coat, with broader shoulders, stepping off the highest viewing platform, heading deeper into the gardens further down the valley. Some man, but he was already in denser cover, walking into the dips and shadows of the gardens. Eleanor followed, her steps light.

In seconds, they'd disappeared, dropping lower into areas out of Gerrard's sight.

He put up the spyglass; he had little doubt of the meaning of what he'd seen. The Hellebore Hall gardens at night, drenched in moonlight, were the perfect setting for a tryst.

Heaven knew, he'd felt the magic himself that afternoon.

Inwardly shrugging, he finished drawing his curtain, and left Eleanor and her beau to themselves.

So tell me—what's he like?" Eleanor looked into Jacqueline's face, her own alive with curiosity.

Smiling, Jacqueline walked on. That morning after breakfast, Eleanor had arrived to stroll the gardens and chat, as she usually did every few days. Jacqueline had expected to have to deny her and devote her time to Gerrard, but when she'd looked his way inquiringly, he'd sensed her question and instead excused himself, saying he wished to look over his sketches from yesterday.

He'd headed upstairs, presumably to his studio, leaving her free to stroll with Eleanor, and appease her friend's rampant curiosity. "You've seen him." She glanced at Eleanor. "You've spoken with him. What did *you* think of him?"

Eleanor mock groaned. "You know very well that's not what I meant, but if you want to know, I was taken by surprise—appreciative surprise, I hasten to add. He's not at all what I'd expected."

Indeed. Jacqueline stepped down from the upper viewing stage onto the path that led through the Garden of Diana and farther to the Garden of Persephone, and the spot where she and Eleanor most often sat and talked.

"He's not quiet, not reserved, but *contained,* isn't he?" Eleanor, eyes on the path, ambled beside her. "He watches, observes, but doesn't react, yet there's all that energy—all that strength and intensity—you can sense it, almost see it, but you can't touch it, and it doesn't touch you."

She shivered delicately; glancing at her, Jacqueline saw an eager, frankly knowing smile playing about her lips.

Eleanor caught her gaze; her eyes shone. "I'd wager Mama's pearls he's a *fantastic* lover."

Jacqueline felt her brows rise. Eleanor had had lovers—she'd never known who, or if there'd been one or more; Eleanor had freely described her experiences, but only in terms of the feelings, the excitement, the physical sensations.

Through Eleanor, she'd learned more than she would otherwise know, yet only in the abstract.

Until now.

He kissed me, and I kissed him.

The words hovered on her tongue, but she drew them back. Held back from sharing that piece of information she knew Eleanor would relish. She could imagine her friend's subsequent questions: how had it felt, what had he done, was he masterful, what had he tasted like?

Wonderful, he'd opened her eyes, yes, he was masterful, but gentle, too—and male—he'd tasted like the essence of male.

Those would be her answers, but she was reluctant to share them. The incident yesterday hadn't been intended, not by either of them. He hadn't played with her hair intending to seduce her into a kiss, of that she was sure. And she . . . she hadn't known that after his lips had touched hers once, she'd ache to feel them again—that she'd want, and be so brazen as to invite, so much more.

Yet he had, and she had. She wasn't yet sure how she felt, or should feel, about either of those happenings.

While Eleanor had always shared the intimate details of many aspects of her life, she had always been more reserved, more circumspect in what she let out. But she knew Eleanor well; she would have to say more.

"Sitting for him has been quite different from what I expected. He's only done pencil sketches so far, and he's very quick with those."

"Do you have to strike a pose? Jordan said he met you and Gerrard in the gardens yesterday, but that he'd finished by then."

"Not finished—we were in between gardens. We strolled through, trying various spots. It's not so much striking a pose as just sitting as he tells me to sit, then talking."

"Talking?" Eleanor drew back to look at her. "About what?"

Jacqueline smiled and kept walking. Their usual bench lay just ahead, set between two flower beds. "Anything, really. The topics aren't all that important. I'm not even sure he listens to what I say, not to my words."

Eleanor frowned. "Why talk, then?" Reaching the bench, they sat.

"It's so I'm thinking of something—because of course I have to think of whatever I'm talking about. He's more interested in what shows in my face."

"Ah." Eleanor nodded. They sat quietly for a few moments, then she said, "Mr. Adair's quite interesting, isn't he?"

Suppressing a cynical smile, Jacqueline agreed.

"He's the third son of an earl, did you know?"

There followed a largely one-sided discussion of Barnaby's character and person, with occasional comparisons to Gerrard. Jacqueline interpreted those with the ease of familiarity; as she'd expected, Eleanor found Gerrard the more attractive, an attraction only heightened by his apparent unattainability, his disinterest, but she viewed Barnaby as the easier conquest.

"Gerrard probably reserves all his intensity for his painting—artists can, I believe, be terribly selfish in that way."

When Eleanor's pause made it clear she expected a response, Jacqueline murmured, "I suspect that's so."

But he hadn't been selfish yesterday. He'd been . . . what? Kind? Generous, certainly. He must be accustomed to dallying with experienced lovers; with her untutored kisses, she was very far from that. Yet he hadn't seemed disappointed. Or had he just been polite?

Inwardly, she frowned.

"Hmm," Eleanor purred. She stretched, raising her arms, pushing them up and out.

Glancing at her face, lifted to the sun, Jacqueline noted again the impression she'd gained the instant she'd seen Eleanor that morning. Eleanor's expression was that of a contented cat stretching languorously in the sunshine.

Jacqueline had seen that expression before; Eleanor had been with her lover last night.

A spurt of some feeling rushed through her, not quite jealousy, for how could one be jealous over something one didn't know—a yearning, perhaps, to . . . live a little. Eleanor was only a year older than she, yet for years Jacqueline had felt the gap between them widening. Before Thomas disappeared, they'd seemed much closer in experience, even though Eleanor had already taken a lover, but when Thomas walked away and never came back . . . from that point on, her life had stalled. Then her mother had died and life had been suspended altogether.

She'd been alive but stationary, going nowhere, learning nothing, not growing, or experiencing any of those things she'd always thought life and living were about.

She was tired of life passing her by.

It would continue to do so—leaving her to experience all that might be only at a vicarious distance—until Gerrard completed her portrait, and forced those around her to see the truth, and start the process of finding who had killed her mother and avenging her death; only once all that had occurred would she be free to move forward and live again.

Restlessness seized her. She stood and shook out her skirts, surprising Eleanor.

"I should get back to the house—I promised Gerrard I would make myself available to sit whenever he wishes, and he must have finished with his sketches by now."

Contrary to her expectations, Gerrard wasn't looking for her; he hadn't sent or come searching for her. Treadle told her he was still in his studio.

She'd told Eleanor that Gerrard had insisted all sittings be private, just her and him, and that he'd made it clear he'd show none of his sketches or preliminary work to anyone; disappointed, but also intrigued, Eleanor had sauntered off, heading home through the gardens.

Jacqueline had returned to the house, only to discover her presence wasn't required—not by anyone, least of all the ton's latest artistic lion.

Disappointed—and irritated that she felt so—she found a novel and sat in the parlor. And tried to read.

When Treadle rang the gong for luncheon, she felt hugely relieved.

But Gerrard didn't appear for the meal. Millicent, bless her, inquired, saving Jacqueline from having to do so; Treadle informed them that Mr. Debbington's man had taken a tray up to the studio. Apparently his master, once engrossed in his work, had been known to miss mealtimes for days; part of Compton's duties was to ensure he didn't starve.

Jacqueline wasn't sure whether to feel impressed or not.

When at the end of the meal, Millicent asked whether she would join her in the parlor, she shook her head. "I'm going to stroll on the terrace."

She did, slowly, from one end to the other, trying not to think about anything—especially artists who kept all their intensity reserved for their art—and failed. Reaching the southern end of the terrace, she looked up—at the balcony she knew to be his, then lifted her gaze higher, to the wide attic windows of the old nursery.

Her eyes narrowed, her lips thinned.

Muttering an unladylike curse, she swung on her heel and headed for the nearest door, and the nursery stairs beyond.

G errard stood by the nursery windows looking out at the gardens—and not seeing a single tree. In his hands, he held the best of the sketches he'd done yesterday. They were good—the promise they held was fabulous—but . . .

How to move forward? What should his next step be?

He'd spent all day weighing the possibilities. Should he, for instance, insist that Millicent be present through each and every sitting from now on?

His painterly instinct rebelled. Millicent would distract, not just him, but Jacqueline. It had to be just the two of them, alone—in intimate communion, albeit of the spiritual sort.

His problem lay in keeping the spiritual from too quickly transforming to the physical. That it would at some point he accepted, but she was an innocent; wisdom dictated he rein in his galloping impulses to a walk.

A tap sounded on the door. "Come." He assumed it was a maid sent to fetch the tray Compton had brought up earlier.

The door opened; Jacqueline walked in. She saw him, met his gaze directly, then, closing the door behind her, looked around.

It was the first time she'd been there since the area had been converted for his use. Her gaze scanned the long trestle table and the various art supplies laid out along its length; she noted the stack of sketches at one end, then glanced at the sheets he held in his hand.

Then her attention deflected, drawn to the large easel and the sized, blank canvas that stood upon it, draped in cheesecloth to protect it from dust.

Walking slowly into the room, she considered the sight, then transferred her gaze to him. "I wondered if you wanted me to sit for you." She halted two paces away, beside the window, and waited.

He looked into her eyes, studied her face, then lightly tossed the sketches he'd been examining—for hours—onto the table; folding his arms across his chest, he leaned against the window frame, and looked at her. "No—you wondered what was wrong."

She eyed him, not so much warily as considering what tack to take.

He sighed, and raked one hand through his hair, a gesture of frustration Vane had broken him of years ago. "I've only just met you, yet I feel I've known you forever." And felt compelled to protect her, even from himself.

She hesitated, puzzled. "So . . . ?"

"So I'm not sure I can do this."

"Paint the portrait?"

He glanced up, saw consternation and fear fill her face. "Yes—but don't look at me like that."

Her eyes locked on his. "How else? I *need* you to paint that portrait. You know that—you know why."

"Indeed, but I also know . . ." With two fingers, he gestured between them. "About this."

The careful look returned to her eyes. "This what?"

Exasperated, he waved between them. "*This,* between us—don't pretend you don't understand, that you don't feel it."

For a long moment, she met his gaze steadily, her lower lip caught between her teeth. Then she drew a tight breath, and lifted her chin. "If this is about that kiss yesterday—"

"*Don't* apologize!"

She jumped.

He pointed a finger at her nose. "That was my fault entirely."

She huffed at him, a derisive sound. "I can't imagine how me kissing you could be your fault. I wasn't under any spell, no matter *what* you might think."

He had to press his lips tight to stop them from curving. He straightened. "I didn't mean to suggest I'd bespelled you."

She narrowed her eyes. "Perhaps you thought I was so blinded by your charms I didn't know what I was doing?"

"No, I didn't think that, either. I do think I shouldn't have kissed you in the first place."

"Why?" She searched his eyes. Her expression grew troubled, sad. She swallowed. "Because of—"

"No!" He suddenly realized what tack her mind had taken; he cut her off with a gesture. "Not because of the suspicion leveled at you— good *God*!" His hand was running through his hair again, thoroughly disarranging the neatly cut locks; he abruptly lowered it. "It's nothing to do with that." It was all to do with him and her. "It's because . . ."

He looked at her, met her green and gold eyes, let whatever it was that was in him reach for her, let the connection rise . . . He could almost feel the passion and desire surge to life, rippling between them.

"It's because of that. *This.*" His voice had lowered, deepened; he spoke slowly, clearly. "Whatever it is that's sprung to life between us."

She didn't say anything; eyes locked with his, she was listening, following.

He stepped away from the window, not directly toward her; slowly, he circled her. "It's because the more I'm with you"—he prowled to stand directly behind her with only an inch separating their bodies—"the more I want to kiss you, and not just your lips."

Reaching around her, he raised his hands; he didn't touch her, but sculpted the air less than an inch from her body, slowly, caressingly running his palms over her shoulders, slowly down, over and around her breasts, her waist, her stomach, hips and thighs. His lips by her ear, he murmured, "I want to kiss your breasts, explore every inch of your body, taste every inch of your skin. I want to possess you utterly—" He broke off, drew in a quick breath, censored the too-explicit words that had leapt to his tongue. "I want to know your passion, *all of it*, and give you mine."

He could feel desire beating at him with wings of heat; certainly she could feel it, too. Passion roiled about them, an almost palpable vortex drawing them in, down, under.

"I can't be near you and not want you—not want to lie with you, to share every secret of your body and make it, and you, mine."

Looking down at her, standing straight and silent before him, listening to and following his every word, he had to fight to lower his hands, to return them to his sides without seizing her.

He succeeded, and let his relief show in a long sigh. Softly, he said, "Doesn't it scare you?" After a moment, he murmured, "God knows, it scares me."

For half a minute, she said nothing, then, slowly, she turned and faced him. Only an inch separated her breasts from his chest.

She looked into his eyes; her expression was open, honest, direct—and determined. "Yes, I can feel it, but I fear death, not life. I fear dying without ever living, without ever knowing, without experiencing this—precisely this. Above all, *this*."

Her eyes steady on his, she drew breath and went on, "I don't know what might or might not happen, or come to be, or what dangers or risks are involved, but I don't care. Because while I'm facing dangers and taking risks, I'll be living, and not simply existing as I have been for so long."

Her honesty demanded his. Her determination undermined his good intentions. "Do you know what you're saying—what you're inviting?"

"Yes." Her lashes fluttered, then she met his eyes again. "You've been blatantly honest."

Not honest enough. "I can't promise . . . anything. I don't know what might develop, how much of me I'll be able to give you. I've never . . ." His lips twisted, but he held her gaze. "Been with a lady like you before."

A lady who affected him so profoundly, in so many ways, in so intense a fashion. He had no idea how a marriage between them would work.

"I didn't ask for any promises."

Her voice remained steady, as did her gaze. He still felt driven to protect her. "Nevertheless, I'll make you one. If at any time you want to call a halt, to retreat to a safer distance for a time, you need only say."

He reached for her as the words fell from his lips. Her eyes widened as he gathered her to him, fully into his arms; her hands gripped his upper arms, yet as he lowered his head, she made no attempt to push back.

Instead, she tilted up her face, and their lips met.

And there was no drawing back. Not for him, not for her.

The vortex closed around them.

Passion rose, a hot wave, and sighed through them, powerful, yet restrained, the steady pull of an undertow beneath the waves. Restrained enough for the novelty to shine—for them both.

His head spun. This was so completely different from any other time, any other kiss... *she* was so completely different from any other woman.

The knowledge rocked him, left him open to a surge of feeling that colored every sensation, that turned her soft lips into a new and enthralling wonderland, transformed her body into a feminine landscape he had to explore—as if it were his first time. Slowly. Savoring every step, every moment.

Jacqueline parted her lips, invited him to take—and gloried when he did. Yet there seemed no rush, no urgency, no overwhelming, grasping passion; this, it seemed, was a time for exploration, for learning.

There was an unadorned, uncomplicated hunger in his kiss; she responded in kind, taking what he offered, taking all she needed. Pushing her arms up, she twined them about his neck, shuddered delicately when his arms tightened in response, drawing her fully against him, tight breasts to the hard wall of his chest, her hips to his rock-hard thighs.

No part of him seemed soft; against her giving flesh, his body was all muscle and bone, powerful, alien—all male. Her rational mind knew she ought to feel frightened, helpless and threatened by that potent strength, yet, bemused, she accepted that she didn't.

If anything, she delighted in the contrast, his maleness emphasizing the female in her; if anything, she felt anticipation rise because of the differences, because of their promise.

His hands, long-fingered and strong, spread over her sides, gripping, then easing and moving over her back.

Spreading heat, a distracting warmth that rose even higher,

spread even more when he angled his head and deepened the kiss. Eagerly, she pressed closer and followed his lead, tempted and very willing.

One hand moved down to the back of her waist, pressing there, locking her to him. The other glided up to curve over her shoulder, lingered there, close to her throat, warm palm against her exposed skin, then smoothly slid down, tantalizingly tracing the bare skin above her bodice before sliding down and around to close over one breast.

She lost what little breath she possessed, felt something akin to lightning streak down her nerves as he weighed her firm flesh, as he blatantly explored the full curves, expertly caressed, then closed his hand and gently kneaded.

A shudder of pure pleasure racked her; worried he might misinterpret, she pressed closer still, slid her hands from his nape into his hair, held his head steady as she kissed him, and with lips and tongue begged for more.

He understood; she felt his lips curve fractionally, then he accepted her unvoiced invitation, kissed her even more deeply, even more intimately, his tongue surging against hers in a rhythm she'd never known yet at some level recognized.

Her head started to spin; her wits slowly sank into a haze of warm delight.

His hands firmed; the one at her breast fondled, then his clever fingers sought out the peak, and rolled it, squeezed until she gasped through the kiss. Until pleasure bloomed and spread under her skin, like a wave rolling through her, pooling low to pulse between her thighs.

He leaned back against the window frame, drawing her with him; his artful fingers continued to play with her nipple, now tightly furled, while his other hand eased from her waist and slid down, over her hips, over her bottom, caressed, increasingly explicitly fondled, then cupped, closed, kneaded.

Her knees buckled. He held her, helpless, increasingly heated, increasingly wanting. Desire flared and spread under her skin; with hands and mouth, lips and tongue, he fed the conflagration.

She clutched his head, kissed him back, felt an unfamiliar urgency rise—

Footsteps pounded on the stairs beyond the door, coming swiftly up.

They broke from the kiss. She heard a muttered curse, realized it wasn't hers, albeit she agreed with the sentiment.

Gerrard gripped her waist and set her back against the window frame; stepping away, he grabbed a sketch pad and pencil.

The door burst open. Barnaby stood in the doorway, breathing hard, his color high.

They blinked at him.

He blinked back, then waved. "Sorry—but . . ." He looked at Gerrard. "We've found a body."

I was out walking—I took the path along the northern ridge." Barnaby glanced over his shoulder as the three of them hurried along the path through the kitchen garden. "The path cuts through the Garden of Hades—it's all cypress trees, a small forest of them. I noticed a section of bank higher up the ridge had crumbled away . . . there looked to be material, and an odd shape, so I climbed up to take a look."

Insatiably curious—Gerrard had said Barnaby was so. Barnaby glanced back at her. Jacqueline met his worried look with grim determination. "Who is it?" she asked.

Barnaby cast an imploring look at Gerrard, then faced forward. "I couldn't say. It's not a . . . a recently deceased body."

Her stomach lurched, but she clenched her teeth. They'd had a brief altercation in the studio, when Barnaby had tried to leave her behind. Gerrard had agreed with him, but wisely hadn't said so; in the end, he'd taken her arm and let her accompany them.

But he wasn't happy about it.

She set her jaw. This was her home, and if there were bodies buried in the garden, she had to know.

Her heart was thudding uncomfortably, high in her chest; she felt slightly dizzy. Heavy clouds had blown over, turning the breezy, sunny morning into an oppressive afternoon, with the rumble of thunder and the metallic tang of lightning a distant threat. As they left the wooden pergola and toiled up the path through the vines of the Garden of Dionysius, she was glad of Gerrard's long fingers clamped about her elbow, steadying her.

Barnaby had alerted her father and Treadle before coming to find them. When they crossed into the Garden of Hades, into the dark shade of the cypress trees, they heard voices ahead. Looking up, they saw a group of men standing around a crumbling bank. The head gardener, Wilcox, was there, along with two of his men, armed with shovels. The head stableman, Richards, was there, too, as were her father and Treadle.

She stopped on the path. Barnaby continued, toiling up the slope. Gerrard glanced at her, and waited by her side.

Her father spoke with Barnaby, then turned and saw her. Barnaby looked at her, and suggested something. Her father hesitated, then nodded; carefully, ponderously, he made his way down the bank, Treadle hovering solicitously at his elbow. Barnaby followed a little way behind.

Her father reached the path; pale, a trifle out of breath, he took a moment to straighten his coat, then he leaned—truly leaned—on his cane. "I'm sorry, my dear—this is most distressing."

She gripped his arm, fingers locking tight. "Who is it?"

Her father met her gaze, then shook his head. "We can't be certain . . ." He sighed; raising his right hand, he opened his closed fist. "Mr. Adair wondered if you recognized this?"

She looked down at the fob watch that lay in his palm.

For a long moment, she said nothing, just stared while her lungs constricted and her heart thudded in her throat. Then she reached out—not to take the watch but with one finger to brush the dirt from the engraving on the closed lid.

She leaned nearer, looked. "It's Thomas's."

A rushing roaring filled her ears and her vision went black.

8

She came to her senses, how much later she didn't know. She was lying on the chaise in the drawing room; Millicent, Gerrard and Barnaby stood nearby, talking in hushed voices.

When she struggled to sit up, Millicent saw and rushed over. "You should stay lying down for a while, dear. You were in a dead faint when Mr. Debbington carried you up."

Jacqueline glanced up at Gerrard, who had come to stand at the back of the chaise. "Thank you."

His expression remained stony. "If you want to thank me, stay where you are."

Millicent blinked, taken aback by his tone. "Ah . . . would you like some water, dear?"

"Tea would be nice."

"Yes, of course." Millicent hurried to the bellpull.

With Gerrard's gaze on her, Jacqueline made a show of relaxing against the cushions. She looked at Barnaby, standing before the fireplace. "What's happening?"

Barnaby glanced at Gerrard, then came closer. "Your father's sent word to the magistrate. Meanwhile, Wilcox and Richards are overseeing the . . . ah, disinterment."

A chill slid through her. "Is it possible to know . . . Can anyone tell when he was killed? Or how?" She focused on Barnaby. "Was he shot?"

Barnaby glanced at Gerrard again. Gerrard sighed and, waving Barnaby to a nearby chair, came around to sit on the end of the chaise. "Perhaps it's better to discuss it, seeing she's so determined."

She shot him a look, but Millicent, taking the other armchair, nodded. "I can see no benefit in pretending we don't have a dead body in the garden, and that it isn't that poor boy, Thomas Entwhistle. I'm sure Jacqueline will be more comfortable if we approach the matter sensibly."

"Yes, precisely." Thank heaven for sensible aunts. Jacqueline looked again at Barnaby; he seemed to be the one with the information. "Is it known when he . . . Thomas, died?"

"Only that it was long ago." Barnaby grimaced. "A year at least, probably more. When was he last seen?"

She thought back, added the months. "Two years and four months ago."

"In that case, there's nothing to say he wasn't killed on that day. He was last seen here, wasn't he?"

She felt the cold intensifying; slowly, she nodded. "Yes. By me." She met Barnaby's gaze, then looked at Gerrard. "I was the last person to speak with him . . . just like with Mama."

Barnaby frowned. "Yes, well, that hardly means you killed them, does it?"

His tone, one of dismissive reasonableness, had her—and Gerrard, too—looking at him.

Barnaby's frown deepened. "What?"

Gerrard shook his head. "Never mind that now. What else have you deduced?"

Barnaby grimaced. "Thomas was killed with a rock. A largish one." With his hands, he outlined an object about twelve inches square. "About that size. Someone picked it up, and smashed it down on the back of his skull."

Jacqueline swallowed. But Thomas was dead; he'd died long ago, and she needed to learn how. "I walked with him along the path to the stables. We parted just inside the Garden of Hercules and he went on. Why . . . how did he end up in the Garden of Hades? It's quite some distance away."

"Indeed." Barnaby tapped the chair arm, then glanced at Jacqueline. "You parted just inside the Garden of Hercules—meaning some way before, and out of sight of, the junction with the side path, the one that follows the northern ridge through Hercules, Demeter, Diony-sius and so to Hades."

She nodded. "I wasn't supposed to go beyond the terrace, but I walked just a little way—the path's open until the edge of the Garden of Hercules."

"Right." Barnaby straightened. "So someone could have met Thomas deeper in the Garden of Hercules without you knowing."

She frowned. "Yes, that's true."

"Would you have heard if he spoke with someone?"

"Not if you mean near the other path—by the time he reached there, I would have been back on the terrace. I wouldn't have known he'd met someone unless he called out, and possibly not even then—the wind usually blows the other way."

"I doubt he called out."

"Why do you say that?" Gerrard asked.

"Because . . . well, Thomas was quite tall, wasn't he?"

Jacqueline nodded; she glanced at Gerrard. "As tall as Gerrard, but thinner."

"Yes, well, from the damage to his skull, whoever hit him was standing close behind him, possibly somewhat higher than he. I don't think that would happen very easily unless that someone was a man Thomas knew."

Gerrard saw the color drain from Jacqueline's face. "A *man*—not a woman?"

Barnaby blinked. "A woman?" He considered, gaze distant, then shook his head. "I can't see it—whoever lifted that rock had to be quite strong. Just grasping a rock that size would be difficult for most women. And as Thomas was tall, then even standing above him on the steepest stretch of the path, they'd have had to lift the rock high to bring it down with such force." He refocused on Gerrard's face. "A single blow, it was."

A small, distressed sound escaped Millicent.

Coloring, Barnaby glanced at her. "Sorry. But, well, it couldn't have been a woman—no ordinary woman, anyway. A giantess might have done it, but unless Thomas was acquainted with one hereabouts, well . . ." Barnaby smiled apologetically, clearly attempting to lighten the moment.

"You're saying," Gerrard reiterated, "that Thomas was killed by a man, almost certainly a man he knew."

Barnaby nodded. "That seems the only reasonable conclusion."

The drawing room doors opened. Barnaby and Gerrard rose as Lord Tregonning and an older gentleman they hadn't previously met came in. Jacqueline swung her legs down; Gerrard gave her his hand and helped her to her feet. He didn't like her pallor, or the way she stiffened; he wound her arm with his and settled her hand on his sleeve, his hand covering hers. Millicent rose, too, and moved to stand on Jacqueline's other side.

The gentleman bowed to Millicent and Jacqueline, who curtsied.

Lord Tregonning waved at Barnaby and Gerrard. "This is Mr. Adair, who found the body, and Mr. Debbington, another guest. Sir Godfrey Marks, our magistrate."

Barnaby and Gerrard shook hands with Sir Godfrey, and exchanged murmured greetings.

Sir Godfrey turned to Jacqueline. "I'm sorry to disturb you, m'dear, but your father showed me this watch, which was found on the body." Sir Godfrey held out the watch. "Are you sure it was Thomas's?"

The last vestige of color drained from Jacqueline's face, along with all expression. She glanced briefly at the watch, then nodded. "I'm sure. Sir Harvey and Lady Entwhistle will recognize it."

Sir Godfrey paused, searching her face, then he nodded and returned the watch to his pocket. "It's a pity it's so long ago now, but just refresh my memory—you walked with him to the stables and parted from him there?"

"No." Jacqueline lifted her chin; Gerrard felt her fingers tighten on his sleeve. "I walked only a little way along the path—we parted where it enters the Garden of Hercules. Thomas went on, and I returned to the house."

Sir Godfrey looked at Lord Tregonning, then glanced briefly at Jacqueline; the expression on his face looked suspiciously like pity. "So you were the last here to see him alive?"

Gerrard felt her fingers flutter beneath his, but her chin set; her expression remained impassive.

"Yes."

Portentously, Sir Godfrey nodded, then turned to Lord Tregonning. "We'll leave it at that." His tone was heavy. "I'll speak to the Entwhistles and let them know. Could have been gypsies or vagabonds, of course. No sense pursuing it—nothing will bring poor young Entwhistle back."

Lord Tregonning's face remained set and unresponsive. "As you wish." His voice was devoid of emotion. He didn't look at Jacqueline, or any of them, but stiffly returned Sir Godfrey's nod and turned with him to the doors.

Jaw slack with amazement, incomprehension in his eyes, Barnaby stared at Gerrard, then glanced at Jacqueline. Before Gerrard could react, Barnaby started after the two men; he touched Sir Godfrey's arm. "Sir Godfrey, about the circumstances of this death—"

Sir Godfrey halted. He frowned fiercely at Barnaby. "I don't believe we need to delve deeper into that, sir." He glanced fleetingly at Jacqueline, then met Barnaby's gaze. "I'm sure I don't need to remind you you're a guest here. No point creating unnecessary distress—a sad occurrence, but there's nothing more to be done."

With that deliberate and emphatic verdict, Sir Godfrey nodded curtly, and departed, Lord Tregonning beside him.

Astounded, Barnaby stared after them.

When the door shut, he turned. "What the devil was that about?" He looked at Gerrard, then transferred his affronted gaze to Jacqueline. "The bounder behaved as if *you'd* killed Thomas! Why on earth would he think that?"

Gerrard felt the stiffness go out of Jacqueline; with a helpless gesture, she sank unsteadily down; he eased her back onto the chaise. "Because," he said, his tone lethal, cutting, "too many people hereabouts believe Jacqueline killed her mother, so why not Thomas, as well?"

"*What?*" Barnaby stared at him, past incredulous. Then he looked at Jacqueline. "But that's ludicrous. You couldn't have killed your mother."

Gerrard fleetingly closed his eyes and thanked the gods for Barnaby. Opening them, he saw Jacqueline, color returning to her cheeks, staring at his friend. She'd been taken aback when he'd seen her innocence, but for someone with no real connection or interest in her to so clearly declare it . . . she was dumbfounded.

Gerrard voiced the question he knew was in her mind. "Why do you say that—why ludicrous? Why couldn't Jacqueline have killed her mother?"

Barnaby almost goggled at him. "Have you taken a good look at the balustrade on the terrace?"

"It's a stone balustrade, the usual sort of thing."

Barnaby nodded. "The usual thing—solid stone, a ten-inches-wide stone top, waist-high to a man, midriff-high to a woman of average height, which I understand Lady Tregonning was.

"A woman of average height"—Barnaby bowed to Jacqueline—"couldn't push, tip or bundle another woman of average height, and, as it happens, greater weight, over such a high *and wide* barrier. It would be as close to impossible as makes no odds."

He looked at Jacqueline, consternation and the beginnings of horrified comprehension dawning in his eyes. "When I say you couldn't have killed your mother, I mean it literally. She had to have been lifted bodily to the top of the balustrade, and then pushed, or more likely thrown, over. I don't think you could physically have managed it, not alone." He hesitated, then asked. "They don't *really* believe you did, do they?"

It was Millicent who answered. "Yes, they do."

Briefly, Millicent explained to a flabbergasted Barnaby how matters had fallen out at the time of Miribelle Tregonning's death.

"And so they all took it into their heads it was Jacqueline." Millicent humphed. "I never subscribed to such nonsense, but by the time I learned of it, it was the general belief. Most of those in the area regard the notion as unproven fact."

Barnaby was appalled. "Unproven facts aren't facts at all!"

Given his belief in the application of logical deduction in solving crimes, Barnaby viewed the making of conjecture into fact as akin to heresy. Gerrard listened as Barnaby questioned, and Millicent elaborated, describing the way local sentiment had evolved, how the notion of Jacqueline as her mother's murderer had taken root in so many minds.

It was frighteningly simple, yet the outcome was devastating. He glanced at Jacqueline. Not only devastating, but difficult to remedy.

She said little. She appeared to be listening; he wasn't sure she was. Treadle brought in the tea tray and Millicent poured. Jacqueline accepted a cup and sat back, sipping. Barnaby and Millicent continued their discussion, moving on to consider how to rectify the situation. Jacqueline listened to that, but there was nothing new, nothing she hadn't already thought of; he watched as her mind turned inward, and her thoughts slid away.

She'd just learned that a young man she'd cared for, and who had cared for her, had been brutally murdered. Even though she wasn't looking at him, watching her face Gerrard sensed, not her thoughts, but her emotions.

Sadness, and more, too many swirling feelings for him to distinguish; one part of him, the polite gentleman, recoiled from intruding on her grief, another part, the painter, noted and cataloged, while the private man wanted to gather her in his arms and comfort her, to soothe and reassure.

He blinked; looking down, he set his cup on its saucer. He couldn't recall such an impulse to comfort afflicting him before, not with such poignant force, with such sharp and clear empathy. Empathy was a necessity for an artist, yet it had never before had such a personal edge.

Never pressed him so keenly to act, to share the burden if not make it his.

From beneath his lashes, he glanced at Jacqueline. If he acted, how would she respond?

He hadn't forgotten that moment in the studio, dramatically interrupted though it had been. They'd moved on, taken a definite step forward together, so where did that leave them—he and she, and what lay between them—now?

She finished her tea. Without glancing at him, she rose. When both he and Barnaby rose, too, Millicent broke off and looked up; Jacqueline smiled fleetingly, distantly. "If you'll excuse me, I think I'll retire for a while. I'm rather fagged."

"Yes, of course, dear." Millicent set down her cup. "I'll look in on you later."

With a nod, a wan smile and a fleeting glance at him, Jacqueline turned to the door. Gerrard watched as she walked out; he didn't like the empty look in her eyes.

He turned back to Millicent and Barnaby.

Barnaby caught his eye. "I'm off to walk the path Thomas must have followed."

He nodded. "I'll come with you." He needed air, and he needed to think.

Leaving Millicent in the drawing room, they walked out onto the terrace. They retraced the route Thomas and Jacqueline had taken more than two years before, then went on, turning down the path along the northern ridge, confirming that all Jacqueline had said was true; she wouldn't have known if someone had met Thomas at the junction of the paths, nor could she have gone so far with him, not with her mother expecting her back.

They walked on through the gardens of Demeter and Dionysius, Barnaby speculating that, if the crime had been committed along the path, given Thomas's height, it would have occurred at the steepest stretch, where the path dipped into the Garden of Hades. Using Gerrard as a model, Barnaby concluded the murderer was at most three inches shorter, a man Thomas had known well enough to be comfortable having close at his back.

Barnaby pulled a face. "I must engineer a meeting with Lady Entwhistle. Mothers always know who their darlings are consorting with. She'll know who Thomas considered a close friend."

They rounded a bend in the path and looked up at the spot where Thomas's body had lain. "Looks like they've taken the body away." Only Wilcox and Richards remained, the former leaning on a shovel.

Barnaby led the way up the steep slope, clambering over the thick roots of the cypresses clinging to the incline.

Wilcox and Richards straightened as they neared and touched their caps. Gerrard nodded in greeting.

Barnaby dusted his hands. "I was just wondering . . . you were both here when Entwhistle disappeared, weren't you?"

"Aye." Both men nodded.

"Do you recall any gentleman being near the gardens about the time Entwhistle left the house?"

Wilcox and Richards shared a glance, then Richards volunteered, "We've all been scratching our heads, trying to remember. Near as we can recall, young Mr. Brisenden was out walking along the cliffs, like he often does. Sir Vincent Perry, another local gentleman, was here calling on Lady Tregonning and Miss Jacqueline—he left the house when young Entwhistle arrived, but he didn't come to get his horse until sometime later. Howsoever, he often walked down to the little bay—not the cove in the gardens, but the one down past the stables—before he came to fetch his horse. As for others . . ." Richards looked at Wilcox, who took up the tale.

"Both Lord Fritham and Master Jordan often walk in the gardens—we're never sure when we'll see one of them about. And there'd a' been plenty of local lads out that day—fishing, hunting, it were the season for both. While they don't normally come into the gardens, they sometimes cut through. Everyone hereabouts knows the paths over the ridges, and how they connect. Fastest way from Tresdale Manor lands across to the cliffs to the north."

Barnaby pulled a face. "Why would any local lads want to kill Entwhistle? Was he well liked?"

"Oh, aye—very amiable young gent, he was."

"We was all hoping he and Miss Jacqueline might marry—everyone knew that was the way things were heading."

Barnaby's gaze sharpened. "So there's no known reason for anyone to kill Entwhistle, other than, just possibly, jealousy over Miss Jacqueline?"

The two older men exchanged a glance, then nodded. "Aye," Richards said, "that's true enough."

Gerrard looked down at the mound of freshly turned earth. "Did you find anything more?"

"Not anything from the poor lad, but"—Wilcox pointed up the slope—"I'd be surprised if that rock there wasn't what had done for him."

To the side some yards upslope lay a heavy rock, roughly rectangular and close to the size Barnaby had postulated.

Barnaby scrambled up and across. He hefted the rock, using both hands, then glanced at Gerrard. "This would have done the trick." He looked around. "That suggests he was killed here, or close by . . ." Noticing Richards and Wilcox exchanging looks, Barnaby stopped. "What is it?"

"Well." Richards waved around them. "There aren't many rocks hereabouts, not big ones like that. It's the trees knit the bank together—the soil's not all that rocky."

"Only place you find rocks like that is up top of the ridge." Wilcox pointed up the slope. "Up there, it's all rocks, just like that one." He indicated the rock Barnaby set down. "We was thinking if young Entwhistle and the blackguard who killed him had climbed to the ridge, then when Entwhistle was struck down, well, he'd roll down to here, most like, and the rock with him."

"Easy enough then to cover him with old cypress needles." Richards kicked at those underfoot. "There's always a carpet of them here. In time, he'd become just part of the bank."

"Nothing much for my lads to do up this way," Wilcox added. "The trees look after themselves, and the needles don't need to be raked."

Gerrard stared up at the ridge; it rose to a point, an outcrop of weathered rock that crumbled away to the edge of the sea cliffs. "Why would any gentleman go up there?"

"Ah, they all do. A bit of a scramble, it is, but all those who grow up hereabouts know—from there you can see the blowhole. When the sea's turned just right, it's a grand sight."

"Aha!" Barnaby's eyes lit.

It didn't take much persuading to get Richards and Wilcox to show them the way—the only way—up to the top of the ridge. From there, it was apparent that the head gardener and head stableman's conjecture had merit; a body falling down the slope would indeed land amid the cypresses.

"And," Barnaby said, his eagerness barely contained as, parting from Wilcox and Richards, they strode back to the house, "it accounts for the one point that stumped me—how did the killer bend down and pick up a huge rock without Entwhistle noticing?"

Gerrard glanced at him. "The killer would still have had to pick up the rock, even if they were standing on the ridge . . ." He broke off as a picture of two men on the ridge formed in his mind.

"Yes, but it would have been easy." Barnaby's voice held a note of triumph. "One, Entwhistle was absorbed, watching Cyclops. Two"— Barnaby caught Gerrard's eyes—"Entwhistle wasn't standing. You saw the area—what's more natural if you were chatting with a friend and looking out into the distance than to sit?"

Gerrard's mind raced. "That means the killer doesn't have to be tall."

"No—any height at all." Barnaby frowned. "Damn! That increases our list of suspects dramatically."

"But he still has to be a he—a man."

"Oh, yes. The size of the rock—and there's a good chance it was that very rock—makes that certain. Even with Thomas sitting down, a woman would have had difficulty picking it up—and with a lady, Thomas would have noticed. More, manners would have ensured if she stood, then he would have, too. No." Barnaby shook his head. "It couldn't have been a woman."

They reached the steps to the terrace; with a fleeting grin, Gerrard took them two at a time.

"What?" Barnaby asked, eyeing that grin.

Gerrard glanced at him. "There's another, even more definitive reason why the murderer wasn't a lady."

Barnaby scrunched up his face, cudgeling his brains, then sighed. "What?"

"Getting onto the ridge—we only just managed without serious damage." Gerrard pointed to a scuff mark on his boot, and a smudge on his trouser leg. "As Wilcox said, it's a scramble. No lady in a tea gown could have managed it, then returned to the house *without* being in the sort of state that would have created a furor. Everyone would have remembered that."

"Excellent point," Barnaby conceded. "It definitely wasn't a lady."

"Therefore," Gerrard concluded, his jaw firming as he led the way into the house, "not Jacqueline."

S he didn't come down to dinner.

"She asked for a tray in her room," Millicent said in response to Gerrard's query. "She said she needed a little time alone to absorb the shock."

He murmured an "Of course," and pretended to accept it, but his mind, his imagination, churned.

As always, dinner was a quiet meal, leaving him plenty of time to think. With a few stilted comments, Lord Tregonning made it clear he considered the subject of Entwhistle's death closed. Barnaby shot Gerrard a questioning look, clearly asking whether they should challenge that; almost imperceptibly, Gerrard shook his head and mouthed, "Not yet."

His first priority was Jacqueline.

After dinner, increasingly restless, he joined Millicent and Barnaby in the drawing room.

"This latest *nonsense*," Millicent declared, "will simply not do! It's dreadful for Jacqueline, and poor Thomas, too. While people assume it's her doing, the real killer goes *free*!"

He and Barnaby assured her they had absolutely no intention of letting the matter rest. Mollified, Millicent confirmed that, although her friends in the neighborhood had always kept her apprised of local happenings, she'd never heard of any dispute involving Thomas, not of the sort that might have led to murder. Dismissing that as a motive, they turned to the other plausible reason, that someone had killed Thomas because he was about to offer for Jacqueline's hand, and would most likely have been accepted.

Gerrard looked at Millicent. "Is that correct—that he was about to offer, and would have been accepted?"

"Oh, yes. The match was a favorable one on all counts."

"So who," Barnaby asked, "were the jealous hopefuls Thomas's success with Jacqueline threatened?"

He suggested Matthew Brisenden, but Millicent dismissed that idea out of hand. She was adamant, even though Barnaby pressed.

"No, no—he's cast himself in the role of her protector—a knight errant. His duty is to serve, not to marry her. You shouldn't take his attitude to mean he has any serious *matrimonial* interest in her—I'm sure he hasn't."

Reluctantly Gerrard confirmed that Jacqueline had said much the same.

"Indeed." Millicent nodded. "I don't think you should imagine Matthew was jealous of Thomas."

"Nevertheless," Barnaby said, "Brisenden might have had some reason to view Thomas as a danger to Jacqueline. That's an equally strong motive for him to attack Thomas, and he was known to be in the vicinity."

Millicent pulled a face. "I hate to admit it, but that *is* a possibility. However, a better bet would be Sir Vincent Perry—he's had his eye on Jacqueline for years."

So Sir Vincent, whom Gerrard and Barnaby had yet to meet, went on their list, along with unknown others yet to be identified let alone discounted. The exercise left them disheartened. Barnaby admitted proving who killed Thomas might not now be possible. On that somber note they retired.

They parted in the gallery and went to their respective rooms.

Gerrard spoke with Compton; he'd heard nothing useful.

"They're a bit shocked. In a day or so, as they mull things over, someone might remember something. I'll keep listening, you may be sure."

According to Compton, the staff had never imagined that Jacqueline was in any way involved with either Thomas's disappearance, or her mother's death. "Doesn't seem to have occurred to them at all."

Dismissing Compton, Gerrard stood before the windows; hands in his pockets, he thought of what they knew about both murders. If people viewed the facts rationally, with an unclouded mind, Jacqueline's innocence shone like a beacon. But people hadn't, and wouldn't, because someone had clouded the issue. Deliberately.

Someone had, with malice aforethought, cast Jacqueline as a scapegoat.

Something dark within him leapt, all gnashing teeth and sharp claws. Muttering a savage curse, he suppressed it; now was not the time for that sort of action—he couldn't see the enemy yet.

He looked out at the dark gardens, at the black and purple sky, at the roiling clouds forming fantastical shapes as they blew in from the west; a landscape artist's dream, he barely saw them.

Rescuing Jacqueline was now critical to him. Not just for her sake, but for his, too.

How she felt, how she was. That was his immediate and all-consuming focus; since Barnaby had told them of the body, the question hadn't left the forefront of his brain. He was worried, concerned, about her—anxious, with his heart uncertain and his gut tight.

Part of him wanted to pretend it was just his painterly instincts wanting to observe her in an emotional state, but that was balderdash. He *cared* for her in the same vein he cared for Patience, and other females like Amanda and Amelia . . . that was closer to the truth, yet still not all of it.

His imagination was too active not to create visions of her alone in her room, grieving, yes, but more—feeling her aloneness, feeling helpless. Thomas would have been her champion once, but he'd disappeared, left her alone—at least now she knew it hadn't been deliberately.

But he was her champion now.

He swung from the windows and paced, frustration growing. The clock struck eleven; he glowered at it, at the reminder of how many more hours he would have to endure before he saw her again, before he could reassure this insistent and strangely vulnerable part of him that she was whole, still well . . . still willing to explore what lay between them with him.

That last part of his motive was there, to be sure, but somewhat to his surprise it wasn't the predominant element; knowing she wasn't weighed down with grief, worry, and especially fear, was.

He wasn't going to get much sleep, not until he knew she was all right. Could he find out now, tonight?

He'd feel ridiculous knocking on her door and asking her outright, not at this hour . . .

Creative imagination was a wonderful thing. Inspiration gleamed; within seconds, his mind had filled in the details.

He didn't stop to think. Turning, he strode to the door, opened it, and closed it quietly behind him.

9

He only needed to see her, to speak with her. To reassure himself that she was all right.

He didn't meet anyone on his way to her room, hardly surprising given the hour. Stalking to her door, he glanced down. Strong light showed beneath it. Grimly encouraged, he rapped on the door. Half a minute passed, then Jacqueline opened it.

Her eyes widened; she stared at him.

He tried not to stare back. She was wearing a fine lawn nightgown with a gauzy robe thrown over it. Her hair was down, a rich brown veil rippling over her shoulders—it was transparently clear she hadn't been abed.

With the lamps blazing behind her, that wasn't the only thing transparently evident.

Her mouth opened, but no words came out.

Jaw clenching, he reached for her arm and moved her back. Stepping into the room, he shut the door.

"What . . . ?" She was still staring at him.

The light now reached her face. He noted her pallor; her stunned, lost and off-balance expression wasn't solely due to his arrival. "I want to look through your wardrobe."

Scanning the room, he saw a large armoire positioned along the side wall. He headed for it.

"My *wardrobe*?" Her tone incredulous but growing stronger, she flitted in a flutter of fine fabrics after him.

"I need to look over your gowns."

"My gowns." Not a question; her tone suggested he'd taken leave of his senses. "You need to see my gowns now."

"Yes." He pulled open the wardrobe doors, revealing a full length of hanging space filled with gowns. "You weren't asleep." He reached for a creation in amber silk.

She tried to peer into his face. "What are you about? Why this burning need to look at my gowns?" She glanced at the clock on the mantelpiece. "It's after eleven!"

He didn't look at her. "I need to gauge what will look best on you."

"At *night*?"

Holding the amber gown before him, he shot her a sidelong glance; arrested, his gaze lingered. "Indeed." He drank in the way the lamplight flowed over her skin, gilding it with the softest of gold washes. He drew in a shallow breath. "I might very well paint you in candlelight. Here—hold this." Thrusting the amber gown into her hands, he dived back amid the rest.

"This"—he pulled out a bronze silk sheath and tossed it at her— "and this." He added a gown in figured green satin to the pile growing in her arms. "Although"—he glanced back at the last gown—"that might be too dark. We'll see."

Returning to the wardrobe, he flipped through the contents, making more selections. "I have a certain look in mind—the color and style of your gown will be critical."

Jacqueline watched him, bemused and suspicious. She accepted the dresses he piled in her arms, and wondered. At last, he stepped back, reached for the wardrobe doors—and shot her a swift glance that was too saber-sharp, too assessing, to be casual.

He met her gaze; she raised a brow.

His lips twisted, rather grimly. He closed the wardrobe doors and reached for her hand. "Come here."

He towed her, her arms full with seven gowns, over to the hearth. Two lamps stood on either end of the mantelpiece, spilling strong, steady light out over the room.

"Here." Drawing her about, he positioned her before the mantel, a foot or so from the lamp on one end. He stood back, looked, then shifted her a fraction closer to the lamp. He seemed to be judging the play of light on her hair.

"That's it. Now turn your face up a little, toward the lamp." His fingers touched, lingered beneath her chin. "Just so." He cleared his throat. "Now." Scooping the gowns out of her arms, he selected one in spring green, and flung the rest over her armchair.

Ignoring the thought of her maid's protests, Jacqueline watched as he shook the spring-green gown out, looking at it, then at her; his gaze drifted down her body . . . she recalled how fine her nightgown and robe were, recalled she was standing before the fire.

Abruptly, he held up the gown, as if to preserve her modesty— although he'd already looked and, she would wager, his keen artist's eyes had seen all there was to see. He handed her the gown. "Hold this against you and let me see."

She did as he asked, mystified, wondering why she was humoring him, yet she stood before the fire, bathed in light, and allowed him to hand her gown after gown. Some he dismissed, others he returned to; the selection he'd chosen covered a range of colors from deepest forest green—a color, once she'd held it up, he rejected out of hand—to old gold, another shade that on examination didn't meet with his approval.

"Somewhere in between," he muttered, returning to a gown of *eau de nil* silk.

That he was in truth evaluating her gowns was plain enough, but the swift searching glances he every now and then directed her way assured her that wasn't his sole aim. Indeed, as he returned to assessing gowns in various shades of bronze, she was increasingly sure his interest in her gowns and on the play of candlelight on her hair was not so much an aim as his excuse.

Finally, he stood back. Hands on hips, he studied her, head tilted, a critical expression in his eyes, a slight frown on his face. "That's the closest you have to the right color—an intense bronze but with more gold than that is what we need. And, of course, the drape is all wrong, but at least now I know what's necessary."

"Indeed." She waited until his gaze rose to her eyes, then asked, "So why are you really here?"

He held her gaze, then opened his mouth.

"And don't tell me it was to study my gowns."

He shut his lips, pressed them tight. His eyes held hers as he debated, then his lips eased and he exhaled through his teeth, not quite a sigh, not quite an exhalation of frustration. "I was worried."

A muttered confession. "About what?"

"About you."

He didn't sound pleased about it. When she looked her befuddlement, he reluctantly elaborated, "About what you might be thinking and feeling." His hand rose, fingers spearing into his hair, but then he stopped and lowered his arm. "I was worried about how the revelations of the day had affected you." He glanced away, his gaze falling on the pile of her discarded gowns. "But I did want to evaluate your gowns. I want to complete the portrait as soon as possible."

A vise of cold iron closed about her chest. "Yes, of course." Turning away, she moved to lay the bronze silk gown she'd been holding over the chair. "I expect you'll want to leave as soon as possible."

Guarding her expression, smoothing her features to rigid impassivity, she turned to face him—and found him, hands on hips, frowning, quite definitely, at her.

"No—I don't want to leave as soon as possible. I want to complete the portrait and free you"—abruptly he gestured—"from all this—the suspicion and the well-meaning prison all around have created for you."

The expression glowing darkly in his eyes made her heart leap, then thud. *Oh* seemed redundant. She moistened her lips—watched his eyes trace the movement of her tongue. "I thought"—she sucked in a breath and steadied her voice—"that perhaps, after this last, you might wish to leave—that you might wish you'd never agreed to paint my portrait."

"No." What rang in his tone brooked no argument. He held her gaze steadily. "I want you free of this intolerable situation . . ." His hesitation was palpable, but then he continued, his words precise and clear, "Free so we—you and I—can pursue what's grown—growing—between us."

Gerrard saw the "*Oh*" form in her mind, more tellingly saw her features ease as the control she'd imposed on them faded. He was searingly aware of an almost overpowering urge to close the distance between them and take her in his arms, to comfort her physically and emotionally, in every way open to him.

Not a good idea.

Dragging in a breath that was too tight for his liking, he forced himself to turn to the fireplace. "So—how do you feel about Thomas's death?"

Not an easy question to make sound idle, not least because it wasn't; he definitely wanted to know. He didn't look at her, but studied the lamp on the mantelpiece. He felt her gaze on him, felt her consider—sensed the change in the atmosphere when she decided to tell him.

She rounded the chair; he turned his head and watched as she smoothed the gown she'd laid over it, then, drawing her robe closed, folding her arms, she paced across the room in a brooding, feminine way. Halting before the windows, she lifted her head and stared out at the dark. "It's odd, but the point that upsets me most is that I can't remember his face."

He leaned back, setting his shoulders against the mantelpiece. "You haven't seen it for over two years."

"I know. But that's a real measure of the fact that he's gone. That he's been gone, dead, for a long time, and I can't change that."

He said nothing, just waited.

After a while, she drew in a deep breath. "He was a nice . . . boy, really." She glanced across the room at him. "He was kind, and we laughed, and I liked him, but . . . whatever might have been, might have come to be between Thomas and me—that I'll never know."

Abruptly, she swung from the windows and came pacing back, her brows knitted, her gaze on the floor. Halting a yard from him, she looked up and met his eyes. "You asked how I feel. I feel *angry.*"

She pushed back the hair that had swung forward, shielding one side of her face. "I'm not sure why I feel so strongly, and not just on Thomas's behalf. The killer took something he wasn't entitled to take—Thomas's life, yes, but that wasn't all. He struck because we—Thomas and I—would have had a marriage and a family, and *that* the killer didn't want us to have. That's why he killed—he wanted to deny us that."

Her breasts swelled as she dragged in a huge breath. "He had *no right.*" Her voice shook with a medley of emotions. "He killed Thomas and stymied me—locked me into a cage of his making. And then he killed my mother." Her face clouded. "Why?"

When she refocused on him, Gerrard pushed away from the mantelpiece. "With your mother, it can't have been jealousy, or any variation of that. Perhaps she learned something the killer didn't want known, either something about Thomas's death, or something entirely different."

She held his gaze. "But it was the same man, wasn't it?"

"Barnaby will tell you that the odds of having two murderers in such a limited area are infinitesimal."

Her gaze grew distant, assessing. "We have to catch him—expose him and trap him—and we need to do it soon."

"Indeed." His crisp tone drew her attention back to him. "And our first step is to complete the portrait."

If anything, the discovery of Thomas's body and their speculation over his death seemed to be hardening her resolve. He remembered thinking that if he were the murderer, he'd be wary of her, of underestimating her strength.

He reached for her arm. "I'm seriously considering painting you in candlelight. Come over here." He drew her to the end of the mantelpiece and positioned her as before. Retrieving the last gown from the chair—the gown closest in hue to what he wanted—he held it out. "Hold that against you."

Jacqueline did. She'd cried all her tears for Thomas long ago; it had been comforting to own to her anger, to be able to admit to it—to speak of it aloud and so give it strength. She watched as Gerrard stepped back, studying her with his painter's eyes. There was an expression in them when he was given over to his art that she was learning to recognize.

That was comforting, too, for it gave her the freedom to think of other things, to acknowledge that he, hearing of her anger—an unconventional response from a young woman over the violent murder of her intended, surely?—hadn't judged. He'd simply accepted, indeed, he'd seemed to understand, or to at least find nothing startling or shocking in her feelings.

He frowned. "The light's too even." He looked at the lamp, then scanned the room. "Candlestick?"

"On the dresser by the door."

He crossed to pick it up and brought it back. He bent to light the wick at the small fire in the grate, then straightened and reached for her right hand. "Here—hold it like that."

Leaving her clutching the gown to her chest, the candlestick held aloft, he went to the lamp at the far end of the mantelpiece. He turned down the wick; the light faded, then died.

Crossing in front of her, he glanced measuringly at her, then doused the other lamp, too. He looked at her, then adjusted her arm. "Hold it there."

He stepped back, then back again. His eyes narrowed, scanning, checking; he spoke softly, vaguely, "I promise I won't make you hold a candle—I'm just trying to get an idea of how it might look if . . ."

His words faded. She watched him look at her, not as a man but as a painter. Watched the change in his expression, the play of the candle-light on his features, watched a sense of awe slowly seize and grip him.

A silent minute passed, then he refocused on her face. "Perfect."

She smiled.

He blinked. Slowly. His lashes rose, and suddenly she knew he was seeing her no longer as a painter, but as a man. He wasn't seeing her as his subject, but as a woman, a woman the look in his dark eyes stated very clearly he desired.

Her heart expanded in her chest; it seemed to slow, then start to thud.

A need to explore his desire swept her. The killer had stolen from her any chance of that with Thomas, yet because of the same killer, Gerrard was now here.

That need took root, grew and filled her. Slowly, she closed her fingers, grasped the gown she'd been holding, and lifted it from her, and away. Extending her arm, she opened her hand and let the gown fall unregarded to the floor; his gaze didn't shift, didn't move from her to follow the silk as it fell.

His gaze, dark and burning, remained locked on her. At his sides, his hands slowly clenched; his jaw set, rocklike; his lips were a chiseled line.

He wasn't going to move, to, as she had no doubt he would see it, take advantage of her; he was holding against it, against the impulse she could see flaring in his eyes.

She tilted her head, studying him as brazenly as he did her. She felt his gaze rake slowly down her body, outlined by the glow of the fire behind her. Her flesh reacted, heated, prickled—as physical a reaction as if he'd touched her. More reaction than if any other man had touched her, yet it was only his gaze, and the hunger she sensed behind it.

The clock ticked; for finite instants, desire held them, a force strong enough for them both to feel. To appreciate. She took a moment to savor it, to experience it, but that was all she dared—he was strong enough to break free, if she let him.

She was still holding the candlestick; other than the small fire, it was the sole source of light remaining in the room. To set it down, she would have to turn, to take her eyes from him, and break the spell.

No. The spell was hers, patently there, hers to use if she chose.

She chose.

Slowly, she extended her other hand, palm up—an unmistakable invitation.

For one heartbeat, as his gaze fixed on her palm, she wondered if he would decline. But then his eyes lifted and locked on hers, and the silly thought slipped away.

He moved to her, slowly, like the predator she'd sensed from the first he truly was. The ton's artistic lion in truth, and he was here with her, in her bedchamber, and it was almost midnight.

He closed his hand about hers, engulfing her fingers with the heat and strength of his; as he stepped nearer, he raised her hand to his lips, and brushed a slow kiss over her knuckles.

His eyes, dark in the poor light, hadn't left hers. He searched them briefly, then turned her hand and pressed a slow, deliberate kiss to the sensitive skin of her palm.

She felt it like a brand, hot, searing, possessive. She couldn't breathe as he took the tilting candlestick from her other hand; reaching past her, he set it on the mantelpiece behind her.

He stepped nearer, releasing her hand to fall on his shoulder, gathering her to him. She was excruciatingly aware of the strength in his muscled arms, of his hand as it spread across the back of her waist, of the insubstantial protection of her nightgown and robe.

Their eyes met, in one glance said all there was to say, then he bent his head as she lifted hers, and their lips met.

Touched, brushed. Fused.

The kiss slid straight into a sea of heat, of pleasured warmth as their lips melded and their tongues twined. She knew this, wanted it, and went forward without reservation, receiving each slow, languorous caress, returning it with abandon and inciting more, inviting even though she had little idea of what, precisely, came next. She wanted to know, wanted to feel; as the kiss deepened, as he angled his head and heat burgeoned, flared and raced through her, spreading under her skin, making her mentally reel until her wits slid away and she gave herself over to feeling, simply feeling, as desire flooded her and grew to a pounding beat, she burned to learn more.

Gerrard sensed the rising tide, the welling of desire, and behind that, a passion that was more—more powerful, more compelling, more enthralling—than any he'd felt before. Her mouth was a haven of feminine delight, soft, giving, beyond tempting; the feel of her body so scantily clad in his arms, leaning into him, sinking against him in naïve surrender, was a potent lure.

With an effort, he lifted his head, broke the kiss enough to look into her face, into her eyes as her lids slowly rose. Enough to realize how rapidly he was breathing, how much his head was spinning . . . already.

Hauling in a breath, he said, "This is dangerous."

And was shocked by how gravelly and harsh his voice sounded.

She didn't blink, but studied his face. He felt her breasts expand against his chest as she drew a steadying breath.

"No." Her gaze remained level, her lips soft, sheening, slightly swollen. "This is right." After a moment, she added, "Can't you feel it?"

He could. Every instinct he possessed was urging him on; not one suggested retreat. If she was willing to move forward, so was he.

She'd been searching his eyes; her lips slowly curved. Her gold-green eyes glowed. "You know it." Sliding her hands up from where they'd rested until then, passive against his chest, she slid her palms along his face, framing it, then stretched upward and breathed against his lips, "Stop denying it. And me." Then she kissed him.

He let her, let her coax, then more blatantly invite.

Then he accepted. Stopped denying what he wanted, what he felt compelled to explore. Her. And their passion.

In every imaginable way.

His arms tightened, urging her closer. She responded, pressing her body to his, her hands sliding back through his hair, then away as she locked her arms about his neck and clung. In his mind, he smiled, purely predatory, then eased his hold on her and let his hands roam.

Heard her breathing hitch as he closed his hands over her gorgeous breasts, full and firm, and kneaded. Sensed the surge of unadulterated desire that rose within her as he played, as he teased her senses awake, as he opened her eyes to sensual pleasure.

Their lips melded, a connection, a communication she clung to; his attention switched from her swollen breasts, from the ruched nipples pressing into his palms, to the succulent delight of her mouth, of her lips and her increasingly educated tongue.

She delighted him, simply and sincerely engaged with him; as he eased his hands from the now tight mounds of her breasts, he gave thanks for her directness, for her straightforward honesty, even in this.

Her clear and unequivocal encouragement wasn't in doubt; she pressed kiss after increasingly scorching kiss on his lips, pressed close and ever closer, sliding her body, all lush curves and supple grace, against his.

He sent his hands sliding, palms beneath her robe, over the fine fabric of her nightgown, so thin it provided a mere whisper of separation between his skin and hers. He traced the indentation of her waist, let his fingers grip her hips, then ease as he explored, then he gave in to temptation and slid both hands down to cup her bottom. Lifting her against him, into him, he flagrantly molded her hips to him, to the rigid column of his erection.

Her breathing fractured, but she didn't draw back. Instead, she gripped his face again, and pressed ever more heated, ever more eager kisses on him.

He thrust against her, suggestive yet restrained, and was rewarded with a gasp, smothered between their lips.

Thinking was no longer necessary. Juggling her, he stripped off her robe, left it lying on the floor as he swung her into his arms and carried her to the bed.

They broke from the kiss as he laid her down, yet when from beneath heavy lids her eyes met his, he detected no hint of second thoughts, of hesitation. Only a steady, unwavering purpose he was coming to recognize as intrinsically her.

Her arms, twined about his neck, had eased; now she tightened them, and drew him back to her—drew him down to the bed and her. He went with no more hesitation than she. After a long-drawn, incendiary kiss, one that left his mind reeling, he drew back and shrugged out of his coat, sat up and leaned down to ease off his boots. As the second boot thudded on the floor, he turned back to her, into the arms she held waiting. Stretching alongside her, he leaned over her, brushed back her hair and framed her face with one hand, found her lips with his, and filled her mouth.

Heat and longing poured through Jacqueline; she'd never felt so alive. So energized, so excited. Whatever he would show her she wanted to know, wherever he led, she wanted to explore. The reciprocity of their kisses had fascinated her before; now, the mutual give and take of their exchange had deepened, extending into a landscape she'd never seen, never even known existed—she wanted with all her heart, all the passion she'd held inside for so long, to go forward with him and learn more.

The candle on the mantelpiece across the room guttered. Shadows closed in, gently cloaking. Their eyes had adjusted; they could both see well enough—enough for her to glimpse his fingers as they undid the buttons down the front of her nightgown, for her to see his hand slide beneath the gaping placket. Then he touched her, and her lids fell; for long minutes, her senses condensed to tactile sensation, to experiencing every thrill his knowing caresses lavished on her willing flesh, to communicating through lips and tongue as he fondled, and taught her.

But then he drew back from the kiss. He held her gaze as he reached up and pushed her nightgown off her shoulder, baring her breast. She quelled a shiver, looked down, lost all ability to breathe as she watched his hand return to her breast, fondling knowingly, pandering to her senses.

A minute passed, and she learned to breathe again, then he shifted, kissed her once, thoroughly, then nudged her chin up and trailed kisses down her throat, and on—to her breast. He caressed the swollen curves, then traced a path to one tightly furled nipple. Licked, laved, then took it into his mouth, and suckled lightly.

Sensation, sharp, powerful as lightning, struck; she gasped, arched, her mind scrambling to absorb and acknowledge the sensations. Then his tongue swept her nipple, languorous and soothing.

Heat spilled through her and she moaned, arching beneath him, clasping his head, wordlessly inviting more.

Which he gave. Unstintingly.

Caught in the landscape he'd conjured, she remained aware, unafraid—eager to go on. Increasingly desperate, although for what she longed she wasn't sure, other than it was more.

He seemed to know. To understand the giddy, rushing tide that had caught her and was sweeping her on. Through quick, assessing glances, through sultry, knowing, measuring looks, he kept watch over her and guided her; this was a place he'd been to many times—he knew the ways.

That he enjoyed his role as mentor and guide she had no doubt. Her breasts seemed to fascinate him as much as his fascination with them enthralled her. He seemed addicted to tasting her—her lips, her skin, every curve of her breasts and throat. In the poor light, she couldn't see the desire glowing in his eyes, yet she felt it; like a flame, it caressed and heated, warmed and reassured. The predatory tension that had infused him, that rode every muscle and turned it to steel, was, she instinctively knew, another sign—there was an aura of leashed aggression in him, one she'd evoked from the first, and increasingly sensed in his response to her.

It didn't frighten her; it excited her.

Almost unbearably.

Seizing his face, she pressed a blatantly inciting kiss on him—and refused to let him go. She demanded he respond; within seconds they were engaged in a heated duel as she wantonly challenged him.

His hand gripped her hip, tensing, then released; she felt his fingers sweep down her thigh, over her knee. Then they slid beneath the hem of her nightgown. Boldly traced upward, lightly brushing the sensitive inner face of her thigh. Heat pooled low within her, throbbing, aching . . . then he touched the curls at the apex of her thighs.

Every nerve leapt; every sense focused, following his touch, tracking each and every light caress. She shifted beneath him, hips lifting, wanting more.

A sense of urgency welled and flooded her.

Shifting over her, he grasped her knee, pressed it wide, anchored it with his as his tongue plunged into her mouth and hotly plundered.

For an instant she was distracted, then she felt his palm sweep inward along her thigh, and he cupped her.

She felt the touch keenly, so intimate, so knowing. She stilled, expecting to be shocked . . . instead, desire surged and rushed through her, a hot tide that swept her into a sea of greedy need and wanton delight. He caressed; beyond thought, totally captured by feeling, she moved against him, wordlessly communing.

He understood her need, her urgency. He intimately explored her as she gasped through their kiss. Left no part of her softness untouched, uncaressed.

And she was spinning, her senses whirling, her nerves coiled tighter than any spring. She wanted to beg for more, to urge him on, but he held her to the kiss, filled her mouth and her senses completely with his maleness, then the kiss eased—as he slid one long finger into her.

She could no longer breathe, no longer think; she could only feel as he explored and learned—and she learned, too. Learned how desperate for his touch she could grow, how hot, how burning, how insistent her need for whatever came next could become.

He knew, and led her unerringly on, until her senses sparked, then ignited, until her nerves unraveled, until her existence fractured and stars rushed down her veins to explode in molten glory.

Spreading pleasure and delight through her.

She found herself floating in a golden sea, physical content lapping over and about her, barely sentient, yet aware that he hadn't left her.

That he hadn't . . .

Gerrard watched completion claim her; he'd never seen any sight so gratifying, so soothing to his male ego. He ached, literally throbbed with the need to take her, to follow their road to its natural end, yet even as he acknowledged the pressure, he knew he wouldn't—not yet.

Despite her certainty, her unwavering sureness, she was too new to this. Too innocent to simply seize. Easing his fingers from the scorching slickness of her body, he gently drew her nightgown down. He continued to ignore his clamoring demons, and simply watched her.

When her lids finally fluttered, then rose, he leaned down and kissed her, openly possessive, then drew back. Even in the dim light, he could sense her confusion, could feel it in the way her fingers gripped his sleeve. He reached for them; taking her hand in his, he kissed her fingers, then leaned over her once more to brush her mouth. "Not yet." He murmured the words against her swollen lips, then drew back and sat up.

Her fingers tensed on his. She frowned. "I . . . don't understand."

He let his lips twist wryly. Sliding his fingers from hers, he reached for his boots. "I know. But there's no need to rush—and going any further now would be rushing."

That was crystal clear in his mind. Regardless, he was a man, not a saint; he wasn't strong enough to hold against any entreaties, especially from her, especially now. Boots on, he rose and reached for his coat. "Sleep well—I'll see you in the morning."

He forced himself to shrug on his coat, then turn and cross to the door. Opening it, without looking back he went out and quietly shut it behind him.

As he walked to his room, he owned to amazement. His nature wasn't gentle or understanding; it certainly wasn't self-sacrificing. In situations such as this, he was commanding and demanding. If a lady offered, he took.

She'd urged him to take her, had wanted him to, her invitation clear and repeated, yet for her, for the sake of what he and she needed to explore, for the sake of what was growing between them, he'd found it, if not easy, then at least possible, more, *desirable,* to walk away.

Quite what that said of what was growing between them, he didn't want to think.

Contrary to his expectations, he slept well enough—the sleep of the righteous, no doubt. By the time he walked into the breakfast parlor, he was focused on one thing—pressing ahead with the portrait.

Elements of it were clear in his mind, yet the exact composition still eluded him. Until he had that clear, he couldn't start.

Immediately after breakfast ended, he commandeered Jacqueline— who seemed perfectly ready to be commandeered—simultaneously rejecting a suggestion from Barnaby that they ought to ride into St.

Just and listen to what was being said about Thomas Entwhistle's murder.

Unperturbed, Barnaby shrugged, and went without them.

Gerrard paced the terrace until Jacqueline joined him, then, her hand locked in his, he towed her into the gardens.

He took her first to the Garden of Apollo, to where the sundial stood in its small section of lawn. Setting down his sketch pad and pencils, he led her to the sundial, and posed her as he wished, standing beside it. He looked at her face; her eyes met his.

For one long instant, they studied each other—he searched for any hint of the maidenly fluster he'd expected but thus far had failed to detect. Last night, she'd bared her breasts to him, let him touch her intimately, writhed and gasped beneath him as he'd brought her to glory; he'd more than half-expected some degree of retreat.

Instead, her customary certainty shone from her eyes. Steady, unwavering, sure. They stood only a foot apart, yet a light smile flirted about her lips . . . as if she knew what he was looking for and was delighting in confounding him.

He humphed, then bent his head and swiftly kissed her. "Stay there." Without meeting her eyes again, he turned and strode back to his sketch pad.

That exchange set the tone for their morning. They talked, but their words remained light, their meaning superficial, their true communication carried by looks, glances, fleeting touches. They were both not on edge, but aware—each hyperaware of the other, but also aware of other sensations, like the lilting breeze, the caress of the sun, the perfumes and colors and shifting shade as they moved about the gardens.

The luncheon gong rang and they returned to the house. Millicent joined them; Barnaby had yet to return and Mitchel remained in his office.

Millicent appeared a trifle distracted. "I'm not at all sure how best to handle the inquiries."

Gerrard frowned. "Inquiries?"

"Well . . ." Millicent waved her fork. "A *body* was found in the gardens. That of a young man who disappeared and who we all thought of as Jacqueline's *fiancé*. We'll have a horde of visitors this afternoon, I assure you. The only reason they haven't appeared yet is that it was probably too late for a morning visit by the time they heard."

As usual, concentrating on his work had driven all other considerations from his head. He looked at Jacqueline, and sensed her drawing back, sealing herself off behind that inner barrier she'd perfected to deal with her world.

"Can you manage alone?" He looked at Millicent. "I'm afraid I need Jacqueline for the rest of the day. I need to define the exact pose before I can start the portrait—and we clearly need the portrait finished without delay."

Millicent thought. "Actually, it might be better if Jacqueline *wasn't* present." With a determined air, she turned to Jacqueline. "I wasn't here when Thomas disappeared, so it's easier for me to stick to the facts without acknowledging any of the speculation. And without you there, they'll find it difficult to introduce any suggestion of involvement on your part. No, indeed." Turning back to Gerrard, she nodded. "By all means devote yourselves to the portrait, and leave me to deal with the rumormongers."

Gerrard smiled, but glanced at Jacqueline, his question in his eyes.

She met his gaze, chin firm, but then nodded. "Perhaps you're right, Aunt. The less opportunity they have to air their mistaken beliefs, the better."

But when he led her back to the gardens, her concern remained. He said nothing; her distance wasn't an issue as today he was working with her body, her pose, not her face and expressions. Those he was coming to know very well. As for her body . . .

Her distraction helped, allowing him to concentrate on her figure, on the lines of her body, without evoking in her the sort of awareness that would, in turn, arouse him. Distract him. He took her into the Garden of Poseidon, posing her again at the head of the long pool, some yards before the entrance to the Garden of Night. He positioned her, then stepped back and sketched, not so much her—he merely outlined her body—but the setting.

Exercising a painter's sleight of hand, he altered the perspective so that in the sketch she appeared to be standing within the entrance, framed by it.

The afternoon light was perfect, illuminating the entrance yet leaving all beyond it in shadow. In the portrait, the scene would be lit by moonlight—the hardest of all lights to use—but today's clarity gave him all the lines he would need, sharply delineating every vine leaf, every twisting, trailing shoot.

Once he had her outline set within the frame, he waved her to a seat nearby. "I'm working on background. I have all I need of you for the present—you can rest."

Jerked from her less-than-heartening reverie, Jacqueline inwardly raised her brows. From his tone, definitely his painter's voice, it sounded more as if she was in his way. Not that she minded; she'd been standing for most of the day. Crossing to the wrought-iron seat set before a thickly planted border, she sank onto it. Leaning on the arm, she looked at him.

She expected her mind to return to wondering how Millicent was coping in the drawing room, and what the attitude of the visiting ladies was. She was very much afraid she knew; they'd assume she was guilty of Thomas's murder, too. The idea hurt almost as much as her realization, when she'd emerged from deep mourning, that they thought she'd killed her mother.

Such matters certainly intruded, but with her eyes on Gerrard, they failed to capture her mind. Instead, she thought of him—not just of last night, and the pleasure he'd introduced her to, not just of his clear expectation that she would succumb to feminine fluster over it, and might regret it, not of the fact that she hadn't, and didn't, but of him. Just him.

The concentration in his face, in his stance, the sense of immense energy he focused on his work, was enthralling. Watching him wield it for her, in the creation of the portrait that by his own words he saw as freeing her from her strange prison, moved her and held her attention completely.

It was, in a way, like watching her champion battle in the lists for her; like any such lady, she couldn't look away.

Eventually, he looked down, and considered his sketches. The fervor that had held him faded; she sensed he was content with what he'd achieved.

She was tempted, but having been warned, she didn't ask to see what he'd done.

As if he'd heard her thoughts, he looked at her. He seemed to consider, then he scooped up his spare pencils, tucked them in a pocket, and strolled across to the seat.

He sat beside her; he met her eyes, then looked down and opened his sketch pad. "I want you to see the concept I'm working on."

Astonished, she shifted to stare at him. "I thought you never, ever, showed your preliminary work to anyone?"

His lips thinned, but his voice remained even, if a trifle irritated. "Normally, I don't, but in your case, you have a sufficiently artistic eye to understand, to see what I see, what I'm trying to capture."

She studied his profile, then shifted closer and looked at the sketch pad. "So what are you trying to capture—"

She broke off as he showed her. The first sheet contained a sketch in barest outline—her, her body, poised within the entrance to the Garden of Night. The next contained details of the entrance; those following filled in various sections of the arched entry, and then came a set defining various elements and aspects.

It was apparent why he so rarely showed such preliminary work; she appreciated his trusting her to be able to interpret it, to fuse all the sketches to get some idea of the final work.

"Me escaping the Garden of Night." Just saying the words, she felt the concept's power. She looked at the entrance, gilded by the late afternoon sun, but with sultry, shadowy, oppressive gloom lurking behind it.

Watching her face, Gerrard saw that she'd seen and grasped his vision, that she understood. He'd broken his absolute, until-now-invariable rule because he'd wanted her to know that the portrait truly would be powerful enough to shatter all preconceived notions of her guilt, that it would speak of her innocence strongly enough to make people rethink, and revisit, their assumptions. Ultimately, that it would be powerful enough to evoke the specter of the real killer.

Her knowing that, believing that, would be important in making the whole work, in bringing life to the portrait that he was beyond convinced would be his greatest yet.

He hadn't wanted her opinion, but her approval, and her support.

The thought was almost shocking; he bundled it out of his mind as she looked at him.

"You haven't yet sketched me in the entrance itself. I'm willing to pose there"—she glanced down at his sketches—"for this."

He shook his head. "I don't need you to do that—I'll pose you in the studio. I want the scene lit by moonlight, and while I've done enough landscapes to know how to manage that for the setting, people are harder. I'll need to work in candlelight, and convert that to moon-light." He caught her gaze. "Your pose will be difficult as it is—indoors will be bad enough."

She looked into his eyes, then pulled a face. "Thank you for the warning." She glanced toward the Garden of Night. "If you're sure."

"I am."

They both turned as footsteps sounded, swinging down through the Garden of Vesta.

"Barnaby." Gerrard closed his sketchbook.

"I wonder if he's been up to the house?"

Barnaby emerged from the path and saw them. He grinned and ambled over. "Richards said he thought you were here. I decided, after the exigencies of my morning, that I shouldn't place any further strain on my temper—according to Richards there's a platoon of local ladies in the drawing room."

Subsiding onto the grass before the seat, Barnaby heaved a long sigh, then stretched out, folding his arms over his chest and closing his eyes.

Gerrard grinned; he prodded Barnaby with his boot. "So report—what did you learn in St. Just?"

Barnaby's features set; it was instantly apparent whatever he'd discovered hadn't made him happy. "It's nonsensical. Well, no, I can—just possibly—understand that people do leap to conclusions based on precious little fact, and the only widely known fact regarding Thomas's disappearance and now death is that the last person to have seen him, and what's more, to have been in the gardens with him, is Jacqueline."

Opening his eyes, Barnaby looked at her. "If I hadn't experienced it myself, I wouldn't have believed how widespread, or indeed how entrenched, suspicion against you is. As it was, I had to be careful what I said—how much I let out and, most importantly, how I reacted to—" Clearly frustrated, he gestured with both hands. " 'Established fact'!"

Looking at Jacqueline, Barnaby assayed a grin. "I assure you, I deserve a medal for discretion." He glanced at Gerrard, met his eyes. "But it was distressing, and rather unnerving."

Gerrard frowned. Barnaby didn't use words like "distressing" and "unnerving" without cause. Indeed, very little unnerved Barnaby.

Lying back, eyes closed, Barnaby refolded his arms, frowning, too. Eventually, Gerrard asked, "What are you thinking?" It was patently obvious something portentous was brewing in Barnaby's brain.

Barnaby sighed. "I honestly think we have to act now—not leave everything until later, until the portrait's finished and we can use it to open people's eyes." Opening his own, he looked up at them both. "The portrait's critical to making people rethink their views of your mother's murder, but Thomas . . ." His gaze rested on Jacqueline. "That's another case, and we can't let them hang the blame on you without cause. If we let it go, let them think what they are without challenging it *now*, then we're going to face a much harder battle to make them open their minds later."

Barnaby looked at Gerrard. "I think we need to speak to Tregonning—lay before him the clear evidence Jacqueline was in no way involved in Thomas's murder, and also the facts demonstrating she's innocent of her mother's murder, too."

Jacqueline drew a not entirely steady breath. "Why do we need to convince Papa?"

Barnaby met her gaze. "Because we need to present a united front, first to last, and when it comes to the local gentry, his attitude is the most crucial. Millicent's, Gerrard's, and my opinions are all very well, but if your father doesn't support you, well, you can see how hard it's going to be."

Abruptly, Barnaby lay back and shook his fists at the sky. "And it shouldn't be hard because you're *not guilty*!"

He glanced at them both. "Sorry, but I really think we need to recruit Lord Tregonning."

10

Barnaby was right. If they allowed the discovery of Thomas's body and the consequent speculation to be used to establish Jacqueline as a disturbed double murderess, then their task of opening all eyes with the portrait would be immeasurably more difficult.

They discussed speaking with Lord Tregonning. Jacqueline vacillated.

"Papa was devastated by my mother's death." She glanced at Gerrard. "It's the pain, the opening up of the wound, that makes him shy away from considering *how* she died. On top of that, he more than anyone is afraid that if he looks too closely, he'll see that it was me."

"That's just it," Barnaby insisted. "The current situation isn't about your mother's death, but Thomas's."

Gerrard reached out, took Jacqueline's hand, captured her gaze when she looked at him. "Barnaby's right—we should approach your father now, when the principal focus is Thomas's murder. However"—with one finger he stroked the back of her hand—"I think you're underestimating your father—he's already moved to address the question of your mother's death. He went to considerable lengths to persuade me to paint your portrait."

He watched her digest that. Eventually, after another glance at Barnaby—who responded with an encouraging, puppy-eager look, making her smile—she looked back at him, and nodded. "Very well. We'll beard Papa."

They bearded Millicent first; when they returned to the house, they found her slumped on the chaise in the drawing room. She jerked to life when they entered, but when she saw who it was, she fell back once more.

"My dear heaven, I've never met such gossipmongers in my life!" She paused, then added, "Of course, that did make it easier to learn their thoughts and raise the questions we want them to consider. I didn't have to introduce the subject of the body—that was what they'd come to talk about."

"How successful were you," Barnaby asked, "in making them wonder who killed Thomas?"

Millicent frowned. "My success varied, I'm sorry to say, but oddly enough it was Marjorie Elcott who grasped the facts most definitely, which is extremely fortunate as she's the biggest gossip in the neighborhood."

"Who else called?" Gerrard asked.

Millicent rattled off a list of names, which included all those local ladies he and Barnaby had met.

"Mrs. Myles and Maria Fritham didn't seem able to absorb the point that if Thomas couldn't have been killed by a woman, then Jacqueline obviously wasn't his killer. Mrs. Hancock and Miss Curtis were more attentive, as was Lady Trewarren, although I fear her ladyship ended simply confused. Others, too, seemed to lose all interest immediately one started talking of *facts*." Millicent grimaced. "Still, it was better than them thinking *I* credited the speculation so many of them seem to have swallowed whole."

Sinking onto the chaise beside Millicent, Jacqueline touched her arm. "Thank you, Aunt."

Millicent humphed and patted Jacqueline's hand. "I only wish there was more we could do. It was distressing to see how widespread—and deeply rooted—this belief in your guilt is, my dear. Most worrying." She glanced at Barnaby, whom she'd unknowingly echoed. "I do wonder, you know, if someone—some specific someone—hasn't been intentionally spreading whispers. Not just recently, but over time. I asked a few of the ladies *why* they thought as they did—I got the same response every time: a blank look, and, 'But everyone knows . . .' "

Barnaby grimaced. "That's a difficult belief to challenge."

"Especially when they delicately refrain from elucidating precisely *what* everyone knows!"

"Indeed." Gerrard sat in the armchair facing the chaise. "That's why we've concluded we need to start a more definite campaign now, rather than wait until the portrait is complete."

Concisely, with a few interjections from Barnaby, he outlined their new tack.

"I agree," Jacqueline said. "As Mr. Debbington pointed out, Papa has already made an effort to address the question of Mama's death by commissioning my portrait."

Millicent nodded. "That's true." She looked at Gerrard. "As I mentioned, I haven't spent much of my life here. Consequently, I don't know Marcus that well. However, I do know he loved Miribelle, not just deeply but as if she were his sun, moon and stars. She was everything to him, but he also loves Jacqueline. Whoever is behind this—not just the two murders but the casting of Jacqueline as scapegoat—has placed my brother in a dreadful position, one I'm sure has been tearing him apart. Suspecting Jacqueline of killing Miribelle . . ." Millicent paused, then gruffly huffed. "Indeed, poor Marcus has been a living and, it seems, quite deliberate victim of this killer, too."

Barnaby softly applauded. "I couldn't agree more."

Gerrard glanced around. "Then I take it we're agreed?"

"Indeed, my boy," Millicent said.

Jacqueline and Barnaby nodded.

"What we need to do next," Barnaby said, "is plan the first step of our campaign."

They didn't just plan, but rehearsed; by the time they climbed the stairs to dress for dinner, they had their approach finely tuned.

The opening move fell to Millicent.

They all gathered in the drawing room as usual; also as usual, Lord Tregonning joined them only a few minutes before Treadle would appear. When her brother bowed to her, Millicent swept up and took his arm. "Marcus, dear"—she kept her voice low—"I wonder if Jacqueline and I could have a word with you after dinner? In your study, if you don't mind?"

Lord Tregonning blinked, but, of course, agreed.

Dinner passed in the customary quiet fashion. Gerrard was grateful; they all had their arguments to hone.

At the end of the meal, rather than lead Jacqueline from the room, Millicent looked pointedly up the table. "If you could, Marcus . . . ?"

Lord Tregonning shook himself. "Oh—yes, of course." He glanced at Gerrard and Barnaby. "If you'll excuse me, gentlemen—"

"Actually, Marcus," Millicent broke in, "it would be helpful if Mr. Debbington and Mr. Adair joined us. What we need to discuss involves them, too."

Lord Tregonning wasn't a slow-top; he glanced from Millicent and Jacqueline, waiting by her side, to Gerrard and Barnaby. His eyes narrowed, but he nodded, somewhat curtly. "As you wish. My study?"

They left Mitchel Cunningham, curious and trying to hide it, in the front hall, and repaired to his lordship's study. With five of them in the room, it was a trifle crowded, but there were chairs enough for all.

Once they were settled, from behind his desk Lord Tregonning let his gaze touch each of their faces, eventually coming to rest on his sister's. "Well, Millicent? What's this about?"

"Quite a number of things, as it happens, but before we get to specifics, I want you to know that I've listened to every argument, every fact and conclusion, and I agree wholeheartedly with them all. Now." She looked at Jacqueline. "My dear?"

Perched on the edge of a large leather armchair, her hands pressed together in her lap, Jacqueline drew in a deep breath, and prayed her voice wouldn't waver. "I realize we've never talked of this, Papa, but I want you to know that I had nothing to do with Thomas's death."

She paused, her eyes on her father's; she felt herself inwardly tense. "And I never harmed Mama—I didn't, and would never have harmed a hair on her head. Yes, we argued that day, but that was all. I didn't see her again after I left her in the breakfast parlor. I have no idea who killed her, or Thomas. But I do know and understand why you asked Mr. Debbington to paint my portrait."

Lord Tregonning's face had turned to stone. Glancing from him to Jacqueline, Gerrard wished he could take her hand, remind her with a touch that he was there, supporting her, but they would already be asking her father to assimilate a lot in one evening.

The atmosphere in the room had thickened, growing heavy with unspoken emotion; Jacqueline drew in a tight breath. "I know of the rumors, the whispers—unfortunately, I didn't know of them early enough to deny them, not when I might have been believed. By the time I realized . . ." Her voice stalled; she gestured helplessly. "I didn't credit them. I didn't see their danger—not until it was too late."

Voice strengthening, she went on, "But I *didn't* kill Mama, and I didn't kill Thomas, either. Someone else did, and we"—she broke off to include Gerrard, Barnaby and Millicent with a glance—"think that same person started, and is continuing creating stories, whispers, about me. I had thought—prayed—that the portrait, once complete, would open people's eyes and start them thinking afresh. But now Thomas's body has been found—if we do nothing, then I'll be blamed for his death, too." She drew breath. "Mr. Debbington and Mr. Adair can explain the details better than I—I beg you to consider all they say."

She looked at Gerrard. Conscious of her father's eye, he didn't smile, but formally inclined his head; she'd given him the perfect introduction.

He met Lord Tregonning's gaze squarely. "I speak from the perspective of a painter, and also that of a businessman. As the latter, I've met evil in my time, faced it eye to eye—I know what true evil looks like. But as a portraitist, I've worked solely with innocents, with the kind, the good and the generous. More than any other attributes or traits, I can unhesitatingly recognize those—I've worked with them for the last seven and more years. When I look at your daughter, that's what I see—to my eyes, innocence and purity of heart shine from her."

He paused, letting silence lend weight to his words, letting them sink into Lord Tregonning's mind. "When I heard of the whispers concerning Miss Tregonning and the death of her mother, I was flabbergasted. It was beyond my comprehension that such suspicions existed—from my point of view, they have no basis. In proof of that, I can assure you that my portrait of Miss Tregonning, once complete, will indeed cast severe doubt over the validity of the rumors. As she patently did not kill her mother, or, indeed, anyone, then the question will arise: *Who did?*"

Lord Tregonning's attention was totally his. Any thought that they might not be able to sway him, that he might insist on remaining aloof and decline to participate in their planned action, evaporated. Gerrard felt the painful intensity in his gaze, for one instant felt the torment the outwardly stoic man had endured, and was humbled by it.

"You're certain she's—" Lord Tregonning glanced at Jacqueline. "Forgive me, my dear, but . . ." He looked again at Gerrard, his dark gaze fixing on his face. "You're sure beyond doubt that she was not involved?"

Gerrard nodded. "However, I'm aware a painter's opinion is not going to sway anyone in authority, although I will guarantee to sway all society. Yet in this case, there are numerous facts, observations and deductions that Mr. Adair has assembled which establish beyond doubt that Jacqueline was in no way involved in the deaths of Thomas Entwhistle, nor your wife, her mother, Miribelle Tregonning."

Gerrard looked at Barnaby, passing the baton in their carefully orchestrated argument.

Accepting it, Barnaby succinctly detailed the evidence he'd gathered that proved it was impossible for a woman, especially any lady, to have killed Thomas Entwhistle, and briefly outlined why Jacqueline could not be a suspect in her mother's death.

"In addition, the rumors have it that she killed her mother in a momentary rage, but there's no evidence whatever, either from the staff, who always know such things, or from friends, many of whom have known her all her life, that she has ever been subject to momentary rages." He glanced at Jacqueline, faintly smiled. "Not even mild furies."

Turning back to Lord Tregonning, Barnaby concluded, "In short, the whisper campaign against your daughter is fashioned from whole cloth, totally unsustainable when examined, yet the killer—assuming, as I think we should, that it is he behind the rumors—was exceedingly clever. He used Jacqueline's standing, more specifically the fact that she's well loved by all about. By raising the possibility that it *might* be she, he ensured all those round about, including yourself, did not pursue the question of who the murderer was."

Barnaby paused, then quietly said, "I have absolutely no doubt that a man killed Thomas Entwhistle, and that the same man killed your wife. His identity remains a mystery, but given these latest rumors—the ones circulating after the discovery of Thomas's body—it's safe to conclude he's still here, in the neighborhood. He hasn't moved away."

Lord Tregonning drew in a deep breath. Slowly, he placed his hands on the desk. "Why have you chosen tonight to tell me this?"

The others looked at Gerrard.

"Because of these latest rumors. It was our intention to follow the plan you'd instigated—to finish the portait, then use it to open people's eyes. With respect to your wife's death, that approach still applies. But now Thomas's body has been discovered, and the killer has grasped the opportunity to extend the suspicion surrounding Jacqueline. If we wait, and allow the web of suspicion ensnaring her to continue to be spun, unchallenged and unchecked, we'll weaken our position, possibly to the extent that when the portrait is complete, even though it will showcase her innocence, that might by then be insufficient to reverse the tide the killer has set running."

For a long minute, Lord Tregonning said nothing, then he turned to Jacqueline. "My dear, I owe you an abject apology. Why I ever listened to the whispers—" His voice quavered and he stopped, but his gaze never left Jacqueline's face. "I should never have doubted you. My only excuse is that when your mother died—was murdered . . . I found it very hard to think. Not for months. I pray you can find it in your heart to forgive me."

The simple words, heartfelt and true, hung in the quiet room.

Then Jacqueline was out of her chair, rounding the desk to hug her father. "Oh, Papa!"

Gerrard looked away, at Barnaby, who was also giving father and daughter a moment alone; Barnaby's blue eyes were alight—he looked positively smug. Millicent dabbed at her eyes with a handkerchief. Gerrard sat back, and thought of Patience, and the twins, and other family moments he'd witnessed in which the females always cried.

The emotion in Lord Tregonning's words replayed in his mind. He cleared his throat, then glanced across to see Lord Tregonning awkwardly patting Jacqueline's shoulder.

"Thank you, my dear." His lordship harrumphed loudly, then whipped out his handkerchief and blew his nose. Jacqueline squeezed his arm, then returned to the armchair, whisking a scrap of fine linen from her sleeve to blot her eyes.

"Yes. Right then." Lord Tregonning realigned his blotter, then looked at Gerrard and Barnaby, and lastly at Millicent. "I thank you all for acting as you have—Jacqueline and I are fortunate to have such supporters. However"—his voice gaining strength, he lifted his head and squared his shoulders—"I assume, given the need to commence countering these insidious whispers immediately, that you have some plan in mind?"

Barnaby leaned forward. "Indeed we have."

He explained.

Lord Tregonning nodded. "I agree. Given so many people imagine Jacqueline responsible for Miribelle's death, and will therefore see her as the most likely to have killed Thomas, too, then *our* behavior becomes critical."

Barnaby glanced around. "We—all of us—need to behave, and be seen to behave, in a manner that doesn't just state but screams our belief in Jacqueline's innocence. Millicent made a good start this afternoon, but we need to go further."

Millicent nodded. "But will that—our behavior—be enough?"

"It could be." Gerrard thought of the power certain ladies of the ton, his Cynster connections, for example, could wield. He wished he could summon a few of them into Cornwall—Helena, Dowager Duchess of St. Ives, Lady Osbaldestone, Minnie and Timms, and perhaps Honoria and Horatia. They'd have Jacqueline on a pedestal, crowned with innocence, in a few days—then they'd whip up the troops to hunt down the real killer. He stirred and looked at Jacqueline. "But in this case, we can be more direct. Whispers can work both ways."

Jacqueline read his eyes. "You mean *we* should spread . . . what?"

"Fact," Barnaby answered. "He spread falsity, we'll spread the truth. Ultimately, our truth will trump his lies. But even more telling, just by starting such hares in people's minds, we'll be chipping away at the base he's built—it'll make it easier, once the portrait's complete, to turn perception around, and raise a hunt for the real killer, for him."

Lord Tregonning slowly nodded. "As this blackguard has grasped the chance afforded by poor Thomas's body being found to restart his whisper campaign against Jacqueline, then if we don't respond we risk being unable to counter him later, *but* if we attack the whispers now, directly, we'll weaken his position even before we show the portrait.

He's given us an opportunity to start pulling down the edifice he's erected—by his own actions, he's strengthened our chances."

Barnaby blinked, then a wide grin split his face. "That's absolutely right. He's started his own downfall—how ironic."

"Indeed." A rare smile curved Lord Tregonning's lips. "Now, how do we go about this?"

"Simple." Gerrard proceeded to outline the tactics he'd seen used to excellent effect by his formidable female connections.

Millicent nodded. "The next major gathering is the Summer Hunt Ball, three days from now. It's hosted by the Trewarrens. It's an annual event, one everyone attends." She looked at her brother. "What do you think, Marcus?"

"I think, in the circumstances, we all should go, myself included." Lord Tregonning glanced at Gerrard and Barnaby. "I dislike the bustle of balls and parties—I've rarely attended such events in the past. For that very reason, my appearance at Trewarren Hall should create all the stir we might wish."

"Indeed!" A martial light glowed in Millicent's eyes. "Everyone will be astonished, and will fall over themselves to learn why you're there. You may be a fusty old creature, Marcus, but you do have your uses—just by appearing, you'll cause a furor."

Lord Tregonning humphed. "Well, I count on you all to make the most of it—I'm not one for conversation, certainly not what passes for such in ballrooms these days."

"Don't worry," Barnaby said. "When it comes to playing social games, Gerrard and I have been trained by experts."

"Speaking of which," Gerrard said, "Jacqueline's gown, her whole presentation, will need to be perfectly gauged."

Millicent nodded. "We must go through your wardrobe, dear. Perhaps, Mr. Debbington, you could assist us with your opinion?"

Gerrard bowed. "I'd be delighted to oblige, ma'am." Jacqueline cast him a sharp glance, but he didn't meet her eyes.

"We'll need to set the stage with minor appearances before the ball," Millicent went on. "Maria Fritham's regular at-home is tomorrow morning—that's an excellent venue for young and old. And in the afternoon, I believe we should call on my old friend Lady Tannahay. She's closely acquainted with the Entwhistles—I think we should ensure that they hear our facts. Aside from all else, they deserve a clear accounting of all we know, and Elsie will deliver that for us."

Gerrard raised a brow at Barnaby, who met it with a resigned look. Gerrard turned to Millicent. "We'll be honored to escort you and Miss Tregonning, ma'am."

Manipulating society's views necessarily meant being socially active. Although he saw painting Jacqueline's portrait as his primary and most important contribution to rescuing her from the situation, Gerrard believed in the arguments they'd expounded. They had to stem the social tide first, before it swept Jacqueline away.

Thus it was that the next morning, he and Barnaby found themselves engaged in precisely the activity they'd fled London to avoid—doing the pretty by various young misses in some lady's drawing room.

Lady Fritham's at-home was well attended. From the sudden hiatus in the conversations and the round-eyed looks cast their way as they entered, the principal topic of interest wasn't hard to guess.

Millicent led them in, sweeping in confidently, a transparently relaxed smile on her lips.

Rising from the chaise to greet her, Lady Fritham wasn't quite sure what to make of that smile. "Millicent, dear." Her ladyship touched cheeks. "I'm delighted to see you." Lady Fritham drew back, eyeing Millicent searchingly. "And in such good spirits."

Her ladyship's gaze deflected to Jacqueline, following Millicent, a similar open and easy expression on her face. Lightly frowning, Lady Fritham looked back at Millicent. "I had wondered if this latest dreadful news would . . . well, *weigh* on you, and Jacqueline, too, of course."

Millicent raised her brows. "Well, dear, while having a dead body discovered moldering in the far-flung reaches of our gardens was certainly a shock, especially when we learned it was that poor boy Thomas, we *did* all suspect foul play years ago, when he disappeared, so finally finding incontrovertible proof of that, while admittedly distressing, is hardly the sort of news to knock one prostrate. It's not as if anyone in the household, nor even the staff, are suspected of the crime."

Lady Fritham blinked. "They aren't—no, well, of course they aren't . . ."

Millicent patted her hand. "I did explain it yesterday—you must not have heard—but it's patently clear poor Thomas was struck down by some man while up on the northern ridge. It seems it could have been anyone—any man, that is—that Thomas knew. That's all we know."

Millicent turned to Gerrard and Barnaby, who had followed Jacqueline. "Mr. Adair and Mr. Debbington know much more of the details than I—I'm sure they'll be happy to elucidate."

As they'd arranged during the drive to Tresdale Manor, Barnaby stepped in to appease the curiosity of the matrons congregated about Lady Fritham while Millicent circulated to spread their news. After exchanging greetings, Gerrard escorted Jacqueline to join the knots of younger callers scattered about the room.

Her hand on his sleeve, she kept her head high and her easy smile in place, yet despite her outward composure, he sensed her tension. This was her first public appearance since Thomas's body had been found; it was important she strike the right note.

They'd briefly discussed how she should behave, that when addressing Thomas's or her mother's death, she had to stop herself from retreating, from withdrawing behind her inner shields. To all who'd known her previously as an openhearted, extroverted soul, the change in her could too easily be—indeed, had so easily been—misperceived as evidence of a guilty conscience.

Three long double windows stood open to the garden; the younger crew had gathered in fluid groups before them. Guiding her to the first group, he murmured, "Just be yourself—that will be enough."

She shot him a swift glance, then looked ahead, smiled and greeted Mary Hancock.

Wide-eyed, Mary returned her greeting. "It must have been a horrible shock to learn the body was Thomas's."

Jacqueline appeared to consult her feelings, then evenly replied, "I think I was more sad than shocked. We'd always suspected he'd met with foul play, but I had hoped there might be some other explanation." She drew in a breath and released it in a sigh. "However, that wasn't the case, and we must now hope that it'll be possible to find the man who murdered him and bring the miscreant to justice."

Sincerity rang in her tone. Mary nodded, clearly struck, as was Roger Myles beside her.

Others were not so perceptive; across the circle, Cecily Hancock's lips thinned, then curled. Gerrard saw a nasty, dismissive comment form on her tongue; she opened her mouth—he caught her eye.

After a moment, she swallowed her comment whole and merely, very quietly, humphed.

Satisfied, he turned his attention to responding to any of the detailed questions they'd agreed Jacqueline should, with proper maidenly reserve, refrain from answering.

Between them, they succeeded in casting doubt on what had been the prevailing if unvoiced suspicion over Thomas's death.

After that first encounter, Jacqueline relaxed a trifle. By the time they'd spoken with and weathered the group before the second set of windows, she'd settled more comfortably into being herself. Her inner barriers, while still present, were less rigid, less formidable. Less apparent.

He'd thought he'd kept his satisfaction in that last to himself, but as they strolled to the third group, she pinched his arm. "What is it?"

He glanced at her, realized she'd sensed his response; keeping his expression impassive, he looked ahead. "Nothing."

Eradicating her inner shields, wiping away the fear and distrust that had fashioned them so that she could once again openly be the woman he knew she was, so that not only her innocence, but her generous heart, her courage, her steadfastness of character could shine . . . that was now a personal goal, one of serious importance to him.

Jordan and Eleanor were in the last group, as was Giles Trewarren. Eleanor and Giles made room for them. They greeted the others, then Jordan smiled at Jacqueline, his attitude supercilious and arrogant as ever, yet he clearly intended to be conciliating. "My dear, don't let the rumors of the ill-formed distress you—none of us who know you believe anything of the sort."

The comment fell into a sudden silence. Some of the others colored, while Clara Myles and Cedric Trewarren, who had chatted earlier with Barnaby, looked confused; they were the only ones in the group who had caught up with recent developments. Gerrard debated stepping in and, as an outsider able to claim complete ignorance, baldly asking what the devil Jordan meant—Jacqueline beat him to it.

She frowned, openly puzzled. "Whatever do you mean, Jordan? What rumors?"

Jordan blinked. He studied her face; his leached of all expression. He glanced around the circle. "I—ah . . . that is . . ."

Eleanor, beside Jacqueline, leaned closer and laid a hand on her arm. "What Jordan means"—she lowered her voice—"is that, what with the discovery of Thomas's body in your gardens, the ill-informed have been indulging in speculation. We just wanted you to know we don't believe a word of it."

Jacqueline met Eleanor's eyes; she held to her puzzled frown for a moment longer, then let it dissolve into an understanding smile. "Dear Eleanor." She patted Eleanor's hand. "You're such a good friend, but truly, now Thomas's body has been found, the only question in the minds of those who know the details is who the man who killed him was."

Eleanor's eyes widened. She searched Jacqueline's face. "Man?"

Jacqueline nodded; she was starting to enjoy this—enjoy tackling the rumors directly. "It seems Thomas went with some man up to the point on the northern ridge, then the man hit him with a rock and killed him. The body rolled down into the garden and the killer covered it with cypress needles."

Clara shivered. "It's horrible even to think of."

"It must have been a shock to realize it was Thomas's body." Giles looked politely inquisitive, but there was also understanding in his gaze. "Mama said it was you who identified Thomas's watch."

Jacqueline nodded. "It was a shock at the time. Now I just feel sad. It's terrible to think of some man killing Thomas like that."

Gerrard listened as she responded to helpful questions, using them to reiterate the facts they wished stressed, steadily dissipating the cloud of, as Eleanor had termed it, ill-informed speculation. Jacqueline referred any who asked for more details to Barnaby.

Jordan and Eleanor exchanged glances; they clearly felt awkward over having commented on rumors that were being so openly debunked. They remained unusually silent, but they listened as the others drew Jacqueline out, and she obliged. She'd grown rock-steady over how to present their case; her assurance and self-confidence increasingly showed.

It was a convincing performance.

By the time Millicent summoned them, declaring herself ready to leave, Gerrard had no doubt that, with steady application, they would lay the killer's whispers to rest.

They returned to the Hall just in time for luncheon. To their surprise, Lord Tregonning joined them; he was eager to hear the results of their first foray. Mitchel Cunningham was out about the estate, allowing a more relaxed exchange of information. Barnaby was in fine fettle—he actually made Lord Tregonning laugh.

Gerrard looked at Jacqueline, saw the change in her face, in her eyes, and knew it had been a long time since she'd heard such a sound from her father. She blinked and looked down. After a moment, she patted her lips with her napkin and looked up once more, composed again.

That moment of fleeting emotion prodded Gerrard; he needed to get started on the painting. When they rose from the table, he confirmed that they would leave at three o'clock for Lady Tannahay's.

In the front hall, he bowed to Millicent and Jacqueline. "I need to sort things out in the studio. I'll join you here at three."

"Yes, of course, dear." Millicent waved him off and swept toward the parlor. Barnaby followed, continuing their conversation regarding the new police force in the capital.

Jacqueline remained. She met his eyes. "Thank you for your support this morning."

He held her gaze, then, reaching out, took her hand, smoothly raised it to his lips and lightly kissed. "It was entirely my pleasure. I'm glad we made such a good fist of it."

He released her. Turning, he left her, but was aware that she watched him walk away, until he turned the corner and passed out of her sight.

What ho?" Barnaby strolled through the studio door, and looked around with interest.

Gerrard glanced up from the sketches he was sorting, grunted, then returned to his task.

Barnaby drifted about the room, eventually stopping by the window. Leaning his shoulders against the frame, he sank his hands into his pockets and looked at Gerrard. "So—how long do you think it's going to take?"

"The portrait?" Gerrard replaced one sketch on the table with one of those he held in his hands. Critically examining the series laid out before him, he murmured, "I think I can do it fairly quickly. Some portraits form a lot faster than others—in this case, I already know exactly what I want to show, how the whole has to look. I just need to get to it."

Head on one side, he studied the sketches. "I'm going to paint the setting first, then pose Jacqueline separately, and place her in it. Given I know how I want to portray both . . . a month might see it done."

"Hmm . . ." Barnaby had been studying him. "I can see you're keen to get started—there's no reason you need to act as social escort."

Gerrard glanced up.

Barnaby struck a pose. "Devoted friend that I am, I'm prepared to make a telling sacrifice and take your place at every blessed afternoon tea."

Gerrard laughed. "I'm not that gullible. You love gossiping, especially being the center of attention when there's a murder to discuss. And although the dear ladies might not know it, *I* know you're sounding them out, ferreting about for any little clues they have tucked away under their bonnets."

Unrepentant, Barnaby grinned. "True. But I meant what I said. If you'd rather stay here and get a start on the portrait, I'll engage to stick by Jacqueline's side. Besides, if I understood Millicent correctly, this afternoon will be a private call."

Perched on his stool, Gerrard stared at his sketches. They called to him, lured him to focus on them, on the painting he would create from them; he was itching to commence. Barnaby's offer was tempting, *except . . .*

He shook his head. "No. I'll play escort, too. We did well this morning, partly because we could divide and conquer. You're a dab hand with the matrons, and I can wield my exotic status to good effect with the younger crew. Together, we're the perfect support for Millicent and Jacqueline."

And if he wasn't with them, by Jacqueline's side, ready and able to ease her path, to ensure no one did anything to damage her emerging confidence . . . he'd never be able to concentrate on painting, anyway. "Let's leave things as they are—I can paint at night."

Barnaby studied his expression, which he kept studiously impassive, then nodded. "If you're sure." Barnaby pushed away from the window. "I'll leave you to it, then—I'll see you in the front hall at three o'clock."

Gerrard nodded, and let his sketches claim him once more.

Their call on Lady Tannahay, at nearby Tannahay Grange, proved to be as Barnaby had foreseen, a private call. Millicent sent in her card; within minutes, they were ushered into the presence of her old friend.

Elsevia—Elsie—Lady Tannahay, was a gracious lady a few years senior to Millicent; she greeted them with unreserved friendliness, and a shrewd look in her eye. She waved them to seats in her comfortable drawing room. "Do sit down. You positively *must* tell me all about this strange business of poor Thomas Entwhistle's body."

Millicent was only too ready to do so; Gerrard sat back and watched while she, with sterling support from Barnaby, explained all that was now known of how Thomas Entwhistle had died.

By the time they'd taken tea, disposed of a plate of delicious cakes, and their tale was told, Lady Tannahay had dropped all pretense of idle interest.

"*Well!*" She sat back and regarded them all, then brought her gaze to rest on Jacqueline. "My dear, I do hope you'll permit me to share this news—all you've told me—with Sir Harvey and Madeline Entwhistle. Poor dears, they've never been sure what to think, and"—Lady Tannahay's bright eyes flashed—"I can imagine only too well what that doddering fool Godfrey Marks would have said—or more to the point, *not* said, if you take my meaning."

Her ladyship fell silent, apparently pondering the failings of Sir Godfrey, then she refocused on Jacqueline. "While knowing Thomas's body has finally been found is a relief in itself, knowing more—especially who they don't have to suspect—will greatly ease Harvey and Maddy's minds. Please do say I may tell them all you've told me?"

Jacqueline smiled, understanding and compassion in her eyes.

"Indeed, ma'am, we had hoped you might consent to act as ambassador. We wouldn't wish to intrude on the Entwhistles at this time, not while the questions that must still be in their minds have yet to be laid to rest."

Lady Tannahay beamed. "You may leave it to me, child. I'll ensure the facts as Mr. Adair and others have determined them are conveyed *accurately* to Harvey and Maddy." She set down her teacup, and looked inquiringly at Millicent. "You will be attending the Summer Hunt Ball, won't you?"

Millicent smiled brilliantly. "Indeed we will. And so will Marcus."

Lady Tannahay's eyes widened. "Oh, *my*!" After a moment, she added, in the tone of one anticipating some excellent entertainment, "How positively delightful."

11

They returned to Hellebore Hall thoroughly satisfied with their afternoon's endeavors. The evening passed quietly. After dinner, Gerrard excused himself, leaving Barnaby to convey his apologies and entertain Jacqueline and Millicent in the drawing room. Climbing the stairs, he imagined Jacqueline laughing gaily at one of Barnaby's tales, and felt something within him stir; as he unlocked the door to the studio and went in, he realized what that something was.

Jealousy.

He stood for a moment, then pocketed the key and closed the door; faintly uneasy, he crossed to the table where the sketches he'd earlier selected lay waiting.

The sight of them helped push his unsettling, uncharacteristic reaction from his mind.

He'd instructed Compton to leave the five lamps stationed about the room alight. The flames had had time to steady; they cast even, unflickering light across his easel, and the large blank canvas clamped upon it. For long moments, he stood staring at the sketches, absorbing all they conveyed—shape, form, energy. Then he shrugged out of his coat and tossed it on a chair. Rolling up his sleeves, he searched through his pencils; selecting one with a lead worn to precisely the right angle, he picked up the first sketch, and turned to the canvas.

He worked steadily, pausing only to exchange one sketch for the next. Each represented another aspect, another layer of the menacing mystery with which he wanted to imbue his setting—the entrance to the Garden of Night. Never had he worked like this before, from the surroundings inward. He was driven by instinct, by unfathomable conviction that that was the way this portrait had to be approached.

It made sense, in a way, although he barely paused to consider it; Jacqueline would be the central and crucial last element—the core, the meaning, the purpose behind the portrait. She would be the life in it; no matter how potent the surroundings, they wouldn't—couldn't—overwhelm her.

The clock doubtless ticked, but he remained oblivious, wholly absorbed in his work. Beyond the window, darkness closed in and night fell. On the floors below, the house quieted as the other occupants settled into their beds.

A slumbering silence enshrouded the house.

He sketched on, his pencil flying ever faster as the surroundings took shape, as he sketched in the barest outline of a figure as a future guide. The tones, the shading, formed in his mind, bringing the collection of fine lines to life, at least to his eyes.

The stairs beyond the studio door creaked, the sound sharp enough to penetrate his absorption. He glanced at the door, frowning. Compton knew better than to interrupt, as did Barnaby, not unless there was some desperate reason, something he had to know.

He heard someone moving beyond the door, then a light tap sounded on the panels.

Not Compton, not Barnaby.

Even while his mind informed him who his midnight visitor most likely was, the knob turned and the door opened.

Jacqueline looked in.

She saw him; raising her brows, she half smiled. "May I come in?"

He looked at the canvas, at the thousand lines he'd laid down in the past hours; he couldn't seem to focus. He looked back at her, half expecting her to be fuzzy, but his vision was clear and sharp; every sense he possessed had no difficulty locking on her.

Laying aside the last sketch, he waved her in, and promptly lost all interest in the canvas; he couldn't drag his eyes from her as she stepped through the door, shut it, then turned and, smiling lightly, came toward him.

She was wearing a heavier robe than last night. This one was of ivory satin, belted at her waist, yet judging from the gauzy glimpses he caught at throat and calf, the nightgown beneath was close to diaphanous.

His mind immediately wanted to find out; his body reacted, not just to the question, but even more to the likely answer.

Dragging his gaze up to her face, fixing his eyes on hers, he stepped away from the easel. Grabbing a sketch pad and pencil in one hand, he grasped her elbow with the other, and turned her down the room. "Since you're here, you have to let me sketch you."

She looked at him; amusement flirted about her lips. "I do?"

He nodded; jaw set, he marched her to the window seat. And managed to release her. "Sit there."

She did, and looked up at him, ivory satin spread about her. Her hair, lit by the lamps, glowed rich and warm and inviting, as were her lips, lush and full, softly sheening . . .

He forced himself to look around, then lifted his coat from the straight-backed chair and dropped it to the floor. Setting the chair at a safe distance, he sat; placing his ankle on his knee, he balanced his sketch pad—and looked at her. Instructed himself to view her as just another subject—and failed.

He made a swirling motion with one finger. "Swing around and lean one elbow on the sill."

She did, shifting her hips, lifting one knee onto the padded seat to accommodate the pose.

The robe gaped, both over her breasts, and below her knees. Her nightgown was indeed diaphanous. The glimpses of pale, smooth skin left his mouth dry.

"Just stay there." His voice had grown gravelly. He shut his lips, and drew—not one of his usual quick sketches but a study, a detailed work of line and shade that showed more, conveyed more.

And captured him fully, in a completely different way than any work before.

Even as he recorded the vulnerable line of her throat, the sirenlike quality of her luscious lips, the provocative curves of breasts, hips and thighs outlined beneath the subtle sheen of satin, he was simultaneously conscious of his own fascination, not, as was usual, with the medium with which he worked, but with his subject.

Conscious of his deepening enthrallment, helpless to resist.

Twenty minutes must have passed, and she made no complaint, but simply watched him steadily with her green-gold eyes. He captured that direct gaze, then studied what he'd drawn—there was no element of challenge in her eyes, but a simple certainty, a reflection of that steadiness of character that had attracted him from the first.

He looked up, and met her gaze. "There's no need to seduce me."

If she could deal in blatant honesty, so could he.

Her eyes widened slightly, then the curve of her lips deepened. "Isn't there?"

"No." After a moment, he added, "You don't seem to realize how dangerous this could be . . . to you." And him. He no longer recognized the landscape into which they'd journeyed; when it came to her, he was no longer sure he recognized himself.

Jacqueline held his gaze, dark and frankly stormy, while she considered his words, his warning. Eventually, she replied, "I have thought of it, but I've decided the greater danger lies in inaction."

He frowned, but she had no intention of explaining further. She had thought, at length; to her, her conclusions were sound. She had no guarantee he would remain in her orbit beyond the completion of her portrait; that evening, Barnaby had told her that that might mean she'd lose Gerrard's company in less than two months.

Going slowly, carefully, was no longer an option. She wanted to know, to explore fully whatever it was that stirred and flared whenever they were close. He'd made it clear he would make no promises; that was as may be—she still had to know, had to grasp the opportunity fate had handed her, to explore this until now unknown arena.

Who knew when next she'd get the chance? He was the first and only man who'd ever made her feel like this.

Even more critically, what if, by not acting but instead taking the safe road, they missed something—unknowingly passed up an experience that, if given a chance to evolve and bloom, might lead to some vital development for them both?

Beyond doubt, not acting was the greater risk.

Lowering her elbow, she shifted, facing him. His gaze lowered, drawn to her full breasts outlined beneath her robe; his frown deepened, a degree of puzzlement quite clear.

"What is it?" she asked.

Lips thinning, he lifted his gaze to her face. "I was wondering if this was the natural outcome of keeping young ladies like you hidden away until the advanced age of twenty-three."

She laughed.

Although patently distracted again, he continued, "If so . . . I can guarantee it'll become all the rage."

His eyes openly roamed, then returned to hers. He looked at her; desire burned steadily in his eyes, yet he didn't move. Gave no sign at all that he would.

She set her feet to the floor, and slowly stood. Paused until her robe and nightgown slithered down, then she walked the few paces to stand before him. Boldly reaching for the sketch pad, she took it; his fingers tightened for an instant, then he let it go.

Turning it, she studied what he'd drawn.

Felt not so much shock as satisfied surprise warm her—was that truly her? There was a quiet sultriness in her face, a sirenlike quality in her gaze. A lush invitation in every line of her body, a body she recognized well enough, but had never before seen as blatantly sexual.

Now she saw through his eyes, understood, and was pleased.

She glanced at him, saw that he'd been tracking her emotions, her thoughts, in her face. "It's very good."

She handed the pad back to him. He took it, but his eyes didn't leave her face. "Accurate, would you say?"

There was something in his eyes that warned her she was standing very close to some edge. She drew breath, found her lungs had constricted, not with fear but anticipation. "Yes."

He dropped the pad; the pencil rolled away across the floor.

He reached for her, and drew her down onto his lap, into his arms—into a kiss that within a minute had set fires alight everywhere under her skin.

Raising one hand, he cradled her head, and pressed her lips wide. Angling his head, he filled her mouth, and took everything she offered, all she freely yielded. She clutched the fine linen of his shirt, fists clenching tight, then realized . . . slowly straightening her fingers, she spread her hands.

Over his chest. Beneath her thighs, his felt like rock, solid and ungiving; the arms about her felt like iron bands, not crushing her yet holding her captive. But his chest felt like cushioned stone, warm, unyielding yet comfortable. She sank her fingers into the heavy muscle and pressed closer, drawn by his heat.

By the urge to get closer still. Pushing her arms up over his shoulders, she pressed her already heavy, already aching breasts to his chest—and felt his pulse leap. Sensed the catch in his breathing, then his fingers shifted about her jaw, his lips firmed—and fire and molten heat poured from him, flooded through their fused lips and into her.

Gerrard's head was spinning. Again. Just being near her when she was thinking sexual thoughts was enough to arouse him. Painfully.

Kissing her was sheer torture.

He couldn't stop.

Yet some part of his mind knew exactly what to do, knew exactly what script he should follow. That he had such a side to him was something of a revelation; more ruthless, more primitive, and passionate, possessive and protective in the extreme, driven by primal instincts and content to be so, such maleness was something he'd associated with Devil and Vane, and the other Cynster males he knew—not him.

Until he'd met her, he hadn't met this side of himself, hadn't known it existed. Now he did.

Now it felt right, and he embraced it; he had no choice.

He tugged the sash of her robe free, slid his palm beneath the satin, skated over warm skin shielded by filmy silk, then closed his hand firmly about her breast, and provocatively, possessively, kneaded.

Instinct informed him what he wanted her to feel, what he needed the interlude to achieve. Settling her more firmly in his arms, his lips on hers, he set out to educate her senses, to educate the passion he sensed in her.

Jacqueline let herself flow on the heated tide he sent rushing through her. She felt no fear, no hesitation, but gave herself up to the wild and thrilling ride. Eagerness buoyed her, anticipation and expectation were a giddy mix roiling through her veins; excitement flowered and desire burgeoned, powerful and compulsive.

His lips and tongue demanded her attention; his hand on her breast shattered it. His long fingers teased, taunted, then soothed. She gasped through their kiss, gripped his head with both hands and with her lips and tongue urged him on.

She wanted to know all; pressing heated kisses on his firm lips, inviting ever more in return, she made that plain.

She was perfectly certain he understood. His hands, palms and fingers spread, traced her body; her robe hung from her shoulders, wide open, no impediment as he pandered to her senses and, she was sure, his. There was hunger in his touch, quite blatant, an element of desire she'd not before encountered — it sent frissons of mindless anticipation sliding through her.

This and more — she wanted to know it all, to experience all there was, all that might be. When his lips left hers she sighed, floating in the warmth they'd created, wits whirling yet able to follow as he bent his head and, nudging her chin up, set his lips to her throat. Paid homage to the sensitive region beneath her ear, then skated down, tracing the long line to her collarbone, pausing to hotly lave the pulse point above it, then his lips glided over the fine silk covering her breast, and fastened about one tightly budded nipple.

She tensed in expectation of a repeat of the sharp sensation she'd felt before, but his ministrations this time only soothed; he licked, laved, dampening the silk until it clung to her skin, then his tongue swirled and her world shook. Trembled.

Her breasts, full and tight, ached; he switched his attention to the other, repeating the subtle torture, then divided his time until she thought she would scream.

The instant before she did, he lifted his head, covered her lips with his, filled her mouth with his tongue and, like a marauding pirate, plundered. His hands slid lower, outlining her waist, gripping momentarily, fracturing her attention, then gliding lower to sculpt her hips. To learn her form as an artist might; for one moment, she wondered . . . then his fingers brazenly pressed between her thighs, stroked her curls, pushed past them to reach the throbbing flesh beyond, then pressed further and probed, and she lost all ability to think.

Discovered to her surprise that she could only feel, that there was such a state as being overwhelmed by her senses. Heightened to almost excruciating sensitivity, they commanded every last ounce of her concentration, held her ruthlessly focused on his touch, on the openly predatory way in which he was caressing her. She'd offered, and he was taking. Despite her whirling wits, that fact registered clearly.

She was in complete agreement.

Reassured he was taking the road she'd wished to take, she dragged in a breath, and turned her attention to him. To other aspects she'd yet to explore.

Like his chest. His shirt was of the finest linen; through it she could feel his flesh, feel the muscles shifting beneath her fingers as like a cat she kneaded. But that wasn't enough; she wanted to feel his skin. Leaning her elbows on his chest, trying not to think too much about the far too evocative play of his fingers between her thighs, she set her hands to his cravat.

Sensually captured by the tactile wonder of the hot, slick flesh his fingers caressed, Gerrard didn't realize what she was about until she wrestled his shirt wide, and laid his chest bare.

She wrenched back from the kiss to look—one glance at her face, at the expression that lit her eyes, and he was lost. Slayed by a desire so deep, so complete, it spared no part of him, left no vestige of his self, his soul, free. From that instant, he was hers, no matter she didn't know it. From beneath heavy lids he watched her face, enthralled by the play of emotions across it, by the directness he'd from the first seen in her, and valued for what it was.

All that it was—the most arousing element in any sexual enounter was the response of the other. With her, he would never need to wonder, not even to think—she lavished her appreciation on him, and in so doing enslaved him.

He let her play as long as he could, as long as he dared. He knew the script—she didn't; control, his control, was vital. And with that, she wasn't helping.

Her hands traced down; her expression plainly stated she was fascinated with his ridged abdomen. Fingers spread, she tested, explored; from beneath her lashes, she threw him a sultry glance, then returned to her avid play. His painter's brain happily re-created the scene in his mind, titled it: *Siren Exulting.*

She was. The sight held him in thrall.

But when her hands eased and drifted lower, his newfound ruthlessness rose to the fore. Catching her hands, he lifted them to his shoulders, released them there; ignoring her questioning glance, he drew her back to him, back into his arms, back into a kiss expressly designed to render her witless.

To plunge her back into the sea of desire, of heady wanton passion, that had been steadily rising about them.

She went eagerly; grasping his head between her hands, she kissed him back with abandon. An abandon that only made him ache all the more, that only made it harder to do what he knew he should.

He had to break her spell, her increasingly strong grip on his senses.

Before he could change his mind—before she could further weaken his resolve—he lifted her, stood, and carried her to the window seat. She drew back from the kiss; he had to let her. From beneath her long lashes, she looked into his eyes, studied his face; he could read her thoughts easily—see the anticipation, the flare of expectation that flamed in her eyes, brilliant emerald and gold, gilded by the fires of passion.

The nursery was old, the window seat wide and liberally supplied with soft cushions; he tumbled her down onto it, and followed, trapping her half beneath him. She laughed softly, a sound of pure abandon that raked his soul, and racked his desire one notch higher. Reaching for him, she drew his head down, drew his lips to hers, parted in flagrant welcome.

He sank into her mouth, for long moments simply indulged, and wallowed in her clear encouragement, in the honest passion that was so much a part of her. He wanted that—wanted to seize—but experience warned that with her, caution and care were imperative. Steeling himself, he mentally drew back, and turned his mind to executing the strategy instinct drove him to employ.

Jacqueline sensed his attention shift; his lips remained fused with hers, a potent distraction, but then his hands were on her, roaming her body, so scantily clad she might as well have been naked.

She wished she were naked—she wanted to feel his hands on her skin, ached for the greater intimacy, wanted that hurdle crossed so there'd be fewer between her and her goal. His touch had grown harder, more demanding, each caress a blatantly sexual act, an intimate claiming.

He touched her as if she was his, sculpted her flesh as he wished, explored without reserve.

Each caress stoked the fires beneath her skin until she writhed beneath him, insensibly sure she needed even more. Exactly what, she wasn't sure, but he responded by running his hand from her collarbone down over her breast, squeezing, swiftly kneading, tweaking the nipple to painful erectness before sweeping down, tracing the indentation of her waist, then passing over her stomach, splaying and pressing possessively, then sweeping lower still, stroking her curls, veiled by fine silk, before gliding down the long line of one thigh—to her knee and the hem of her nightgown.

He drew it up, up to her hips, then he tugged and drew it higher still, to her waist. Cool air played over her bare skin as with one knee he nudged her thighs apart; through their kiss, she gasped—she would have pulled back, broken the kiss to drag in air and steady her giddy senses, but he didn't permit it. He held her to the kiss as the exchange turned scorching, as he set his hand to her bare knee, then ran his palm up, over her thigh, and found her.

Cupped her, then his fingers stroked and he parted her soft flesh, and slid not one but two fingers into her.

She felt the intimate penetration to her soul, felt her body arch, not in protest but in welcome. He stroked, possessive and sure; her every sense locked on the movement. On the sensations he evoked, that he drew from her, pressed on her. She had to cling to the kiss as her world spun; he held her to it, her lips beneath his, feeding her kisses laden with passion, with a desire that burned as bright as her own. More than anything else, that desire, his blatant wanting, buoyed and reassured.

She wanted him, and he wanted her. That seemed totally right.

Gradually, he eased back from the kiss; lifting his head, he looked down at her, studied her face from beneath heavy lids, then his lips quirked in smug, wholly male satisfaction. Between her thighs, his hand worked, knowingly stroking, stoking a need that was already threatening to sweep her away. She sank her fingers into his shoulders and tried to pull him back, but he moved lower, then shifted—with his free hand caught her nightgown hem and raised it higher still, then bent his head.

His mouth, hot and wet, closed over her nipple. She almost screamed, the sound only half smothered; the sensation wasn't new, but had grown immeasurably sharper. And only swelled more as he feasted, as he made free with all she'd willingly offered. Steadily he drew her, body and senses, into deeper waters, into the hot, surging tide of passion unrestrained.

She went willingly, aware her horizons were rapidly expanding, that she'd lost touch with the world she knew, and would have to rely on him to guide her back.

Her body was no longer hers to command. Her world had reduced to the window seat; she was acutely aware of how her body, all but naked, writhed beneath his experienced caresses, how it rose, responding to every ardent touch, how the lamplight played over the valleys and hollows—how he watched, and saw, and was pleased.

Grimly pleased. She sensed that last as he lifted his head and looked down at her breasts, firm, swollen and aching, nipples tightly furled, skin flushed with desire. He moved lower still, and let his gaze wander, down over her waist, her stomach, to the damp curls one thumb idly stroked, to the junction of her thighs, to where his hand worked, constantly caressing, probing, but never quite pressing as he had once before.

Slowly, he traced his way back to her face, met her eyes, then the light of sheer conquest gleamed in his, and he bent his head.

His lips touched her navel; his tongue swirled, then probed. She shrieked, but the sound came out as a breathless squeak. She felt him chuckle, then he drew back and blew gently on her damp flesh, then touched his lips once more to her skin, and set about trailing hot, wet, open-mouthed kisses down over her stomach.

To her curls.

To—

She screamed, but she'd lost her breath entirely—no sound came out at all. She twisted, but he'd grasped her hips, anchoring her while he pleased himself, and pleasured her.

"*Gerrard!*" She finally managed a shocked whisper.

"Mmm?" He didn't lift his head, barely paused in his ministrations.

Her wits had spun away; her mind was blank. "You . . . *can't.*" She felt like she was dying, her chest so tight she couldn't breathe, her every nerve coiled and shrieking.

"I can."

He demonstrated, and her world shuddered. Closing her fists in the cushions beneath her, she clung for dear life. She'd thought they'd been following the usual pattern of events—the pattern as Eleanor had described it more than once. But *this* had never featured in Eleanor's experience.

His hands gripped and he lifted her to him.

She felt her body react, felt the intimate surrender to her bones.

Felt the mind-numbing pleasure to her toes.

She moaned his name, closed her eyes tight. Gave up the fight to do anything other than give herself to him, to let him do with her as he wished.

And he knew.

He lavished sensation and more upon her, intimacy beyond her wildest dreams, until, quite suddenly, it was all too much. The glory built to an unbearable degree and she broke apart—flew apart in a cascade of pleasure and physical joy, and gold and silver glory.

Heat pulsed through her, flooded her mind and her soul, buoyed her as he lapped, then laid her gently down.

Blindly, she reached for him; after an instant's hesitation, he came to her, let her draw him to her, but then he settled beside her, his hand soothing her flushed body, gently drawing her back to earth.

Something was wrong. Her body was drowning in the languorous aftermath of the pleasure he'd brought her, yet all he did was draw her nightgown down and lift her robe over her, protecting her cooling skin. Raising her lids, heavy with satiation, she watched his face, the planes still etched with the desire he'd held back—that he was still holding back.

She waited until his eyes met hers, then simply asked, "Why?"

He couldn't pretend not to understand. She may be a novice, yet for him to have given her such pleasure, yet taken none for himself . . . that wasn't the way things should be.

For a moment, he studied her eyes, then to her surprise, he caught her hands, one in each of his, pressed them to the cushions on either side of her head and leaned over her. Leaned close—his face was inches from hers, his lips a handbreadth away.

He looked at her lips, then lifted his gaze and met her eyes. "I want you. You know I do."

She did; his desire for her screamed, not just from his eyes, not just in the deepened, roughened tone of his voice, but from the tightly leashed tension that invested every muscle in his large lean body. If that wasn't evidence enough, his erection rode against her hip, rampant and rigid.

Moistening her lips, she kept her eyes on his. "Why, then?"

"Because . . ." He searched her eyes. "You've offered yourself to me twice. Twice, I've given you the chance to step back, to retreat to safer ground." His gaze lowered to her lips, then again returned to her eyes. "To escape me, and the demands I'll make of you if I make you mine."

Her body was still throbbing with the aftermath of what he'd wrought; between them, she could feel not only her own heart, but his, too, thudding. Pounding. "Do you want me to escape?"

His lips lifted, but it wasn't in a smile. "No. I want to have you." His head lowered, his lips brushed hers. "But what I want, what I'll demand and take if you surrender yourself to me, might be more than you're prepared to give."

The words feathered over her lips, promise and warning combined.

She met his eyes again, felt herself drowning in their depths. "What, exactly, would you demand of me?"

"Everything. All of you." He shifted, looking down; his hand brushed the side of her breast, instantly stirring her body to life. "What I've taken so far is much less than I want. I want every scintilla of passion you have in you, every iota of desire you have to give." He paused, then raised his lids and again met her eyes. "I want to, and will, possess you utterly."

About them, all was silent and still; between them, passion arced, desire burned. The predator in him was starkly evident, in the lines of his face, in the intensity of his gaze.

She knew what she wanted. She opened her mouth—

He kissed her. Kissed her with all the passion he'd held back, ravished her mouth and her senses, plundered and took, giving her a taste—just a taste—of his ravenous hunger, then he pulled back.

"Be in no doubt." His voice grated, a sexual rumble that rasped her senses. "If you offer a third time, I'll take, and there'll be no going back. I won't play the gentleman and turn you away. I want you—if you tempt me again, you'll be mine. Every inch of you. With every gasp, every moan, every heartbeat, you'll be mine."

Straightening his arms, he lifted himself over her; looking down, he held her gaze. "Think about it." His eyes searched hers. "If you decide you truly want that, I'll be here. Waiting."

Prowling. The energy that crackled beneath his skin was new. Something beyond his experience, as he was beyond hers.

Gerrard paced before the darkened windows of his bedroom, still aching, still driven.

One part of him, the primitive prowling part of him that now gave him no surcease, hadn't wanted to warn her—had wanted instead to seize and be damned.

But he'd known better. The more sophisticated part of him that had evolved through the years, that had watched and seen and, it now seemed, absorbed, knew the price he was paying for warning her and letting her go—letting her go to make her own decision—was a bargain in terms of what he would gain.

Her. Committed by her own act, not swept into his arms by his more powerful libido.

He knew, to his bones, what he felt for her. Something he'd never expected to feel. He now understood what he never had before—the driven quality behind the protective possessiveness of the Cynster men, especially Devil and Vane, the two whose marriages he'd most closely observed. Devil, being Devil, was forever arrogantly blatant, while Vane was quieter, stubborn and immovable, yet the force driving their behavior was the same. He hadn't expected to feel the same compulsion, but now he did . . . his approach would be more subtle.

He knew women, had interacted more closely with them than most—he knew enough to cloak his driving need, to veil his vulnerability by insisting Jacqueline make her own decision to give herself to him, to commit herself through her own, considered act.

Now he'd chosen, fought and succeeded in following that tack, when the time came, she would view the consequences of becoming his as something she'd invited, and, he hoped, accept them without complaint.

His plan was sound, well grounded. It would work.

Smothering an inclination to growl, he swung on his heel and paced across the room. His blood was still coursing too fast through his veins, desire still lashed and passion prodded—leashed, for now.

But not for long.

He was as arrogant as Devil or Vane, enough to feel confident of her decision—of what she'd choose. She'd choose to be his, and then he'd have her.

Without her knowing she'd been seized.

12

The following morning, with Gerrard in attendance, Millicent reviewed Jacqueline's wardrobe. Jacqueline was unsurprised when her bronze silk sheath was declared most suitable for the Summer Hunt Ball; a present from her mother just before she'd died, it was her most sophisticated and revealing gown, but she'd yet to wear it apparently, its time had come.

It was the middle of summer; in that corner of the world so distant from the capital, it was customary for the local families to entertain themselves and their youth with some event every few days. Today, Mrs. Hancock was hosting a picnic, or as she more grandly termed it, an "alfresco luncheon."

They left the Hall at noon; by the time they reached the Hancocks' house beyond St. Just, most of the guests had arrived.

Once again, Jacqueline found herself tensing as they emerged onto the Hancocks' terrace and all eyes swung her way. Some of the guests had been at the Frithams' yesterday, but there were others who had yet to assimilate their new direction. She held her head high, kept a smile of precisely the right, unconcerned degree on her lips, and followed Millicent, Gerrard and Barnaby's leads. She was grateful for their support, especially Gerrard's; as at the Frithams', he remained by her side.

Somewhat to her surprise, Mrs. Elcott, the vicar's wife, usually so severe, unbent enough to compliment her on her spring-green muslin. "I'm delighted to see that you're not hiding yourself away. No doubt the discovery of poor Mr. Entwhistle's body has caused you distress, but it never does to overindulge such passions. Facing forward is precisely what a young lady of your standing must do."

Mrs. Elcott pursed her lips, as if holding back further comment, then surrendered to temptation. "Have you spoken with the Entwhistles yet?"

Jacqueline managed to look unconcerned. "Not yet."

Gerrard smoothly cut in with a distracting remark. A minute later, he drew her away.

"She wanted to know so she could be first with the news." She allowed him to lead her to the trestle table where refreshments had been laid out.

Reaching for the lemonade jug, he glanced at her. "True, but it seems she's shrewd enough not to credit the killer's whispers—or if she has in the past, she's now willing to run with the truth instead."

Jacqueline accepted the glass of lemonade he'd poured for her. "To give the devil his due—or in this case the vicar's wife her due—I've never heard her gossip maliciously. She's simply addicted to being up with the latest, to understanding what's going on."

She could relate to the impulse. Over the rim of her glass, she glanced at Gerrard; she wished she knew what, precisely, was going on between them. Last night . . . once she'd returned to her bed, she'd fallen deeply asleep. She'd assumed she'd have time today to assess his proposition, his veiled ultimatum. She was certain she ought to think before she allowed her, where he was concerned, too impulsive desire to sweep her into his arms. Especially now he'd informed her the step would involve irrevocable surrender, at least on her part.

Unfortunately, it was impossible to consider him and his lionlike propensities while he was beside her, or even in the vicinity, which meant there was nothing to be gained by attempting to think of such things now; she might as well enjoy the moment, and his company.

He was the perfect escort—always there, yet never crowding her. Supporting, guiding, but not directing, he played the perfect foil in helping her project just the right image—the impression, as he'd said, of being herself.

By the time they settled on picnic rugs to sample the delicacies Mrs. Hancock's cook had prepared, she'd relaxed enough not just to laugh, but to do so spontaneously, without reserve. As Barnaby, the inveterate storyteller, continued his tale, she sipped from the flute of champagne Gerrard had handed her, then glanced at him. He caught her eye, held her gaze for an instant, then raised his flute to hers, clinked, and sipped, too.

Suddenly a touch breathless, giddy as if the champagne had gone to her head, she looked away, at Barnaby, and drew in a tight breath. Her breasts rose above the scooped neckline of her gown; she felt Gerrard's warm gaze sweep her exposed skin.

Raising her glass again, she sipped, and fought to slow her pulse; she wished she had a fan.

"You're such an accomplished raconteur." Opposite Barnaby, Eleanor bestowed on him an openly inviting smile. "Why, your adventures seem almost legendary."

Beside Jacqueline, Barnaby stiffened. "Oh, no," he airily replied. "I've just seen a thing or two—inevitable in the capital."

"Ah, yes, the capital." Eleanor was not the least deterred by the less than encouraging response. "Do you spend most of your time there?"

Barnaby murmured a noncommittal response, immediately capping it with a general question, drawing the others—Clara, Cedric and Hugo and Thomasina Crabbe—into the conversation. On Jacqueline's other side, Gerrard shifted, then glibly deflected a question from Eleanor designed to once again fix Barnaby's attention on her.

Despite the undercurrents—primarily Eleanor's doing—the mood remained light. Eleanor, Jacqueline knew, was merely amusing herself; she wished to see Barnaby wound about her little finger, but then she would discard him. Aside from her mystery lover, gaining power over the males who hove on her horizon was Eleanor's chief amusement.

Jacqueline had seen that for years, but she hadn't, until now, thought much of it. Now . . . she couldn't help but feel Eleanor's behavior wasn't very ladylike, or kind. Luckily, Barnaby, the male currently in Eleanor's sights, showed no signs of succumbing.

The picnic consumed, the matrons sat back in the shade and chatted. Everyone else elected to go on a ramble through the adjoining woods. They set off in a large, rambunctious group; before long, they'd strung out along the path.

Whether by luck or good management, she and Gerrard brought

up the rear. That didn't please Matthew Brisenden. He was swept ahead with the others yet, whenever the curve of the path allowed, stared back at her strolling on Gerrard's arm.

Gerrard was aware—more aware than he liked—of Matthew's dark looks. The boy was ridiculously possessive; Gerrard recognized and labeled his attitude instantly, and was in no way amused by it. He was also screamingly conscious of Jacqueline beside him, strolling along with, it seemed, not a care in the world. He was pleased that she'd relaxed, that she was more and more able to show her true colors to the world, yet . . .

Step by step, they fell further behind. She seemed absorbed with the flowers and trees, for which he gave thanks; he wasn't in the mood for idle chatter. Increasingly, he watched her face, felt himself falling ever deeper under her spell.

"Oh!" She stopped, looking ahead.

He followed her gaze; the rest of the party had disappeared out of sight around the next bend.

She glanced at him; a challenging light danced in her eyes. "There's a shortcut, if you're willing to risk it."

He was willing to risk a great deal for a few minutes alone with her. He waved. "Lead on."

She smiled and turned aside, pushing past a thick bush onto a minor path. "This leads to the stream. The main path crosses it at a wooden bridge further on, then curves back on the other side, but it's a long way around."

"So what's the risk?"

Even as he voiced the question the bushes before them thinned, and he saw the stream gurgling along the middle of a wide bed and spanned by an old fallen tree.

"Behold." Jacqueline waved at the tree. "The challenge."

She started down the slight slope. Gerrard followed. The stream had shrunk to within its summer banks, leaving the lush green of its winter flood plain ten yards wide on either side. Yet the stream was still too wide to jump, and too deep to wade through, and the tree trunk wasn't large.

Jacqueline turned to him. "Are you game?"

He looked down at her. "Do I get a reward if I succeed?"

Jacqueline studied all she could see in his eyes, and wondered why he and only he made her feel like a siren. She let her lashes veil her eyes and looked back at the tree. "Possibly."

"In that case"—he leaned down so his words wafted past her ear—"after you, my dear."

To her hyperaware senses, he even sounded like a lion.

She drew breath, took the hand he offered to step up to the narrow bole, paused to catch her balance, then ran lightly across. She'd performed the same feat countless times. Jumping down to solid ground at the other end, she turned—and found Gerrard stepping off the tree immediately behind her.

He caught her; hands locking about her waist, he whirled her, then lowered her until her feet touched earth. For one finite instant, they stared into each other's eyes, then he drew her—fully—against him. He looked into her eyes, briefly searched, then his gaze lowered to her lips. "Reward time, I believe."

He swooped, captured her lips with his, and plunged them both into a fiery kiss, one that stirred them both, that sent flames spreading beneath her skin, that left her breasts firm and aching, that spilled heat down her veins to pool low, to pulse with a longing she now understood.

She held tight, fingers clutching his upper arms as their lips and tongues dueled, not for supremacy but for pleasured delight.

The moment spun on, and on.

Eventually, he drew back. They were both breathing too quickly as he looked into her eyes. "Have you made your decision yet?"

Gerrard had told himself he wouldn't push, wouldn't ask—but he ached to know.

She tried to frown, couldn't manage it. "No. I . . . got the impression I'd be wise to think seriously about . . . what agreeing would entail."

Her gaze dropped to his lips. He fought against the urge to kiss her again.

"You should." He couldn't keep his voice from deepening. The thought of what would follow her decision—

Footsteps. They both heard the steady crunch of boots heading their way.

Turning to the sound, they stepped apart—just as Eleanor and Matthew Brisenden came into view.

"There you are!" Eleanor looked delighted.

Gerrard could quite happily have consigned her to perdition. Along with her companion, who was looking daggers at him.

"I told Matthew you would have taken the shortcut and be waiting for us here." Patently pleased with her perspicaciousness, Eleanor swept forward, her gaze locked on Gerrard.

Smoothly, he linked his arm with Jacqueline's. "Just so—we knew the rest of you wouldn't be long."

"The others are up on the main path." Matthew came up, frowning at Gerrard, openly disapproving. "We should join them."

Gerrard smiled easily. "Indeed. Do lead the way."

Matthew blinked, but, with tight lips and a curt nod, had to do so. Gerrard steered Jacqueline in his wake.

To his amazement, Eleanor took his other arm.

He stared at her, but she seemed totally oblivious of her impertinence.

"We've been talking about the traditional gathering tomorrow." Eleanor glanced across him at Jacqueline. "Will you come, do you think?"

Jacqueline met her gaze. "Oh, I think so."

"Well, regardless, Mr. Debbington, you really should attend. It's almost as much fun as the ball itself. Indeed"—Eleanor's eyes gleamed as she looked up at Gerrard—"sometimes more."

"The tradition," Jacqueline informed him, "is that all the younger people gather at Trewarren Hall in the morning and decorate the ballroom."

"And the terrace and gardens," Eleanor put in.

Jacqueline nodded.

"So"—Eleanor fixed her gaze on Gerrard's face—"will you be joining us?"

Gerrard glanced at Jacqueline; he wouldn't be letting her out of his sight any time soon. Particularly not if Matthew Brisenden would be anywhere near. "I believe I will," he murmured, addressing Jacqueline. He caught her gaze when she glanced up. "All work and no play will very likely make me a dull painter."

Her lips quirked; she looked ahead.

"Excellent!" Eleanor said.

. . .

That evening, at the dinner table, Lord Tregonning shocked them all. Looking down the table, he asked Millicent, "How did your excursion go today?"

Millicent stared at him, then hurried to answer. "It was an excellent outing, Marcus—quite gratifying." She rattled off a list of the ladies who'd been present. "While I wouldn't go so far as to say we've *convinced* anyone of anything, I do think we've started hares in a good many minds, and set the stage for pushing matters further."

Lord Tregonning nodded. "Good, good." He glanced at Jacqueline, Gerrard, then Barnaby. "So everything's going as planned?"

"Quite smoothly." Barnaby reached for his wineglass. "I understand there's a gathering of the younger folk tomorrow, which will be our last event before the ball."

"Ah, yes—the decorating party." Lord Tregonning turned a sympathetic gaze on Jacqueline. "Are you comfortable attending that, my dear?"

"Oh, yes. Indeed, I haven't encountered as much difficulty as I'd imagined, and"—Jacqueline glanced at Gerrard, then across the table at Barnaby—"with Mr. Debbington's and Mr. Adair's support, I doubt I'll encounter any challenge I can't meet."

She toyed with her fork, then went on, "While most are a trifle confused at first, all thus far have seemed . . . *receptive* to thinking again. However, I don't think that would have been so had we not challenged their preconceived notions."

Lord Tregonning nodded again.

Gerrard noticed the puzzled look on Mitchel Cunningham's face. He had no notion of what they were discussing; no doubt he'd work it out soon enough. Turning to Jacqueline, Gerrard asked, "What form does the Summer Hunt Ball take?"

"It's a proper ball with musicians and dancing. As for the rest . . ." Briefly she described the usual other attractions—a card room, and a salon for conversation. "The terrace and garden walks are lit for the night, too."

From there, with Barnaby's help, Gerrard steered the first conversation they'd had over the dinner table at Hellebore Hall into a more general discussion of the amenities of the area.

· · ·

Later that night, Jacqueline stood at the balcony window of her bedroom, and wondered if Gerrard was painting. Her windows overlooked the orchards of the Garden of Demeter; she couldn't tell if light was spilling from the windows of the old nursery, yet she felt sure he'd be there, standing before his easel creating the setting in which her innocence would shine.

Even last night, as she'd left the studio she'd glanced back and seen him returning to the easel, to the canvas on it, as if drawn to it.

His devotion to the portrait, to rescuing her, touched her. Buoyed her.

She recalled, very well, all that had passed between them the night before. That he wanted her she didn't doubt, and she wanted him. Her reasons for grasping the opportunity to learn what that mutual wanting truly meant remained valid, yet his insistence she decide, that she make what would amount to a declaration of unrestricted acceptance . . . He was right; about *that* she needed to think.

He'd said he wanted *everything*, all she was, to possess her utterly; that was a very wide claim—she wasn't sure she understood the implications.

To agree to that . . . to do so, she would need to trust him, to trust that, to whatever extent his "everything" stretched, he wouldn't hurt or harm her. Not in her wildest imaginings did she think he would, yet in trusting him that much, in specifically and openly acknowledging such trust, as he was demanding, it would help to know why—why had he asked that of her.

Why was he, as he demonstrably was, so deeply interested in her?

The obvious, transparently real answer was that he was fascinated with her as a subject, yet was that the whole answer? Reviewing his absorption with painting her, contrasting that with the intensity he focused on her when he held her in his arms, whether the force that drove him was one and the same she couldn't tell, and could see no ready way of discerning.

Did she truly care whether his interest in her was driven solely by an artist's fascination?

The question slid into her mind, and revolved there—yet another question with no easy answer.

Minutes ticked by as she mentally circled. What did *she* want of this, of him, of what had flared between them?

That she knew—she wanted experience. Of the physical, the sensual, all the aspects of a woman's life of which, due to the events of recent years, she remained ignorant. At its simplest, she wanted to know. Now he'd arrived and unexpectedly offered her the chance to learn, was she going to take it?

All her instincts sang "yes!" yet she clung to caution and the sensible approach. Was there any reason she shouldn't accept his terms?

Mentally, she looked ahead, thinking of how a liaison with him as he'd described it would affect her life . . . and discovered a void.

Her future.

Frowning, she tried to bring her expectations into focus, but the emptiness in her mind remained; she had no vision of her future at all.

Staring unseeing at the night, she felt oddly hollow as realization solidified. The killer had stolen her expectations; her future was a blank canvas, and she had no idea of the picture she wished to see upon it.

It was a shock to discover such complete and utter nothingness where surely something should have been.

She was twenty-three, well dowered and attractive enough, yet she'd been frozen—was still frozen—on the threshold of her life. What dreams she'd nurtured when Thomas had lived had vanished with him; not even a ghostly vestige remained. Presumably once she was free of the nightmare of her mother's and Thomas's deaths, her mind would turn from its fixation on the past and present and attend to the future, and sketch in some details. Until then . . . she had no expectations of her future to guide her.

But Gerrard and his offer were there, before her now; how should she respond?

By agreeing. He'd made it plain he wasn't asking for her future, but her present; he'd talked in terms of a physical liaison, with no defined strings attached.

If she'd been younger, or felt more a part of the usual round of social life, she might have felt shocked, might have felt she was risking something, might have hesitated. But now?

Given all fate had denied her, given what might yet be denied her forever more, the compulsion to accept his terms burgeoned and grew.

"I want to *live.*" The whisper fell from her lips, a potent exhortation. A direction. If she waited . . . until when? Once she was an old maid, would such a chance come again?

Conviction welled. Instinct, yes, but that was all she had to guide her. Yet in this arena, she had so little previous knowledge, so little practice in listening to her heart . . .

Arms folded, lips set, she tapped one slippered toe. She felt a strong urge to have done with thinking, to open her door, slip through the quiet corridors and return to his lair and his arms. She'd never been an impulsive person, yet in this, with him, instinct was urging her on.

Innate caution held her back.

Turning from the window, she paced into the room and stopped, her gaze fixed on the corridor door. For long minutes, she debated: to yield and accept now, or wait for some further sign?

Or, perhaps, ask more questions?

It took effort to turn aside, but she did. Shedding her robe, she climbed into bed, slid under the covers, tugged them up, closed her eyes, and willed herself to sleep.

Not terribly successfully, but she felt rested enough when she joined the others in the breakfast parlor the next morning. She was conscious of the intentness of Gerrard's gaze on her face, but merely bade him a good morning, and applied herself to tea and toast.

Intentness of gaze didn't qualify as a sign.

The day was fine. She, Gerrard and Barnaby decided to drive Gerrard's curricle to Trewarren Hall; his pair needed exercising. They bowled down the lanes toward Portscatho and the cliffs along the Channel. Trewarren Hall lay a few miles back from the cliffs—far enough so the trees in the park grew tall and straight, not bent and twisted by the Channel winds.

Lady Trewarren was briefly taken aback when she realized Gerrard and Barnaby intended joining the group, but she rallied, setting Barnaby to assist with garlanding the ballroom while Gerrard was dispatched with Jacqueline to oversee the stringing of lanterns through the trees.

Two gardeners were waiting with the crate of lanterns; all she and Gerrard had to do was point out the most suitable positions, something Gerrard with his landscape artist's eye accomplished with barely a thought.

The first half of the morning passed in pleasant endeavor, then other members of the decorating party, having completed their chores indoors and elsewhere, found them. A laughing group comprising Roger, Mary, Clara and Rosa were the first; they paused to comment excitedly, looking forward to the night, before waving and heading off along the path to the lake.

Gerrard watched them go, then arched a brow at her. "I take it the tradition ends with a party by the lake?"

She smiled. "We gather there, in and around the summerhouse, until the gong sounds for luncheon on the terrace."

The next group of decorators to come down from the house included Cecily Hancock. Pausing beside Jacqueline, she asked Giles Trewarren, also in the group, if the Entwhistles were expected that evening; she ingenuously pointed out that Sir Harvey was Master of the Hunt.

Glancing apologetically at Jacqueline, Giles admitted Thomas's parents had sent word they would attend, although they'd leave before the dancing.

Everyone looked to see how she'd react. Jacqueline fought not to retreat behind her usual poker face. Sensing Gerrard beside her helped. She met Cecily's eyes and kept her expression open, allowing her sympathy for the Entwhistles to show. "I'm looking forward to speaking with them. They've had so much to bear. What with being in mourning, I haven't had a chance to talk with them recently, and now with Thomas's body being found, I do feel for them."

Glancing at Gerrard, she found encouragement in his gaze. She looked at Cecily. "And, of course, I must introduce Mr. Debbington and Mr. Adair, who found the body and discovered so much about how Thomas died."

Cecily searched her face. A spark of surprise showed in her eyes.

The others, too, were watching her, yet they clearly accepted her words as fact. Giles assured Gerrard he'd make sure his father introduced them to Sir Harvey, then the group made their farewells and headed on to the lake, Cecily subdued, apparently thinking.

Jacqueline felt a surge of satisfaction over that.

Turning back to Gerrard, she found him waiting to catch her eye, approval in his. "You handled that well. Every person who shifts their view is one more the killer has lost his hold over. After tonight, I predict he'll be cursing and gnashing his teeth."

She smiled, but sobered quickly. "We can but hope."

Three more groups trailing down from the house found them. After successfully dealing with Cecily, Jacqueline handled the careful comments—about her joining in the decorating again, about her dancing again after her mother's death, of the dreadful finding of Thomas's body and speculation over his death, and his parents' likely feelings—with aplomb.

Yet every mention of Thomas, of the suspicions that lingered in people's minds, was a reminder of how widely the poison had spread.

Gerrard saw that realization grow, read it in her more sober demeanor when the others moved on. When the last lantern was up and the gardeners left them, he pulled out his watch. "There's half an hour left before luncheon."

All those who'd passed had gone to the lake; they could glimpse it glinting through the trees.

"I could use a moment away from the throng." Pocketing his watch, he glanced around. "In all these acres, there must be somewhere else we can go for a moment of rustic peace?"

She smiled. "There's a pond upstream. None of the others will have gone there—they always head for the summerhouse."

"I've a fondness for ponds." He waved her on.

She led him down a path lined with tall trees; within minutes they were out of sight and sound of the lake.

"You're doing very well."

She glanced at him, but said nothing. She was growing more comfortable, more consistently leaving her inner barriers down. More consistently and confidently being herself.

That was part of the reason he'd come, to simply be here if she'd needed help. But she'd weathered Cecily Hancock's malicious spite well; she hadn't needed him to intervene, yet he'd had to be there.

He glanced at her, very conscious of the other, more major part of his reason for remaining by her side.

She hadn't yet agreed to be his.

He'd thought that by now she would have, or at least would have given him some sign of acceptance, of intent. His strategy dictated he shouldn't pressure her. He'd weakened once; he remained determined not to do so again.

But . . .

He glanced briefly at her profile as she walked beside him. That night in the nursery . . . had he, perhaps, overplayed his hand? He looked ahead, matching his strides to her shorter ones. He'd been so utterly confident she would come to him; last night, even while he was painting, he'd broken off, again and again, to glance past the canvas at the door, and its knob.

Every little sound had had him focusing on that knob, waiting for it to turn. But it hadn't.

Had he read her wrongly?

Two seconds of remembering how she'd writhed under his hands, under his mouth, eliminated that as a possibility. Which meant that something—some thought, some consideration—was holding her back.

Causing her to hesitate, to rethink and assess.

He drew in a breath, felt a tightness reminiscent of desperation close about his chest. Nonsense—it could only be a temporary hesitation. If she needed reassurance, he was willing and able to give it; if it transpired he needed to adjust his approach, to modify his stance, his declared position, he was willing to do that, too.

Perhaps she simply needed a little encouragement?

Jacqueline kept her gaze on the trees ahead, on the path as she led him on, yet she was acutely aware of the glances he threw her, of the way his gaze lingered on her face.

As if he found her as puzzling as she found him. Just as she was so constantly aware of him, he, too, was absorbed with her; his attention, his focus on her, never really wavered.

The trees thinned; the path opened out into a clearing, dividing to encircle a deep pond fed by the stream that ultimately flowed on to fill the lake. The surface of the pond was still, reflecting the surrounding canopies and the sky. Rushes fringed the edge; waterlilies spread in patches, white and pink splotches floating on dark green leaves.

"We've circled around—the house isn't far." She indicated another path on the far side of the pond, then led the way to a large flat rock on which a stone bench sat, the perfect place to sit and look out over the pool, and reflect.

He paused beside the rock, looking at the other path, then back at the path they'd come down. "I see." Stepping onto the rock, he waited for her to sit and draw in her skirts, then sat beside her. He pointed across the pond to where in the middle distance water shimmered silver through the trees. "The lake, I take it?"

"Yes." She managed not to jump when he took her hand. Her nerves flickered, then pulled tight. She shifted to face him as he raised her hand to his lips, turned it and, catching her eye, holding her gaze, pressed an ardent kiss to her palm.

She felt the lingering caress to her toes, had to fight to quell a reactive shiver.

Before she was free of the effect, he shifted and reached for her face. His long fingers curled about her nape, his thumb cradling her jaw as he drew her to him.

Drew her lips to his, and kissed her.

Ardently.

Making no secret of his desire for her, or of what he wanted.

Richly textured, his tongue found hers and stroked, caressed, then commanded her response. Demanded it, drew her to him and into their play. Into a passionate exchange, an exploration of another degree, on yet another level of their evolving interaction, of their mutual desire.

Hot, increasingly urgent, hungry, yet contained.

Not restrained yet limited, delimited; there was no sense of being swept away, but of meeting him, matching him, of sharing control.

The kiss drew her in, lured her deeper. Quite how it happened she didn't know, yet when she managed to lift her head enough to draw in a shallow breath, she discovered he'd leaned back against the stone bench and she was leaning over him, his face clasped between her hands, her lips parted as she looked down into his eyes.

"Why?" She searched his eyes, glowing richly brown beneath the distracting fringe of his lashes. "You want so much from me, but why do you want me to decide?"

Beneath her, he stilled—a stillness that communicated the intent focus of his thoughts. Her question had caught him off balance; he was rapidly searching for an answer.

She resisted the urge to press, to reframe the question; it was clear enough and she knew he understood.

He moistened his lips. His gaze lowered to hers, then his hands firmed about her waist. He didn't lift her from him, but simply held her, then he raised his gaze to her eyes. "I told you—I want all, everything that's in you to give."

"What do you mean by that, and why do you want it?"

"Because . . . that's what desire is, between a man and a woman. A wanting."

"You told me yourself, intimated at least, that what you wanted from me was more. More than the usual, the norm." Whatever that might be. She waited. And sensed for the first time a degree of uncertainty, of, not confusion but wariness in him.

Why would he be wary of her?

When he said nothing, just ran his large, warm palms up and down her back, she arched her brows. "You're being very mysterious."

Something flared in his eyes. "There's nothing mysterious about *this.*"

He must at some point have lifted her; she was half sitting on his lap. She could feel his erection riding against her hip. The growl that had edged his voice, the strength in his hands, only emphasized the aura of danger, of being in the arms of a sexual predator.

Yet she felt no fear, not the slightest lick of trepidation. She looked down into his darkening eyes, and knew that no matter how blatantly he hungered for her, no matter how frankly he displayed his ardor, harming her, hurting her, either physically or emotionally, wasn't any part of his game.

Why she felt so safe, so secure, so *sure* when in his arms, she didn't know, couldn't explain.

She kept her eyes locked on his. "You haven't answered my question."

When his lips remained sealed, she reiterated, "Why do you want *more* from me? Why is it important I agree to that?"

He exhaled. His gaze dropped to her lips; his own remained set in a stubborn line.

She leaned closer, boldly skated her parted lips over his. "I'm seriously considering not making my decision until you answer my question."

She'd breathed the words over his lips; she felt his chest swell, knew she'd succeeded in twisting the rack. Two could play at ultimatums. Pressing closer, she kissed him, held his face between her hands, covered his lips with hers and challenged him to take . . .

The rustle of leaves was soft. She heard, but didn't react, too caught up in evoking his reaction, in the promise of his rapacious mouth.

A theatrical gasp had her jerking upright, turning to see—

One hand clamped over her lips, Eleanor stood at the edge of the clearing, eyes wide, locked on her.

Beside Eleanor stood Matthew Brisenden, an expression like a thundercloud darkening his face.

Jacqueline could happily have strangled them both.

Biting back an unladylike curse, she tensed to struggle from Gerrard's arms, to slide from his lap, but his hands firmed, and she obeyed the instruction.

Smoothly, unhurriedly, he lifted her and set her on her feet. Retaining one hand, he rose and stood beside her.

With unshakable savoir faire, he nodded to Eleanor and Matthew. "Miss Fritham. Mr. Brisenden. Have you been down by the lake?"

Gerrard kept his tone polite, faintly bored, as if he was discussing a stroll in the park. A kiss did not qualify as a major indiscretion; he refused to allow them to treat it as such.

Matthew glowered at him. Gerrard quashed the impulse to smile in return. He'd never expected to be thankful to see Brisenden's disapproving countenance, yet he was. Who knew what he might have revealed if Jacqueline had continued her persuasion?

A gong sounded, resonating through the trees.

"Ah—luncheon." Setting Jacqueline's hand on his sleeve, he raised his brows in polite query at Eleanor and Matthew, and waved to the path leading to the house. "Shall we?"

They had no option but to follow as he led Jacqueline up the path; Eleanor did so quite readily; Matthew would, Gerrard suspected, have preferred to call him out, but, still glowering darkly, tramped reluctantly behind them.

Eleanor, unsurprisingly, came up on his other side. Acknowledging her with the most distant of nods, he kept his attention on Jacqueline, instituting a conversation about the various trees they passed; there were times when his hobby was distinctly useful.

Jacqueline responded glibly; far from being embarrassed or trepidatious over being discovered indulging, he sensed she was irritated, sharply annoyed with her importunate friends.

The observation gave him heart; perhaps he'd achieved something today.

Something aside from having attracted Eleanor's attention in a way he'd up to now avoided.

He'd known his share of predatory females; Eleanor was definitely one. Now that she'd seen evidence of his interest in Jacqueline, specifically the nature of that interest, her blood was up. She thought he was interested in dalliance, and was about to offer her charms.

He was defensively aware of the speculative glances Eleanor threw him as they walked back to the terrace. She didn't attempt to join his and Jacqueline's conversation, but eyed him as if she was measuring him to the last inch, and deciding just how to harness him.

She was destined for disappointment, but what intrigued him more was that Jacqueline was aware of Eleanor's avid interest. He saw it, saw Jacqueline notice Eleanor's assessing looks, saw comprehension and more in Jacqueline's eyes.

But she didn't look at him. Didn't glance up to see if he'd noticed, or if he was responding. Not a hint of jealousy, or possessiveness, invested her demeanor, but she was watching, noting, nonetheless.

Was she so sure of him, of her hold on his senses?

Or did she truly not care?

The latter option bothered him more than he liked. Even more than her earlier question and her threat of waiting for him to answer before she declared herself his. That was definitely not part of his plan.

They were first to the terrace, but to his relief, the others came up in a laughing, chattering throng before they'd finished helping themselves to the cold meats and pastries set out on a table.

Barnaby was among those returning from the lake. Gerrard summoned him with a look; encouraging Jacqueline to draw the younger girls to their table, they endeavored to hold Eleanor at bay.

Temporarily defeated, she joined Jordan's circle, but she paid scant attention to her brother's discourse. Her eyes remained fixed on Gerrard, occasionally sliding to Barnaby, but returning, always, to Gerrard. Jordan's gaze also frequently came his way.

Inwardly, Gerrard swore and remained on guard.

Just as well; as they all left, going down the front steps in a gay, noisy group, exchanging promises and challenges for when they met again that evening, Eleanor maneuvered to come up beside him. He led Jacqueline to his curricle. His grays stamped, unimpressed by the high-pitched voices; a groom held on to their bits, reverently crooning.

Barnaby had gone to the other side of the curricle; it was just roomy enough to accommodate three.

Alongside, Jordan's curricle stood waiting with a pair of showy bays between the shafts.

"I wonder, Mr. Debbington . . ." Boldly, Eleanor gripped his arm, forcing him to halt and face her. She smiled. "I wonder if I might suggest Jacqueline and I swap places, at least until the turnoff to the manor." She let her gaze sweep his horses, then turned her eyes on him. "I've a great penchant for powerful beasts. I find them quite fascinating."

Gerrard resisted the urge to roll his eyes; even more smoothly than she, he replied, "I'm afraid that won't be possible. We've arranged to take an alternative route."

"Oh?" Eleanor's gaze and tone sharpened. "To where?"

In a different direction to the one she was heading in; beyond that, Gerrard had no clue. It hadn't occurred to him that she would so impertinently question him.

Before he could utter the annihilating setdown spontaneously forming on his tongue, Jacqueline's fingers tightened on his sleeve; leaning forward, she spoke across him. "Mr. Debbington expressed an interest in viewing the church at Trewithian. With luck, we'll just have time to head that way, then return to the Hall."

Eleanor deflated. "Oh. I see."

Jacqueline smiled lightly; reaching out, she lifted Eleanor's hand from Gerrard's other sleeve, squeezed it in farewell and released it. "We'll see you tonight."

Eleanor nodded, disappointed, but amiable enough. "Yes, of course."

Gerrard blinked, and hurriedly added an abbreviated farewell; Barnaby, already in the curricle, waved. With not the slightest sign she understood that she'd just been put in her place, Eleanor inclined her head, and turned away.

For one instant, Gerrard stared. Then he inwardly shook himself, turned and helped Jacqueline into his curricle, followed, gathered the reins, sat, and set his horses trotting.

"Phew!" Barnaby leaned back as the wheels rolled smoothly down the drive. "That was a near-run thing." He glanced at Jacqueline. "Quick thinking, too. You have my heartfelt gratitude for saving us, m'dear."

"Indeed." Gerrard glanced at Jacqueline, and caught her eyes; they were lightly dancing. "Should I really turn east?"

She looked at the gates, rapidly approaching. "I think we'd better. But it's a pleasant drive and not that much further. Especially with such"—she gestured to his grays—"*powerful beasts.*"

Gerrard laughed; so did Barnaby.

Her smile deepening, Jacqueline looked ahead.

Despite the roundabout route, they returned to Hellebore Hall in good time. Gerrard drove straight to the stables, then he, Jacqueline and Barnaby walked across the field toward the house. Pegasus watched over them; Jacqueline smiled as they passed the statue.

Over her head, Gerrard glanced at Barnaby. "Did you learn anything?"

Barnaby had intended subtly sounding out the younger generation over the source of the whispers. He'd questioned Lord Tregonning; thinking back, all his lordship could recall was that after he'd emerged from his grief over his wife's death, Sir Godfrey and Lord Fritham had both behaved as if everyone *knew* that Jacqueline had been responsible. Everyone had behaved in that way, avoiding speaking of the incident, and if they couldn't, referring to it as an accident. Lord Tregonning had accepted the unspoken verdict; his grief had left him unable to question it, and without detailed knowledge to challenge it.

Only later, when the pall of grief had fully lifted, had he come to find that unspoken verdict hard to swallow.

Barnaby had been hunting, bloodhoundlike trying to track the whispers to their source. Gerrard wasn't sure it would prove possible, but he was grateful Barnaby was so tirelessly investigating every possible avenue.

Hands in his pockets, Barnaby grimaced. "Only that the whispers have been spread over a long time—no one remembers from whom they first heard the suggestion that Jacqueline was responsible for her mother's death. The association with Thomas's death is an extension of that." After a moment, he went on, "Jordan and Eleanor are the most open in their support." He glanced at Jacqueline. "I gathered they've always been quick to take your part."

She shrugged. "We're next to siblings—they're my closest friends."

Barnaby nodded. "So we're no further ahead on that front, but the older generation might remember more. Until now, the younger ones haven't spent much time thinking of the deaths. They weren't that important to them."

Wise to his friend's phrasing, Gerrard asked, "What other snippets have you gleaned?"

Barnaby's grin flashed. "Not so much gleaned as thought through. I've been wrestling with the motive for Lady Tregonning's murder." He met Jacqueline's gaze. "At present, we don't have one, which is in large part the reason it was so easy to cast suspicion on you—you were the only one with any whiff of a cause, no matter how unlikely."

Looking ahead, he continued, "If we accept that the same person killed Thomas and Miribelle, and that the reason Thomas was killed was because he was about to become engaged to Jacqueline, then isn't it likely Miribelle was killed for a similar reason?"

"Such as?" Gerrard prompted.

"What if some gentleman had had his eye on Jacqueline all along, and had approached Miribelle to gain her support for his suit?"

Gerrard turned the notion over in his mind. "The relative timing's always bothered me, but that . . . it fits."

Barnaby nodded. "When Thomas disappeared, you"—with his head he indicated Jacqueline—"went into half-mourning. That stymied the killer for a while, but then, when you were accepting callers again, what more natural than that he should seek your mother's support?"

Jacqueline briefly glanced at Gerrard, then turned to Barnaby. "You're suggesting she refused her support, and because of that, he killed her?"

Barnaby pursed his lips, then shook his head. "I think it would have to be more than that—I think she must have flatly rejected the proposal, refused to countenance it, and said so. Declared she would forever oppose the match. *That,* I think, would have been enough to make someone who'd already committed murder to secure your hand resort to murder again."

Continuing toward the Garden of Hercules and the house, they reviewed old points from that new perspective.

"Murdering your mother meant you went into mourning for a year," Gerrard said, "but time passing doesn't seem to worry this villain."

Jacqueline nodded. "But now I'm out of mourning again, by a few months." They were still in the sunshine, yet she shivered.

He caught her hand, engulfed it in his, lightly squeezed. "No one's asked for your hand lately, have they?"

Without looking at him, she shook her head. "I'm sure Papa would have told me if they had. Other than Thomas, and that hadn't been done formally, no one has ever asked permission to marry me."

The Garden of Hercules loomed ahead. Shadows engulfed them as they descended toward the terrace. When they reached the steps, Gerrard stood back to let Jacqueline precede him, but as she took the first step, her hand still in his, he halted her and drew her to face him.

He met her eyes. "If any gentleman should ask for your hand, you will remember to mention it, won't you?"

She held his gaze, then glanced at Barnaby, before looking back at him. "If any gentleman should ask, you'll be one of the first to know." Turning, she started up the steps.

Releasing her hand, Gerrard followed, not at all sure how to interpret that. At face value? Or because, by then, she would be his?

13

It's one thing to have won over those who know me well," Jacqueline whispered to Gerrard as, her hand on his arm, they followed her father and Millicent up the front steps of Trewarren Hall. Dragging in a tight breath, she resisted the urge to clamp a gloved hand to her fluttering stomach and plastered a delighted smile on her lips. "Wider society is liable to be another matter entirely."

"Nonsense." He smiled at her. "Stop worrying. Just act as you feel you should." His gaze lingered on hers, then he murmured, "Listen to your heart."

Difficult when it was thudding. She drew in another breath, aware when his attention shifted to her breasts; she felt warmed by the fleeting touch of his gaze, oddly reassured.

She didn't need to ask if he would stay by her side; she knew he would. She didn't need to wonder if his attention would cause comment; in this setting, that was a given. Her mind was racing faster than a bolting pair; she felt starved of breath, yet exhilarated and excitedly expectant.

No wonder her head was spinning.

As they joined the receiving line, she tried not to dwell on the moment in the drawing room when Gerrard had entered in full evening dress. Barnaby had followed him in, but she hadn't even noticed him for some time. Gerrard in black and crisp white, with a silk waistcoat in subtle swirls of amber and brown, had captured her senses to the exclusion of all else.

The sharp contrast of the black and white emphasized the breadth of his shoulders, the lean, hard lines of his long frame and the austere, patriarchal planes of his face. The harnessed power she'd so often glimpsed in him was tonight on full show, the intensity that was an inherent part of him blatant and unrestrained. Sexuality shimmered, an invisible cloak about him; she could almost taste the raw power and his aggressive brand of passion.

Eleanor was going to swallow her tongue.

They'd never competed for the attention of any gentleman; she wasn't sure they'd be competing over Gerrard, yet Eleanor's attempt to monopolize him earlier that day had raised the unwelcome specter in her mind, one factor contributing to the manic frenzy of butterflies swarming in her stomach.

The man beside her—not the gentleman, but the man—was another.

She wasn't sure of him, either, not now she'd seen him in his true colors. Not now she was standing beside him, her gloved hand on his black sleeve, so very aware of his physical presence—and so very aware of her own.

Since the bronze sheath had been made, she'd gained several inches. One at least in height, which left the hem flirting about her ankles in a decidedly provocative fashion. That was the least of her worries. She'd also gained about her hips and breasts, of all places; if she drew in a large breath too quickly, she might be in serious trouble.

As she infused her smile with even greater brightness and curtsied to Lady Trewarren, she made a mental note to locate the withdrawing room before any disaster could occur, so she would know where to run when it did.

Rising from her curtsy, she saw an arrested look in Lady Trewarren's eyes, and only just suppressed the urge to glance down and check, but her ladyship's gaze rose smoothly to her face; her eyes lit with real warmth. They touched fingers and cheeks, then Gerrard led her on in Millicent's wake.

As predicted, her father's presence instantly created a stir; guests peered over heads and peeked around others to confirm that yes, Tregonning was there, in the flesh. She was grateful for the distraction he provided.

She was about to glance around when she met Gerrard's gaze, and realized he'd been watching her.

He leaned closer. "Relax." His hand closed over hers on his sleeve, a warm and reassuring clasp. "You look superb." His gaze lazily, and quite brazenly, drifted lower, over her breasts, and down. His lips quirked; fleetingly his eyes met hers again, then he looked ahead. "So nice to be proved right. That color is delectable on you."

Delectable? Was that why he'd looked, just for an instant in that fleeting glance, as if he'd like to . . .

She refused to let herself finish the thought; she had distractions enough as it was.

Gerrard knew his role; it was imperative Jacqueline didn't focus on the whispers, on how people viewed her. Didn't retreat. Her self-protective shields gave credence to the whispers, hiding what she truly was—a young lady patently incapable of murder.

He was there to distract her; he knew how to do it.

They moved into the throng filling the ballroom. Leaving directly challenging the whispers to Lord Tregonning and Millicent, supported by Barnaby and his deduced facts, they parted from the others; Lord Tregonning and Millicent went one way, Barnaby another. Gerrard turned his attention to keeping Jacqueline absorbed in the whirl of a major ball.

Lady Trewarren had handed all the unmarried young ladies dance cards; the old custom was useful in ensuring, as her ladyship had put it, "No disputes for me to settle."

"I'll take the first waltz," he murmured. "If you'd be so kind."

She glanced up, met his eyes, then inclined her head. "If you wish." Catching the tiny pencil attached to the card, she duly inscribed his name on the appropriate line.

"And the supper waltz, too."

She cast him a glance, but wrote that down, too.

"Jacqueline!" Giles Trewarren appeared out of the crowd. His face was alight with good cheer, and definite approval. "Excellent! I've caught you in time. I'd be honored if you would grant me the first country dance."

In less than a minute, they were surrounded by the unmarried gentlemen of the district, all eager to have their names on her card. Gerrard stood beside her, amused by the surprise he glimpsed in her eyes—she truly had no idea of the effect she, gowned as she was, had on impressionable males.

On less impressionable ones, too.

A certain possessiveness had crept into his manner; he knew it. He said little, but monitored the conversation, ready to step in and redirect it if need be. He didn't want anyone mentioning Thomas or her mother, and sobering her. Her eyes were alight; she was blossoming, just as he'd known she could.

Matthew Brisenden came up. He cast a dark glance Gerrard's way, but to Jacqueline his behavior was gentlemanly and deferential; inwardly Gerrard acknowledged it always was. The lad—he had difficulty thinking of Matthew as a peer—continued to act as if he'd elected himself Jacqueline's champion.

Gerrard quashed the impulse to point out, forcefully, that the position was already filled.

"My dear Miss Tregonning." A gentleman some years older than Gerrard, well built but tending portly, shouldered through the growing crowd to bow flourishingly before Jacqueline. "You outshine the moon tonight, my dear. Dare I hope to claim the supper waltz?"

Jacqueline smiled and gave the man her hand. Gerrard detected no change in her manner, but to his eyes, the fellow was an aging Romeo.

"Sir Vincent, I would indeed have been delighted, but I fear Mr. Debbington was before you."

Gerrard recognized the name and was instantly alert. This was the gentleman Millicent had said had his eye on Jacqueline.

Jacqueline glanced at him, then at Sir Vincent. "I don't believe you've met. May I introduce you?"

She did. Sir Vincent Perry eyed him measuringly, but returned his bow. "Debbington." Sir Vincent turned back to Jacqueline. "Then perhaps you would honor me with the dance after supper, Miss Tregonning?"

Consulting her card, she nodded and wrote in Sir Vincent's name. "Indeed, sir—the honor will be mine."

Other gentlemen came and went, joining their circle, securing a dance with Jacqueline, then moving on to meet with other young ladies, but Sir Vincent remained. Jacqueline responded readily to his sallies, but treated him as she did all the others; she did nothing to encourage him.

Gerrard was aware of the increasingly narrow-eyed glances Sir Vincent threw his way.

He ignored them, but kept a mental eye on Sir Vincent while over the heads he tracked the progress of the rest of their party. While crossing the room, Lord Tregonning had paused beside various groups to acknowledge the interest his presence evoked; his attitude, that of a gentleman expecting to be pleasantly entertained without any concern clouding his mind, caused those he spoke with, once he'd moved on, to look at Jacqueline—Gerrard hoped with new eyes.

His lordship had set a steady course for Sir Godfrey, eventually engaging the magistrate; Millicent and Barnaby had swept up in support. Gerrard knew their strategy. Lord Tregonning had introduced Barnaby and his findings, then left it to Barnaby to explain. Barnaby was still explaining. Sir Godfrey seemed to be making heavy weather of absorbing Barnaby's deductions.

Lord Tregonning excused himself and made his slow, regal way to the cardroom; there, he'd engage the older gentlemen like himself, expressing his shock at the discovery of Thomas's body and his views on the person responsible, slaying any thought that he entertained the notion that Jacqueline had been in any way involved.

Barnaby and Millicent remained talking, low-voiced and serious, with Sir Godfrey. Then Millicent looked up, clearly exasperated. She pointed to a door, linked her arm in Sir Godfrey's, and all but forcibly towed him off to the library, there, Gerrard guessed, to lecture him at length and make sure he understood the Tregonnings' stance. Barnaby followed, quietly determined. Gerrard had every confidence the pair would succeed in clarifying Sir Godfrey's mind.

"Ah, my dear Jacqueline."

Jordan Fritham's arrogant drawl recalled Gerrard to nearer events.

Jacqueline smiled and gave Jordan her hand. "Jordan. Where's Eleanor? I haven't sighted her yet."

"Oh, she's over there somewhere, busily filling up her dance card." With a nonchalant wave, Jordan dismissed his sister. "I thought I should come and do my part to fill yours." Assured, he glanced idly over the crowd. "The cotillion, I think, if you please?"

Gerrard tensed; Sir Vincent openly bristled. Jordan's attitude—tone, stance and clear assumption—was so ineffably superior it bordered on the rude. Yet Gerrard was prepared to wager the egotistical prick didn't even realize; he was considering ways to puncture Jordan's ego when Jacqueline spoke.

"I'm so sorry, Jordan, but you're too late." With a gentle smile, she held up her card. "My card's already full."

Stunned surprise filled Jordan's face; Gerrard had to fight to keep his lips straight, especially when his eyes met Sir Vincent's.

"Oh." Jordan blinked; he seemed to be having trouble assimilating the blindingly obvious—that Jacqueline was a popular young lady who didn't need his patronage to fill her evening with dance partners. He blinked again. "I see. Well, then, I'll . . . leave you to it."

With an abrupt bow, he swung around and walked away.

"Jacqueline, dear." They turned to see Millicent sweeping down on them, resplendent in lilac bombazine. She smiled at the circle of attentive males, then announced, "Lady Tannahay and the Entwhistles have arrived, my dear, and they'd very much like to speak with you. And Mr. Debbington, too, of course." She flashed a smile at the others. "I'm sure these gentlemen will excuse you."

They did, with swift bows and intrigued expressions.

Taking Jacqueline's hand, Gerrard laid it on his sleeve, covering it with his. He looked down at her, encouragement in his eyes. "Just be yourself—that's all you need to do. Don't be afraid to let what you feel show."

He felt her fingers quiver beneath his; she drew in a breath, and stiffened her spine. Her attention was already fixed on their destination, a corner of the room where Lady Tannahay stood beside an older gentleman, tall, imposing, but with bowed shoulders, a smaller, rotund lady by his side. The lady wore dark gray, her gown severely cut.

Jacqueline held her head high; Gerrard's whispered words echoed in her mind. What she felt for the Entwhistles, for Thomas . . . As they drew near, she concentrated on that, let her emotions well.

Gerrard halted before Sir Harvey and Madeline, Lady Entwhistle. Jacqueline's eyes locked with her ladyship's; she was distantly aware of Millicent introducing Gerrard to Sir Harvey, but Lady Entwhistle searched her eyes—in her ladyship's face she saw understanding, compassion, and the same sense of loss she herself still felt.

"My dear." With a wavering smile, Lady Entwhistle reached for her hands.

Jacqueline surrendered them readily, returning the light pressure of her ladyship's fingers.

"I know you share our loss, my dear—that you've grieved for Thomas as have we. He was a dear, dear boy and we miss him every day, but you . . ." Lady Entwhistle struggled to find a smile and squeezed Jacqueline's hands. "While finding his body is a shock, I hope you can now leave poor Thomas to rest, and go on with your life. We were very happy when he chose you, but we wouldn't wish his death to ruin your life. I had no idea until Elsie spoke with us that some had even considered . . . But with what I hear these gentlemen"—her ladyship's gaze shifted briefly to Gerrard and she smiled faintly—"have learned, the situation should be plain to all."

Lady Entwhistle drew in a steadying breath, and smiled more definitely at Jacqueline. Then she impulsively drew her closer and touched cheeks. "My dear," she murmured, "I do hope you'll put all this behind you and go on. I know Thomas would have wanted that."

Jacqueline drew back; ignoring the tears in her eyes, she smiled at Lady Entwhistle. "Thank you." Their gazes held. Nothing more needed to be said.

"Ahem." Sir Harvey cleared his throat. He nodded at Jacqueline. "Good to see you looking so well, m'dear." He looked at his wife. "I've just been talking to Debbington here."

Gerrard shook hands with Lady Entwhistle, then Sir Harvey continued, "He tells me his friend, Mr. Adair, can explain the details better—ah, here he is now."

Barnaby, whom Gerrard had beckoned to join them, came up and was introduced to the Entwhistles. Sir Harvey and Lady Entwhistle decided to retire to the library to hear all Barnaby could tell them.

With Gerrard, Jacqueline took her leave of them. As she turned back to the room, Elsie Tannahay caught her eye. "Come walk with me for a little, my dear. It'll save you from the overly interested, at least until the dancing starts."

Gerrard offered Lady Tannahay his arm; with a gracious smile, she took it. He offered his other arm to Jacqueline.

Millicent waved them on. "I'm off to talk to that reprobate Godfrey. I want to keep my eye on him."

They parted. As they strolled down the room, Lady Tannahay relentlessly claimed Jacqueline's attention, chatting about inconsequential matters; her position in local society ensured that no one attempted to interrupt, but everyone was watching.

Many had witnessed the scene earlier, and had understood the implications; they were now busily explaining to those who hadn't seen.

Lady Tannahay directed them onto the terrace; they admired the lights strung through the trees. On hearing it was in part Gerrard's work, Lady Tannahay complimented him on the effect. "Quite a magical creation."

Music drifted out from the ballroom, summoning the dancers. Accompanying them back inside, Lady Tannahay halted and smiled. "Well, we've done our part for the evening's entertainment—Gertie Trewarren should be thoroughly grateful. Now we can give ourselves over to amusement—enjoy the rest of your evening, my dears."

With a gracious nod, she moved away.

Roger Myles pushed through the crowd; grinning, he bowed before Jacqueline. "My dance, fairest one."

Jacqueline laughed, and gave him her hand.

Gerrard squeezed the hand that lay on his sleeve and leaned closer to whisper, "Come back to me here at the end of the dance."

She cast him a glance, but nodded. He let her go, and watched Roger gaily claim her attention.

Deciding such light relief was precisely what she needed—what would most effectively lighten her mood—he retreated to the side of the room. All was going as planned, and Lady Tannahay had turned up trumps for them. Noting the many ladies and gentlemen who glanced appraisingly at Jacqueline, he felt confident their strategy was working; after tonight, no one would credit any tale of Jacqueline being involved in Thomas's death.

Barnaby rolled up while the dancers were still whirling. "Sir Harvey's a shrewd one—he grasped all I had to say immediately. Like Jacqueline, they've already mourned Thomas. They have other children, and want to see this put to rest for everybody's sake. In terms of Jacqueline, they're definitely in our camp. They'll help in any way they can in learning who's behind all this."

Gerrard nodded, his gaze on Jacqueline twirling down the line of dancers.

Beside him, Barnaby surveyed the nondancers, most of whom were of the older generation. "I'd forgotten what it's like in the country—the discovery of Thomas's body is the main topic of conversation." He caught Gerrard's eye. "I'm going to circulate and see if, using my status as ignorant outsider, I can draw a bead on who's behind the whispers."

Gerrard looked back at the dancers. "Do you think there's any chance that way?"

"I don't know, but the more I run up against the effects, the more I realize the whispers have been both subtle and very pervasive. Whoever's behind it, they have access to a large number of ears."

With that, Barnaby drifted away. The music came to a triumphant end. Laughing, the dancers halted; the lines wavered, then broke up.

Gerrard saw Jacqueline turn and look for him. Roger Myles went up in his estimation by taking her hand and leading her back. Yet she'd barely regained his side before the musicians struck up again, and Giles Trewarren appeared to claim her hand.

He suffered through that dance, but the next was the first waltz. Meeting Jacqueline and Giles at the edge of the dance floor, he claimed Jacqueline's hand, chatted with Giles until the first squeak of the violins, then swept Jacqueline into his arms and onto the floor the instant the first familiar strains floated out.

And felt something within him ease as the sensation of having her in his arms once more permeated his brain.

They'd revolved four times before Jacqueline caught her breath. Aware of the subtle shushing of the heavy silk of her gown against his coat, the brush of his long legs against her skirts, the intensity of his gaze as he looked down at her, his attention so focused . . . she dragged in a huge breath, and gave thanks when his eyes remained locked on her face. "You're very good at this."

She didn't just mean waltzing.

The faint curve of his long lips suggested he understood, but all he said in reply was, "So are you."

Looking up, he whirled them through the turn at the end of the long ballroom, his hand at her back, heated and heavy, drawing her fractionally closer; when they were precessing once more up the room, he looked down at her once more. "You can't have been dancing all that much in recent times."

"No." Eyes locked with his, she thought back. "Not since before Thomas died."

And even then, never with a partner so assured, so confident in his ability that she could without a qualm resign all control and simply enjoy the moment, the movement, the indefinable energy of the dance.

"I like to waltz." The admission slipped past her lips without thought.

His eyes held hers. "So do I."

They'd reached the other end of the ballroom, and an even tighter turn. While others paused and adjusted, he drew her closer still; she sensed his strength as he swept them through and past.

Exhilaration flared, and raced down her veins.

Desire followed, tempted forth by the look in his eyes, by the knowledge of what he was thinking, seeing in his painter's mind. She studied his eyes, felt herself falling, drowning in the glowing brown—drawn into his vision, under his spell.

A sensual shiver slithered down her spine; her skin flushed, then prickled. Her nipples furled tight. Heat, not from without but within, burgeoned.

"If I dance much more with you, I'll need to carry a fan."

He laughed; his eyes glinted. Yet his gaze, to her unscreened, remained passionate and intense, not an invitation but a promise.

A clear statement that between them there would be much more.

She wondered why she wasn't frightened, not even trepidatious. With him, such emotions had never surfaced, never colored her view of him, or, more particularly, of them. Of what might be . . . would be, once she agreed.

The music was building to its culmination; his expression grew more serious, his gaze more intense. "Have you decided yet?"

The words were deep, even, but not demanding. More enticing.

"No." She held his gaze as they swirled to a halt. "But I will. Soon."

He studied her eyes for an instant longer, then nodded.

Gerrard forced himself to release her. He led her to the side of the dance floor. Her next partner promptly appeared to claim her hand.

He relinquished it with growing reluctance; he would much rather have led her to some private place where he could spend the next hours convincing her to be his. Instead, mindful of his other goal, he danced with other young ladies, and made sure they had as many of the facts regarding Thomas's death as he felt they could keep straight.

Then Eleanor came up and made it clear she'd saved a dance for him. Ordinarily, he'd have ruthlessly quashed such presumption, but against the risk of giving her even such minor encouragement, he decided to accept, to see, in light of Jacqueline's appearance tonight, what Eleanor now thought of the circumstances of Thomas's death.

But Eleanor wasn't interested in dead bodies. "It's all so long ago. I'm sure Jacqueline, poor dear, wouldn't have had anything to do with it, so there's really nothing more to be said, is there?" Eyes bright, fixed on his face, she tried to press closer, but he prevented it. Lowering her lids, she favored him with a sultry glance. "I'd much rather talk of more *exciting* things."

He managed to steer her through the rest of the dance without uttering a blistering setdown; releasing her with relief, he wondered that Lady Fritham—who seemed the usual sort of matron—wasn't aware of Eleanor's startlingly improper propensities. He might be doing his best to seduce Jacqueline, yet he was quite certain she was a virgin. Eleanor . . . there was something in her eyes, a blatantness in her behavior, that left him perfectly certain she'd already dipped her toes in Eros's fountain.

Normally, he wouldn't hold that against any lady—he wasn't such a hypocrite—yet in Eleanor's salacity there was something that repulsed him, and not just him but Barnaby, too. They hadn't discussed it; they didn't need to—one shared glance was enough. Neither felt at all attracted to Eleanor, which was mildly strange as she was physically very beautiful.

The thought had him searching the throng for Jacqueline; the sight of her heading his way lightened his mood, even if she was on Matthew Brisenden's arm. But Matthew was another who failed to see any attraction in Eleanor; unlike Gerrard, he was open in his disapproval, and Eleanor took herself off.

Gerrard swallowed an impulse to thank Matthew, but did catch his eye and incline his head in approval. The evening continued; increasingly guests moved back and forth between the terrace and the gardens, and the ballroom and reception rooms beyond.

At last, the opening bars of the supper waltz sounded; with real relief—real if hopeful anticipation—Gerrard drew Jacqueline into his arms and started them revolving down the floor.

But she smiled, sighed softly and relaxed in his hold, and he didn't have the heart to press her. Instead, he held her close, but gently, and let his eyes, and their silence, speak.

Between them, that level of communication was growing, deepening, becoming more acute. By the end of the dance, although they'd uttered not a word, Jacqueline's mind was filled once more with thoughts of him, of them, and the decision she'd yet to make.

Of the sign she'd yet to see, the answer she'd yet to receive.

Gerrard led her into the supper room. Once they'd filled their plates, they were joined at a table by Giles, Cedric, Clara and Mary, and later Barnaby. The conversation was light and breezy; acutely aware of Gerrard beside her, her mind drifted to more private concerns.

They were talking of returning to the ballroom when Eleanor and Jordan came up. Jacqueline smiled at them as they stopped beside the table; it occurred to her that in the past, at any ball, they would have been together. Not tonight; indeed, no longer. Her absence from ballrooms and parties in recent years had meant she and her childhood friends had grown apart. While not so evident when they visited at the Hall, in situations such as this, their divergence was clear.

Jordan and Eleanor joined in the chatter. Then Jordan caught her eye; moving around the table, he came to stand beside her.

Leaning down, he spoke confidentially. "I say, there's a host of whispers doing the rounds over who killed Thomas—it seems at long last they've realized it wasn't you. Of course, there's still a lot of ill-informed nonsense about over your mother's death, but you may be sure I set all those I heard speculating straight."

Looking down his nose, he straightened. "Nothing more than gossipmongering, of course—we all know there's nothing to it."

Her gaze on his face, Jacqueline was excruciatingly aware of the sudden silence about her. Although Jordan had lowered his voice, he'd still been heard.

She didn't know how to respond.

Her heart grew colder, and sank. A familiar vise tightened about her chest. Briefly she inclined her head. "Thank you."

Turning back, she forced herself to glance at the others' faces. And saw uncertainty, puzzlement, frowns that could have denoted any number of reactions.

The lighthearted atmosphere was gone.

Smiling easily, Gerrard pushed back his chair and stood; Barnaby did the same.

"It's time to get back to the dancing." Gerrard closed his hand over hers, gently squeezed. "The musicians are tuning their instruments."

The others followed his lead with alacrity. Talk erupted on all sides. It sounded false to Jacqueline's ears, but at least it dispersed the awful silence.

On Gerrard's arm she walked back into the ballroom. Sir Vincent appeared through the regathering crowd. He smiled delightedly, and swept her a bow in his usual florid fashion. "My dance, I believe, my dear."

She conjured a smile and gave him her hand, noting that he hadn't acknowledged Gerrard, as if he wasn't there. She glanced back as Sir Vincent led her to the floor. Gerrard stood where she'd left him, his gaze locked on her.

Then Eleanor appeared by his side, and slid her hand onto his arm. Gerrard turned to her.

Jacqueline looked ahead, amazed at the sharp feeling that lanced through her, at the sudden tensing of her muscles, and the way her mind reacted. She'd expected Jordan's words and their effect to claim her, to drag her thoughts back into the uncertain vortex of how people saw her. Instead, while her dance with Sir Vincent did indeed pass in a blur, her mind was wholly occupied with Gerrard.

With what Eleanor was almost certainly doing, and how Gerrard might respond.

With the possibilities, with her decision. With how much of a sign she was waiting for . . . and why.

The music finally ceased, and she blinked back to her surroundings. They were close by the terrace doors at the other end of the ballroom from where she'd left Gerrard.

"My dear, I wonder if I can claim a few minutes of your time? The next dance won't start immediately." Sir Vincent gestured to the doors to the terrace. "Perhaps we could stroll in the quiet—others are out there, too. Quite proper, I assure you."

The ballroom was stuffy; a few minutes of cooler, fresher air sounded like an excellent idea. She needed to clear her head so she could think. "That would be pleasant."

On Sir Vincent's arm, she walked onto the terrace. They paused to look around. Lantern-lit paths led away, crossing the lawn to meander between the shrubs and trees. A light breeze blew, shifting leaves; the lanterns winked and blinked, myriad tiny stars.

Numerous other couples were strolling the terrace and lawns. Glancing along the terrace, Jacqueline felt her heart stop. Gerrard stood at the other end with Eleanor on his arm; from her gestures, she was attempting to entice him down the steps and into the gardens.

She and Sir Vincent stood in relative shadow, but Gerrard and Eleanor were lit by light pouring from the ballroom. Eleanor was facing their way, but hadn't seen them. Her attention was focused on Gerrard, on . . . seducing him. Apparently he didn't wish to be seduced; curtly he shook his head and shifted back, attempting to disengage, but Eleanor brazenly clung to his arm—even more brazenly raised her face to his and tried to step closer still.

Gerrard stepped back. With icy precision, he lifted Eleanor's arm from his and dropped it.

He said something; Eleanor's face fell.

Turning brusquely on his heel, Gerrard strode back into the ballroom.

"Ahem!" Sir Vincent cleared his throat, and belatedly turned Jacqueline in the opposite direction. "I have to say I did wonder—never do know with London bloods—but Debbington seems to have his head on straight. I wouldn't mention it normally—I know she's a friend of yours—but Miss Fritham needs to take a powder."

They'd reached the end of the terrace. Sir Vincent looked around the corner of the building. "Ah, yes. Just the ticket."

He continued around the corner. Absorbed with what she'd just witnessed, with her relief that Gerrard had dismissed Eleanor so ruthlessly even though he hadn't known she'd been watching—and with the kernel of competitive pleasure that was blossoming, nurtured by the thought that he preferred her less fashionable beauty to Eleanor's—it was an instant or two before Jacqueline registered the oddity in Sir Vincent's words.

Just the ticket for what?

By then he'd led her, unresisting, to the French doors leading into one of the minor parlors. The doors were unlocked; Sir Vincent opened them wide, and guided her in with his usual courtly suavity . . . She went, uncertain, suspicions flickering.

The moon shed enough light to see by, but Sir Vincent immediately lit a lamp; the glow spread, easing Jacqueline's nascent fears. This, after all, was Sir Vincent; despite his occasionally too particular attentions, he'd always accepted her rebuffs like a gentleman. As he turned to face her, his expression resolute, she wondered if perhaps he was going to warn her about the whispers; mentally composing a suitable reply, she waited for him to speak.

To her shock, he threw himself on his knees before her.

"My dear!" He grasped her hands.

Stunned, she tugged, but he tightened his grip.

"No, no—don't fear! You must excuse my intemperate passion, sweet Jacqueline, but I can no longer stand by without speaking."

"Sir Vincent! Do, please, get up, sir." Jacqueline cast a glance at the side terrace. Just because no one had been there didn't mean no one would venture that way, and the lamplight was now shining out through the open doors, a beacon.

Instead of rising, Sir Vincent lifted her hands to his lips and pressed impassioned kisses to her knuckles. "*Dear* Jacqueline, you must listen. I cannot allow you to become infatuated with these London bloods—they're not worthy of you."

"What?" She stared down at him. "Sir—"

"I've waited too long not to speak. At first I thought you too young." Still holding her hands, Sir Vincent clambered to his feet. "Then came that unfortunate incident with Entwhistle, and then, just as you were going about once more, Miribelle died, and I had to wait again. But I'll wait no more. My dear, I desire to make you my wife."

Jacqueline felt her jaw drop. "Ah . . ." She struggled to marshal her wits. "Sir Vincent, I never dreamed—"

"No? Well, why would you? I'm a man of the world, while you've little experience of it, but I've had my eye on you for some time—your mama was aware of my intentions. She insisted I wait before addressing you, and so I have." Stepping nearer, he tightened his grip on her hands and looked down at her. "So, my dear, what do you say?"

Jacqueline dragged in a huge breath. "Sir Vincent, you do me a very great honor, but I cannot agree to marry you."

Sir Vincent blinked.

She tugged, but he still wouldn't release her. He seemed to be thinking—too hard for her liking. "Sir Vincent—"

"No, no—I see my mistake. No doubt you have dreams of being swept away by passion." He pulled her to him.

Her heart rising to her throat, she braced her arms and fought to keep her distance. "Sir Vincent—*no!*"

"No need to fear, my dear." Inexorably, he drew her closer. "Just a kiss to show you—"

"*Perry.*"

The single word fell with the crushing weight of a millstone. Clipped, hard, resonant with menace, it shook Sir Vincent to his toes. Jacqueline felt alarm ripple through him; she wasn't surprised.

Gerrard stepped into the room. "I suggest you unhand Miss Tregonning immediately."

There was a quality to his voice that rendered any "or" redundant.

Sir Vincent blinked, then, as if abruptly coming to his senses, released Jacqueline.

She stepped away, closer to Gerrard, flexing her crushed fingers.

Gerrard turned to her. "Did he hurt you?"

She looked into his face; a primitive promise of immediate retribution was etched in the austere lines, unforgivingly hard in the moonlight. She was relieved she could say, "No. I was just . . . surprised."

Looking back at Sir Vincent, she saw he was blushing furiously, shaken, embarrassed and, she suspected, annoyed. "Sir Vincent, I repeat, you do me a great honor, but I have no wish to become your wife. Please believe that nothing, no persuasions of any kind, will change my mind." She thought, but there was nothing more she wished to add. Inclining her head, she held out her hand to Gerrard. "Mr. Debbington?"

His eyes were locked on Sir Vincent. She waited; transparently reluctant to leave without administering appropriate justice, Gerrard eventually glanced at her face, then, accepting her unspoken edict, he took her hand, set it on his sleeve and, turning, escorted her from the room.

Behind them, she heard Sir Vincent exhale.

Barnaby was waiting by the door. He fell back to let them through.

Once on the terrace, Jacqueline dragged in a huge breath. Beneath her fingertips, the steel that had infused Gerrard's muscles remained. They walked slowly back to the main terrace. Barnaby strolled beside them.

She sighed, trying to lighten the atmosphere. "Thank you. I had no idea he was intending that."

"Hmm." Barnaby was frowning. "I did hear correctly, didn't I? He just asked for your hand?"

Jacqueline recalled their hypothesis; she shivered. "Yes. But I can't believe—" She broke off, remembering.

Gerrard's gaze raked her face. "What?"

Could it be? "He said he'd told Mama. And he was at the house the last time Thomas called. Sir Vincent left before Thomas . . . or at least we thought he did."

Barnaby shook his head. "Your stablemen said he didn't come to fetch his horse until later—they assumed he'd been down to the cove."

They reached the main terrace and paused.

"Down to the cove, or in the Garden of Hercules." Gerrard glanced at Barnaby, then at her. "Who's to say?"

14

Once back in the ballroom, Barnaby drifted off, intent on pursuing his inquiries. The musicians had finished for the evening, yet the gathering was still in full swing.

Gerrard strolled with Jacqueline, but when they stopped to chat with a group of fellow guests, he realized that wasn't the sort of diversion she needed. The incident with Sir Vincent and its implications were distracting her, making her appear distant and enigmatic once more.

He inwardly cursed. Except for that moment at supper, she'd done a superb job of being open, transparently herself, of keeping her inner shields down; she didn't need, courtesy of Sir Vincent, to tarnish her success this late in the night.

Grasping the first opportunity, he excused them and drew her back toward the terrace. "Come and walk in the gardens." Glancing down, he met her eyes. "We should at least assess our creation."

She smiled; he saw the relief in her eyes and was content.

It was mild outside; many couples and small groups were still ambling about the paths. They descended the terrace steps and followed a path across the lawn, then took the extension that led to the pond.

Lanterns bobbed overhead. Jacqueline looked about, studying the pattern of glimmering lights through the screening trees. "It's the best I've ever seen it."

Turning, she smiled up at him.

Lowering his arm, he closed his hand about hers, and they walked on.

The lanterns stopped halfway to the pond; they'd deliberately not lit the clearing, not wanting to encourage anyone to venture close to the deep water at night. Reaching the shadows, they exchanged a glance, then walked on.

The night embraced them. Their eyes adjusted to the silvery moonlight. The moon wasn't full, but had waxed enough to cast a faint glow over the landscape. When they strolled into the clearing, the pond was a dark, still expanse; the distant trickle of the stream running down to the lake was the only sound to punctuate the silence.

The tall trees ringing the clearing, the shrubs and bushes beneath, created the illusion of a private room in the night, one that was exclusively theirs.

Jacqueline went to the stone bench. Gerrard handed her to it and watched her sit on one end. He didn't trust himself to sit beside her. Pensive, she looked across the pool; he studied her face, then sank his hands in his pockets and remained where he was, like her, staring at the black water.

The coolness of the stone and the pleasant night soothed Jacqueline's chaotic thoughts. She'd been keyed up when they'd first entered the ballroom; since then, her feelings had veered through growing confidence in the way she appeared, and the way others responded to her, through the meeting with the Entwhistles, the moment of shared sorrow, then the laying of that sorrow to rest. Lady Entwhistle's encouragement to look forward and live echoed in her mind. After that . . .

She'd enjoyed the dancing more than previously. The waltzes with Gerrard had been highlights, moments that had reflected the undercurrent of thoughts, of emotions, that had run beneath all else through the evening. Indeed, through the last days.

Jordan's comment, albeit intended in support, had disrupted that pleasant and positive train, throwing her back into the uncertainties of before, but then Eleanor's behavior with Gerrard, and his reaction, had brought her obsession with him racing back.

As for Sir Vincent . . .

She sighed softly, then drew in a deep breath, enjoying the sweet, night-stock-scented air. Could Barnaby and Gerrard be right? Was Sir Vincent more sinister than he seemed?

She'd known him for most of her life. She honestly couldn't see him as Thomas's, let alone her mother's, killer, yet she hadn't thought of him as a would-be suitor, either. And there was no gainsaying that the killer was someone she knew.

She paused, feeling her thoughts settle like leaves stirred by a wind; despite the distractions, one subject remained uppermost, most compelling, continually capturing her.

Gerrard.

Only a few minutes had passed since she'd sat, yet all else had slid away, unimportant in a relative sense given he was standing beside her.

Given she'd yet to make her decision, and the declaration he'd demanded.

Facets of the evening resurfaced, flotsam thrown up by her questing mind. When Sir Vincent had hauled her into his arms, when he'd pressed passionate kisses to her fingers, she'd felt nothing beyond mild revulsion. All Gerrard had to do was look at her, meet her eyes and *think*—and she responded, ardently, instinctively.

The relief she'd felt when she'd heard his voice, and known he was there, glowed again. How was it that in a mere week he'd come to represent safety and, more, protection, to her?

Was that the sign she was looking for?

And what of his turning from Eleanor? Her friend was unquestionably more beautiful than she, and certainly more experienced in the ways of attracting men, yet he hadn't shown the slightest interest in any of Eleanor's offers, even when those offers had grown blatant.

Another sign? Perhaps.

Gerrard watched her thoughts flow over her face. Some he identified, others . . .

He wanted to know them all, wanted to understand, to know and so be certain of her, in every way. He was a long way from achieving that goal. Standing beside her in the night, he still had no idea if she would agree to be his—his as he wished, as he'd—increasingly he suspected unwisely—stipulated.

It was time, perhaps, to alter his stance.

Looking down, he shifted, drawing her attention. "When we were here this afternoon, you asked me why I wanted a clear decision from you." He met her eyes, shadowed and unreadable, and selected his words with care. "In the sense of sweeping you off your feet, of sweeping you into bed on a tide of desire—primarily mine . . . I don't want to seduce you."

She blinked.

Ruthlessly, his voice hardening, he went on, "I know I could. That all I need do is push a little harder. But—" He broke off. Looking away, he drew in a breath. "I don't want just that from you." He looked back and caught her gaze. "I don't want what's between you and me to be like that."

A seduction driven solely by me.

He didn't say the words, but Jacqueline heard them. The light was sufficient to limn the planes of his face, to confirm that there was absolutely no lightness in his expression.

From the first, he'd made it clear he couldn't promise anything, yet equally clearly, he viewed her as different. As something more than just another conquest, one, she knew, of many.

Couldn't promise, not *wouldn't.*

Looking into his face, hard, unyielding, yet in the soft moonlight perhaps more revealing, she sensed for the first time that behind his confident, polished exterior lay someone with uncertainties, just like her.

What if he couldn't promise because he didn't know? Because, no more than she, was he sure of what lay between them, how it might evolve, what it might become?

What if she refused and walked away, and neither of them ever learned the answer?

She rose, all hesitation falling from her. Leaving the bench, she closed the distance between them; he watched her every step of the way, desire and more naked in his face. Drawing his hands from his pockets, he reached for her as she neared. She stopped only when her breasts brushed his chest.

For one moment, feeling his hands slide about her waist, feeling their heat seep through the shot silk, she gazed into his eyes . . . and found not the slightest change in his stance—no intention to seize, no inclination to step back. He was waiting on her—on her decision.

He wanted her to want him as much as he wanted her.

Reaching up, she set her hands on either side of the strong column of his throat, then eased them back; stretching up, she drew his head down to hers, drew his lips to hers, and fused them.

She kissed him, not the other way around, and he let her. Let her press her lips to his, slide her tongue between, and take, let her set the pace, let her explore. He followed, accepting all she gave, offering all she wished in return, angling his head to deepen the kiss when she urged him to do so.

It was intoxicating. To have him at her command, to have him metaphorically by her side, hand in hand, going forward into what she sensed was a landscape as mysterious to him as it was to her.

Desire, warm and now familiar, rose and washed through them, heating, welling, buoying.

Beckoning.

He dragged his lips from hers. In the shadowy light, from beneath heavy lids, their eyes met, held. One of his hands had risen to cradle her head; his other arm held her locked against him. "I don't know where this will lead, but I want to follow the path on, with you."

With the fingers of one hand, she traced his cheek. "Yes. I need to know, too."

She sensed more than saw, felt more than knew, that he was no more in control of "this" than she; he wasn't dictating it, wasn't directing it—he was searching for answers, driven to it, as was she.

What lay between them was a shimmering temptation, both physical and emotional; he, too, could see it, and its promise, but the whole was as unknown to him as it was to her, and, it seemed, as confusing. With this, he was no more experienced than she.

That was a potent attraction—to know that if, in going forward, she was taking a risk, then so was he.

His breath brushed her lips and she yearned, not just for a kiss but for so much more.

"You know my decision." Her voice was low, sultry, the siren he and only he evoked coloring her tone. Boldly, she pressed closer, lifting her lips to breathe over his, "Convince me I'm doing the right thing."

She sensed his impulse to devour, to take her lips in a scorching kiss, but he refrained. Instead, from under heavy lids his eyes held hers as he raised his hands, sliding his palms slowly up until through the heavy silk he cupped her breasts, then his thumbs cruised knowingly over her ruched nipples.

Sensation lanced through her; a silent, tight gasp escaped her. For an instant he played, then he bent his head, took her lips in a long, lingering kiss, while with his hands, his strong fingers, he pandered to her senses.

When he eventually lifted his head, her body was aflame, senses stretched tight, nerves coiled, wanting. Waiting.

"I will." In the weak light, she saw him grimace. "But not here, not now."

She blinked, and returned to the real world, to the clearing by the pond. He was right. Not here, not now; they had to go back, had to thank their hosts and bid them farewell, had to journey home in the carriage with the others.

Her lips throbbed, her flesh ached with sweet anticipation. With one finger, she caressed the corner of his lips, then stepped back, out of his arms. "Later."

She turned; together, they walked back to the house.

The waiting was going to kill him.

Gerrard paced before the windows in his bedchamber, and willed the minutes to tick by. He and Jacqueline had returned to the ballroom, behaved with appropriate decorum, then endured the journey home, opposite each other in the blessedly dark carriage.

Lord Tregonning had parted from them in the front hall. Jacqueline and her aunt had climbed the stairs. With Barnaby, he'd followed; turning his feet toward his room, not hers, had required considerable willpower.

He'd dismissed Compton; the house was slowly settling into slumber. Once it did, he would go to Jacqueline's room.

How long should he give her to get rid of her maid?

Muttering a curse, he swung around and stalked to the hearth, staring—glaring—at the mantelpiece clock. Not enough minutes had elapsed.

He should have told her not to undress; a great deal of his fondness for her bronze silk sheath revolved about a vision of peeling it from her. He'd give a great deal for the chance to transform that vision to reality, but he doubted she'd realize—

Soft footsteps reached him. An instant later, his door opened and Jacqueline whisked in. She saw him, shut the door, and then she was flying to him—bronze silk sheath and all.

He caught her.

Wrapped his arms about her, lifted her from her feet, straight into an incendiary kiss.

Twining her arms about his neck, she parted her lips, surrendered her mouth, and sank against him.

Without thought, his hands shifted, one splaying over her back below her waist, angling her hips to his, the other rising to cradle her head, holding her steady so he could ravish her mouth.

No holds barred.

He'd warned her; now he could only marvel at his presentiment, for not in his wildest dreams had he imagined it would be like this.

Instant conflagration.

An immediate need more primitive than anything he'd felt before. He was a polished sophisticate, an experienced lover, yet she never seemed to connect with that side of him. The touch of her lips, the feel of her in his arms, the tentative, innocent trace of her fingers along his cheek, and he was lost to all sanity, all gentlemanly dictates, overwhelmed by an urgent and elemental need to make her his.

Totally.

As he'd warned her, completely. In every way.

Jacqueline sensed the passion in him, felt the barriers dissolve before its power, tasted its rapacious urgency on his lips, felt it in the flagrant possessiveness of his hands, of his body hard against hers. The thought of quailing before that elemental hunger never entered her head; instead she exulted, gloried in the knowledge she could provoke him to that, that she, her body, could be desired like that.

Beyond reason. Beyond all words. Where they now were, only deeds spoke, only actions had meaning.

His tongue dueled with hers; surrendering wholly to the moment, she clung to the passionately intense exchange. His hands shifted over her back, a minute later, her bodice loosened. He'd undone her laces.

She drew in a tight breath as his lips left hers; he skated kisses along her jaw, then nudged her head up, pressing a kiss to the sensitive spot beneath her ear before dipping his head to follow the long line of her throat to where her pulse thudded at its base. He laved, lightly sucked; heat rose through her and spread in a melting wave beneath her skin.

Flushed, nerves coiling, she felt his palm slide, gliding over bronze silk to cup her breast. His fingers closed, kneaded provocatively, then rose to trace the neckline of her gown; she felt immeasurably grateful when he eased the heavy fabric down. Once clear of her breasts, the silk fell in folds to her waist. The tiny, off-the-shoulder sleeves were mere scraps of gauze across her upper arms. Sliding her arms free, she draped them over his shoulders.

She could barely breathe as he lifted his head and looked down. Her breasts were still screened by her filmy chemise, gathered just above them.

One tug, and the drawstring was loose. He hooked his fingers in the fine fabric and drew it down.

The room was filled with shadows; he hadn't lit any lamps. Yet there was light enough for her to see his face, to make out his expression as he blatantly surveyed what he'd uncovered.

He'd seen her breasts before; she reminded herself of that, yet as, starved of breath, lungs inexorably tightening, she studied his face, she saw something far more potent than approval in the harsh planes.

Absorbed, he lifted his hand and cupped one breast, weighing, assessing, then he closed his fingers and kneaded knowingly, tightening her nerves still further, then he eased his hold and stroked, not simply observing but learning, as if the texture of her skin was a wonder, as if her tightly ruched nipple was worthy of his most earnest attention.

Enthrallment. She sensed, all but saw him fall under the spell—her spell, the fascination her body, it seemed, held for him.

She stood unmoving, watching him examine her; a feminine power unlike anything she'd known slowly welled within her.

A true sign, surely, that this was right. That this, here and now, was the way forward for her.

The joy swelling inside her assured her it was so.

He bent his head and pressed a hot kiss to the upper curve of one breast, and any thought of retreating, of doing anything other than going forward with abandon, slid from her mind. His lips trailed over her now aching and swollen flesh, then he took one tightly furled nipple into his mouth, and lightly suckled.

Then he feasted.

She gasped, let her head fall back. Eyes closed, she clutched his shoulders, then eased her fingers and slid them to his nape, then into the silky wonder of his hair, gripping tight as he pleasured her, thankful that his hard hand pressed to the small of her back held her to him, and kept her upright.

Her senses started to spin; a kaleidoscope of sensations buffeted her mind. There was an emotion in his touch that went far beyond wonder, that was more intense, more ruthless than simple desire, a driven passion that, innocent though she was, she recognized as possessiveness.

Gerrard was far beyond thinking, far beyond disguising his feelings or his intentions in any way. She'd come to him; that was all the agreement he needed, all the encouragement his demons required to slip their leashes and devour.

The only thing holding him back from summarily stripping her, laying her across the bed and sheathing himself in her softness, claiming her, branding her in the most primitive way, was a strange and novel merging of the two halves of himself. The demons of his maleness, driven by passion and rampant possessiveness, were, with her, being directed, not overridden but working in concert with the more subtle demands of his aesthetic mind.

She and only she had ever called to both.

While his demons still slavered, turning his every touch demanding, making every action a command, a seizing, no request, he was conscious of a greater fascination, of a need to go slowly, to fully explore and experience every shred of passion, of desire, that her surrendering herself to him evoked.

To wallow in the physical, to gorge on the sensual.

He was more educated than most in both.

When he finally drew his lips from her breasts, she was heated, urgent, driven beyond innocence to make demands of her own. He acquiesced to her tugs, shrugging out of his coat, first one arm, then the other, letting the garment fall unheeded to the floor. His waistcoat followed.

Her hands spread across his chest and he caught his breath, not so much from the touch itself as the urgency behind it. At the feminine desire he glimpsed in her eyes as she reached for his cravat, at the focus in her face as with unsteady hands she unraveled the folds, then drew the long linen strip away.

She dropped it, and stepped closer, eliminating the last inches between them as she boldly tugged his shirt from his waistband and slid her hands, small palms to bare skin, beneath. She touched, then spread her fingers and ran her hands up his chest. Leaning in, she lifted her face; he lowered his head and their lips met. Melded.

For long moments, he savored the taste of her escalating passion, sweet, hot, and exquisitely female. An evocative blend of the innocent and sultry, of untried promise.

His. All his.

His to educate, to awaken.

To possess.

Closing his arms around her, he slid one hand down, over her back, down over the curve of her hips, pushing the stiff silk lower, then down.

The gown fell to the floor, sinking about her feet, taking her chemise with it. He closed one hand over her bottom, drew her fully to him, and settled to explore. To arouse her still further. Tracing, fondling, he felt the dew of desire rise to his touch as he caressed the sweet curves, felt her initial shock drown beneath a wave of heated yearning.

Of increasingly urgent desire.

He held her to their kiss, plundered her mouth as he wished, ravaged her senses, and filled his with her surrender. A surrender even more explicit as she sank against him, and let him have his way.

Naked in his arms, held against a body whose very hardness embodied a potent promise, Jacqueline gave up trying to steady her giddy senses and let them whirl. Swirl. They danced to his touch, to the increasingly intimate caresses he pressed on her, to his flagrant exploration, to the rapacious need that, held back, was still evident in every driven touch.

A threat, but not one of pain. Of possession, yes, but she now longed for that.

Ached for it, with an urgency that only grew more desperate, that had her sinking her nails into his sides to urge him on.

The wash of night air over her bare skin left her acutely aware of her naked state; she should have felt unsteady, uncertain—in reality, she didn't care; she reveled in the shocking intimacy. Reservation, shyness, modesty, all were fading at the edges of her mind, overwhelmed by a need more physical than she'd foreseen, and more powerful. She wanted it all—she wanted him naked, too, wanted to feel his skin against hers, needed that degree of physical closeness, needed him entwined with her.

Now.

Sinking against him, blatantly offering her mouth, yielding to his every demand, she ran her hands, splayed until then across the wide muscles of his chest, down. Over the hot, flickering skin of his abdomen, over the shifting muscles, down to the waistband of his trousers. And further. Briefly, boldly, she traced his erection.

And felt his breath hitch. Sensed the sudden hiatus in his concentration. Pressing her palm to him, she stroked, lingeringly, then reached for the buttons at his waist.

Gerrard dragged in a breath and caught her hands. Shackled them with his, drew them away, to her sides, then released them, broke their kiss and swept her into his arms. He would have preferred to go more slowly, but she'd already rushed ahead.

He carried her the few paces to the bed, knelt and laid her across it. Pausing, he looked down at her, his mind almost blank as he drank in the sight of her naked and heated, flushed with desire and wanting him so blatantly, then he grabbed his shirt, drew it over his head and tossed it away, then stepped back and swiftly dealt with the buttons at his waist.

Toeing off his shoes, he stripped off his trousers and stockings; naked, he joined her, coming down beside her propped on one elbow the better to view her. Intent, she reached for him; again he caught her hands. Once again shackled them, this time in one of his; shifting, he drew her hands up and anchored them over her head.

She was breathing rapidly. She frowned, opened her lips—

"Don't speak." Briefly, he met her eyes, noted how wide they were. "I know what you need."

And what I need.

He looked down, let his gaze roam her body, laid out beside him, a delectable gift. The truth crashed through him. Just taking would be so much less than either of them needed, or deserved.

Her breasts remained swollen, firm and tight, the ruched peaks begging for his attention. Her skin, pearly white, almost glowed, satin soft, tinted with desire, an elementally evocative sight. The indentation of her waist, the teardrop-shaped hollow of her navel, tempted him to taste. Below her taut belly, tawny curls covered her mons, veiling the delicate flesh between her thighs.

His gaze swept her thighs, sweetly curving to her knees, followed the subtle swell of her calf to where it tapered to narrow ankles and finely boned feet. To him that long line held the essence of femininity; he reached out and with his palm sculpted. Caressed.

She shivered.

Returning his gaze to her face, he watched her response as he ran his hand slowly upward, from her calf to her knee, up her thigh and over the swell of her hip, sliding through the curve at her waist to glide over her breast to her shoulder, and on, up the exposed inner face of her arm to her fingers. Then he reversed direction, sweeping his fingers around her face, then spreading his palm, now tingling and hot, below her throat, then running it more heavily, more possessively, down, over the center of her body, fingers trailing over her breasts, over her navel to splay over her taut stomach.

He pressed gently, watched her eyes darken. Watched her moisten her lower lip, lush and swollen from his kisses. He shifted over her, leaning down to take her lips, her mouth, again, while his hand slid lower, fingers spearing slowly through her curls to the slick, swollen flesh beyond.

Her body lifted; her thighs parted, wordlessly inviting. He slid one knee between hers, cupped her fully, evocatively stroked, then slowly pressed two fingers deep, into the lush haven of her body.

She moaned, the sound trapped between their lips. He filled her welcoming mouth with his tongue while between her thighs he pressed her on.

Until she writhed beneath him. Until, heated and desperate, she tugged against his hold, but still he held her hands. He shuddered when, denied them, she used her body, all womanly curves and sweet, flushed skin, to caress his, and tempt him.

He held against her for long moments, then released her hands and moved over her. She spread her hands over his shoulders, his chest, greedily grasping. Inciting.

Yet still he held back. Spreading her thighs, he settled between, yet he wanted, and knew he could have, even more from her.

She broke from the kiss, pressing her head back, panting, gasping. Before she could catch her wits, he lowered his mouth to her breast.

Jacqueline jerked; the voracious contact sent sensation lancing through her, sharp, passion sweet. She closed her eyes and almost sobbed. The wet heat of his mouth expertly applied to the excruciatingly sensitive peaks of her breasts was both pleasure and punishment. She wanted more, so much more—she knew exactly what.

She could feel the heavy weight of his erection riding against her inner thigh. She wanted that inside her, wanted him to take her.

Wanted to be conscious when he did.

His hand hard about one breast, he suckled more powerfully, simultaneously probed deeply between her thighs.

"Gerrard!" She arched against him, her fingers sinking into his shoulders, the hardness of his body, the crisp, crinkly hairs adorning it, meeting her softer, smoother skin, evocatively abrading it.

Poised above her, his weight, the inherent power in his naked, muscled frame, the ruthlessly intimate touch of his hands and mouth, sent realization of her vulnerability crashing through her. Dragging in a breath, she cracked open her lids. Caught the gleam of his eyes beneath his lashes as he lifted his head.

"Now—*please!* Take me now."

The plea fell from her lips on a breathless gasp.

His face was an angular mask, graven with desire; he searched her eyes, then his gaze lowered. He bent his head once more, shifting back to place a hot, openmouthed kiss on her navel.

She sobbed, clutching desperately at his shoulders, thinking he meant to caress her as he had before.

Instead, he rose above her, adjusting his hips between her widespread thighs; bracing his weight on his arms, he nudged into her.

She caught her breath, felt her eyes grow wide as the broad head of his erection pressed into her. Stretching her.

She blinked. For one instant wondered how . . .

He flexed his spine and thrust in. Inexorably. Hard, deep.

Pain lanced through her—she gasped, closed her eyes. Her breath tangled in her throat; her lungs seized.

He held still, embedded within her, impossibly large, impossibly heavy. Totally alien.

So male.

Amazingly welcome . . .

The sharp sting was already fading; her body eased beneath his. She straightened her fingers from where they'd curled about his biceps, nails biting in in instinctive reaction.

He bent his head, found her lips, breathed over them, "There's no rush," then covered them.

But he was wrong. She returned his kiss with all the hunger she possessed. Sliding her hands around his body, she clung; the instant he started to move within her, she knew what she wanted, what she needed. Now.

He thrust deep, and she was with him, rising beneath him, urging him on. Wanting more. Wanting all; if she had to give him that, she wanted the same in return.

And she got it.

He groaned and surrendered, and all control evaporated. They broke from the kiss, gasping, breaths mingling. The dance caught them, trapped them. Heat poured through them, rushed down their veins, pulsed between them. His body moved over hers, into hers, repetitively stroking inside and out; hers seemed to know the rhythm—she moved with him, against him, without conscious thought.

The tempo steadily escalated, a pagan crescendo of motion and searing heat. A constant striving to a fiery climax that for long desperate moments seemed out of reach.

And then they were there.

In the eye of desire's storm, surrounded by passion's whirlwind, by flames that left them gasping, nerves coiling, tightening as sensation spiraled and coalesced.

From beneath heavy lids, their gazes met, locked; every nerve she possessed was alive, exquisitely abraded as he drove deeply, powerfully into her, as he moved against her and her body responded, ardent and abandoned.

Beneath him, she rode each thrust, each forceful penetration. Desperately clinging.

Then she broke apart.

She cried out, felt perception shatter as her nerves unraveled and her body melted. In one clear instant, she saw him above her, his expression blank as passion claimed him, too, as with her body she claimed his, as with his he'd claimed hers.

Then completion swept her, caught her, buoyed her on, into a golden sea. Satiation swamped her; she felt warmth deep within her as with a groan he joined her, then collapsed across her. She drifted on the waves, his weight surrounding her, holding her, securing her.

In the last instant before she sank into pleasured oblivion, she turned her head and brushed her lips to his temple. "Thank you."

Into those simple words she let all she felt flow, then surrendered to the tide and let ecstasy claim her.

*T*hank you.

Her words and the emotions carried in them echoed through Gerrard's brain; he returned to the living slowly, savoring them, feeling them sink to his soul, the headiest, most contentment-making balm he'd ever known.

His strategy had worked; the waiting had been worth it. She'd come to him, and now she was his.

Disengaging, he lifted from her, then slumped beside her. He studied her face; he couldn't truly see but she seemed sunk in bliss. After a moment, he lay back, and gently, carefully, eased her over, into his arms. She came, not quite awake, turning to him, one arm sliding across his waist, her head pillowed on his chest.

He was accustomed to the moment, to the warmth of a boneless female draped over him, yet this time was different, acutely so. He was more aware of her, of her skin, her limbs, of the soft cloud of her hair, the gentle huff of her breathing. Of her weight, her warmth—of all she meant to him—as if through the act of joining they'd created a linkage that ran deeper, and was more tightly meshed, than the norm.

Closing his eyes, he considered that. Wondered if perhaps that was what happened when a man found his mate.

His lips lazily, openly arrogantly, curved. He replayed her words again . . .

He stilled; his lips straightened. *Thank you?*

He kept his eyes closed, but his mind raced. Why had she thanked him? It was she who'd given herself to him, not the other way around. She who'd accepted him as her lover and husband-elect—shouldn't he be thanking her?

Abruptly he recalled his earlier errors in assuming how she would think or react. If she'd had the temerity, and the audacity, to judge his ability as a portraitist, there was no telling what tack her mind might take.

He replayed her "thank you" again; a disquieting thought took hold. *Surely* she knew he intended marrying her—that he saw her coming to his bed as agreeing to their marriage?

Even as his mind posed the question, he knew the answer—it was perfectly possible she didn't.

His direction was crystal clear to *him.* He couldn't recall when he'd decided, but he'd embraced the path to marriage with absolute commitment regardless of his until recently deeply entrenched antipathy.

Nothing about him had changed; he'd simply seen an undeniable light. His reservations over engaging with love still existed, but were of insufficient weight to turn him from his path, to diminish in any way the compulsion that now drove him.

However, his conversion to the ranks of the matrimonially minded hadn't come about through any action of Jacqueline's. His antennae were well honed, well educated in detecting husband-hunting young ladies; he'd detected no sign of such intent in her. Her fascination with him, and with what had grown between them, was innocent and true, free of any calculation.

That was one of the reasons she'd captured him.

Well and good, yet although she was twenty-three, even by the standards of a county backwater she was socially inexperienced. Thanks to Thomas's and her mother's deaths, she hadn't been exposed to wider society, much less the circles in which he moved. She didn't appreciate how, in such circles, things were done, how matters were arranged.

She didn't know the ways.

And with her only close contemporary being Eleanor Fritham . . .

His lips set. Hardly surprising if Jacqueline hadn't, yet, understood his tack.

The pleasure thrumming through his veins was slowly fading; sleep beckoned, but his mind ranged on—to what now loomed as his next step.

If she wasn't yet thinking of marriage, then it clearly behooved him to steer her mind in that direction *before* he specifically stated his objective. He knew women, at least in general; they preferred to think they made their own decisions in such matters. Jacqueline, he felt sure, would have the same prejudice, so he'd introduce the subject and let her decide—let her see the light as he had—before uttering the formal words and offering for her hand.

The one question remaining was how. His mind circled the problem; sleep fogged his thoughts and drew them down.

One conclusion shone through the veils of slumber.

He had experience aplenty in discouraging young ladies, and none whatever in persuading them to the altar.

Jacqueline's senses drifted hazily, swirling through mists of pleasure, gradually focusing on the here and now, on her body, on what it felt.

On the hands that so slowly, so skillfully caressed, on the lips that touched her shoulder, lingered, then disappeared.

On the phantom lover who in the dark of the night stirred her to life. Lured her to join him.

She was lying on her side, almost on her stomach; lifting lids languid and heavy, she looked, but even her night-adjusted eyes couldn't see.

It was the dark depths of the night. The moon had set; there was no light to guide her.

Only sensation. Only the hard, hot reality of the man beside her.

And the desire that flared between them.

She turned to him, into his arms. Reached for him.

Found heavy muscle and bone, and, as one blind, traced. Saw through her fingertips, through the palms she smoothed over his upper arms as he loomed over her in the dark, over his broad shoulders as he surrounded her with his strength.

He was anonymous, and so was she, sundered from their identities by the absolute dark, and so free to allow their desires full rein, to give and take as they would, without restraint.

Tactile sensation was their only communion, that and the incoherent sounds of passion. Neither spoke; for her part, she had no need for words. With sight denied her, her other senses expanded, until every caress, every trailing brush of fingers held her complete and unwavering attention. Effortlessly.

He took her further than before, higher, deeper into the realms of physical desire and sensual need. She heard her own gasps echo in the dark, heard the harried sound of her breathing.

She was acutely aware of how her body responded to each explicit caress, to the increasingly intimate knowing. She was aware of how she surrendered herself utterly, to him, to his passion.

He knew the boundaries well; although he pushed her to them, again and again he drew her back. In between, he let her explore, let her learn of him; he allowed her to pleasure him, guided her, taught her the ways.

Eventually, when she was giddy with need and both their skins were slick with desire, he pressed her back into the bed, spread her thighs wide and settled between. And joined them.

And it was different than before, with not even an echo of pain to dim the pleasure. With their skins so alive, their tactile senses so heightened, their passions already so inflamed, the fires roared, and the conflagration consumed them, yet still they clung, breaths mingling as they reached for the peak—and found ecstasy.

It shattered them, flung them far, left them to burn in glory among the stars, until, uncounted heartbeats later, they drifted back to the world, to the rumpled bed, to the sanctuary of each other's arms. And slept.

15

Gerrard awoke, then mentally cursed, lifted his head and squinted across the room. The clock stated it was nearly six o'clock. Too late to . . .

Swallowing a resigned sigh, he raised a hand to Jacqueline's shoulder and gently shook. "Wake up, sweetheart. You have to get back to your room before the maids are about."

She roused slowly, dreamily, then opened her eyes and blinked up at him. Then she smiled, a cat drunk on cream; before he could restrain her, she stretched against him, angling up to press her lips to his.

With predictable results.

He inwardly groaned, but couldn't resist the sweetness, the simple unalloyed delight. But when she drew back on a happy sigh, he gritted his teeth and set her from him. "We have to get you back. Now."

She grumbled, but he held firm; bundling her from the bed, he scrambled into his clothes, then went to lace her gown.

Still floating on the aftermath of pleasure, Jacqueline leaned back against him, thrilled to be able to so brazenly claim the hardness of his body, and its heat. Tilting her head back, she caught his eyes, lifted her lips.

He hesitated, but then obliged . . . she inwardly exulted; he couldn't resist, it seemed.

Just as well; after all she'd experienced last night, she feared she was addicted—it would be comforting if he was, too.

The kiss ended and he lifted his head, but only partially. His lips brushed her temple; she sighed and looked forward, relaxed and nearly boneless against him.

"What was your 'thank you' for?" His words, soft and deep, floated past her ear. "Just so I know."

Her smile grew, softened. "For so unstintingly and devotedly showing me so much that I'd wanted to know."

He straightened, steadying her on her feet; she felt him tightening her laces. "Are you grateful enough to bestow a reward?"

He liked claiming rewards, but . . . "Assuredly your efforts deserve one, but . . ." He finished tying her laces. His hands fell away and she turned to face him. "What more could I possibly give that you would want?"

Her gaze reached his face. To her surprise, his expression was unreadable; there was no teasing glint in his eyes.

He held her gaze for a moment, then murmured, "I'll think of something. But now"—taking her arm, he turned her to the door—"let's get you safely to your room."

Gerrard escorted her all the way. They could hear the distant sounds of the household stirring belowstairs, but no staff had yet ventured to the upper floors. At her door, they parted with one last, passionate kiss, then he swiftly retraced his route through the still quiet corridors.

As he'd suspected, she wasn't thinking of marriage. Regardless, she was going to have to start, and soon. He might not have any experience in influencing females in such a direction, yet how hard could it be to turn an unmarried twenty-three-year-old, gently reared lady's mind to matrimony?

In her room, Jacqueline stripped off her gown—again—then slumped into bed, and instantly fell asleep.

She woke late. As she hurried through her morning ablutions, it wasn't the events of the night that claimed her mind, but rather their consequences.

Given the intimacies they'd shared, how should she behave toward Gerrard? Prior to him, she'd done nothing more than kiss a man. Now . . .

She had no idea; regardless, five minutes later, in a gown of sprig muslin becomingly flounced, she glided into the breakfast parlor.

Seated at his usual place at the table, Gerrard looked up and met her eyes. His expression remained mild, yet his eyes held memories that sent a pleasurable shiver down her spine.

He inclined his head. "Good morning."

Surreptitiously, she cleared her throat. "Good morning."

Dragging her eyes from him, she nodded to Barnaby, who returned her greeting with a guileless smile. After helping herself to sustenance, she returned to the table and sat. Millicent poured tea for her; Mitchel passed the cup. Jacqueline took it, sipped, and gathered her wits. So far, so good.

Millicent launched into a review of their various successes at the ball. "I'm still not sure Godfrey has correctly grasped the *wider* implications." She, Gerrard and Barnaby filled the minutes trading observations.

"I warn you," Millicent said, setting down her napkin, "we'll have a small army of callers this afternoon. They'll all want to learn more—it would be helpful if you gentlemen could be present to assist."

"Yes, of course," Barnaby said.

Gerrard's agreement came more slowly. With a glance at Jacqueline, he pushed back his chair. "If I'm to spend the afternoon in the drawing room, I must get some painting done. If you'll excuse me?"

Millicent waved a gracious dismissal. Stifling a twinge of regret, Jacqueline smiled and let him go.

If he was going to spend the morning painting . . . She turned to Millicent. "I need to check through the linen closets. If you have no special need of me, I'll do that this morning."

Millicent agreed. Her aunt engaged Barnaby in a discussion of mutual acquaintances in Bath.

Mitchel Cunningham rose as she did, and accompanied her to the door. "I gather," he said, "that last night was enjoyable?"

Mitchel occasionally attended such events, but not always; he hadn't attended last night. She smiled. "It was, more so than I'd expected."

He hesitated, then asked, "The Entwhistles were there?"

"Yes." She met his eyes. "It was a relief to be able to speak with them. They're as determined as we are to find poor Thomas's killer."

Mitchel studied her; he appeared perplexed. "I see."

A frown in his eyes, he bowed and they parted.

Wondering—for quite the first time—how Mitchel viewed her, Jacqueline headed for Mrs. Carpenter's room.

After conferring with the housekeeper, she summoned the appropriate maids and went to attend to the mundane chore of assessing the sheets and towels. That done, she extended her purview to include all the napery.

She was running her eye over a linen tablecloth when the clocks struck twelve, and she realized with some surprise that Eleanor hadn't turned up for one of their customary walks in the gardens. She couldn't recall the last local ball she'd attended after which Eleanor hadn't appeared the following morning to review, often in salacious vein, the highlights of the previous night.

Uttering a mental thank-you to fate, Jacqueline owned to significant relief. She had no wish to listen to a diatribe against Gerrard for refusing Eleanor's advances. And while she might privately preen at having captured his attentions herself, she saw no reason to let Eleanor know she had succeeded where Eleanor had failed.

That would not be nice. It also struck her as potentially unwise. Eleanor could be vindictive when thwarted. Although she'd never been the target of Eleanor's ire, she was relieved not to have their long friendship put to that particular test.

Lunch came, and went, with no sign of Gerrard.

As Millicent had predicted, when the clocks struck three, the callers descended. A veritable horde, they filled the drawing room and overflowed onto the terrace.

Barnaby had joined them just before the rush to glibly lend his aid. Scanning the heads, he paused beside Jacqueline. "I'll go and fetch Gerrard. I think he's actually painting, which means he'll have no notion of the time."

After last night, she was much more confident of playing her part in their plan; she hesitated, conscious of a wish to have Gerrard by her side, yet also reluctant to interfere with his crucial work on her portrait. "If he's absorbed"—she looked up at Barnaby—"perhaps we should leave him to paint in peace. I'm sure I'll be able to manage—and you'll be here, too."

Barnaby met her eyes, then smiled. "I doubt Gerrard would agree. With a choice between being by your side in such a situation, and painting your portrait undisturbed in the attic, I suspect he'll toss his brushes aside without a thought." His smile deepened. "I'll slip up and remind him—aside from all else, he'll have my head if I don't."

Jacqueline watched him ease his way through the crowd. Eyes narrowing, she wondered how much he'd guessed.

Wondered if his words were true. He knew Gerrard rather well, after all.

"Where's Mr. Adair off to?"

Jacqueline swung to face Eleanor. She'd arrived with her mother, sullen and sulking, presumably over Gerrard, who, of course, wasn't present to squirm over her mope. "He'll return in a moment—he's gone to fetch Mr. Debbington from the nursery."

Eyes on the doorway through which Barnaby had gone, Eleanor tilted her head. "Is he painting, then? Mr. Debbington?"

"Yes. He's commenced the portrait."

"Have you seen it?" Eleanor turned to study her face.

"No—he doesn't show his work until it's completed, even to the subject."

"How . . . arrogant." Eleanor's eyes narrowed; she glanced again at the doorway. "He refused point-blank to dally with me in the gardens last night—he was quite curt about it, too. Indeed, I'm starting to wonder about Mr. Debbington—about whether he's a trifle queer."

"Oh?" Jacqueline heard the defensive note in her voice; she fought to convert it to simple curiosity. "Queer in what way?"

"Well, you know what they say about artists." Eleanor lowered her voice. "Perhaps he's one of those who prefer boys rather than women."

Jacqueline was thankful Eleanor was still looking at the doorway, and so missed her slack jaw. Words of denial leapt to her tongue; she swallowed them just in time. "Ah . . . surely not."

How could she defend Gerrard over such a charge—how could she explain how she knew?

Another thought struck. Was this how rumors, damaging whispers without any foundation, started? Just a spiteful, speculative comment, and . . .

She glanced around, confirming no one else stood close enough to have heard.

Lady Tannahay caught her eye and beckoned.

"Come." Jacqueline wound her arm in Eleanor's, determined to distract her from her latest tack. "Lady Tannahay wishes to speak with us."

Ruthlessly, she drew Eleanor with her, away from other, less well informed minds.

Through the open nursery window, Gerrard had heard the chatter of many voices drifting up from the terrace. He'd glanced at the small clock Compton had placed on the scarred mantelpiece, sighed and set aside his brushes, then headed downstairs to change his shirt.

He was striding down the corridor to the gallery when Barnaby appeared, heading his way. "How is it?" he asked.

"Interesting." Halting, Barnaby waited until he joined him. "They're all eager to hear more. From the prevailing attitude, I'd say we're well on the way to ensuring no one suspects Jacqueline of any involvement in Thomas's murder."

Turning to walk beside him, Barnaby went on, "As for her mother's death, some of the ladies are indeed wondering whether that, too, is a conclusion that needs revisiting."

Gerrard glanced at him. "Have any of them broached the subject?"

"No. It's more a case of them suddenly being struck by the possibility, but as yet no one is game to openly question the accepted truth."

Gerrard looked ahead. "So we still need the portrait."

"Indubitably. The portrait will give them precisely the right opportunity to voice their wonderings aloud." Reaching the stairs, they went quickly down. "And that," Barnaby declared, "is the opening we need."

They stepped off the stairs, both concealing their resolution behind the affable masks they used to charm. With assured ease, they strolled into the drawing room; exchanging a glance, they parted.

Gerrard saw Jacqueline speaking with Lady Tannahay, Eleanor beside her. Both were facing away; neither had seen him. Deeming Jacqueline for the moment safe, he paused to chat to the numerous other ladies keen to pass the time—to politely inquire about his family, his stay in the area, but most importantly to learn all he knew of Thomas Entwhistle's death.

Barnaby was similarly engaged on the opposite side of the room. Seated on the central chaise, Millicent held court. The entire gathering, including those who'd stepped out onto the terrace to admire the view—and stare at the cypresses in the Garden of Hades—exuded a significantly different tone to that which had held sway when they'd first set foot in Lady Trewarren's ballroom. Eyes had been opened, perceptions turned around. Barnaby was right; over the matter of Thomas's death, they'd succeeded in lifting suspicion from Jacqueline.

Buoyed, Gerrard smiled; reassured, increasingly relaxed, he circled the room to join Jacqueline.

She looked up when he halted beside her, and smiled. Warmth leapt to her eyes and set them glowing; her lips softened. "Hello."

He met her eyes, inclined his head.

A heartbeat passed, then she blinked, recollected herself and faced forward. "Lady Tannahay has been asking after you—after the portrait."

"Indeed." Her lips curving, her eyes twinkling, Lady Tannahay extended her hand.

Gerrard took it and bowed. He answered her ladyship's queries readily, and was rewarded with her suggestion that he take the two young ladies for a stroll on the terrace. They parted from her ladyship with a bow and curtsies. Gerrard drew Jacqueline closer, his hand at the back of her waist as he turned her toward the French doors.

She looked up at him, that same open, transparently trusting expression softening her countenance; he felt as if he was literally basking in the glow, then he looked past her, to Eleanor Fritham.

Eleanor's expression had blanked; she looked from him to Jacqueline, then, eyes narrowing, glanced once more at him before turning her attention, now acute and frankly chilly, to Jacqueline. "I *thought—*"

"Ladies." He spoke over Eleanor, drowning her words, deflecting their edge. Smiling charmingly, he took Jacqueline's arm. "Shall we stroll?"

Smiling in return, Jacqueline nodded, then looked at Eleanor.

Over Jacqueline's head, he met Eleanor's eyes.

She'd heard the warning in his tone, read the same message in his eyes. She hesitated, then nodded, thin-lipped. "By all means—let's walk on the terrace."

He didn't like her tone, and even less the impression that she was planning to pay him back for his rejection of her—and his preference for Jacqueline.

But by the time they'd gained the terrace, Eleanor had reverted to her customary friendliness, at least toward Jacqueline. Toward him, she remained watchful and sharp-eyed. Like a stalking cat.

Jacqueline was lighthearted, relaxed, her gaze warming whenever it rested on him. He was certain she wasn't aware of it, or of how easily Eleanor at least was reading her reaction and, he would swear, interpreting it correctly. Jacqueline's innate openness left her blind to Eleanor's two faces.

He was alert, on guard, but they moved through the ladies gathered on the terrace, chatting here and there, and nothing happened. He'd started to relax again when abruptly Eleanor halted and, smiling, turned to Jacqueline.

"Let's go down and stroll through the Garden of Night." They were standing before the main garden stairs. Eleanor spread her arms, attracting the attention of other ladies nearby. "It's a lovely afternoon, and I'm sure Mr. Debbington would like to view the garden with a guide who knows it well." She focused on Jacqueline. "You haven't taken him through it, have you?"

He glanced at Jacqueline; her expression had grown stony, rigid—distant. Her inner shields had sprung up.

"No." The word was flat, expressionless.

Her fingers had tightened on his arm.

Eleanor shook her head, smiling in fond exasperation. "I don't know why you won't walk there anymore—your mama's been gone for over a year. You'll have to venture in there again sometime."

With a bold, brazen smile, Eleanor reached to take his arm.

Jacqueline caught her wrist.

Eleanor jerked, taken aback. Her eyes widened.

Releasing Eleanor, Jacqueline drew a deep breath. Gerrard glanced at her, concerned, and saw her walls come down, saw her deliberately lower them, leaving her emotions exposed, letting what she felt—all she felt—show.

"I will walk there again—someday. But in case you've forgotten, my mother didn't *go*—someone flung her to her death, into the Garden of Night. And that someone wasn't me. Mama died down there, alone. I won't walk there again until we learn who her killer was, until he's been exposed, and has paid for what he did. Then, yes, I'll walk again in the Garden of Night, and perhaps show Mr. Debbington its treasures. Until then . . . I fear you'll have to excuse me."

Her voice had gained strength with every word. Her last sentence was a regal declaration. With a cold nod to Eleanor, Jacqueline turned away. He turned, too, retaking her hand and placing it on his sleeve.

She glanced up at him, determination and resolution clear in her face. "I believe we've strolled long enough out here."

"Indeed." He glanced over the heads, into the drawing room. "Tea has been served. We should go in."

She nodded. Head high, she didn't look back as he steered her over the threshold. About to follow, he glanced back, noting the barely suppressed surprise—and the welling approval—in the eyes of the ladies who'd overheard the exchange. Noted, too, the stunned, utterly dumbfounded look on Eleanor Fritham's face.

He guided Jacqueline to a quiet spot a little way from the central chaise. Leaving her for a moment, he fetched her a cup of tea. Handing it to her, he smiled—not his charming smile but a private, totally sincere expression. "Bravo!" He kept his voice low as he turned to stand beside her, facing the room. "That was very well done."

She sipped, then set her cup on the saucer. "Do you think so?"

She didn't look up, but glanced at the guests—at the ripple of conversation that was spreading from the French doors through the room.

"I would describe it as a command performance, except it wasn't a performance. You spoke the truth, from the heart—everyone who heard realized how hard that was to do."

He looked down, caught her gaze as she glanced up. "No matter how annoying Eleanor might be, in this case, she set the stage for you perfectly—and you had the courage to seize the moment and play the most difficult role."

Jacqueline studied his eyes, drank in the undisguised, patently sincere admiration she read in them. Felt her heart lift. "I thought you said it wasn't a performance?"

"It wasn't." His eyes remained steady on hers. "The role you had to play was you."

•　　•　　•

He understood her so well. Far better than any other ever had. Jacqueline had no idea what she'd done to deserve such a boon from fate, but she wasn't about to refuse it.

Wasn't about to waste one precious minute she might spend in his arms.

That night, she waited until Holly left her room, counted to twenty, then rose from her dressing stool, tightened her robe's sash, and all but flew from the room.

To his. To him.

To the pleasure she knew she would find there, and to learn more, to delve deeper into the mysterious realm that had opened between them.

Of that, she wanted to know a great deal more.

On swift, slippered feet, she sped through the gallery. Remembering the fraught scene of the afternoon—the scene she'd not simply suffered through, as until now had been her habit, but had grasped and turned to her advantage, all because Gerrard had shown her the need to be herself, and had convinced her she had the strength to do it, to play that most difficult of roles—she glanced out of the windows, down at the terrace, at the glimmer of marble that was the steps leading down, at the dark conglomeration of canopies that marked the Garden of Night, rustling in the breeze.

Frowning, she slowed, then stopped and stepped to the window. She looked to left and right, confirming that there was no breeze. Not even the tips of the tall, feathery herbs in the Garden of Vesta were stirring.

She looked again at the bushes surrounding the upper entrance to the Garden of Night. They'd definitely moved, but now were as still as the rest of the gardens. She pulled a face. "One of the kitchen cats—must be."

Turning, she continued along the gallery, her attention reverting to her goal.

See? I told you! She's off to his room—the *trollop*."

"Keep your voice down."

A long moment passed. Cloaked in the heavy shadows of the entrance to the Garden of Night, the first speaker stirred, and glanced, sharply, at the other. "Did you know he's started her portrait?"

The other shrugged and made no reply.

"I tell you, it's *serious*! You should hear what the old biddies are saying—how if the portrait shows her as innocent, they'll have to think again. They're starting to *expect* to have to think again."

"Are they?" The words were softly uttered. A moment passed. "Now, that won't do."

"Precisely! So what are we going to do to stop it?"

Another long silence ensued. Eventually, the other spoke, voice flat, even, cold. "Don't worry—I'll take care of it."

"How?"

"You'll see. Come on." The larger figure turned into the enshrouding darkness of Venus's garden. "Let's go in."

J acqueline reached Gerrard's room and whisked through the door. Shutting it, she looked across the room, and saw him standing by the windows.

He'd been looking out, but had turned. No lamps were lit; cloaked in shadow, he watched as she crossed the room to him.

As she neared, she looked into his face. The planes were hard-edged, angular and unreadable. Impassive and implacable. Boldly, she walked to him. Walked into his embrace as he reached for her; his hands slid around her waist, fingers flexing, grasping, drawing her to him and holding her.

He studied her. After a moment he said, "I wasn't sure you'd come."

She arched a brow. "Did you think I'd be satisfied with one night?"

His shoulders lifted slightly, but she saw the ends of his lips curve as he bent his head. "It's an unwise man who claims to read a female mind."

His lips brushed, then covered hers, and she decided his caution was just as well—her mind held precious few thoughts, and even those were spinning away. She sighed into the kiss, then went to sink against him, but he held her back, keeping a space of inches between them.

She didn't know why, but followed his lead as he deepened the kiss, parted her lips and claimed her mouth—intently, completely. No quarter, but also no hurry. He took everything he could from the kiss, and left her gasping.

Reeling.

"I think," he murmured, his eyes dark beneath the screen of his lashes, "that before we go any further we should agree on some rules."

She blinked. "Rules?"

"Hmm. Such as . . . you remember I warned you that if you came to me I would expect to possess you—all of you—utterly?"

She was hardly likely to forget. "Yes."

He drank her answer from her lips in a long, lingering sip.

"There's a corollary to that rule." He drew back enough to catch her eyes again. Slowly let his hands slide up until they cupped her breasts. His fingers found the tight peaks and played—delicately, too knowingly.

She could barely breathe. "What?"

"Having agreed to be mine utterly, you can't rescind that state—you can't not be mine until I release you, until I let you go."

He never would. Gerrard waited, watched her fight to hold on to sufficient wit to consider his decree . . . Releasing her breasts, he loosened her sash, parted her robe and slid his hands beneath. Around, past her waist to slide down, over her hips to possessively caress the lush curves of her bottom.

Her gaze grew more distant, her senses following his wandering hands.

"Do you agree?" he prompted.

She refocused on his face, studied his eyes. "Do I have any choice?"

He eased her closer, moving deliberately into her. "No."

Hands rising to his shoulders, she tipped back her head to keep her eyes on his. "Then why ask?"

"Because I wanted you to know the answer. To understand how things are . . . will be."

"I see." Jacqueline held his gaze as he drew her against him, quelled a reactive shiver at the strength in his hands, wondered what it was she saw burning behind the rich brown of his eyes. "And now I know . . . what next?"

"Now you know . . ." He bent his head. "We go on."

On. That was precisely where she wanted to go; Jacqueline returned his kiss with fervor, eager to learn what path he'd chosen, what sensual avenue he'd set his mind upon.

He shifted, angling his head; the kiss turned heated, demanding. His arms closed around her, locking her to him, then his hands spread, molding her to him, leaving her in no doubt whatever of his rapacious need.

To her surprise, he drew back from the kiss, unhurriedly, as if he knew she was his and intended taking all the time he wished to savor her. Eventually he raised his head; she lifted her lids and looked up at him. He studied her face, searching, she didn't know for what.

His hand tightened about her bottom, lifting her to him, blatantly shifting her hips against the ridge of his erection.

"The lamps—do you mind if I light them?"

His tone and the predatory look in his eyes suggested the question had sprung from ingrained manners; it was no true request.

"If you wish" was on the tip of her tongue; she caught it back, asked instead, "Why?"

His roving gaze returned to her eyes. "Because I want to see you." Smoothly, gracefully, he released her, and clasped her hand. "To view you as I make love to you."

Her senses leapt; she felt giddy. The heat in his eyes beckoned, caressed—promised all manner of illicit delights.

Eyes locked on hers, he raised her hand, brushed his lips across her fingers, then unfurled them and pressed a burningly hot kiss to her palm.

She swallowed, nodded. "Very well."

Her voice wasn't entirely steady. He turned her; she dragged in a breath as he led her across the room to where a pair of bronze lamps stood on either end of a narrow side table. On the wall behind the table hung a rectangular mirror, wide and high within an ornate gilt frame.

He halted before the table. Releasing her, he lit one lamp; she tracked him in the mirror as he crossed behind her to light the other. The flames flared, then steadied; he glanced at her, clearly gauging the golden light bathing her. To her surprise, he turned the lamp lower, checking the level of light, then crossed to adjust the other.

When he turned, she swung to face him. He took her hand; she expected him to lead her to the bed—instead, he moved her back, turning her, positioning her before the center of the table, facing the mirror midway between the lamps. He moved to stand behind her; over her head, he looked into the mirror—at her, her body—then lifted his gaze to her eyes. And smiled.

Not his charming social smile but that slight curving of the corners of his lips that was far more sincere—and infinitely more predatory.

"Perfect." Reaching for her shoulders, he drew her robe down and away. He tossed it aside, over an armchair, but his eyes never left her; as he stepped closer, his gaze lowered from her face. In the mirror she followed his gaze, and saw what he did, the tight peaks of her full breasts standing proud through the fine lawn of her nightgown.

The gown was virginal white, thin and soft, now gilded by the warm glow from the lamps. She'd fastened the long placket to just above her breasts. His gaze drifted lower, over the indentation of her waist and the flare of her hips, and lower, over her stomach to the faint shadow that was the curls at the apex of her thighs. His gaze lingered, then swept slowly on and down, then unhurriedly returned to her face.

The lengthy perusal had heated her; as he studied her eyes she wondered if it showed. She was tensing to turn and face him when he shifted, and lifted her hair. She'd brushed it out; a thick rippling river, she'd left it running down her back. He speared his fingers through it, then raised his hands and lifted the spread veil forward, over her shoulders.

His face a mask, hard, unreadable, he laid the long tresses down. Shaking his fingers free, he studied the result, then artfully shifted this strand, then that, until he was satisfied.

Until her bright brown hair lay partially over her breasts, an inadequate but distracting screen, burnished by the lamplight.

Before she could comment, he reached for her; sliding his hands about her waist, he closed the last inches between them. She felt his hard warmth at her back and relaxed, but his hold on her waist prevented her from sinking back against him.

Holding her before him, he bent his head; through the strands of her hair, with his lips he found and traced her lobe, then dipped to press a long kiss to the sensitive spot behind her jaw.

"Unbutton your nightgown."

The words whispered past her ear, distilled seduction. She inwardly smiled; catching his eye as he glanced up, into the mirror, she willingly raised her fingers to the highest button, and slid it free.

His hands rode at her waist, hot and strong, fingers tensing as her hands descended. He watched, unblinking, as she slipped each button free.

"Open it. Wide."

Gravelly, forceful, the quiet words sent a shiver spiraling down her spine. Her gaze locked on the vision in the mirror, she grasped the sides of the nightgown and slowly lifted them apart, drew them aside, revealing her breasts, full, firm, already tight.

The lamplight flowed over her, highlighting planes and curves, casting others in shadow. His gaze didn't race, but perused her bared flesh in an intense yet leisurely appraisal; under that blatantly assessing, flagrantly male gaze, her nipples furled into painfully tight buds.

He straightened, lifting his head. Still close behind her, he raised his hands—caught her gaze as he closed the fingers of each about the rucked shoulders of her nightgown, and eased it off, and down.

Glancing down, he ran his hands down her arms, freeing them from the gown's sleeves. "Put your hands on the edge of the table."

He looked up, met her eyes as, wondering, she slowly obeyed, leaning forward to place her hands on the wooden tabletop, lightly gripping the edge.

"Don't shift your hands until I give you leave."

Give her leave . . . She was suddenly very certain he was choosing his words deliberately; he was uttering them evenly, as orders, not mere directions. Instructions he expected her to obey . . . as if she were . . . his utterly.

His to do with as he pleased.

A shudder racked her, yet she felt no trepidation, not the lightest lick of fear. What she felt was excitement, the dark thrill of wanton desire.

And he was feeding that, scripting the moment—as he wished, perhaps, but why did he wish it? She glanced at his face, the planes austere in the lamplight, his expression stark, not so much impassive as set.

His gaze had left her face to wander down over her breasts, then lower. Her nightgown had gathered in loose folds about her hips. His hands returned, palms sliding bare across her naked skin, warm yet hard, long-fingered, strong as they lightly gripped her waist, then swept, slowly, down.

Over her hips, taking her nightgown with them until it slipped over her thighs and slid to the floor, a soft puddle at her feet.

Leaving her naked, bathed in lamplight.

Her breath caught, her lungs seized. Her nerves coiled tight, every thought, all reaction, frozen as she drank in the sight. Of herself, a golden nymph poised in the lamplight, a faerie being trapped in this world—unreal, ephemeral. Magical.

She recognized her face, her hair, her form. This was her, yet not; what was reflected in the mirror was a truth she'd never seen, a woman she'd never before known.

A siren unveiled.

She felt his gaze, hot as a flame, rove her skin, following her own as, stunned, she examined. Then he looked at her face, studied it; she realized and raised her gaze, met his dark eyes.

He raised his hands, again spanned her waist, then slowly slid them up, palms to her heating skin. Spreading his fingers over her midriff, he gripped and eased her back against him; bending his head, he set his lips to the tip of her shoulder, then traced lightly inward, nudging her head aside so he could lave the pulse thundering at the base of her throat. "Don't speak, or move. Just look. Watch. And feel."

She had no choice; fascination held her spellbound, trapped in the fantasy he'd created. A fantasy in which every inhibition had flown, and there was just her, him, and need.

His need to possess her utterly, hers to fulfill that need.

Desire.

It welled as his hands rose beneath the curtain of her hair and closed about her breasts. Her head fell back against his shoulder as his fingers flexed, kneaded; her breath shivered, then suspended on a gasp as he found her nipples, and squeezed. Played.

He knew how to make her frantic, how to call to her desire and send it rushing through her, sweeping all reservations away. It thrummed through her veins, heated her skin until her body glowed with its flame.

From beneath lids suddenly heavy, through the tracery of her lashes she watched as he aroused her, then, as if satisfied with some private assessment, he brushed aside the screening veil of her hair to fully expose her breasts, filling his hands.

Possessed. His to savor as he pleased.

He lifted his head, joined her in her rapt contemplation. His hands moved, pandering to her senses, to his desire. The lamplight touched his face, hard and unyielding; it washed over the flushed curves of her body, painting them soft, giving — vulnerable in their nakedness.

One tanned hand left her breast, splayed across her midriff, then moved down, stroking heavily as if savoring the texture of her skin, then angling over her taut stomach and tensing, pressing in.

Pressing her hips, her bottom, against his hard thighs, tilting them so his rigid erection rode against her, an insistent pressure in the small of her back.

Her senses swelled, her breaths were short, shallow; her head was whirling. The promise of pleasure was so potent she could taste it. Briefly she studied his face, wondered again why he wanted her like this. She could sense the control he was exerting, the grim determination that held him back from simply having her, that allowed him to take her along this road, into an illicit paradise.

It was a type of bondage, one with no physical chains, yet the chains were there — Gerrard knew it. He sensed her gaze on his face, sensed the question forming in her mind. He lowered his gaze, lowered his hand, felt her attention shift, leaving his face to lock on his questing fingers.

He speared them through the tawny curls, caught a few between his fingertips and rubbed, as if gauging their texture. Then he fluffed the curls, and noted she'd stopped breathing. He paused, fingertips poised over the shadowed hollow at the apex of her thighs, to knead her breast, to again squeeze her nipple, tight, then tighter, until her concentration fractured. Until she gasped. Writhed.

All but begged. Her hips angled forward, lifted, her curls brushing his fingers in open entreaty.

He accepted the invitation. Slid two fingers into the heated hollow, stroked, found the sensitive pearl throbbing beneath its hood and swirled, then pressed deeper and probed.

She started to shift, to part her thighs to give him better access.

"No. Don't move. Remain exactly as you are."

Panting lightly, eyes wide, pupils distended, she obeyed. With her thighs together, he couldn't penetrate more than an inch past the slick, swollen lips of her sheath.

Far enough for his purpose, far enough to reduce her to desperation. Ruthlessly he wound her tight, gave her just so much and no more . . .

Abruptly, she dragged in a breath and caught his eyes. "What do you want from me?"

"More."

"More how?"

Suddenly, he knew. It was as if her question had opened a door in his mind; he'd intended to show her her own sensual nature—it seemed that in doing so, she would teach him of his own. The vision that formed in his mind stole his breath; her lips were parted, her skin already flushed, yet she waited . . . for his answer.

To learn what he truly wished of her.

"I want to watch you reach ecstasy. Here, with the lamplight pouring over you. I want you to let me view you as I push you over the peak."

Three heartbeats passed; her eyes locked on his, she knew exactly what he asked. Even, perhaps, why he asked.

She nodded. "All right."

Again she shifted to part her thighs.

"No. Not like that."

She looked up at him, her question in her eyes.

He released her breast, spread that hand over her stomach and drew her hips back; still gripping the table's edge, she had to lean further forward. Releasing her, he gripped her hip, anchoring her before him, then withdrew his fingers from the hot haven beneath her curls, shifted back, reached beneath the sweet swell of her bottom, into the dark hollow between the backs of her thighs, and slid his fingers deep into her sheath.

She gasped, spine tensing, head arching back; his hand clamped about her hip, he held her in place as he worked his fingers deep. Her slickness scorched; the musky scent of her rose to tease him.

He ignored it. Gave all his attention to pleasuring her, to watching her while he did. He found the right rhythm, the perfect angle, the correct length of penetration; stroking in and back, blatantly intent, he set about driving her on.

She responded, skin suffused, muscles fluidly shifting as she rode his fingers. She'd understood what he desired, and was unstinting in yielding all he'd wished for, bringing his wild, illicit vision to life.

He couldn't tear his gaze from her, had to fight to dissociate his mind from the firm and giving softness of her body, from the hot slickness of her sheath, from the scent of passion that wreathed about them and tried to draw him in. He found desire fracturing as like a man parched he drank in the beauty of her shifting form, of the naked desire she so freely let show.

Despite giving herself up so completely to passion, despite the physical absorption, she still watched him; he caught the glint of her bright eyes under her lowered lids, and realized she wasn't the only one exposed.

She seemed steady on her feet. He released her hip, then stepped back and to the side—so she lost any contact with him beyond his hand buried between her thighs, so he could with greater detachment better view her body as she responded.

Without reserve.

She raised her head and shook back her hair. Her eyes met his, her breasts thrust forward, nipples proudly erect. With his free hand he reached out, slid his fingers around one pert peak, and played.

Pushed her further.

For long moments he pandered to her need, and watched her scale the peak. Her eyes closed, her knuckles tightened on the table; inexorably he drove her on.

Until she was almost there. She gasped, opened eyes dark and wild and found his. "Come with me. Now."

An unbelievably evocative plea—half sob, half command. He hadn't intended it, yet the lure of the visual, of all she'd allowed him to see, the allure of her body, so female and flushed with desire, the evocative lines and even more evocative scent of passion, coalesced like a net and dragged him in. Detachment was beyond him.

His fingers were flicking open the buttons at his waist as he moved to stand directly behind her. Awareness of all he'd blocked out rushed back. He was rigid, aching; it was an inexpressible relief to withdraw his fingers from her body, and replace them with that part of his anatomy he'd been ignoring for the last hour.

Untold relief to sink his throbbing staff into the heated heaven between her thighs.

He groaned, the sound revealing more than he'd expected. He cracked open lids that had fallen closed, and in the mirror found her eyes. Still watching him.

A small, slight smile curved her lips.

He tightened his hands about her hips, lifted her up, onto her toes, drew back, and plunged in.

She asked for no quarter, neither with words, sobs or moans; if anything, she pressed back against him, meeting his thrusts and urging him on.

He rode her deep, hard, unrestrained, freed from the shackles of the conventional—by her. By her willingness to give him all he wished, by her openness, her unlimited honesty in this, in the enjoyment she took, the pleasure she found, in engaging in sex with him, in taking him into her body, and lavishing pleasure on him.

Her face showed it all, eyes now closed, a witchy little smile curving her parted lips, a small, luscious indent between her brows as she concentrated, her senses wholly focused on where they joined.

On the hot pleasure of his filling her.

The peak beckoned, loomed ever nearer, then she was there. He thrust harder, deeper, prolonging the moment, with her through every panting gasp—then the rippling contractions of her surrender caught him; she tightened about him, and took him with her.

Over the edge and into sheer delight.

He had no idea how he managed to keep them upright, but eventually he withdrew from her, swept her up in his arms and carried her to the bed. He went back to douse the lamps, then stripped and joined her beneath the covers.

She murmured, a soft, sleepy declaration of contentment; lips still curved, she settled in his arms.

He lay back, listening to the heavy beat of his heart as it slowed from the thundering cadence of a sexual adventure that had extended far beyond his expectations. He'd set the stage, his aim crystal clear;

she'd accepted his challenge, yielded all he'd asked, but then something else had overtaken them.

It wasn't the first time that had occurred. With no other woman had he found himself, not out of control yet under the direction, or so it seemed, of some power greater than himself.

Not that he was complaining.

Closing his eyes, he sank into the mattress, felt deep and complete satiation claim him, and let his own lips curve. He'd achieved what he'd set out to do—to create sexual, sensual chains between them, and bind her to him. The concept was primitive, frankly possessive, but that suited his mood. Even more importantly, with her and him, the chains were real; they would work. Because she was so freely ardent, so open and honest in her passions, he could bind her through her senses' delight. Through pleasure.

Through the very act of possession—hers . . . and, it occurred to him, his. The realization drifted across his mind as sleep slipped in and drew him down.

16

Iff she was bound to him, then, *ipso facto,* he was equally bound to her. Gerrard wondered why he hadn't seen that before. He was even more astonished that, having now realized, he didn't actually care.

After rising early, then eventually escorting a sated and sleepy Jacqueline back to her room, he'd felt too awake, too alive to return to bed. He'd dressed and come down for an early breakfast.

To his surprise, Barnaby joined him.

"What ho?" Strolling into the parlor, Barnaby headed for the sideboard. "Is it your devotion to the painting that has you up so early, or did something else disturb your slumber?"

Refusing to react to the none-too-subtle glint in Barnaby's eyes, Gerrard shook his head. "I can't paint in the morning—the light's too deceptive. I was thinking of going for a walk to refresh my memory of the Garden of Night."

Plate in hand, Barnaby came to the table. "Are you using it as the setting, then?"

"Yes, the lower entrance. It's appropriate, therefore evocative."

Engaged with a sausage, Barnaby nodded his understanding.

When they'd both satisfied their hunger, they rose and ambled out onto the terrace. The air was cool, but held the promise of warmth; the gardens lay before them, serene and inviting.

"Just think what we'd be doing if we weren't here."

As they strolled, they tossed comments back and forth, the usual banter about acquaintances and events that would have filled such an interlude in the capital. They were very much men-about-town, as distinct from country squires.

Reaching the north end of the terrace, they eschewed the path to the Garden of Hercules, opting for the pleasanter path through the orchards of the Garden of Demeter, then from the wooden pergola angling along the upper boundary of the Garden of Apollo, lying basking in the early morning sunshine, and so through the Garden of Poseidon to the lower entrance to the Garden of Night.

Barnaby dawdled. Hands in his pockets, with his eyes he followed the line of the tinkling brook as it ran through the Garden of Poseidon and then down the valley; lifting his gaze, he squinted toward the cove.

Leaving him observing, Gerrard walked on toward the Garden of Night. Ten paces from the entrance, heavily wreathed in creepers, he paused to examine the layering of the leaves and branches.

He'd captured the effect correctly on his canvas; satisfied, he walked on. Halting just before the arched entrance, hands on his hips, he looked up, head back as he studied the detail of the leaves.

Unmoving, he ran his eyes down, confirming the way the different creepers intertwined. Noticing a new shoot, pale, almost white, thrusting up through the densely packed leaves just above the ground, he lowered his arms and crouched to examine it.

Whizz—rustle—crump!

He tensed to spring up, but before he could an arrow tumbled out of the vines and fell at his feet.

"Go inside!"

He swiveled to see Barnaby frantically waving him into the Garden of Night. Then Barnaby pelted off back up the path in the direction from which the arrow had come.

For one second, Gerrard remained frozen, then, the arrow in his hand, he smoothly rose and walked into the humid enclosure of the Garden of Night.

Rampant growth solidly screened the area; no one could shoot at him while he was inside, not without him seeing them. And whoever it was didn't intend being seen, which most likely meant he had met them.

Gerrard paused by the grotto's pool, deep in the garden, half over-hung by the terrace. He felt decidedly odd. Detached. There was no doubt in his mind that had he not bent down to examine the new creeper shoot, the arrow would have lodged in his back.

Would he have died? Possibly. There was a good chance he'd have lost the ability to paint—for him, another, potentially worse death.

Chilled, he turned and sat on the stone coping edging the pool. Leaning his elbows on his thighs, he studied the arrow, twisting it between his hands. It was well made, decently fletched, and carried a killing point, one that would have sliced through muscle, deflected off bone, and lodged deep. The sort of point used to slay deer.

His jaw set. He was sure Barnaby wouldn't see anyone, let alone catch them. The arrow could have come from a considerable swath of the gardens along the northern slope. Still . . . he waited for Barnaby to return.

His gaze wandered across the clearing before him, the central portion of the Garden of Night. The grotto behind him was the principal focus of interest, drawing the eye; the stream filled the pool, then ran underground beneath the clearing to the winding path, then along a rocky culvert beside it, eventually emerging into the sunlight as the path entered the Garden of Poseidon.

Without conscious direction, his artist's eye noted the lines, measured distances; in his mind, a plan of the garden took shape, much as the designer would have laid it out. Sitting on the pool's edge, swinging the arrow between his fingers, he looked across the clearing, and frowned.

For balance, there should have been something there—a statue in an alcove or some such thing. Instead, the side opposite the pool was a dense mass of creeper . . . or was it?

He rose and crossed to look more closely. Once within arm's reach of the apparently dense mound, he saw it was in fact two weeping trees, their canopies overgrown by the vines; it was easy to push aside the creeper veil and look in . . . to what had clearly been intended as a serene and pleasant bower in which to sit and observe the fountain in the grotto pool.

Gerrard glanced back and forth, checking the angles. He felt sure

he was right; that was what the original design had been. Now, however, the creepers had grown rampant and converted the bower to a
green chamber, secret and concealed . . . and in use.

The moss planted there had withered long ago, but there was a
thick cushion of straw covered by a layer of soft, dried moss, with
dried flowers, heads of lavender and other herbs mixed in.

It was a trysting place.

The flowers and herbs weren't that old, and the thick layer of
moss had recently been disturbed.

Footsteps sounded on the path, heading his way. Barnaby.

Gerrard let the creeper curtain fall. He could guess who used the
green chamber to meet with her lover after dark.

Barnaby came through the archway. He grimaced. "No luck."

Gerrard's lips twisted. "It was a long chance."

"Indeed." Crossing to the pool, Barnaby sat. As Gerrard neared,
he reached for the arrow; Gerrard handed it over.

Barnaby examined it; his expression grew grimmer. "I'm seeing a
pattern here."

"All those the killer has targeted have . . ." Gerrard paused.

"Loved Jacqueline?" Assessing the arrow point, Barnaby nodded.
"True, but I don't think that's it—or not all of it."

Gerrard let Barnaby's description pass; taking exception would be
too revealing, as well as pointless—Barnaby knew him well. "If not
that, what?"

"Murdering you and Thomas because you'd grown close to
Jacqueline I can understand, but why kill her mother?"

"We've already answered that." Gerrard started to pace.

"Perhaps, but we have to remember what's commonly known."
Barnaby looked up. "From that, what links you to the others is that
you're *protecting* Jacqueline."

Gerrard met his eyes. "Which means you, too, are at risk."

"Possibly, but I'm not the most urgent threat to this killer. You
are." Barnaby locked eyes with him. "You're also the key to Jacqueline's freedom—without you, there'll be no portrait and no revision of
the accepted truth."

Gerrard halted. Gazing at Barnaby, he thought through all he
knew; he wasn't convinced the killer hadn't targeted him purely because he'd grown close to Jacqueline.

Barnaby studied his expression, then grimaced. "Regardless, we need to return to London."

Gerrard blinked. "London? Why?"

Barnaby told him. Initially he made much of the danger to Gerrard.

He dismissed that. "It's safe enough here now we're on guard."

"Yes, and no—what if the killer doesn't truly care if he kills you, only that he stops you from completing the portrait?" Barnaby held his gaze pointedly. "There are many more ways to accomplish that, which will make it that much harder to prevent. Are you sure you want to risk it?"

His imagination ran wild; he could instantly envisage any number of ways of halting the portrait—burning down the house, harming Jacqueline.

Barnaby's expression set. "No matter what arguments you make, one fact remains. Without your completing her portrait, Jacqueline is trapped. Only you, with it, can free her."

Gerrard stared into Barnaby's steady blue eyes. Then he hauled in a huge breath, and nodded. "You're right. London it is. Us, Millicent and Jacqueline."

"When?" Barnaby stood. "Can you finish the portrait there?"

Gerrard nodded. "Once I finish the setting, it'll be easier—and faster—to do the sittings in my studio. As things stand . . . if I do nothing but paint for the next two days, we can leave after that."

"Two days from now?"

Gerrard nodded, suddenly eager to have Jacqueline safe in his own territory. He and Barnaby started back toward the house.

"I'd suggest," Barnaby said, "that there's no benefit in scaring the ladies." He caught Gerrard's eye. "We'll square things with Tregonning, and then cast it as a jaunt to the capital."

"That," Gerrard declared, "will be easy. I've already paved the way for taking Jacqueline to town—she needs a new gown for the portrait."

Barnaby grinned, grimly determined. "Excellent."

Reaching the steps to the terrace, they went quickly up.

Jacqueline spent the next two days in what seemed a constant whirl. Not since her mother's death had the household been plunged into such frenetic activity.

They were going to London—her, Millicent, Gerrard and Barnaby. So her father had informed them at luncheon on the second day after the ball. Apparently Gerrard had spoken to him about the need for a new gown for the portrait, and her father had agreed, not only to the trip but to Gerrard's completing the portrait in his studio in town.

She'd only been to Bath before, never to the capital. Now, courtesy of Gerrard, she and Millicent could look forward to at least two weeks, most likely more, in which to sample fashionable life.

All but dizzy contemplating the possibilities, she and Millicent had much to do to prepare for both the journey and their stay, all in the day and a half her father and Gerrard had allowed them. Males both, they didn't seem to comprehend how much time it required to sort, freshen and pack a wardrobe, select and pack hats, shoes, gloves, shawls, reticules, stockings, jewelry and all the other accessories necessary for putting on a creditable show in town.

On that both she and Millicent were determined. They were clearly destined to meet at least some of Gerrard's fashionable relatives; they had no intention of appearing as provincials, insofar as they could avoid it.

And then there were the household duties to delegate.

She was almost glad that Gerrard retreated to the old nursery. After the announcement, he didn't appear again, not for dinner, nor for breakfast or lunch the next day.

Of course, at night, she visited his room. On the first night, discovering him absent, she'd quietly climbed the stairs, avoiding Compton's room to open the nursery door.

The night had been warm and sultry. Clad only in breeches, his feet bare, he'd stood poised before the canvas. But his gaze had deflected to her. As before, she'd sensed the complete shift in his attention, the total distraction she was to him, and had hidden a wholly feminine smile.

She'd gone in and closed the door. He'd run his hand through his hair, then, as she walked to him, he'd set his palette down. And turned to her.

Later, she'd dozed on the window seat, her flushed skin protected from the cool night air by her robe and his shirt. She'd watched him paint, bare-chested, muscles shifting in the steady light thrown by six lamps turned high.

In those moments, his concentration had been absolute, focused on his work. Powerful, potent. Intense.

It was the same intensity, both physical and mental, that he brought to their lovemaking, but then, as its object, she couldn't so clearly observe and appreciate. What she'd seen as he'd painted had made her shiver. Deliciously.

When they were together, all that was hers.

He'd returned to her when the sky was lightening, stirring her awake as the shades shifted through blues to grays before the soft pastels of dawn. Kneeling on the window seat, straddling him, under his direction sinking down and taking him deep inside her, she'd seen the reflection of the dawn on the sea, just as he drove her to glory.

Later, she'd slipped away and left him sleeping.

That day, he didn't appear at all.

She caught Compton in the corridor and learned that when in a painting frenzy, his master slept through the morning when the light wasn't strong, waking before midday to pick up his brushes again. Instructing Compton to ensure adequate food and drink were provided, and if at all possible, consumed, she returned to the myriad tasks awaiting her.

She'd expected Eleanor to appear for one of their walks, expected to tell her of their trip then. But Eleanor didn't appear. Recalling their last exchange, Jacqueline inwardly shrugged. She and Eleanor had fallen out before, always over some action of Eleanor's; eventually, Eleanor always came around, even if she never apologized.

So Eleanor would learn of their departure for London after the fact.

The following morning at eight o'clock sharp, Gerrard escorted Millicent and herself down the steps to her father's traveling coach. The four horses stamped and shifted; harness jingled as the coachman climbed up. Her father, who'd been waiting by the carriage, kissed her cheek. "Send me a letter when you're settled."

She promised, kissed him, and he handed her up. Millicent followed, then Gerrard; he took the seat opposite, with his back to the horses.

Her father exchanged a look and a nod with Gerrard, then shut the door. The coachman flicked the reins and the coach jerked, then ponderously rolled on. Barnaby would be just behind, in the curricle driving Gerrard's grays. Sometime later, Compton would set out with Gerrard's luggage, including his equipment and the all-important portrait.

She felt a thrill of excitement course through her veins. Her anticipation showed in her face; she knew from the affectionate light in Gerrard's eyes as he watched her.

Then he closed his eyes and fell asleep.

The journey was not nearly as exciting as she'd hoped. Gerrard slept for most of the time, doubtless catching up on all the sleep he'd gone without over recent days. In truth, there was no point doing otherwise; in the carriage with Millicent, in the inns at which they stopped both at midday and at night, there was precious little opportunity for dalliance.

Still, she was going to London.

Eventually, they arrived.

Gerrard had explained, and convinced her father and Millicent, that it was perfectly acceptable for her and Millicent to stay in his house in Brook Street. He, it transpired, didn't live there, but in lodgings nearby; he'd bought the house for the attics, which now housed his studio, and kept the house, too large for a single gentleman, for family members when they came up to town.

There were two older ladies currently in residence, Gerrard's aunt Minnie, Lady Bellamy, and her lady companion, known to all as Timms.

By the time the heavy coach rolled into Brook Street, Jacqueline felt that her eyes had grown so round they'd never be normal again. There'd been so much to see as they'd entered the capital—the shops!—the people!—Hyde Park and the carriages of the fashionable, the nattily dressed gentlemen riding along Rotten Row. Gerrard had leaned forward and pointed out the sights to her. Millicent had sat back, smiling, taking it all in her stride.

The coach slowed, then rocked to a halt. Gerrard didn't wait for the footman, but opened the door and stepped down to the pavement, then turned, took her hand, and helped her down.

She looked up at the town house before her. It was large, two stories above the street, one below, and attics with dormer windows high above. The stonework was in excellent repair, the woodwork neatly painted, with a bright brass knocker on the forest-green front door. A short set of steps led up to the front porch.

Barnaby had driven ahead that morning; the front door opened and he looked out. He waved and came quickly down, smiling. "There's a reception committee waiting."

She heard the sotto voce warning, intended for Gerrard; he didn't look at all surprised. Indeed, he looked resignedly amused. Barnaby helped Millicent out. With a brief, bolstering smile, Gerrard set Jacqueline's hand on his sleeve and turned her to the door.

It swung wide as they climbed the steps.

"Good afternoon, sir." An ancient and imposing butler stood at attention, ready to bow them in.

Gerrard grinned. "Good afternoon, Masters. I gather the ladies are lying in wait?"

"Indeed, sir. As are Mrs. Patience and Mr. Vane."

"Ah. I see." His smile deepening, Gerrard turned to her. "This is Miss Tregonning. She'll be staying here with my aunt and her aunt"—he included Millicent as she joined them—"also Miss Tregonning. This is Masters—he's Minnie's butler, and will organize anything and everything as if by magic."

Straightening from his very correct bow, Masters accepted the tribute without a blink. "Miss, ma'am—both myself and Mrs. Welborne will be honored to assist you in any way."

"I take it tea will be served in the drawing room?" Gerrard asked.

"Indeed, sir." Masters directed a footman to close the front door. "Our orders were for as soon as you arrived, to refresh you after the long journey." He turned to Millicent and Jacqueline. "Mrs. Welborne has your rooms prepared. I'll have your boxes taken up straight-away."

They murmured their thanks.

"I'll take the ladies in." Gerrard glanced at Barnaby. "Are you staying?"

Barnaby grinned. "In the interests of experience, I rather think I will."

Gerrard raised his brows, but made no reply. He led the way to a pair of double doors, opened them, then stepped back and ushered Jacqueline and Millicent in.

Beside Millicent, Jacqueline stepped into an elegantly proportioned room, its walls hung with dusky pink paper warmed by the late afternoon sunshine pouring in through long windows left open to a flagged terrace; beyond, the green of lawns and shrubs was patterned with splashes of summer blooms.

The furniture was lovely—wooden, none of it spindly, yet equally none of it overly ornate. Much of it was rosewood, and glowed with a luster that screamed of care. It took an instant for her eyes to travel to the long chaise further down the room, set at an angle to the hearth. A smaller chaise and three armchairs completed the grouping. Two older ladies sat on the larger chaise, avidly watching them. Another lady, younger and beautifully gowned, sat in one armchair; a gentleman, handsome and severely elegant, uncrossed his long legs and rose from its mate.

Even as, a polite smile on her lips, she went forward with Millicent to meet Gerrard's family, something—some observation—nagged at Jacqueline's mind. Just before she reached those waiting, it came clear; there was a clock on the mantelpiece and two statues made into lamps flanking the terrace windows, but beyond that, other than an ancient tatting bag resting beside the feet of one of the older ladies, there were no ornaments, and no signs of habitation—no journal or playbill lying on a table, no softening touches. The room seemed strangely sterile.

Gerrard didn't live there, so it lacked any evidence of him. Despite its elegance, the lovely furniture and the attractive paper, curtains and upholstery, the room felt rather cold, not neglected physically but lacking a certain energy. Lacking life.

Reaching the long chaise, Gerrard introduced Millicent, then Jacqueline, to his aunt, Lady Bellamy.

"Good afternoon, my dear—I'm so very glad to meet you." Lady Bellamy, with curly, white hair, many chins and bright if faded blue eyes, reached for Jacqueline's hand, clasping it between hers. "I hope you and your aunt will excuse me if I don't rise—my old bones aren't what they were."

Her smile growing warmer, Jacqueline bobbed a curtsy. "I'm delighted to make your acquaintance, ma'am."

Lady Bellamy beamed, but wagged a pudgy, beringed finger. "Everyone calls me Minnie, my dear, and I hope you and Millicent will do the same. No need to stand on ceremony."

Jacqueline smiled her acquiescence; Gerrard had told her about his aunt. She was of an age where guessing her years was impossible; she was over sixty, but how far over was anyone's guess.

"And," Minnie said, patting her hand before releasing it, "this is Timms. No one calls her anything else, either."

"Indeed." Her gray hair pulled back from her plain-featured face, Timms took Jacqueline's hand in a surprisingly strong grip. Her gaze was warm, friendly and disconcertingly direct. "Very glad you needed to come to town, else no doubt we'd have developed a reason for jauntering down to Cornwall. Not that I have anything against Cornwall in summer, but such a journey at our age . . . well, better not."

Jacqueline felt her smile deepen, felt all reserve slide from her. "Indeed, it's a very long way. I'm glad we needed to visit."

Timms grinned and released her. Taking her arm, Gerrard steered her to the other lady, who had risen and was speaking with Millicent.

Millicent glanced around as they neared, smiled and stepped back, allowing Gerrard to introduce her.

"Miss Jacqueline Tregonning—my sister, Patience Cynster, and her husband, Vane."

Jacqueline went to curtsy, but Patience caught both her hands.

"No, no—as Minnie declared, we need no ceremony." Patience's hazel eyes met Jacqueline's gaze with greater warmth than she'd expected; when, after an instant studying her, Patience again spoke, there was no doubt of the sincerity behind her words. "I'm so very pleased to meet you, my dear."

Echoing the sentiment, frankly amazed at how truly welcome she did indeed feel, Jacqueline turned to the gentleman, who, lips curving, smoothly lifted her hand from his wife's grasp and elegantly bowed over it.

"Vane Cynster, my dear." His voice was deep, sonorous. "I trust the journey down wasn't overly fatiguing?"

The question encouraged an answer; in less than a minute, Jacqueline found herself seated on the end of the smaller chaise, engaged in a surprisingly easy exchange with Patience and Vane. Gerrard hovered beside her. Millicent, next to her, was chatting animatedly with Minnie.

Jacqueline had never felt so unreservedly welcomed, so warmly accepted; reassured, she relaxed.

Gerrard watched her, pleased to see that her inner reserve hadn't materialized, not at all. As far as she knew, none of his family were aware of the circumstances of her mother's death; she clearly found no difficulty in engaging openly with them.

That was something of a relief; the same would no doubt hold true when she met the rest of the clan, and the members of wider society who, once it became known she was here, staying in his house under Minnie's aegis, would make it their business to meet her.

Which meant he could relax, and concentrate on painting. She would take his London acquaintance by storm; he was looking forward to observing the action from a safe, if watchful, distance.

The tea trolley arrived. Patience did the honors. Barnaby and Gerrard ferried the cups, then Barnaby joined Millicent, Minnie and Timms in discussing which of London's many sights were most impressive and thus not to be missed.

Gerrard drew up a chair beside Vane. While Patience talked with Jacqueline, comparing country life in Cornwall and Derbyshire, where his and Patience's childhood home lay, he picked Vane's brains over what had occurred in their mutual business circles over the weeks he'd been away.

Sipping his tea, he made a firm if silent vow not to, under any circumstances, divulge the name of the modiste to whom he intended to take Jacqueline the next morning.

He tried, but failed. At eleven the next morning, Millicent, Patience, Minnie and Timms accompanied him and Jacqueline to Helen Purfett's salon.

The salon was in unfashionable Paddington, in a narrow house on a street leading north from the park. Minnie, Timms and Patience exchanged glances as Patience's carriage rocked to a halt on the cobblestones outside. Gerrard had led the way, driving his curricle and grays, Jacqueline on the seat beside him, transparently excited, her eyes enormous as she glanced about.

Her reaction soothed his already abraded temper. He reined it in as he handed Patience and the three older ladies to the pavement. He wasn't surprised when, after looking about her, Minnie asked, "Are you sure this dressmaker is suitable, dear?"

"Helen isn't a modiste in the sense of making ball gowns. She specializes in making gowns for artist's models."

Four pairs of lips formed an "Oh."

With a wave, he herded them all up the steps to the door. Helen would be expecting him and Jacqueline; he hoped she'd cope with the unexpected crowd.

He'd painted all night in his studio in the attic; only when it was too late—the small hours of the morning—and he realized Jacqueline hadn't arrived, did he recall he'd forgotten to tell her how to access the attics from the lower part of the house. The conversion had made the attics into separate quarters, reached by stairs from the alley alongside. There was a connecting door and stairs from the house proper, but they were concealed.

He sincerely hoped she hadn't gone wandering about in the night, trying to find her way up. Minnie was a frighteningly light sleeper.

There was nothing to be done but paint on; he hadn't thought to ask which room she'd been given. So he'd returned to laying the last layer of detail into the creepers and vines about the entrance to the Garden of Night.

Due to the appointment with Helen, he hadn't been able to sleep for long this morning. Consequently, he was in no good mood to deal gently with the sort of feminine helpfulness with which he coped when necessary, but more normally avoided like a pinching boot.

He loved Patience, Minnie and Timms, but he didn't need their "help" in this instance.

Helen blinked when they all trooped into her salon upstairs, but she recovered well. After he'd introduced her, she showed the four observers to a long sofa before the front windows, ordered tea and scones for them, then, with a smile, excused herself, Gerrard and Jacqueline, and whisked them into a smaller, more cluttered workroom.

"Better?" She raised a questioning brow at Gerrard.

He sighed, and nodded. "Yes, thank you. Are these the satins?" He picked up a stack of fabric swatches.

Jacqueline, Helen and he stood at her worktable; Helen and he discussed lines and made sketches while Jacqueline quietly listened, but when, design and drape agreed, they turned to choosing the fabric, she joined in with decided views of her own.

Her eye for color was as good as his, and she had a sound appreciation of what suited her. They all quickly agreed that a certain brassy bronze shot-silk shantung was perfect.

"See—with the drape, it'll catch the light differently, so you'll get all the curves highlighted, especially in lamplight." Helen draped a long swatch of the material over Jacqueline's shoulder, angling over her breasts to her waist, then stood behind her and pulled the material tight. "There." Reaching forward, Helen adjusted the silk. "What do you think?"

Gerrard looked; his lips slowly curved. "Perfect."

They made arrangements for fittings over the next four days, then Gerrard led Jacqueline out to join their now thoroughly bored supporters. In a much better mood than when they'd arrived, he ushered them out to the carriages.

He drove Jacqueline back to Brook Street, only to find an unmarked black town carriage waiting outside his house, with a too familiar groom in attendance.

"Her Grace?" he resignedly asked Matthews, one of Devil Cynster's grooms.

Matthews grinned sympathetically. "The Dowager and Lady Horatia, sir."

Heaven help him. He loved them all, *but* . . .

Beneath all else, he was just a tad worried that Jacqueline would find his female connections, especially *en masse,* too overpowering, and take flight. Yet as he squired her inside and into the drawing room, he reminded himself that this—her introduction to his extensive family circle before he asked her to marry him—was only fair. If she accepted him, she'd be accepting them, too.

He'd debated mentioning marriage before they'd left Cornwall, but he'd only just started his campaign to illustrate the benefits of matrimony sufficiently for the idea to occur to her before he broached it; he was perfectly sure she'd yet to start thinking along his required lines. The visit to the capital would provide both settings and circumstances to extend his campaign beyond the sensual—he intended her to see and appreciate what life as his wife would be like—but he hadn't until now considered how she, used to being very much alone, would react to a family framework in which ladies were never alone, but part of a large familial group whose members frequently visited, openly shared experiences and were perennially interested.

In everything.

Evidence of that last gleamed in two pairs of aging but still handsome eyes as he guided Jacqueline to the chaise on which the Dowager Duchess of St. Ives and Lady Horatia Cynster sat, waiting to greet them.

"I am enchanted, my dear, to meet with you." Helena's eyes danced as, releasing Jacqueline's hand, she raised her pale eyes to his face. "Gerrard—such a happy circumstance that Lord Tregonning chose you to paint this so important portrait, *n'est-ce pas?*"

He returned a noncommittal murmur; it was never wise to give the Dowager more information than strictly necessary. That was the rule the family's males had learned to live by; unfortunately, there was very little the Dowager's pale green eyes missed—and even less that her exceedingly sharp mind failed to correctly interpret.

Lady Horatia Cynster, Vane's mother, the Dowager's sister-in-law and most frequent companion, was less overtly intimidating, but almost equally dangerous. "I remember meeting your mother, my dear, many years ago at a ball. She was exceedingly beautiful—there's much I can see in you that I remember in her."

"Really?" Eyes lighting, Jacqueline sat in the armchair before the chaise. "Other than from Lady Fritham, our neighbor who was Mama's childhood friend, I've never heard much of Mama before she married Papa."

"Ah, I remember." The Dowager nodded. "It caused quite a stir, that marriage—that she, such a diamond, chose to leave the ton so completely and retire to Cornwall. Horatia, do you recall . . ."

Between them, Helena and Horatia recalled a number of stories of Jacqueline's mother during the short time she'd graced the capital's ballrooms. Leaning forward, asking questions, Jacqueline eagerly absorbed all they said.

Gerrard found himself redundant. Found himself swallowing a certain surprise at how easily Jacqueline had found her feet with such ladies.

He wasn't, of course, at all surprised by their eager embracing of her.

From the moment Barnaby had suggested visiting London, he'd known he'd have no chance of disguising his interest in Jacqueline as purely professional. Within the family, it wasn't even worthwhile making the attempt; they'd see right through him, and laugh and pat his cheek—and tease him even more unmercifully.

It was bad enough when Horatia turned from the conversation to smile up at him, and say, "Dear boy, such excitement! The whole tale is so romantic. Of course, none of us will breathe a word, not until the deed is done and all settled, but you've certainly enlivened what was shaping up to be a deathly dull summer."

Her eyes twinkled up at him; he inclined his head—she could have been talking about the portrait and his rescuing Jacqueline, or about his impending nuptials—it was impossible to tell. To his relief, sounds of an arrival heralded the return of Patience, Minnie and Timms, and spared him having to answer. They all bustled in, ready to tell Helena and Horatia about their visit to the unusual dressmaker—and even more eager to quiz Jacqueline on all that took place in Helen's work-room.

The level of feminine chatter rose, blanketing the room. Minnie called for tea; Gerrard seized the opportunity to make his excuses and escape.

Before he could, Patience stopped him with a raised hand. "Dinner tonight," she informed him. "Just the family." She saw the look in his eyes and smiled, understanding, yet in no way relenting. "It's so quiet at present, everyone is only too glad to have an excuse not to eat at their own board."

By "the family" she meant any of the wider Cynster clan in town; during the Season, most lived in London, but during the summer, they came and went as business and family affairs dictated.

He could refuse, citing his work on the portrait, but . . . He glanced at Jacqueline, then looked back at Patience and nodded. "Usual time?"

She smiled, an all-knowing older sister. "Seven, but you might come a trifle earlier and visit the nursery. There have been complaints regarding your absence."

The thought made him grin. "I'll try."

With a general nod, he turned away, and made good his escape. Within that circle, Jacqueline clearly needed no protection.

He, on the other hand, needed to protect his sanity. Climbing the stairs, he took refuge in his studio.

17

Later that night, Jacqueline stood in Gerrard's studio, and watched him sketch her into the portrait. Everyone else had retired to their beds.

In the front hall when they'd returned from dinner, he'd explained the routine he intended to follow, working through the nights as the scene was set in moonlight, then sleeping through the morning before rising to reassess and prepare through the afternoon, so that at night he could paint again. His clear aim was to complete the portrait as soon as possible.

Everyone understood why that was desirable. On the journey to town, they'd discussed and agreed that while there was no need to bruit the purpose behind the portrait to society at large, it was necessary that Gerrard's family understood both the urgency and importance behind the work. As he'd explained, their discretion could be relied on, and their knowing would ensure that no vestige of scandal attached to her because of her attendance in his studio, whatever the hours, regardless of the privacy.

Having met his family, *she* now fully understood. It was comforting knowing they were so supportive, indeed, so interested and determined that all would go well for Gerrard and their endeavor, and her, too.

He'd posed her beside a plaster column, her right hand raised, palm placed lightly to the column's surface; in the portrait, the column would be the side of the archway that was the lower entrance to the Garden of Night. Her hand would be holding aside a piece of creeper.

He'd shown her what he'd done so far; she could see the effect he was aiming for. It would be powerful, evocative. Convincing.

All she needed the portrait to be.

She stood unmoving, her gaze fixed as he'd instructed, to the left of where he worked behind his easel; her mind roamed, to all else she'd seen and learned that day.

The visit to Helen Purfett's salon had been interesting; they would return tomorrow afternoon, and the three afternoons after that, for fittings, but it would be just the two of them. Millicent, Minnie, Timms and Patience had lost interest in the process, although they were still exceedingly keen to see her in the finished product.

She hesitated, then remembered Gerrard was not yet sketching any details, just the lines of her body, her limbs. He'd promised tonight would be a short session, a training for the hours that would come; for now she could let her expression relax—let her lips curve as she recalled the rest of her day.

During their journey, she'd wondered whether she would find his relatives, especially the ladies, intimidating; they were, after all, members of the haut ton, and had been all their lives. Admittedly, she wasn't all that easily intimidated, yet the transparently warm welcome they'd accorded her, and the ease with which she'd found herself relaxing into, as it were, the bosom of his family, had not just surprised her, but left her feeling amazingly buoyed.

Not just reassured, but more—as if she was one of them, accepted and embraced.

Millicent, too, seemed happy and gratified. Her aunt had already formed a bond with Minnie and Timms; they were much of a kind, absorbed with observing the lives of those around them.

By the time she'd gone up to dress for dinner, she'd lost every last trepidatious reservation. She'd looked forward to the prospect of his family dinner with genuine anticipation.

To her surprise, he'd arrived at the house while she was dressing. He'd paced in the drawing room, then whisked her into his carriage the instant she was ready, leaving Millicent to follow later with Minnie and Timms. They'd driven to Patience's house in Curzon Street—and gone straight to the nursery.

Her smile deepened. She hadn't until then thought of Gerrard with children, but the trio who'd yelled and come pelting toward him had been totally sure of their reception. With, it had proved, complete justification. He'd devoted half an hour to them. After quelling their rowdy greetings, he'd introduced her; the children had smiled and accepted her in the same, trusting manner their parents had—as if, because she was with Gerrard, she was beyond question a rightful member of their circle.

He'd filled their ears with tales of the gardens of Hellebore Hall. She'd sat quietly and listened; the little girl, Therese, had climbed onto her lap with sublime confidence that she would be welcome. She'd smiled and settled the warm bundle of soft limbs and body, then rested her cheek on the child's head and listened to Gerrard paint her home as she'd never seen it.

Yet she recognized it. That was his talent, to see and be able to convey the magic in landscapes, in the combined creations of nature and man.

When they heard the gong summoning them downstairs, she'd been as reluctant to leave as the children had been to let them go. To her surprise, Therese had kissed her cheek and solemnly informed her she had to come with Gerrard when next he visited.

Touched, she'd smiled. Leaning down, she'd brushed a kiss to Therese's forehead, then lightly ruffled her golden curls. A strange feeling, warm and appealing, had bloomed inside her—even now, reliving it, she wasn't sure what it had meant.

They'd gone down to dinner. It should have been an ordeal, a test she'd had to face. Instead, it had been a relaxed and entertaining affair with much laughter, conversation unlimited, and goodwill on all sides.

She hadn't expected the men to be so charming. No one had had to tell her that they wielded considerable power, not just in society but in wider spheres. Devil Cynster, Duke of St. Ives, was the head of the family, a mantle he'd been born to and carried with flair. He was impressive, yet he'd smiled and teased her; his duchess, Honoria, had dismissed her powerful husband with a haughty wave and welcomed her warmly.

Yet despite their outward ease, in the drawing room after dinner she'd noticed the men—Devil, Vane and Horatia's husband, George—gathering around Gerrard with their port glasses in hand. The subject of the discussion had been serious; she was certain she knew what it had been.

Unconditional, instinctive support—that's what had been behind that purposeful discussion. From the corner of her eye, she focused on Gerrard, still wielding his pencil, absorbed; she wondered if he knew how lucky he was to have a family like that. Not just behind him but all around him.

Always there to lend a hand.

He looked up, caught her eye, then he looked back at his work; a moment later, he stepped back. Head tilted, he glanced from it to her and back again, then he sighed, waved her to him, and turned aside to lay down his pencil.

She lowered her hand, worked her arm back and forth as she walked to him.

He met her before she rounded the easel, caught her waist and steered her back from the canvas. "There's not enough there to make sense of yet."

From a distance of inches, she met his eyes, searched them. "I can pose for longer—I'm not that tired."

He shook his head. His gaze dropped to her lips. "I don't want to overtax you."

He bent his head and his lips found hers; as he whirled her senses into the flames, she wondered if her potential tiredness had prompted him to call a halt, or whether the strength of his desire—which apparently had escalated over five nights of abstinence—wasn't instead the principal force driving him.

Regardless, he wanted her—here, now, as desperately as, within mere seconds, she wanted him. Their desire was mutual, wonderfully so, freeing them both from any hesitation. She offered her mouth, willingly offered her body; she was his to possess.

Gerrard knew it; her eager surrender was pure joy, the vital element that again and again reassured him, that soothed his primitively possessive soul—that side of his nature only she connected with. Only with her had he experienced it; only with her could he explore it and, it seemed, be whole, complete in a way he never had been before.

Between them, passion rose, heated and demanding. Without

breaking the kiss, he stooped and swung her up into his arms. Her hands clutching his shoulders, urgently gripping, he carried her down the long narrow room. Ducking a shoulder between the tapestry hangings screening the room's end, he walked through—to the wide boxed bed set under a pair of dormer windows on the western end of the house. If he'd been painting all night and couldn't face the short walk home, this was where he collapsed.

Compton had made up the bed; with clean sheets, white pillows and a green satin comforter, it sat waiting.

Lifting his head, he waited for Jacqueline's eyes to open, held her gaze for an instant, then smiled, wickedly, and tossed her on the bed.

She half swallowed a shriek, then laughed as, in a froth of skirts, she sank into the soft mattress; he'd had her pose in the gown she'd worn to dinner. Eagerly she looked to right and left, noting the sparse furniture in the alcove. He shrugged out of his shirt, then bent and eased off his boots, watching her all the while.

By the time her gaze returned to him, he was unbuttoning his trousers. She watched, her gaze steady, direct, then she lifted her eyes to his, and raised her hands to the buttons of her bodice.

Undid them, not shyly but with the sultry deliberation of a siren.

His lips curved, not in a smile but in blatant expectation. He stripped off his trousers. Naked, he stood at the end of the bed and flipped her skirts up to her hips. Reaching out, he let his fingertips glide down the fascinating curves of her legs, tracing, then he caught one garter and rolled it down, removing it, her stocking and slipper in one smooth caress. He repeated the action on her other leg, paused for a moment to admire the result, then joined her on the mattress. Pushing her skirts to her waist, he straddled her thighs, and reached for the gown's shoulders as, on her elbows, she struggled to slide her arms free. Between them, they managed it; he drew the gown off over her head and tossed it aside.

Before he could, she tugged the drawstring of her chemise loose, and drew the fine garment up and off.

He had no idea where it landed, had no eyes for anything except her. Here, naked in his bed beneath him. He leaned forward, covered her lips and kissed her with all the passion in his soul, then he closed his hands about her waist, and lifted her.

Sitting back, he set her down straddling his thighs; he didn't need to urge but simply guide her as she shifted forward, over his erection, then sank down and took him deep.

Into the heavenly heat of her body. Their eyes locked, held, and he felt as if she drew him into her soul.

He thrust in, deeper, nudging her womb. Her sheath was a velvet clamp, tight yet giving, slick and scorching as it contracted about his rigid length.

She spread her knees wider, pressed lower, then, satisfied she'd taken him all, she leaned forward; hands splaying, needy and greedy across his chest, she licked one nipple.

He caught his breath, then bent his head and nudged hers up. Their lips met, and the intimate fusion they both craved began.

Without reservation. Without restriction.

Hotter, harder, more intense, ultimately more primal, more primitive and powerful. It was as if with every day that passed they grew closer, learned more of the other, appreciated and thus knew there was yet more they could ask, more they could give. More they could give that the other would want. Would value.

In the last gasping moments when from under heavy lids, their gazes met and desperately clung, that last was beyond obvious. This was special, to them both unique. With no other could they give this much; no other could touch and take, no other would so wantonly seize.

No other could desire to this reckless extent.

They crested the peak in a tumultuous rush, blinded by glory, together they fell, swirling and sinking through their fragmented senses into the void of earthly bliss. Together, still, wrapped in each other's arms they lay as the waves of satiation lapped about them.

The truth had never been so starkly clear.

For each of them, there was no other.

He left her slumped, exhausted in the bed, and returned to the portrait. Jacqueline had no idea where he got the strength, yet, as she reviewed recent events, she could possibly understand his inspiration.

Staring up at the segment of sky visible through the dormer windows, she tried to think, convinced she should, about their liaison—

about how it had evolved, its all-consuming fire—but sleep wouldn't be denied, and she succumbed.

He stirred her awake when the sky was still dark, when stars still sparkled, diamonds scattered by a god's hand. He was a dark god, a shadow blocking out the stars as he rose above her, a night god claiming her, swift, certain, and sure, devastating and divine. In the dark of the night, he demanded and drove her; she sobbed, surrendered, and gave all he asked. Everything he desired. All she wanted.

Pleasure thrummed, hot and sweet through her veins, down her nerves, then completion took her and she shattered.

Later, when dawn was coloring the sky, he led her down to her room. He kissed her, then turned and went back up the hidden stairs. A silly smile on her lips, she watched until he disappeared, then waltzed across the room, and fell into bed.

As she'd arranged, no maid came to wake her until she rang. She slept until midday, then, thoroughly refreshed, rose and prepared for her day.

While Gerrard reviewed his work and planned what he would paint that night, she had a luncheon to attend, then he and she would visit Helen Purfett, after which she, Millicent, Minnie and Timms had been invited to a select afternoon tea at the Marchioness of Huntly's London home.

That day proved a pattern card for those that followed. Other than for the fittings at Helen Purfett's salon, she didn't see Gerrard until he joined them for dinner. After that, he accompanied them to whatever evening engagement they'd accepted, but at ten o'clock, when the summer twilight had faded from the sky, he and she returned to Brook Street and his studio.

Her sessions posing beside the column grew steadily longer.

Their bouts of lovemaking grew progressively more intense.

More intensely intimate.

The brassy bronze gown was completed; clad in it, she stood beside the column. Courtesy of what he'd already painted, she could readily imagine she stood poised on the threshold of the Garden of Night.

About to step free of its cloying embrace.

When she needed a rest, he had her sit on a stool, her face at the same angle as when she was posed, and talk to him of the past—of her mother and Thomas, all she'd felt about their deaths and the hurt of the whisper campaign against her.

It no longer bothered her to speak of it, yet when she did, she could feel the old emotions rising through her—knew that was why he needed her to talk of it, so he could capture those feelings, all that showed in her face, for his canvas.

Increasingly, far more than she'd expected, the portrait became a shared enterprise; she hadn't imagined that painter and subject could work together in such a way, yet with him and her, between them, they did.

She grew steadily more familiar with his work, more critically appreciative of his genius. For genius it was; the figure that took shape on the canvas was so vibrantly alive, every time she looked at it, it was a shock to realize it was her.

Since the day they'd arrived in London, she hadn't seen Barnaby, but one evening at the end of the first week, he sought her and Gerrard out as they were strolling between the guests at Lady Chartwell's soirée.

"There you are!" Joining them, Barnaby looked around the room. "You know, town's not so bad in summer after all—despite the heat, it's a dashed sight more comfortable than any damned house party."

"And whose house party have you been attending?" Jacqueline asked.

Barnaby grimaced. "M'sister's." He met Gerrard's eyes. "And she had, indeed, invited the dreadful Melissa."

Gerrard grinned. "How did you escape?"

"Silently, in the dead of night."

Jacqueline laughed.

Barnaby placed a hand over his heart. "Word of honor."

"But why did you go?" she asked.

"I was chasing m'father. Ran him to earth there, and dashed if he didn't join me in my clandestine bolt to the capital. He's holed up in Bedford Square, swearing not to venture forth other than on official business. Useful, as it happened—I had plenty of time to bend his ear while on the way to town."

"What did you learn?" Gerrard asked. Barnaby's father, the Earl of Sanford, was one of the committee of peers overseeing the newly established metropolitan police force.

Barnaby glanced around, confirming that no one else stood near enough to overhear. "The pater thinks as we do—he's rather impressed by your talents, incidentally." Barnaby grinned briefly, then sobered. "But more to the point, he agreed I should talk to Stokes."

"Who's Stokes?" Jacqueline asked.

"An investigator—I understand his title will now be inspector—with Bow Street. He's more or less a gentleman, but rather more importantly, he's made a name for himself solving convoluted crimes of the sort we're dealing with." Barnaby met Jacqueline's eyes. "I can vouch for his discretion, but given we can't, at this stage, lay any formal complaint, all I'm hoping to get from him is some indication as to which direction his experience suggests we look in for our murderer."

Barnaby fell silent, his gaze on Jacqueline. Understanding what Barnaby wanted—why he'd sought them out—Gerrard asked, "Are you comfortable with Barnaby discussing all we know and believe with Stokes?"

She refocused on Barnaby. "Yes. If he can help, or suggest who might be behind the murders, then of course, do speak with him."

"Just let us know what he says," Gerrard added.

Barnaby grinned. "Righto. I don't plan on going back to the Hall until you're ready with the portrait. I'll be skulking around the traps. Send for me if you need me."

With a snappy salute, he left them. Within minutes he was making his excuses to a disappointed Lady Chartwell.

Ten minutes later, her ladyship's clocks struck the hour—ten o'clock. Gerrard steered Jacqueline to her ladyship's side, and with his customary charm, excused them without, in fact, giving any real excuse. Lady Chartwell smiled, patted Jacqueline's hand, and let them go. His town carriage was waiting; in minutes, they were on their way back to his studio.

D ays passed. Jacqueline posed, Gerrard painted, and the portrait came to life.

It increasingly absorbed him, all but obsessed him. The only distraction capable of disrupting its hold was its subject, Jacqueline herself.

She commanded his attention on a level that effortlessly overrode all else, even his need to paint. How it had happened he didn't know, but she, her nearness, knowing she was his, had become vital, the linchpin of his existence, the very essence of his future. Even while he threw his energies into her portrait, that vulnerability nagged. He hadn't yet secured her—hadn't yet offered for her hand and been accepted.

Time and again, he thought of mentioning it, doing the deed so it was over and done. Accomplished.

Time and again, he remembered she was, in a fashion, in his debt in terms of the portrait—she needed him and his talents to win free, to win back her life. The idea she might feel obliged to accept his offer because of that filled him with creeping horror.

If he asked her now, before the portrait was completed, how would he know, or ever be sure of, her reasons for accepting him?

Which left him facing the single, central source of his uncertainty—he still couldn't guess what she thought. What she truly felt for him, how she saw him. For a man who'd imagined he'd understood women well, it was a humbling situation.

M y dear, I'm so *glad* Gerrard has chosen you."

Jacqueline blinked. She stared at the extremely old, distinctly vague but sweet old lady she'd only met five minutes before.

Aunt Clara reached out, and with her ancient claw lightly patted Jacqueline's hand. "It's always such a relief when our young men make *sensible* decisions—they're all such *good* boys, but they do sometimes seem to drag their heels . . ."

It was the middle of their third week in London; Jacqueline and Millicent had found their social feet. This afternoon they were attending a tea party at St. Ives House in Grosvenor Square.

In introducing Jacqueline to Aunt Clara, who was very, very old, a Cynster by birth, Honoria had whispered that the old lady's mind, while lucid enough, did occasionally wander. So Jacqueline smiled and, leaning closer, whispered, "I'm afraid you've misunderstood. Gerrard and I aren't betrothed."

Swallowing a sip of tea, Aunt Clara nodded. "No, no—of course not. Quite right." She set her cup on its saucer, then serenely continued, "Not that we have many betrothals in this family—quite rare, in fact. While they do drag their heels, once they make up their minds, they tend to want everything settled yesterday—and their chosen wife warming their bed, you see."

An indulgent smile curved the old lady's lips. Fascinated, Jacqueline studied it.

"Quite besotted, they become. And in this case, of course, what with this dreadful business hanging over your head, and dear Gerrard working day and night on the painting, all to free you, I daresay the notion of a betrothal just now isn't his primary concern. Indeed"— Aunt Clara leaned closer and lowered her voice to a quavery whisper—"all things considered, I very much doubt a betrothal of any length will find much favor with him at all."

Jacqueline realized she'd failed to make her point. "Actually—"

"I heard Patience say just yesterday that she wouldn't be surprised if, after you and Gerrard leave to take the painting down to Cornwall to put all right down there, the next time she saw you, you'd be married."

Patience said? Jacqueline stared. Her mind froze, then abruptly raced, in no specific direction. After a moment, she drew in a deep breath, focused again on Aunt Clara's lined face, and carefully asked, "What do the others think?"

Clara made a noise that was half laugh, half snort. "My dear, if we weren't ladies, there'd be wagers exchanged. *Nothing* so delights us as a new marriage in the family. Why"—she waved one crabbed hand to indicate the entire room—"everyone has their own view of the when, and of course we all hope there'll be a wedding to attend, but even if not, and it's done by special license—and I have to say that's very common in this clan—then you may rest assured we'll still have a celebration."

Clara met Jacqueline's eyes and smiled, sweetly charming. "I'm so glad, dear, that you'll be joining us."

Jacqueline smiled weakly, and held her tongue.

S he should have been paying more attention from the first. Later that day, as afternoon edged into evening, Jacqueline paced in her room, agitated yet determined to set things right.

Aunt Clara's comments had opened her eyes. Mentally revisiting all her interactions with Gerrard's family, especially the female members, reinterpreting what had transpired in light of Clara's words had made it perfectly clear Clara's assumptions were shared by many, if not all.

If she'd paid more attention, if she hadn't been so thrilled by their ready acceptance of her, if she'd had more experience of large families, especially tonnish families . . . but she hadn't. She now faced a serious misinterpretation, on a major scale, one honesty let alone honor demanded she correct.

But how to do that?

She racked her brain, yet there seemed only one way forward.

Halting her pacing, she consulted the clock. It wasn't yet time to dress for dinner. Millicent was taking a nap. Minnie and Timms hadn't accompanied them today, but had remained at home; they would have napped earlier. At this hour, they were usually to be found in the back parlor.

They were there, Timms tatting as always, Minnie sitting in a chair in the waning sunshine. They looked up as she entered, smiling in greeting.

Halting before them, she pressed her hands tightly together and drew in a deep breath. "I wonder if I might speak with you both for a moment."

They exchanged a quick glance, then Minnie beamed. "Of course, dear. Sit beside Timms there—we're all ears."

"You have our undivided attention," Timms confirmed, although her fingers never slackened.

Jacqueline sank onto the chaise. Minnie's faded eyes fixed on her; anticipation lit her face. Now she was here . . . "I'm really not sure where to begin."

"Try the beginning," Timms advised. "That usually works best."

"Yes, well . . . you've all been so kind, to both myself and Millicent, so welcoming. I'm so grateful—you've made coming up to town so much easier for us both."

"But of course, dear." Minnie's eyes twinkled.

"Yes, well, you see . . ." Jacqueline drew in another breath and plunged on. "I've just realized that there seems to be some confusion over the . . . ah, *connection* between myself and Gerrard." She looked from Timms to Minnie; no comprehension yet showed in their eyes.

"Gerrard is helping me break free of my problems at home, helping to rescue me if you will, but his reasons for doing so—for painting my portrait—are, well, *professional,* and of course he's motivated to assist a lady as a true gentleman should. That's all that connects us, yet I fear an . . . an *expectation* has arisen that's based on the notion that there's some link of a more *personal* nature between him and me."

Both Minnie and Timms were frowning, but lightly, as if her pronouncement merely puzzled them. "Do you mean," Timms asked, "that you aren't thinking of marrying him?"

Jacqueline stared at her; she couldn't think of any way to answer but equally bluntly. "No. That is," she quickly amended, "it's not a question of my wanting to marry him so much as there's never been any suggestion of marriage between us. We've never discussed it."

"*Ah.*" Timms turned to exchange a look denoting some deep understanding with Minnie.

Minnie's smile returned, brighter than ever. "I wouldn't let that worry you, dear. They—our men—are chronically backward in coming forward, at least when it comes to *discussing* matrimony." Her gaze grew considering. "Indeed, I can't, off the top of my head, remember one who ever has . . ."

After a moment, Minnie returned her gaze to Jacqueline's face, her expression unquenchably cheery. "But don't let it trouble you, dear. We've known Gerrard from the cradle, and he definitely intends to marry you."

She managed not to show any sign of exasperation—or of the strange panic slowly brewing inside. She kept her gaze fixed on Minnie's twinkling eyes. "Indeed, ma'am, I do assure you there's nothing like that between us. Gerrard is merely interested in me in terms of the portrait."

"*Pfft!*" Timms caught her eye. "Nonsense." Her sharp eyes studied Jacqueline's face, then she gruffly continued, "However, I can see that you believe it, which perhaps isn't surprising, stubborn nodcock that Gerrard can be—supercilious and arrogant, too, although I suspect he'll have hidden that side of himself, at least from you. Humph!" She paused to tug a piece of yarn free. "Regardless, I'd strongly advise you to start thinking of how you'll answer when he asks whether you want a big wedding, or if you'd rather be married by special license. Incidentally"—Timms caught Jacqueline's eye—"we'll all be most disappointed if you opt for the special license."

She couldn't simply smile weakly and retreat, and leave things as they were. Jacqueline opened her lips —

"Indeed, dear." Minnie leaned forward and patted her hand. "I do understand that perhaps, from your point of view, we've jumped the gun a trifle, and I can quite see that coming from the country, you wouldn't have immediately realized, and it's very sweet of you to think to explain now, but I do assure you that in reading Gerrard's intentions toward you we haven't made any mistake."

Jacqueline stared into Minnie's steady blue eyes. "He isn't thinking of marrying me."

"Oh, yes he is," Timms averred. "I've known him since he was a squalling infant, and he's definitely set his sights on you." She met Jacqueline's eyes, and grinned. "Mind you, given he's done such an excellent job of hiding his intentions from you, I wouldn't want to be in his boots when he finally asks for your hand."

Minnie chuckled. "Indeed, not."

Jacqueline looked from one to the other; both were clearly enjoying imagining Gerrard's difficulties when he proposed. But he wasn't going to . . .

It was hopeless. She sighed and sat back, then rose and excused herself. They let her go with fond smiles, and reassurances that all would be well — she would see.

She returned to her room; she spent the hour before dinner bathing — and thinking.

It was impossible not to wonder, just for a moment, if they could be right and she wrong. Minnie, Timms and Patience — and the rest of them — indisputably knew Gerrard, knew gentlemen of his ilk, much better than she; they all had much more experience in correctly interpreting male behavior.

That was all very well, yet in this case . . .

Head back on the edge of the tub, steam wreathing about her face, she closed her eyes and thought back to all she and he had ever said on the subject. She couldn't be sure she recalled his words verbatim, but he'd insisted he could make no promises. She'd accepted his attentions on that basis; he'd said nothing since to suggest he'd changed his mind.

Yet Minnie, Timms and Patience were convinced . . . and they didn't even know of the interludes in the alcove off Gerrard's studio.

Didn't know of all that had grown between them.

Cocooned in the warm water, veiled by the steam, detached from the world, she looked inward. And asked herself, in light of all that had evolved between them over the past weeks, what she wished now. She thought, considered, weighed as well as she could the connection, the link, the indescribable communion that between them transformed the physical act into an emotional, almost spiritual experience. A transcendent moment of glory, for which she now yearned.

She'd wanted to know, to learn, and he'd shown her, taught her, and more. He'd given her all that; she was more grateful than she could say. Simply thinking of the feelings that welled and spilled through her when they joined was wonderful. Joyous.

He'd shown her that—all a woman could be.

She was grateful, happy, and would gladly sup further at his table. For herself, yes, she would accept any extension of their time together, and take full pleasure in all they could share, but would she go so far as marriage?

To that, no ready answer sprang to mind. She hadn't considered the concept, not for years; she was no longer sure how she felt in that regard.

Yet with regard to him, how he felt, she *knew* he'd accepted the commission to paint her because of the professional challenge, and he'd stuck with it because of a chivalrous determination to see her free. He hadn't seduced her—she'd insisted on it. As her portraitist, he'd wanted to learn more of her, all he could of her; that their interaction had subsequently evolved to its present extent wasn't something she could, or wished to, lay at his door.

It had simply happened. It simply was.

She couldn't hold him responsible. To her mind, there was no justification to even mention the subject of marriage, let alone expect him to be thinking of it. Even if, on reflection, she decided marriage to him might suit her, it wouldn't, to her mind, be honorable to even raise the matter, much less expect him to agree.

The water had grown cold. Rising, she stepped onto the rug spread before the hearth, and reached for the towel the maid had left ready. Drying herself, she followed her thoughts. Between them, all seemed clear and straightforward. However . . .

She couldn't leave the ladies who'd been so kind to her, who'd so openly taken her to their hearts, believing there was a wedding in the wind. That would be deceitful, and she'd never been that—Eleanor's province, not hers.

Yes, she'd tried to correct their mistake, and yes, they'd routed her comprehensively, but that didn't absolve her from doing all she could to convince them that she wasn't, as they clearly supposed, Gerrard's intended, his fiancée in all but name.

So how was she to convince them they were wrong?

Proof. She needed some words, action or evidence that clearly indicated he wasn't thinking of marrying her. Something actual, factual . . .

She brightened; crossing to the bellpull, she rang for the maid. After dinner, they were to attend a party, with dancing, at Lady Sommerville's. Collecting suitable, citable evidence in such a venue shouldn't be too hard.

18

One of the great attractions of a trip to London was the chance of visiting the very best modistes. With Millicent, Jacqueline had taken full advantage of the capital's amenities; when, that evening, she climbed Lady Sommerville's staircase on Gerrard's arm, she felt positively glowing in a gown of amber silk surprinted with a delicate dark bronze tracery.

She'd donned the new gown to bolster her confidence; she also hoped it would make her task that evening easier by attracting the attention of other gentlemen.

During their evenings' entertainments, Gerrard always hovered by her side, presumably to ensure she remained untroubled, and so he could whisk her away when the clocks struck ten. She was his subject; naturally, he wanted her in the right frame of mind to pose for him. There was nothing more behind his attentiveness, his hovering, than that. They were lovers, true, and he was possessive in that sphere, but in general in society, she could see no reason for him to be so.

Not unless he was thinking of marrying her, which he wasn't. That was what she needed to prove.

After greeting Lord and Lady Sommerville, she and Gerrard swept into the ballroom. It wasn't a huge room, and this wasn't, she'd been told, a large party, yet she was pleased to note numerous dark coats dotted amid the bright satins and silks.

Gerrard steered her in Millicent's wake; they eventually stopped beside a chaise on which Lady Horatia Cynster sat. Exchanging pleasantries, Millicent settled beside her ladyship; with Gerrard, Jacqueline moved to stand to one side of the chaise.

Intent on her plan, she lifted her head and eagerly scanned the guests.

Gerrard seized the moment to less than approvingly scan her. Where the devil had she gotten that gown? The silk hugged her figure, clung to her breasts, outlined the quintessentially feminine curve of her waist and the evocative flare of her hips. As for the long line of her legs that always transfixed him, the fine material flirted and seduced, first revealing, then concealing as she moved. Worse, whenever she moved, the light corruscated over the complex fabric, drawing the eye to her delectable curves.

And not just his eye.

Mental alarm bells rang. Glancing around, he inwardly swore. It was summer. The crowd was small and commensurately more select—and of quite a different caliber to that of a ball during the Season. There were few bright young things in evidence; they were all attending country house parties in the hope of snaring a husband. Likewise, the younger gentlemen had in the main been hauled off by their fond mamas, to either do their duty by their sisters, or to look over the field, also at those same house parties.

The vast majority of those left in town, including all those strolling or prowling through Lady Sommerville's ballroom, weren't interested in snaring a husband or wife. They were, however, definitely interested in members of the opposite sex.

Too many of the gentlemen had already noticed Jacqueline.

He used the term "gentlemen" generically; many of the males present were wolves of the ton. He knew them; on the rare occasions he could be persuaded to attend such affairs, he was normally classed among their number.

Some dark emotion, one that made him feel like snarling, rose when he saw one of his peers cast his eye assessingly over Jacqueline. This would definitely be the last time she wore that gown in public, at least not until they were married, and perhaps not even then.

The intrigued gentleman noticed his hard stare; they locked eyes. After a moment, the gentleman's lips curved; he inclined his head and moved on.

Just as well.

Gerrard glanced at Jacqueline, then surreptitiously drew out his watch and checked. It was just nine o'clock; he had an hour to endure before he could legitimately whisk her away. The obvious alternative tempted, but Horatia was there. Patience's mama-in-law, she regarded him as a cross between a nephew and a grandson; she would notice any change in his schedule and report it.

Beside him, Jacqueline shifted; she slid her hand onto his arm. "Let's stroll. Most others are."

She started walking; he fell in beside her, not at all sure mingling with his strutting peers was a wise idea. But she was on his arm; he could steer her clear of any—

Halting, she half turned and smiled, inviting the attention of a couple nearby. "Good evening."

Gerrard looked, and inwardly groaned.

Two unquestionably eager steps brought Perry Somerset, Lord Castleton, to Jacqueline's side. Beside Perry, rather more reluctantly, came Mrs. Lucy Atwell, Perry's current paramour.

Tall and stylishly handsome, Perry reached for Jacqueline's hand, and threw Gerrard a glance. "Do introduce us, old chap."

Inwardly gritting his teeth, he did; Perry bowed elegantly.

Lucy and Jacqueline exchanged polite nods.

"I'm delighted to meet you, Miss Tregonning." Lucy's fine eyes roved Jacqueline's gown. "I must compliment you on your attire— Cerise?"

"No, Celeste."

"Ah." Lucy flashed him a measuring look. "I've heard Mr. Debbington has been burning the midnight oil—literally—in painting a fabulous portrait of you. Do you find his demands difficult to meet?"

"Not at all." Jacqueline's smile was transparently assured. "I quite enjoy it."

"Indeed?" Lucy's brows arched; the look she threw him was arch, too. She knew that prior to Jacqueline, he'd only painted people he was close to; she was searching for some reason—the most obvious reason—as to why he was painting Jacqueline, but had refused to paint her, stunning though she was.

Before he could steer the conversation into safer, less ambiguous waters, Perry asked if they'd visited Kew Gardens.

That was such a strange question to hear coming from Perry, a rakehell who rarely saw the sun, both Gerrard and Lucy stared at him.

"No," Jacqueline brightly replied. "But I've heard they're impressive."

"I've heard the same about the gardens at your home," Perry said. "Perhaps you'd like to view Kew one afternoon, to compare?"

"No." Gerrard laid his hand over Jacqueline's on his sleeve. "I'm afraid we don't have time—the sittings are quite arduous."

Jacqueline looked at him. "But I don't sit in the afternoons."

He met her eyes. "You will be, starting tomorrow."

"But—"

"And the very last thing we need is more freckles."

She stared at him; she didn't possess a single freckle, not anywhere, and he knew it.

The squeak of violins cut through the room.

"Perhaps some other time," Perry said cheerily. "Meanwhile, if you would grant me the honor—"

"I'm afraid I'm before you, old boy." Gerrard clamped his fingers about Jacqueline's hand; catching her eye, he raised her fingers to his lips. "My dance, I believe?"

She thought—actively *thought*—about refusing him. He saw it in her eyes. What she saw in his—the emotion that flared in response—apparently convinced her to acquiesce with good grace.

He returned his gaze to Lucy and Perry. "If you'll excuse us?"

"Of course." Lucy was looking daggers at Perry, who hadn't yet noticed.

Gerrard led Jacqueline to the dance floor, then swung her into his arms and stepped into the swirling throng. If he was wise, he wouldn't make any comment. After all, what could he say?

"Why this sudden urge to consort with strangers?" Even to his ears, the question sounded ludicrous; worse, his tone registered as aggrieved.

He wasn't surprised when she looked at him, her eyes wide. "What on earth do you mean? They're other guests. I thought we should be sociable."

Why? He bit his tongue and looked over her head, steering her into a turn. The soft shush of her skirts against his trousers, the feel of her supple body, pliant under his hand at her back, soothed his unexpected irritation. What was he so agitated over? A few words?

Or because she'd sought Perry's attention?

He didn't like the answer. Drawing her fractionally closer, he im-

mersed himself in the dance, gave himself up to the predictable pleasure of waltzing her around the room. The whirling left them cocooned in time and space, alone in the middle of a crowd.

Alone with her—that was how he preferred to be. Until now he'd
thought himself a social animal, at least when he wasn't painting, but
with her, when it came to her, he was discovering new aspects of himself every day.

Jacqueline remained silent, content to whirl safe in his arms while
she thought through what had just occurred. Eventually, she looked
up at Gerrard. "Is there an understanding between Lord Castleton
and Mrs. Atwell?"

His lips thinned. "Yes."

"Ah. I see." She looked away. In stopping Castleton from claiming her hand, Gerrard had been steering her clear of stepping on Mrs.
Atwell's toes. Very properly. He hadn't been acting possessively but
protectively; it was sometimes difficult to tell.

She revisited her plan; it still seemed viable, but she clearly needed
to make a few adjustments. Next time, she would have to find someone to entertain Gerrard, someone he was willing to be entertained by.

At the end of the dance, by mutual accord they resumed their
stroll.

Finding someone she could be certain Gerrard would be willing
to be entertained by wasn't as easy as she'd hoped, but by dint of
steady application, she finally set eyes on the perfect group.

"Mrs. Wainwright, what a pleasure to see you." She smiled at the
stylish matron and bobbed a curtsy, then exchanged greetings with the
lady's two unmarried daughters, Chloe and Claire. Jacqueline had met
the trio at a number of afternoon engagements, and at a musicale.

The family knew Patience and Gerrard well; their home lay near
Gerrard's estate in Derbyshire. Gerrard shook hands and bowed.
Chloe and Claire's eyes lit; they responded warmly, and asked after
his horses.

Delighted to have found such young ladies, of suitable age and
perfectly sensible, to keep Gerrard company, Jacqueline turned her
smile on the last member of the group—a handsome, well-dressed
gentleman whose features declared him to be Chloe and Claire's older
brother, Rupert. Jacqueline recalled some mention of him.

"Hello!" Smiling, she gave him her hand. "You must be Rupert."

"I confess I am." With a delighted smile, Rupert bowed, all long-limbed grace. His eyes twinkled as he straightened. "Whatever tales they've told of me are probably true."

She laughed.

"I heard you're in town sitting for Gerrard—that's quite a coup. Have you had time to see much of London?"

"A little—not perhaps as much as I'd have liked, but . . ."

Gerrard chatted with the Wainwright girls, simultaneously monitoring Jacqueline's exchange with Rupert. He knew Rupert, knew his propensities, but Rupert was behaving himself—as usual when under his mother's eagle eye.

Confirming that Mrs. Wainwright did indeed have her eye on Rupert, Gerrard relaxed, and gave his attention to Chole and Claire; he'd known them all their lives.

He didn't see the danger, until it was too late.

"There's the musicians again." Rupert swept Jacqueline a bow. "Can I tempt you onto the floor, Miss Tregonning?"

Gerrard whipped around—but he'd danced the last dance with Jacqueline.

"Thank you." Jacqueline smiled gloriously and gave Rupert her hand. "That would be delightful."

No, it wouldn't be. Gerrard inwardly swore; Mrs. Wainwright tensed, and shifted nervously. In something close to mounting panic, he watched Jacqueline, oblivious, smile and chat to Rupert as he led her to the floor . . .

Turning to Chloe, he reached for her hand. "If you would grant me the honor of this dance, Miss Wainwright?" He barely waited for her agreement before leading her in her brother's wake.

The music swelled as they reached the floor; he swung Chloe into his arms, his gaze fixed on Jacqueline. They started revolving; he steered them as close to Jacqueline and Rupert as he could.

Chloe sighed. "Nothing will happen until the end of the dance."

When he looked down at her, she rolled her eyes resignedly. "He uses the dance to butter them up—you know what he's like. When the music ends, she'll be curious to see whatever it is he's invented this time, but still convinced he's perfectly trustworthy."

"As most of us know, he's not."

"Indeed. But there's nothing you can do until the dance finishes, so I'd appreciate it if you'd stop staring at them, and pay attention to where we're *going*!" Chloe tugged at his shoulder; they barely avoided another couple.

Gerrard colored. "Sorry." He hadn't blushed in decades.

He tried to comply with Chloe's edict—he knew she was right—but logic couldn't prevail against the dark impulses surfacing; time and again, he darted glances at Jacqueline as, laughing and smiling gaily, she circled the floor in Rupert's expert arms.

Jaw clenched, his teeth almost grinding, Gerrard waited for the waltz to wind to its conclusion.

Whirling around the room, Jacqueline wondered if any other man was ever going to meet, let alone eclipse, the standards Gerrard had set. Her senses assessed Rupert, and despite his obvious expertise, found him wanting. In just what way, she couldn't say, but it was simply not the same as waltzing with Gerrard. Inwardly sighing, she continued to respond to Rupert's conversation. He certainly had a glib tongue. They'd touched on various topics; he'd now steered the conversation to gardens.

Why they all thought she must be interested in gardens she had no idea. Yes, the gardens of Hellebore Hall were fantastic, but she'd grown up with them; she took their extravagant beauty and power largely for granted.

As if sensing how mild was her interest, Rupert shifted the conversation to statuary, specifically statues of Greek and Roman gods.

"I say." His hazel eyes lit. "There's a fascinating statue in the library here. Have you seen it?"

She shook her head. "This is only the second time I've visited here."

"Ah, well—this is not to be missed. I'm sure Lady Sommerville, if she'd thought of it, would have suggested you view it. Coming from a house surrounded by gardens devoted to various gods, you'll appreciate it—it's a fabulously lifelike depiction of a thoroughly remarkable naked god. I've never been able to decide which one—perhaps you could hazard a guess."

The music slowed; their feet halted. Rupert took her hand. "Come—let me show it to you. I assure you, it'll take your breath away."

He looked so eager, she hadn't the heart to argue, let alone refuse. Especially as Rupert was helping her prove her point. She glanced back as he led her out into a corridor; she couldn't see Gerrard. When last she'd glimpsed him, he'd been waltzing with Chloe.

The sight had caused her an unexpected pang, yet if, as she contended, his interest in her derived solely from her being his subject, and not at all because he saw her as his intended bride, then naturally, given the right opportunity, his attention should wander.

If she spent the next hour with Rupert and other gentlemen, quite apart from Gerrard, while he spent that time enjoying the company of some other lady or ladies, then surely she could cite that as tangible evidence—as factual, actual proof—that he didn't see her as his future wife.

Rupert halted, threw open a door and waved her through. Crossing the threshold, she heaved an inward sigh. She felt certain that if Gerrard did see her as his bride, he wouldn't allow her to be alone with Rupert.

Yet he had. So . . . here she was, in a darkened library. Actually alone with Rupert. She'd assumed the room would be open to guests, with lamps lit and maybe a few older gentlemen snoozing in armchairs. Instead, it was deserted, the dark shadows thrown by packed bookcases and heavily curtained windows encroaching on a desk and chairs grouped in the room's center.

Rupert closed the door, plunging the room into deeper darkness. It took a moment for her eyes to adjust.

She looked about, swiveling to scan the room. "Where's the statue?"

Rupert drew near. "Well, my dear, just give me a few minutes, and I'll create it—to your abundant satisfaction."

His tone warned her; clearly she'd made a serious error in judgment. Swinging to face him, she stared. "*What?*"

Rupert shrugged off his coat and tossed it on the desk. He smiled, his hands rising to his cravat. "Confess. You didn't *really* think there was a statue, not one of marble, did you?"

His attempt at a seductive purr grated on her nerves. "Yes! I did!" She glared at him. "And here—" Grabbing his coat, she thrust it at him. "Put that back on."

Rupert waggled his eyebrows. "No." His cravat half undone, he undid his waistcoat and tugged his shirt from his waistband. "I promised you a naked god, and I always keep my promises."

She narrowed her eyes at him, then nodded. "Very well. But I never promised I'd stay and watch."

She darted to the side, intending to slip past him and race to the door.

He was quick, too quick; stepping sideways, he blocked her path.

Then he smiled, cynical yet still stupidly eager, and moved nearer. Pressing her, herding her, back toward the desk.

He took her out this way." Gerrard stalked into the corridor, towing Chloe behind him. He wanted a witness, especially one of Rupert's family, so there'd be someone who'd know the reason for him thrashing Rupert to within an inch of his life.

"Are you sure?" Chloe asked, her tone beyond resigned.

"Yes." Gerrard paused and looked up and down the corridor. "Where the devil have they gone? There's no rooms open this way."

"Rupert won't be looking for an *open* room."

Gerrard swore, and headed down the corridor, Chloe's hand in his. "Your brother's incorrigible."

"You're one to talk."

"*Me? I* don't waltz young ladies out of ballrooms."

"Precisely."

Chloe's tone was tart. Gerrard threw her a warning glance, which she met with a sour look.

"*Ooooow!!*" *Crash!*

The commotion came from a room further down the corridor. Gerrard dropped Chloe's hand and ran.

"*No!*"

As he flung open the door, he realized it was Rupert shrieking.

"*Stop* it! That's enough. Put the damned thing down!"

The sight that met his eyes brought Gerrard up short. Rupert, his shirt hanging open and cravat askew, was on the floor, on his arse, desperately scrabbling backward from Jacqueline, a virago wielding a long wooden ruler.

Protecting his head with his raised arms, Rupert wasn't escaping.

"You *fiend*!" Jacqueline laid into him, slapping the ruler against his thigh. "You *witless . . .*" Words failed her. Dragging in a breath, she brandished the ruler. "Put your clothes back on this instant! Do you hear me? *Now!*"

Gerrard had known she had a temper; he hadn't previously seen it totally unleashed.

Her eyes blazed as, unimpressed with Rupert's bumbling attempts to find his buttonholes, she stepped nearer and raised her arm.

"No, *no* — see, I'm dressing — I *am!*"

"Good!" She stood over him and glared. "Don't you ever — *ever!* — try such a thing with any other young lady. If you do, I'll hear of it, and I'll . . . I'll — "

"I have a horsewhip you can borrow."

Jacqueline jerked her head up, stared at Gerrard as he calmly — too calmly, with far too much control — strolled into the room. Snapping her mouth shut, she straightened, and slipped the ruler behind her, into the folds of her skirts. "Ah . . ." She really didn't like the feral look in Gerrard's eyes, which were fixed unwaveringly on Rupert. "Rupert had an accident."

Gerrard's lips curved, not in a smile. "I know just what sort of accident Rupert had. What, incidentally, caused the crash?"

"He fell over a stool."

After she'd pushed him, then whacked him with the ruler.

"How unfortunate."

Gerrard's drawl was deepening — worsening.

"Yes, well . . ." Jacqueline blew out a breath, puffing aside a lock of hair her tussle with Rupert had loosened. "As you can see" — she went to gesture at the cowering Rupert, then realized she had the ruler in that hand and switched to using her other — "he's . . . getting himself together again."

Much as she was tempted to leave Rupert to whatever fate Gerrard might mete out, it was, in a way, at her instigation that Rupert had come to be alone with her. She'd never imagined he'd do anything so patently silly, but . . . He was nearly finished buttoning his shirt. He didn't seem able to look away from them, his eyes wide, resting first on her, then on Gerrard; he looked like he was struggling not to whimper. "And then he's leaving," she pointedly said, hoping he'd take the hint and go with all speed.

"Oh, he's definitely leaving."

Gerrard took one step, grasped Rupert's arm and hauled him to his feet.

"Here! I say, old chap—"

Resisting the urge to shake Rupert, Gerrard marched him to the door. "Just be thankful there are ladies present."

Rupert goggled at Chloe, a silent martyr in the doorway, and shut up.

Chloe stepped back. Gerrard thrust Rupert, still struggling to tuck his shirttails in, through the door, then nodded to Chloe. "If you'll excuse us?"

No real question; he shut the door on Chloe's suddenly interested face and turned back into the room.

Jacqueline watched Gerrard stalk, slowly, toward her. While he'd been occupied, she'd tossed the ruler back on the desk, and quickly smoothed down her skirts. Pressing her hands together, she lifted her chin.

"What the *devil* were you thinking, going off alone with Rupert?" Gerrard halted immediately before her, his expression hard, a definite scowl in his eyes. His tone was harsh, rather flat.

She tilted her chin higher, and suppressed an answering frown. "He said there was a special statue in here. I had no idea he had such a . . . a salacious scheme in mind."

"Well, he did." Gerrard's eyes bored into hers; his accents were exceedingly clipped. "Indeed, I think it safe to say most of the gentlemen you'll meet in this season will be entertaining salacious thoughts of you. Most, however, won't act on them, not unless you encourage them—for instance, by going apart with them in a setting such as this!"

He paused; she saw something—some emotion—roiling behind his eyes. Instead of giving voice to it, lips compressing, he reached for her hand, turned and headed for the door. "I would be exceedingly grateful if in the remaining few days we're in town, you could refrain from consorting with other men."

Towed behind him, she almost tripped. "No." She pulled back on his hand, then almost tipped backward as with a low growl, he swung to face her. "What I mean," she hastily amended, eyeing his harsh expression, "is *why*?"

For a moment, he said nothing, just stared at her. Then, "In case it's slipped your mind, we're lovers."

His tone had grown dangerous again; for one fanciful instant she felt as if she was in a darkened room with a large wild animal. Her nerves flickered. Her eyes locked on his, she carefully said, "Yes, but that's . . . private. Just because we're lovers shouldn't mean I don't dance or speak with other gentlemen. No one else knows we're lovers—it looks odd if I cling to your arm all the time."

And you cling to mine. People are getting quite the wrong idea . . . But she didn't wish to be quite so forthright. He might feel obliged to marry her if society expected it, but once the portrait was finished, she'd return to Cornwall, and society would be irrelevant.

She could see thoughts shifting behind his eyes.

His expression hardened, his jaw set. "We'll only be in town for a few more days—any additional *oddity* will be neither here nor there."

Turning, he started towing her to the door again.

Her grand plan lay in shreds, and if he adhered to his pigheaded edict and insisted she remain by his side, she'd never be able to correct the mistaken impression they'd given the ladies of his family—and possibly everyone else.

They were nearing the door. She dug in her heels and tugged back. "No. What you don't understand—"

He halted; his chest swelled, then he rounded on her. His eyes blazed; his features resembled a granite mask. The air between them shimmered with aggression, and poorly concealed possessiveness. "Do you recall"—his voice had lowered, his diction precise, his tone a dark warning—"agreeing to be mine *until I released you?*"

She had to nod. "Yes, but—"

"I haven't released you." His eyes burned, holding hers. "Until I do, you're mine—and—no—other's."

She stared at him, stunned; she'd never imagined he'd draw such a line.

Apparently believing her silence denoted agreement, he continued in a fractionally less domineering vein as he turned and opened the door, "Specifically, you will not encourage any other gentlemen—you won't seek their company, nor encourage them to seek yours."

Drawing her through the door, he reached back, shut it—and to her continuing dumbfounded astonishment went on as he led her back to the ballroom, "And most importantly, you will not go anywhere alone with cads like Rupert—"

She shook aside her astonishment; it was doing her no good.

"How the *devil* was I to know he was a cad?" Her temper rose. "If you want my opinion, Rupert's a handsome lackwit. For the good of young ladies everywhere he should be locked up in Derbyshire—"

"If you'd remembered your promise—"

"I *didn't* promise you my every hour!"

"I have news for you. You did." His voice had gone dangerously flat. The gaze he bent on her was hard and unyielding. "Even if you didn't mean it, I'm claiming exactly that—every last hour of every day."

She searched his eyes; her jaw fell.

He held her gaze for a pregnant instant, then looked ahead and whisked her into the ballroom.

Jacqueline snapped her mouth shut, bit her tongue, swallowed her scream of frustration; too many pairs of eyes had fastened on them.

Setting her hand on his arm, Gerrard led her through the guests; only she was aware of his glamour, the contradiction between his outward languid elegance as he nodded to others, and the tension in the muscles beneath her fingers, the rampant possessiveness in the hand covering hers on his sleeve.

She plastered a light smile over her clenched teeth. Bloody-minded, arrogant, *obstreporous man*! She was only trying to make all right with his family—

It hit her. Suddenly, just like that, in the middle of Lady Sommerville's ballroom.

The scales fell from her eyes with a resounding crash. She halted abruptly, almost swaying from the shock.

Gerrard smoothly shifted; long fingers closing about her elbow, he propelled her on. "We're leaving."

"Now?" A species of panic clutched at her stomach. She looked for Millicent. "But it's not yet ten."

"Close enough. Millicent will know we've left. Horatia will drive her home."

It was a routine they'd followed for the last week, but . . . She needed to think. Desperately needed time to straighten her tangled thoughts.

Her frighteningly dizzying novel thoughts.

In no mood to brook any resistance, Gerrard escorted her out of the ballroom and down the stairs. In the foyer, they waited while his carriage was summoned, then he handed her in and joined her. The door was shut, the horses given the office. The carriage rattled out along the road, and they were alone, sitting side by side in the warm dark.

Teeth gritted, he held his demons down, soothed them with the fact that she was with him, beside him, unharmed, and would remain so, with him, from now on. Until he'd finished the portrait, extricated her from the web of suspicion in Cornwall—and carried her off and married her.

That was his plan, and it was set in stone. Immutable, not open to modification.

Thank heavens Timms had, in her inimitable fashion, warned him. If she hadn't met him in the corridor that evening and twitted him over allowing Jacqueline to remain in ignorance of his intentions, if Timms hadn't mentioned the conversation she and Minnie had had with Jacqueline, he'd never have guessed what Jacqueline was about, what was behind her seeking to spend time with other men—and his reaction would have been a great deal less controlled.

Given how fraught, how provoked he'd still felt, even guessing her reasons, the gods only knew what horrors Timms and her teasing had averted.

Sitting in the carriage as it rocked along, excruciatingly aware of Jacqueline beside him, warm, feminine, the perfect answer to his every desire, no matter how deep or dark, guilt seeped through him; the blame for her uncertainty over his intentions lay squarely at his door.

He'd shied away from speaking—of his wish to marry her and even more of his *need* to marry her—and part of that, definitely, had been a craven wish to protect his own heart, by not acknowledging it, to conceal the vulnerability he felt over loving her.

Be that as it may, he still couldn't speak, not until the portrait was finished, and she—her winning free of the suspicions over her mother's death—no longer depended on him, on his talents, and his exercising those in her cause. Waiting was still the honorable way forward.

Imagining it—putting his proposal to the test, laying his future at her feet—sent apprehension snaking down his spine. To him his future might be immutable, but it would only be so if she agreed.

He still had no real idea of her feelings, felt no certainty over how she would react. Did she love him? He still didn't know.

Drawing in a breath, he shifted to glance at her. She'd been staring straight ahead, unusually silent. The flare from a street lamp fleetingly lit her face. Her expression looked . . . unreadable.

He frowned. "I expect the portrait to take two, possibly three, more days to complete. After that, I suggest we return to Cornwall with all speed. We set the stage before we left—no sense delaying and letting the questions we successfully raised fade from people's minds."

Through the gloom, Jacqueline studied his face. "Only three days?" She hadn't seen the portrait in the last day or so, hadn't realized he was so close to finishing it.

He nodded, and looked ahead. "I'd appreciate it if you could remain at the house over that time. In case I need to check a line or adjust the shading."

She felt her expression harden. "And you'll be able to concentrate better if you know I'm in the house, and not gallivanting about falling prey to gentlemen cads?"

His jaw tightened. A fraught moment passed, then he nodded. "Precisely."

He glanced, sharply, at her; even through the dimness she felt the lancing quality of his gaze. "Three days, and the portrait will be finished . . ." His voice faded; he cleared his throat and looked away. "As for what's between us, we'll talk of that later."

She narrowed her eyes, glared through the gloom, but he was looking out of the window. *Later?* Damn him! He *was* intending to marry her.

Just thinking the words left her shaken, as if the earth had tilted beneath her feet. In some ways it had.

Everyone else had seen it; only she hadn't.

She wasn't at all sure how she felt about that.

The carriage rocked to a halt in Brook Street. He descended to the pavement and handed her down, then escorted her up the steps and into the front hall.

Masters shut the door behind them. Jacqueline smiled at him. "Aunt Millicent will return later. I doubt she'll be late."

"Indeed, miss—she rarely is." Masters bowed and retreated.

Gerrard took her arm. Grasping her skirts, she climbed the stairs beside him.

In the gallery, she paused. Drawing breath, she faced him. "I'm really not feeling all that well—a bit . . . unsteady." True enough; her wits were whirling giddily. "I know you're in a rush to complete the portrait, but I wonder if you can manage without me for tonight."

The lamps were turned low, yet even in the weak light, the concern that filled his eyes, his whole face, was visible. His grip on her arm firmed, as if he thought she might faint. "Damn! I knew I was pushing you too hard. You should have said."

That last was uttered through gritted teeth, but there was enough self-censure in his tone for her to let it pass; he was irate with himself, not her.

"Come—let's get you to bed." He glanced at her as he steered her along the corridor. "It isn't something you ate?"

She shook her head. It was something she'd heard, something she'd realized. "I'm just . . . overtired." And she needed time alone to think.

His lips set; he opened her door and guided her in. She'd expected him to ring for her maid and leave her. Instead, he led her to her dressing stool, sat her gently down, and proceeded to pull the pins from her hair.

She stared at him in the mirror. "Ah . . . my maid can do that. You should go to the studio."

He shook his head. "I want to see you settled."

She tried twice more to get him to leave, to no avail. Then, to her even greater astonishment, after tucking her into bed, he hesitated, frowning down at her, then shrugged out of his coat. "I'll sleep with you for a while. The portrait will go faster if I take a break, and without you . . ."

The suspicion that he knew she wasn't truly ill and was calling her bluff, as it were, occurred only to be dismissed; the look on his face was a transparent medley of concern and worry.

Guilt jabbed at her, but she desperately needed time to think. How she was to accomplish that with him lying naked beside her . . .

He slid under the covers and reached for her. She half expected him to make love to her; instead, he gathered her gently into his arms, settling her against his warmth. He bent his head, searched for her lips, but there was no passion in his kiss, only gentleness.

"Go to sleep."

With that order, he relaxed beside her, around her, sinking deeper into the soft mattress.

He fell asleep in minutes.

She didn't.

Listening to his breathing, she turned her mind to all she had to sort through—the observations, the revelations, the inescapable conclusion.

He did, indeed, intend to marry her.

That much was now beyond doubt. Viewing his behavior from that perspective, there was no contradiction, no reason to question the conclusion everyone, it seemed, had reached.

What was in question was how she felt, not just about his wanting to marry her, but about his failure to mention the matter despite having opportunities aplenty.

She felt she should be angry, yet that seemed too simple, too superficial a response. Decisions on marriage were too serious, too important, to be governed by such reactions.

Timms had warned her to think of her answer; that was assuredly sound advice. Yet in evaluating him, and his desire for her, the one uncertainty she even now could not resolve was the element that had, from the first, been a complicating factor between them. Was his interest in her, passionate and intense though it was, primarily a painter's fascination, something that would dissipate once he'd painted her enough to satisfy his obsession—or was there something deeper, more enduring, behind it?

She couldn't answer that question, no matter how she examined, analyzed and thought. Unless he told her which alternative was the truth, she wouldn't see it, not until it was too late. Without him telling her, without him being willing to reveal that much to her, she wouldn't be able to answer him.

Stalemate. She turned her mind to the other aspect she had to resolve. He hadn't said anything, had given not the slightest indication he wanted her for his bride, yet it wasn't hard to see that should she wish to refuse him, her position—thanks to him—was now seriously weak.

She glanced at him, lying slumped beside her, one heavy arm thrown over her waist. He was lying on his stomach, his face by her shoulder . . . She had to resist a sudden urge to run her fingers through his heavily tousled hair.

He'd manipulated her. She was increasingly sure that was true. Increasingly sure that he'd made the decision to marry her relatively early in their acquaintance, perhaps even before he'd taken her to his bed. At her insistence, true enough, yet she wasn't sure, any longer, just who had been inciting whom.

It was patently obvious he'd realized she hadn't read his direction, that she hadn't understood his ultimate aim. Studying his profile in the dimness, she wasn't the least bit amused by what was in effect deceit by omission. Admittedly, he, and many others, too, would consider his actions as being "for her own good"; that in no way excused them, not to her.

Almost as if he could feel her disapproval, even in his sleep, he stirred, heavy and warm beside her. His arm tightened about her as if checking . . . with a soft gusty sigh, all tension left him and he slipped into deep sleep again.

Even asleep, he was possessive. And protective.

She looked at him, felt him half surrounding her. A warm feeling, part elation, part simple joy, rose within her, spread, then flooded through her, slowly subsiding.

How was she to answer him when he asked?

Was she prepared to cut off her nose to spite her face?

Was she prepared to live her life without him, without experiencing that warm feeling in the night, that elation—that simple joy?

The answer to that wasn't one she needed to search for; it was there, in her mind, clear and shining, unequivocally true.

Was that love? Did she love him?

She still wasn't entirely sure. She would think more on that, yet for now, how was she to manage this—manage him? How was she to cope?

She sighed and turned her mind to that—and fell asleep.

19

Jacqueline walked into the breakfast parlor the next morning—and found Gerrard seated at the table, working his way through a plate of ham and sausages. He met her gaze, and murmured a greeting.

She returned it; wondering, she went to the sideboard.

The older ladies didn't come down for breakfast; normally she was the only one there. Gerrard had been gone from her bed when she'd woken. Given the shifting landscape between them, she felt rather odd taking the chair opposite him at the otherwise empty table and nodding to Masters as he poured her tea. Almost a preview of how things might be.

Masters stepped back. Lowering his coffee cup, Gerrard caught her eye. "I received a message from Patience this morning. She, Vane and their brood are returning to Kent this afternoon. Given I'm not sleeping away the morning, I thought I'd go around and bid them farewell. I wondered if you were free to accompany me? You did promise Therese, and she won't forget."

Jacqueline's expectation of a boring morning spent indoors evaporated. "Yes, thank you. I will come." Aside from all else, it would give her a chance to reassess Patience's view of her and Gerrard; his sister knew him better than anyone.

They left after breakfast, as soon as she'd changed her gown. The day was fine and sunny; they elected to walk the few blocks to Curzon Street.

Bradshaw opened the door to them. The atmosphere within the house was one step away from bedlam. Piles of boxes were already growing on the hall floor; footmen and maids were scurrying frantically.

"There you are!" From the gallery, Patience waved and came hurrying down the stairs. "What a blessing!" She embraced Gerrard, then Jacqueline, with equal fervor.

"We thought we'd come and bid the monsters adieu," Gerrard said.

Patience put her hand over her heart. "If you can distract them for half an hour, I'll be forever in your debt. They want to *help,* but they're driving the staff demented."

Smiling, Jacqueline turned to the stairs. "Are they in the nursery?"

"Yes—do go up. You know the way." Patience turned away as her housekeeper bustled up.

Gerrard joined Jacqueline on the stairs and together they went up.

They spent nearly an hour with the children, Gerrard on the floor with the boys, drawing and talking of manly activities, Jacqueline with Therese in her lap, sitting in the window seat telling stories of princesses and unicorns, and playing with ribbons.

Retying Therese's ribbons for the third time, Jacqueline watched Gerrard deal with the two boys. He was clearly first oars with them. And with Therese, but the little girl seemed determined to redirect her attention to Jacqueline, demanding acknowledgment in return, totally assured, as if convinced she had the right.

As if she saw Jacqueline as the female half of Gerrard.

Jacqueline would have dismissed the thought as reading too much into the actions of a small child, but she couldn't. Therese's certainty shone in her big blue eyes . . . and she hadn't even seen Gerrard and Jacqueline in any social setting. Was it truly that obvious, even to babes?

Eventually, two nursemaids came to take the children down for luncheon. They made their good-byes, boisterous on the part of the boys, more dignified from Therese.

"And you'll come with Uncle Gerrard when he visits us in the country."

Crouching down, Jacqueline smiled and tweaked Therese's ribbons. "I'll come if I can, but that might not be possible."

Therese frowned. Gerrard came to say good-bye. Brightening, she waved her arms; he obliged, and swung her up.

Jacqueline rose. Therese wrapped her arms tight about Gerrard's neck and whispered something into his ear. His eyes shifted to Jacqueline, then he looked back at Therese as she eased her hold and leaned back.

He smiled. "All right. But..." He tickled Therese and she squealed. "You're a devil's imp, I'm sure."

Therese giggled and squirmed. Gerrard set her down, and watched her hurry to join her waiting nursemaid. In the doorway, Therese blew kisses to both Jacqueline and him, then ran off; her laughter echoed back along the corridor, then faded.

Gerrard took Jacqueline's arm. She glanced at his face; he was still smiling. "What did she ask?"

He met her eyes, then shrugged. "Just about when I'll next come down to visit them."

She wanted to press for details, but wasn't quite game; she didn't want to precipitate a decision she hadn't yet made.

Downstairs, they found Patience and bade her farewell; clearly distracted, she hugged them both. "We'll see you at the summer celebration."

The comment was general; Jacqueline made no response. She'd heard of the summer gathering of the Cynster clan held at the ducal estate.

They found Vane in his study, up to his ears in investment reports. He smiled, rose and shook their hands; his gaze rested on her warmly, as if he, too, saw her as someone rather closer than a friend.

Indeed, as Gerrard followed her from the study, leaving Vane to his work, she realized no one would describe her as Gerrard's "friend." That label had never fitted, but just what she was . . .

What she might be, what she would consent to be, she hadn't yet decided.

They strolled back to the front hall. Gerrard paused amid the chaos. He glanced around, then took her hand. "Come—I want to show you something."

He led her into the dining room, yet to be stripped of its plate and cocooned under Holland covers. Guiding her around the table, he halted before the hearth, looking up at the picture hanging over the mantelpiece.

It had already commanded her eyes, her attention. It was a portrait of Patience, seated, with her three elder children gathered about her. Who had painted it was not in doubt.

Jacqueline stared, her gaze drawn again and again to Patience's face as she gazed down at her children. The emotion that glowed there was remarkable; it tugged at the heart, soothed the soul—reassured that the world was right, would be right, as long as such encompassing, all-powerful feeling existed within it.

"Of all the portraits I've done with children, this meant the most to me." Beside her, his gaze on the portrait, Gerrard spoke quietly. "Patience was my surrogate mother for years—for me, painting this was the final step in growing up. As if in recognizing and bringing to the canvas what she feels for her children, the infinite depth that isn't duplicated in any other relationship, I let her go." His lips quirked. "And possibly let her let go, too."

She said nothing, but looked again at the evocative portrait.

He shifted. "I have to admit, in painting that, I learned a great deal about motherhood."

After a moment, he wound her arm with his; they left the room, and with a good-bye to Bradshaw, quit the house.

They walked briskly back. Gerrard glanced at her as they turned into Brook Street. "I'm going to the studio—I'll want you to pose this afternoon, and then through the evening. You'll have to cry off any engagement." He frowned, looking ahead, not waiting for any agreement. "I'll need the next two evenings entire from you to complete it as it should be."

She could hardly argue; she nodded and climbed the front steps beside him. "I'll tell Millicent." And then send cards to the ladies whose entertainments they'd agreed to attend.

He paused before the door, met her eyes. All lightness had flown from his. After a moment, he murmured, "It won't be long now."

She nodded; Masters opened the door and they went in. The portrait would soon be finished—and then, between them, they'd have to face whatever was destined to be.

He was a font of ambiguous comments, utterances she could interpret in at least two ways, if not three.

That afternoon, Jacqueline posed beside the column in the studio, while Gerrard, with complete and utter absorption, painted her onto his canvas.

He'd let her peek before she'd taken up her position; there wasn't that much more to do, but these final stages would be crucial to the overall quality and impact of the work.

She'd learned to be silent, to let her mind wander while keeping absolutely still, keeping her hand raised, her head tilted just so. Her expression didn't matter; her face and features would be the last things he would paint, working from the multitude of sketches he'd already done. So she didn't have to guard her thoughts. At present, his interest was fixed on her raised hand.

His focus had always intrigued her; it reached deeper, signified far more than mere concentration. Devotion and dedication were the concepts that sprang to mind, along with ruthless, relentless determination. He brought all three to the task, driven, quite clearly compelled.

From the corner of her eye, she glanced at him, briefly let her gaze drink in the sight of him standing poised behind his easel in shirtsleeves, breeches and boots, wielding his brushes with consummate skill.

In arranging to have him paint her portrait, she hadn't been searching for a champion, but she'd got one. He'd driven up and claimed the position, just like a knight of old, sworn to defend her honor, her reputation, against the world. That was the commitment he brought to her portrait; she no longer questioned that for him—as with the portrait of Patience and her children—this work meant more. He was painting it for her, in defense of her, yet the doing of it gave something to him, too.

The ability to vanquish those who'd dared threaten her.

Her gaze rested on him; now her eyes had been opened, she could see so much more. A chivalrous protectiveness he might feel for any lady, but the possessiveness that in her case went hand in hand with a protectiveness that was rigid, absolute, and knew no bounds, made it impossible to imagine that, success achieved and her dragons vanquished, he would simply shake her hand and drive away.

She hadn't looked for marriage, not to him or any other, yet it seemed he was intent on bringing that to her, too.

As her successful champion, he could request a reward. Shifting her gaze, she wondered when he would ask. Of what he would ask, she no longer had any doubt.

How she would answer, she still didn't know.

It all hinged on whether she loved him.

She felt like a Shakespearean heroine, gazing at the moon, asking: What is love?

Two nights had passed since the morning they'd farewelled Patience, since Gerrard had informed her he would be painting for longer hours. She'd posed through the afternoon and into the late evening of both days. He'd retired with her to the bed in the alcove, but later had returned to his canvas.

This morning, when at dawn he'd walked her back to her room, he'd told her he wouldn't need her again. He was painting her face, her features; not only didn't he need her for that, but he'd explained he didn't want the distraction of setting eyes on her during the process.

She'd borne her banishment with good grace, but she'd grown accustomed to being awake at dawn. To being with him through the dark watches of the night.

Restless, she'd come to her window, to stare at the waning moon and ask the ancient question. Much good had it done her.

The lamps were still burning in the attics; she could see the reflection in the glasshouse panes. He was still working . . . Lips setting, she straightened. If he was, he needed to rest. He'd been painting almost around the clock for more than two days.

The night was hot and sultry; a thunderstorm grumbled in the distance as she slipped through the shadows of the upper corridor and eased open the door to the hidden stair. The boards didn't creak as she quietly climbed; at the top, she opened the door to the studio, and peered in.

He wasn't in front of the canvas. She looked around, then slipped in and closed the door. He wasn't in the main section—but the portrait was.

It was complete, finished; she didn't need him to tell her so.

It was remarkable, powerful. It drew her. She stood before it and stared, transfixed. The woman in the painting was her, yet a her with so much on show, so much plainly at stake, emotion welled and blocked her throat.

Amazing. She would never have believed he'd seen all that, much less that he could with mere paints depict it—her inner fears, the sense of imprisonment that had dogged her for the past year, her desperation to escape it, to flee. To leave it all behind, knowing, simultaneously, that she couldn't.

He hadn't painted simple innocence, although innocence was plainly there, but the emotions that gave innocence its credibility. Loss, confusion, and a sense of betrayal that had sunk to the soul.

She shivered; despite the heat, she wrapped her arms about her and clutched her wrapper close.

The setting was potent, frightening. Even safe in London in the attics of his house, she could taste the danger, the suffocating tension. Raw menace seeped from the dark leaves of the garden, trying to engulf her and draw her back, into the shadows. The moonlight was faint, a mere suggestion of illumination, not strong enough to light the path ahead.

Darkness predominated, not mere black but a palette of shifting colors, not passive but active evil, alive, still hungry, still wanting her.

The woman in the painting desperately needed someone to reach out and haul her free of the cloying web that miasmalike held her trapped.

The woman in the portrait was her.

She let out a shuddering breath. Drew another in, and looked away, slowly stepped away, out of the portrait's hold. Beyond evocative, it would free her. Looking around, she searched for its creator.

For her champion who would succeed.

She found him in the alcove, asleep.

Stripped, he'd sprawled facedown across the bed. Standing in the gap between the tapestries, she let her gaze roam, over his muscled shoulders, over the sweep of his back, the indentations below his waist, the swell of his buttocks, the long, muscled lines of his legs.

Moving inside, she let the tapestry close behind her, shutting off the lamplight. Moonlight fell softly, illuminating the scene as she paused by the bed and let her wrapper fall. Raising her hands, she undid the ties of her loose nightgown, and let it slide down to puddle at her feet. Stepping free, she lifted one knee to the bed and crawled across it, to him.

He knew her touch; he didn't wake when she set her palm to his side, and slowly, lovingly, ran it down. She didn't stop to think, to question her heart; instead, she let it guide her, and followed it to its desire.

Gently, she urged him onto his back; obligingly he rolled over, still asleep.

Gerrard awoke to sensation. To the touch of her lips, to the heat of her mouth as she closed it around him. To the caress of her hands on his bare hip, on his balls. To the scent of her in the steamy night. To the swish of her hair like silk across his thighs, across his groin.

To the knowledge that she was there, naked, kneeling between his spread thighs, ministering to him. Evocatively. Devotedly.

The shuddering breath he drew in wasn't enough, not nearly enough to steady his whirling head. Blindly, he reached down, touched her head, helplessly slid his fingers into the thick locks and clutched as his hips rose, thrusting to her tune.

To the music that rose about them.

Pleasure cascaded through him; eons passed as she played, then at his fevered urging rose up, straddled him, and took him in.

She rode him through the night, swept high on the wild winds of ecstasy, through a storm of passion while desire rained down and swamped them. Swirled, built, then dragged them under.

He rose and flipped her over, thrust deep and filled her.

Their bodies merged, slick and heated, in the relentless primal dance.

Total surrender.

It came on the moonlight, whispered through them both, and took them. Racked them.

At the last drew back and left them, sated and exhausted, together in the tangled ruins of his bed.

He woke the next morning with sunshine on his face. Pleasure in his mind. Memories washing through him.

He lay on his back, sprawled naked beneath the dormer windows. He'd never felt so decadently alive.

His lips curved, then he smiled, lifted his head and looked around.

She was no longer there, but her scent lingered. Her taste was still on his lips. He had a vague recollection of her whispering that she had to go back to her room, but that he should remain, and sleep.

In the hours prior to that they'd forsaken slumber, too hungry for each other. The minutes had spun out, desire drenched, stoked with passion. In the heat of the night, they'd burned. Soared. Shattered.

The pleasure of her abandoned loving had been soul-shatteringly sweet.

Swinging his legs over the edge of the bed, he sat up. He ran his hands over his face, then remembered, rose and walked through the tapestries into the studio. To the portrait that sat, complete in its last detail, on his easel.

It was done, and it was, as he'd always known it would be, the finest thing he'd yet accomplished.

Triumph welled, yet it wasn't solely the triumph of achievement, of pride in a painting well done. It went deeper than that, ranged on a more fundamental plane.

After last night, he knew what she felt for him. There'd been a joy and a rightness in their joining that she'd seen and acknowledged, that she'd openheartedly embraced as strongly as he.

All the necessary pieces were falling into place.

She loved him. She would marry him.

All he had to do was take the portrait back to Cornwall, slay the specters of her past, expose the murderer if they could and win her free.

The future thereafter would be, not his, but theirs.

Turning, he strode to the bellpull and rang for Masters.

Jacqueline slept late. After rising and donning a new gown of sprigged muslin, she consumed a late breakfast in her room, then went downstairs.

Minnie, Timms and Millicent were in the drawing room, heads together, discussing their arrangements for the evening. When they'd learned that the portrait would be completed that day, and that Gerrard was set on returning to Cornwall with it as soon as possible, Millicent, urged on by Minnie and Timms, had declared they would hold a farewell dinner for all those of his family who had helped and supported them during their stay.

And, of course, have a private unveiling of the portrait, in reward as it were.

Gerrard had grimaced, but to her surprise agreed. To her, he'd admitted, "I'm curious to see how they'll react."

Patience and Vane had already left town, but most of the others who'd rallied around, encouraged Gerrard and lent her countenance, were still there, although most were, indeed, planning to leave for their estates any day.

Jacqueline confirmed that Gerrard hadn't yet appeared downstairs. She listened to the guest list, made a few suggestions as the three older ladies wrestled with their seating plan, then excused herself and slipped away.

Going upstairs, she wondered if Gerrard was still sleeping. But as she climbed the hidden stairs to the studio, she heard voices. Looking up, she saw that the studio door had been left ajar.

In the same moment, she recognized Barnaby's voice.

"Stokes was most exercised over the incident with the arrow."

Arrow? Jacqueline halted on the last step, a yard from the door.

"Like us," Barnaby continued, "he thinks the murderer attempting to kill *you* is an indication that the entire series of murders revolves about Jacqueline herself. She's the only common link between the victims."

Jacqueline stilled; she stared at the door, unseeing.

Barnaby went on, "*Unlike* us, Stokes doesn't think it's anything as simple as a jealous suitor."

Jacqueline heard a swishing sound; Gerrard was cleaning his brushes.

"What does Stokes think?"

The question was flat; his tone held a menacing quality.

"Oh, he acknowledges the *possibility* of a jealous suitor, but as he points out, none have stepped forward to claim Jacqueline's hand."

"Except Sir Vincent."

"True, but Sir Vincent's behavior doesn't suggest any deep and desperate passion. After Jacqueline refused him, he hasn't shown his face again, hasn't attempted to press his suit."

After a moment, Gerrard prompted, "So?"

"So Stokes suggests we look further—what if the motive behind the murders is not for the murderer to marry Jacqueline himself, but to stop her marrying at all? She's Tregonning's heiress, after all."

Gerrard grunted. "I checked. If she dies without issue—or is condemned for murder—on her father's demise the estate entire goes to a distant cousin in Scotland. Said cousin hasn't been south of the border for decades, and is, apparently, unaware of his potential good fortune."

Jacqueline's jaw dropped.

Silence reigned, then Barnaby asked, his tone reflecting the same stunned amazement she felt, "How the devil did you learn all that? I thought you've been painting nonstop?"

"I have been. My brother-in-law, and others, haven't been."

"Ah." After a moment, Barnaby added, "I wish I knew how they ferreted out such things."

A dark smile colored Gerrard's voice as he said, "Remind me to introduce you to the Duke of St. Ives."

"Hmm, yes, well, none of that gets us any further, unfortunately. Whoever it is who wants Jacqueline free of any potential husband is still lurking around Hellebore Hall, waiting for her to return."

"It's interesting, don't you think, that they haven't followed us to town?"

"Indeed—which is another reason to think it isn't Sir Vincent. He's known about town, and could have come up easily enough."

"Matthew Brisenden couldn't have."

"True, but I've never seen him as our murderer."

Gerrard sighed. "I hate to agree with you, but Jacqueline says he's protective of her, and I think she's right."

Outside the door, Jacqueline set her lips. How kind of him to agree with her, but why hadn't he told her someone had shot an arrow at him? When?

As to why . . .

"Regardless of our villain's identity, our way forward is clear." Gerrard's voice held steely determination, and a quiet, unshakable resolution. "The portrait is both the key and the bait. We take it back to Hellebore Hall, arrange to show it, and wait for him to strike."

Jacqueline heard footsteps, Barnaby walking around.

A pause ensued, then he said, "You know, I didn't entirely believe you could achieve this with a portrait. Damned if it isn't as good as a real clue. Everyone seeing it will know—and start thinking of who the real murderer might be. And yes, you're right—it's bait. He'll come for it—if at all possible, he'll destroy it."

Barnaby's voice strengthened as he swung around. "But he'll also come after you."

"I know." Gerrard's voice held a note of imperturbable anticipation. "I'll be waiting for him."

Jacqueline stood on the stair, those words revolving in her head. Gerrard and Barnaby discussed the dinner that evening, then the logistics of returning with all speed to Cornwall; she paid little attention, too absorbed with their earlier revelations.

Then Barnaby made to leave. He hadn't come through the house; he must have used the external stairs. On a spike of relief, she heard them both moving across the studio to the outside door.

Quietly, she turned, and slipped down into the house.

G errard gave her precious little time to straighten her tangled thoughts, to steady her whirling head.

Fifteen minutes later, he found her in the back parlor where she'd taken refuge to think without distraction.

She stopped thinking the moment he walked in.

He smiled, all his effortless charm to the fore, a light that was solely for her glowing in his eyes.

That private warmth, the intimate connection, brought memories of the past night crashing back.

She'd thought, last night, that she'd discovered what love was—a surrender, a selfless giving, a devotion that could edge into worship.

From her position on the chaise, she watched him cross the room to her, and it was crystal clear she had a great deal yet to learn.

She drew a tight breath. "Is it completely finished?"

He nodded. "Yes." He halted a few paces before her, standing easily, his hands sliding into his pockets as his eyes, still glowing brown, searched her face. "I—"

"I've been thinking." She cut across him without compunction. It was imperative she take control of this interview; she knew it was important to keep her gaze steady on his face, but she had to fight to do it. "Millicent and I can take the portrait back—now it's finished your commission is completed. There's no need for you and Mr. Adair to trouble yourselves with the long journey back and forth."

His face changed; in the blink of an eye, his expression turned to stone, his warm gaze to one sharp as a surgeon's knife.

The silence lengthened, then he said, his tone even and deceptively mild, "I came to ask for your hand—to ask you to be my wife."

The words were a blow in the center of her chest. Her eyes started to close, to shut out the pain; she forced them open, forced herself to meet and hold his gaze. "I . . . haven't, don't, think of marriage."

A moment passed, then he said, "I know that initially, when we first became lovers, you weren't thinking of marriage, not at all. But since then, since coming to London . . . I think if you consult your memories, you'll see that you have been, if only instinctively, considering the prospect for some time."

A straightforward denial leapt to her lips; her gaze trapped in his, she held it back. She recalled Minnie and Timms's meddling; if they'd prodded her, how much more likely were they to have prodded him? And in doing so accurately informed him of her state. Those two saw far too much.

"I won't marry you. I don't wish you to return to Hellebore Hall." She sat on the chaise, her hands clasped in her lap, and looked up at him steadily. He remained standing, studying her; the intensity of his gaze held her caged.

Love, it seemed, sometimes demanded sacrifice, even after surrender. If that was how it was, then for him, she would be strong enough, even for that.

His eyes narrowed; his gaze didn't waver. "Was it a dream then, last night? And early this morning? I thought it was you, the angel who visited me in my bed beneath the stars." Abruptly he moved, a predator circling before her, his eyes never leaving her, never releasing her. "You who took me into her mouth, into her body—"

"Don't." She shut her eyes, seized the moment to breathe in and out. "You know it was me." Opening her eyes, she met his gaze, now darkly burning. "It changes nothing. It won't happen again."

The ends of his lips lifted, the half-smile wholly intent. "Oh, but it will—again, and again. Because you love me—and I love you."

She rose to her feet, opened her mouth, but no words came. Nothing good enough to challenge the knowledge in his eyes.

Her hesitation was all the confirmation Gerrard needed; the look in her eyes, as if she was desperately casting about for some argument to counter his, and failing, placed the matter of their mutual state beyond doubt. A weight lifted from his shoulders; relief was a heady draft coursing through his veins. That much, then, was as he'd thought. What remained a mystery was the reason for her sudden—and if he were truthful, unnerving—tack.

This wasn't how he'd imagined his proposal would go.

He stepped closer, close enough for their senses to flare.

She locked her eyes on his, narrowed them. Her jaw tightened. "I will *not* marry you—you can't make me say yes. And under no circumstances are you to return to Hellebore Hall."

He held her gaze, slowly arched one brow. "How do you plan to stop me?"

She frowned.

He went on, "I've no intention of letting you refuse my suit. I'll keep after you, keep seducing you—you'll have to agree in the end." Resolution rang in his tone; to him there was no other option. "As for returning to the Hall, either with you in your father's coach, or ahead of you in my curricle—either way, I'll be there to hand you down."

Still frowning, she looked down, staring at his waistcoat. A moment ticked past, then she looked up and met his eyes. "I won't agree to marry you—I won't acknowledge that I love you in any way. I can't stop you from returning to the Hall, but I can speak with my father and make him understand why he must turn you away, and insist you return to London."

The stony determination he saw in her eyes chilled him. "Why don't you explain that to me?"

Her features tightened. "Very well. Think of this—I've loved, and lost twice to this murderer. First with Thomas, a young girl's love, which was bad enough, and then with Mama—and that was devastating." Her voice shook, her lashes flickered, but she drew breath and went on, lifting her eyes to his, the green and gold burning with a fire he took a moment to place, to recognize, "Now there's you. This murderer is waiting at the Hall—we both know that. To love and lose a third time . . ."

Dragging in a breath, she shook her head. "No—I won't risk it. If you understand at all, you won't ask that of me."

He held her gaze for a long moment, then quietly replied, "I do understand." He reached for her hand, let his fingers slide over hers, then twine. Lock. "But I'm not asking you to love and lose a third time. I'm asking you to love, and have the courage to embrace it and fight for it, with me."

She opened her mouth—he squeezed her fingers to silence her. "Before you argue, consider this—whatever you say, whatever you do, no longer matters. I know you love me—you've shown me you do—and I love you. I'll follow you to the ends of the earth if need be, and badger you until you accept me as your husband."

Her eyes searched his, then he sensed her inner sigh. "I know he tried to kill you—I know about the arrow."

"Ah." He held her gaze as perception swung, revolved, then settled again. He remembered the door to the stairs, left open by the footman who'd come to remove his shaving water; he'd been on his way to shut it when Barnaby had knocked on the other door. Suddenly all was clear.

She tried to tug her hand from his; when he didn't let go, she glared at him. Belligerently. "When were you going to tell me? Never? But if we're considering things, then you ought to consider this—*if* I loved you, *I'd* move heaven and earth to keep you from this madman."

He searched her eyes, then he smiled.

Jacqueline's heart melted; there was no charm in the gesture, no artful seduction, just an overflowing understanding, acceptance, and love. It glowed in the rich brown of his eyes, a light she couldn't mistake, a light he made no effort to conceal.

He raised his free hand and cradled her cheek, tipping her face up so he could study her eyes more closely. When he spoke, it was with awe, as if he'd made some great discovery. "It's not your heart you're trying to shield by denying you love me—it's me. You're trying to protect me."

Of course. "Perhaps. But—"

His smile deepened; he bent his head and kissed her.

She tried to hold aloof, apart, tried desperately to simply exist and not be swayed . . . and failed. A shuddering sigh escaped her, and she sank into his arms, parted her lips and welcomed him in.

And felt, again, the power rise between them, felt it swell and whirl and cocoon them. Felt it bind them, hold them, fuse them until they were not the same separate beings they once had been.

When he lifted his head, she was defeated—not by him, but by that power. He, too, seemed caught. When he spoke, his voice was raspy, gravelly. "I thank you for the thought, sweetheart." He brushed a kiss to her knuckles, then met her eyes. "But that's not how it's going to be."

For a long moment, she felt as if she was drowning in his eyes, then he said, "Timms said something, not long ago, when she was twitting me about love and my attitude to it. I can't remember her words, but I remember her meaning: when it comes to love, what will be will be—it's not up to us to decree."

Those words were patently, self-evidently true. There was no point arguing. However . . . "I won't agree to marry you."

He held her gaze, then nodded. "Very well. If you insist, we won't make the announcement yet."

She narrowed her eyes at him. He met her look blankly. Unyield-ingly. But she could be unyielding, too; if she gave in, even to a secret betrothal, he would use it to, as he would see it, protect her. "No, I am *not* agreeing. Not yet. Once we've exposed our madman, you can ask me again." A memory stirred. "Knights who champion ladies can't claim their reward until after the dragon is slain."

His eyes narrowed; the look in them held more than a touch of hard arrogance, of his customary ruthlessness. His lips thinned, but then he nodded. "Very well." He drew a deep breath, his chest swelling against her breasts. "We'll take the portrait back to Hellebore Hall and, hand in hand, side by side, wait for the murderer to appear."

But first they had a family dinner to attend, all the while concealing the complex web of emotions that, it seemed, hour by hour steadily grew, wove and twined more tightly, linking them ever more incontrovertibly.

He, of course, encouraged it, and she was helpless to prevent it.

They'd arranged to show the portrait in the drawing room; it stood in pride of place before the empty hearth. Before any others ar-rived, Minnie, Timms and Millicent stood in a semicircle in front of it—and simply stared.

Then Minnie turned to Jacqueline, and took her hand. "My dear, I confess I had no idea matters were quite so bad." She glanced back at the portrait. "But I can see they are." She looked up at Gerrard. "Dear boy, this is the best you've ever done—and for more than one reason."

Timms gruffly concurred. "It conveys so much—there's so much of you both in it—hopefully it'll accomplish all you need."

The doorbell pealed; guests started to arrive. Without exception, all were amazed and somewhat stunned by the portrait. Jacqueline's head spun with all the comments, but she'd met everyone before, knew them, felt comfortable in their company, felt at home within their circle.

Despite all the portrait so eloquently revealed, although she did indeed feel her emotions exposed, she didn't feel vulnerable. In part it was a matter of trust—of trusting all those around her—but it was also a reflection of the strength she drew from the light in Gerrard's eyes when they rested on her, from the touch of his fingers lightly trailing her arm as he passed by.

Nothing occurred to mar the evening. The conversation about the dinner table was all about the portrait, of what others saw in it, of their hopes for it. Of the situation that awaited her, Gerrard, Millicent and Barnaby at the Hall, and how they planned to resolve it.

Warm wishes flowed all around them, but in the glances the men shared, Jacqueline read a seriousness, and a readiness to support in whatever manner was required, that was almost medieval. A rallying to the clarion call, a warriorlike response from elegant gentlemen who were clearly only one small step removed from their sword-wielding ancestors.

It was obvious that Gerrard was cut from the same cloth.

None of the men dallied about the table; all rose and followed the ladies back to the drawing room, back to the portrait. Powerful and evocative, it dominated the gathering.

"It takes my breath away." Amelia stood before it, examining it anew. "But not in a pleasant way."

Jacqueline had met the twins, Amanda, Countess of Dexter, and Amelia, Viscountess Calverton, at a number of functions. They were a few years older than she, but so full of life she'd been immediately drawn to them. Their husbands, both tall, handsome men, cousins in fact, stood nearby; they'd been teased over the dinner table about their rivalry over who would fill their nursery first—both twins had given birth to firstborn sons within a month of each other, then, later, to daughters, again within the space of a month.

"It gives me the shivers." Standing beside Amelia, Amanda realistically demonstrated. She turned to Jacqueline. "I hope that whatever that represents"—she pointed to the louring, threatening Garden of Night—"is defeated and behind you."

Jacqueline looked at the painting. "Not yet." She met the twins' eyes. "We hope it soon will be."

"Humph!" Amanda swung to Gerrard. "All I can say is, if you can see all that well enough to paint it, you'd better be intending to take her hand and pull her out of there."

Gerrard's lips curved in a relaxed and open smile. "Rest assured, I fully intend to do just that." He shot a glance at Jacqueline. "And, indeed, lead her rather further."

Into a new life. His eyes stated that clearly; for a moment, Jacqueline was lost in the promise that glowed in his brown eyes.

Amelia made a strangled sound, smothering some comment. Both Jacqueline and Gerrard looked to see the twins exchanging glances, then Amanda shook her head with mock severity at Amelia, and took her sister's arm. "No—don't say a word. Whatever word we do say will be taken amiss, so . . . let's retire and leave these two to their own devices."

With smiles that could only be construed as regally smug, the twins swept off to join their husbands.

"*Grandes dames* in the making," Gerrard muttered.

Another Cynster lady Jacqueline had grown close to was Flick—Felicity—Demon Cynster's wife. Demon Harry was Vane's younger brother, an ex-hellion if ever there was one. The resemblance between him and Vane was not strong physically, but Jacqueline saw it in myriad little things. Like the hard glint in Demon's blue eyes when he paused beside Gerrard to discuss their return to Hellebore Hall.

Flick tugged her hand, distracting her. "You must promise to come to Newmarket later in the year." She held up a hand, imperious for all she was a slip of a thing. "With Gerrard or without him, regardless, I'll expect to see you."

She could only smile, and agree. Dillon Caxton, Flick's cousin and, as Jacqueline understood it, Demon's protégé in many ways, joined them. He was startlingly handsome in Byronic fashion; his manners were assured, his address polished, but Jacqueline sensed he held himself back, behind an inner wall of reserve.

Nevertheless, he was a close friend of Gerrard's; after chatting easily with Flick and herself, Dillon turned to Gerrard and asked if he would introduce him to Barnaby. "Demon mentioned his hobby. There's a little matter at Newmarket that I think might interest him."

Gerrard raised his brows, but readily agreed.

He left her with Flick, but returned within minutes, much to Flick's amusement.

The rest of the evening passed in a pleasant whirl. The last guests to depart were Horatia and her husband, George.

"Take care, dear." Horatia touched cheeks. "And we'll see you later in the month."

Without waiting for a response, Horatia turned to Gerrard. "Whatever you need to do in Cornwall, don't take too long about it. We'll expect to hear the end of this story when we see you both at Somersham."

Gerrard innocently swore he wouldn't drag his heels.

Jacqueline narrowed her eyes at him; another of his ambiguous comments, or so she suspected.

When, later, he joined her in her bed, when, later, she was lying pleasured witless and at peace in his arms, she realized she'd started seeing her—their—future from his family's perspective. And coveting what she saw.

Yet . . .

Gerrard shifted, then pressed a kiss to her temple. "What is it?"

She hesitated; when the words came, she let them fall as they would—nothing but honesty between them. "I haven't had a future for so long, I'm finding it hard, difficult, to believe in what might be."

"Us?"

That simple little word encompassed so much.

"Yes."

She wondered if he would reassure her with the obvious phrases. Instead, after some minutes, he murmured, "It's as Timms said: what will be will be. All we can do is go forward, together, and see what lies along our path—what fate has in store for us."

If she'd had any doubt that he was following her thoughts accurately, they were banished when his voice hardened.

"But first, together, we have to catch a murderer."

The next day they set out to do just that with single-minded focus. Gerrard seemed even more driven than over painting the portrait in the first place; his impatience infected her.

The day flew with preparations. By evening, all was ready for their departure early the following morn. Barnaby, of course, was to join them. If it hadn't been for the distance, Minnie and Timms would have come, too.

"You'll have to tell us *everything* when you return." Minnie drew Jacqueline down, kissed her cheek, patted her hand, then released her.

She and Millicent retired early.

Later, Gerrard came to her room. To her bed. To her.

There were no longer any shields, any doubts, any questions between them. Only the unvoiced threat of a murderer.

That only made them more determined, more open and defiant in their ardor. Their bodies twined, their hearts soared, their senses steeped in the pleasure of the other, giving, taking, lavishing, receiving, until the world shattered, and the glory took them.

And their souls flew, hand in hand, side by side.

20

"W e were thinking of a ball," Millicent said. She drew a deep breath, then added, "Here."

"Here?" Lord Tregonning shot her a startled look, then returned to studying the portrait.

Gerrard exchanged a glance with Jacqueline, then Barnaby. They hung back in a semicircle in the drawing room. They'd arrived that afternoon, and decided to hold this, the first display of the work, before dinner.

Eventually, Lord Tregonning nodded. "Yes. You're right. A ball held here will bring out the entire county."

Millicent let out the breath she'd been holding. "Precisely. And with this on show"—with an extravagant gesture she indicated the portrait—"they'll be *avid* to see it. We won't need to do anything more."

"Indeed." Lord Tregonning turned to Gerrard, and held out his hand. "I had hoped, but I never imagined it could be this . . . *impressive*. So unquestionably the truth."

Mitchel Cunningham had joined them. He stood a little back, but he, too, was staring at the portrait. Recalling her earlier suspicion that Mitchel hadn't believed in her innocence, Jacqueline moved to stand beside him; when he glanced her way, she nodded at the portrait. "What do you think?"

He looked again at the canvas, then his expression grew grim. "Frankly, I owe you an apology." He glanced at her. "I was never sure . . . but now." He looked at the portrait, shook his head. "This slays all doubt."

Jacqueline smiled. She wouldn't have called Mitchel a sensitive soul, yet the portrait had shaken him. "I'm hoping others will see that as clearly."

"I'm sure they will." Mitchel continued to stare at the painting. "Indeed, this leaves them no choice."

Treadle appeared to announce dinner. Gerrard, who'd been speaking with her father and Millicent, motioned to Compton, standing unobtrusively by, to remove the portrait, then turned to look for her.

Still smiling, she went to join him. Together, they headed for the dining room, discussing how best to manage the portrait's public unveiling.

Millicent was adamant it had to be kept hidden until the ball. "If we let it be seen before, rumors will abound. Some will judge it before they see it, and seek to sway others with their opinions, and so on. After all the effort put into its creation, we should ensure we use it to greatest advantage."

"Indeed." Barnaby paused in eating his soup. "I have to say I'm still amazed by its power—it'll drive home our point in dramatic fashion."

"Lady Tannahay is one we should invite to a private showing." Gerrard set down his spoon. "Are there any others we need on our side?"

Everyone agreed on the Entwhistles, but when Lord Tregonning suggested Sir Godfrey, Millicent was emphatic in excluding him. "Best we give him the shock of his life in a social setting. Privately, he'll dither, and not be sure what to think."

Her tone was caustic; the rest of them exchanged glances, and let the matter of Sir Godfrey lie.

"How soon?" his lordship asked. "One can hardly organize a ball in one day."

"Three days," Millicent declared. "Three nights from now, we'll throw open the doors and invite everyone to admire Jacqueline's innocence, and think of what that means. If anything's going to rattle our murderer, knowing everyone will be wondering who he is should do it."

Their plans filled the following hours; they retired at eleven. At half past the hour, Jacqueline slipped into Gerrard's room, and into his arms.

She was late leaving the next morning. Deeming it easier to explain her presence wandering the corridors in nightgown and robe if he wasn't by her side, she insisted he let her return to her room by herself. It wasn't as if she didn't know the way.

Her caution proved wise; she met Barnaby within twenty feet of Gerrard's door. She blushed, but Barnaby greeted her without a blink, explaining he was on his way for a walk in the gardens. Then she encountered two maids in the corridor; they blushed—for her, she presumed. Glancing in a wall mirror, she saw her eyes were slumbrous, her hair beyond disarranged, her lips subtly swollen. No point pretending how she'd spent her night. Crossing the gallery to the other wing, she saw Treadle in the hall below—and he saw her. That was what came of succumbing to reckless passion.

Not that she regretted it.

Reaching her room, she decided she didn't care what anyone thought. If the murderer had taught her one thing, it was to grab love with both hands and enjoy it. Celebrate it when it was there, offered to her.

What will be will be. Timms was very wise.

Given her recent activities, she ought to have been exhausted. Instead, she felt energized—fired by impatience to identify her mother's murderer. Thomas's murderer. He who had held her life in thrall for too long.

She rang for Holly. As she washed and dressed, she felt confidence well. Not since Thomas died had she felt so positive, so eager to face the day. She felt as if, after a long night, the sun was finally rising once more on her world—and she had Gerrard to thank for it.

Her champion. She grinned, gave her curls a last tweak, then headed for the breakfast parlor.

Gerrard was already seated, along with Mitchel. Barnaby had arrived just ahead of her. He held the chair beside Gerrard for her, then sat alongside.

The three of them chatted, tossing ideas back and forth about the ball. Considering all that had to be done. Mitchel was subdued. After cleaning his plate, he rose and bid them a good day. Barnaby asked if he would be around later, in case they needed assistance with arrangements for the ball.

Mitchel shook his head. "I'm afraid not. I'll be out for most of the day—we've the rotation of crops to organize."

Nodding, Barnaby raised a hand in acknowledgment. Jacqueline smiled; Mitchel bowed and left.

She, Gerrard and Barnaby fell to organizing with a vengeance, expecting Millicent to join them any minute.

But Millicent didn't appear.

Jacqueline had just registered that her aunt was unusually late when Millicent's maid peeked into the parlor. Jacqueline saw her. "Gemma?" The maid looked shaken. Jacqueline pushed back her chair. "Is anything wrong?"

Gemma edged into the room, bobbing a curtsy. "It's Miss Tregonning, miss. I don't rightly know where she is." Gemma's eyes were wide. "Have you seen her?"

A chill touched Jacqueline's heart, then spread. She rose. Chairs scraped as Gerrard and Barnaby rose, too.

It was Barnaby who spoke, calmly, evenly. "She must be somewhere. We'll come and help look."

It didn't take long to find her.

Gemma and another maid had already searched upstairs. Gerrard asked Treadle to gather the footmen, then went with Jacqueline and Barnaby out onto the terrace, to look, and then to plan.

They walked to the main steps leading down to the gardens, searching the various areas they could see. Jacqueline called; Gerrard filled his lungs and shouted, "Millicent!" but there was no answering wave, no reply.

Beside Jacqueline, he halted at the top of the steps. Glancing down, he saw marks, dirt streaked across the pale marble.

There'd been a light shower during the night. He looked down the steps, confirming that the well-worn patch of path at the bottom was damp. There were similar, small, telltale streaks all the way up the steps.

"Barnaby." He wasn't sure if it was his artist's imagination running amok, but . . . when Barnaby looked at him he pointed to the streaks.

Barnaby crouched down, with his eyes followed the trail up the steps, then swiveled and looked along the terrace. The faint streaks led on, smudged here and there, but then ended—where the balustrade overlooked the Garden of Night.

Gerrard felt his face harden; Barnaby's was grim as he rose.

"What is it?" Jacqueline asked, looking from one to the other.

Gerrard pressed her arm. "Wait here."

Quickly, he went down the steps, and turned into the Garden of Night. Barnaby was on his heels.

Jacqueline froze. In her head, a voice screamed, *No!* It was a battle to get her limbs to work, to move. Gripping the balustrade, she forced herself forward; step by step, she followed the men down.

Her gaze locked on the entrance to the Garden of Night, not the one Gerrard had painted, but the upper one. The entrance she'd stood at over a year ago, and seen her mother lying dead, flung like a broken bird, her legs trailing in the pool, her back broken on the stone coping.

The archway drew nearer. Nearer. Then she was standing in it, within the cool touch of the garden's shadows.

Gerrard and Barnaby were bending over the body of her aunt. As with her mother, her aunt lay half across the coping. White as death. One hand trailed, fingers lax, on the gravel.

A choked sound escaped her. She wanted to scream, to call for help, but she couldn't get her throat to work. Her lungs felt as if they were caving in.

Gerrard heard; he turned and saw her. He said something to Barnaby, then rose and swiftly came to her.

She pressed both hands to her lips. Couldn't form the words to ask. Asked with her eyes instead.

"She's alive." Gerrard gathered her to him, hugged her reassuringly. "Unconscious, but alive." He lifted his head, yelled, "Treadle!"

An instant later, the butler appeared at the top of the steps. "Sir? Miss? What . . . ?"

"Send for the doctor, then send some footmen down here with a door."

Alive. Millicent was alive. Jacqueline's legs gave way.

Gerrard swore, and tightened his arms about her.

She rested her head against his chest, forced her lungs to work, dragged in a huge breath. Gulped. "I'm sorry." She hauled in another breath, then locked her legs and lifted her head. "Go back and stay with her. She's badly hurt. I'll wait here." She sensed his hesitation. "I'll be all right. Truly. The best help you can give me is to help her—I can't. I can't go in there."

He understood; she saw it in his eyes. He steadied her against the end of the balustrade. "Stay there—don't move."

She nodded. He turned and plunged back into the Garden of Night.

Millicent was carried up to her room and laid on her bed.

Lord Tregonning was informed; Sir Godfrey was summoned.

The doctor arrived. He was taken straight up to Millicent. When he entered the drawing room half an hour later, he looked grave.

"She's unconscious, but she was lucky. A branch broke her fall. It broke off beneath her and prevented her spine or skull from cracking. Her arm's broken, but will mend well enough. However, she did hit her head. How long she'll be unconscious I can't say."

"But she'll live?" Jacqueline leaned forward, hands clasped in her lap.

"God willing, I believe so. But we can't take that for granted, I'm afraid. She's still with us, but we'll need to take one day at a time— she's not young, and the fall was—"

"Horrific." Lord Tregonning was pale, stunned; his knuckles showed white as he gripped his cane.

"I've made her as comfortable as I can. Mrs. Carpenter knows what to do. I'll call again this afternoon to see if there's any change, but it may well be a day or more before she regains consciousness."

Barnaby shifted; he spoke in an undertone to Lord Tregonning. His lordship nodded, then focused on the doctor. "I'd appreciate it, Manning, if you kept this entire episode under your hat. At least until we know more."

The doctor hesitated, then nodded; his gaze flicked to Jacqueline for the briefest of moments, then he bowed and left.

Barnaby stared, all but openmouthed, after him; the instant the door shut, he flatly stated, "I don't believe it."

Gerrard forced his hands to relax from the fists they'd curled into. "Believe it." His growl sounded feral. "But this time, that's not how things are going to be."

He turned to Jacqueline; he didn't like the empty look in her eyes. "When she regains consciousness, Millicent will tell us who flung her over the balustrade, but we can't sit and wait until then." He looked at Lord Tregonning. "The murderer thinks Millicent's dead—if he realizes she isn't, but is unconscious, he'll be desperate to silence her. We need to keep her safe."

Lord Tregonning's eyes widened. He had Barnaby summon Treadle, and they quickly conferred. Footmen would guard Millicent night and day. Barnaby suggested and all agreed that the most useful way forward was to behave as if nothing untoward had occurred. Treadle assured them the staff would keep mum; he withdrew to ensure it.

"It'll confuse the blackguard, and the portrait is bait enough." Barnaby looked at Gerrard.

Who nodded. "Indeed. But nevertheless, we need to piece together what happened."

Barnaby met Gerrard's eyes, then turned to Lord Tregonning. "With your permission, sir, I'd like to interview the staff before Sir Godfrey arrives."

Lord Tregonning met his gaze, then nodded. His jaw setting, he looked at Jacqueline. "Whatever permission you need, consider it given." He moved to sit beside Jacqueline, awkwardly taking her hand and patting it. "My dear, do you think we might go up and sit with Millicent? When she wakes, I think she'd like us to be there."

To Gerrard's relief, Jacqueline focused on her father, then nodded. They both rose. He escorted them to Millicent's room, saw them settled, then returned to Barnaby, still standing in the drawing room, a determined frown on his face.

Barnaby glanced up as he shut the door. "We are *not* going to allow this incident to be obscured by people trying to protect others."

"My thoughts precisely. What do you suggest?"

"That we take charge. That we gather all the facts, then present them to Sir Godfrey so there's no chance of him sidestepping logic."

Gerrard nodded. "What's first?"

Barnaby raised a brow at him. "Establishing when Millicent went outside, and if we can, why, and then making sure we can, if need be, prove Jacqueline was elsewhere between that time and dawn."

Gerrard held his friend's gaze, then said, "She was with me."

Barnaby grinned. "I know. I met her leaving your room this morning—I heard the door and thought it was you, so I came out . . . but it was her. And she must have been seen by others. So—when did she arrive?"

"About half past eleven."

"Good—so we have that fixed. Now let's see what that maid can tell us."

Shocked, but now growing angry on her mistress's behalf, Gemma was very ready to tell them all she knew. "She always fussed over getting ready for bed—creams, potions, and I had to put her hair in curling rags every night. It was after midnight that I left her room, and she wasn't in bed even then. She was restless—old ladies often are, you know. They don't settle easy, so they often walk about. If it was clear, she'd go down to the terrace—since we've been back here anyways—I've seen her walking there in the moonlight."

Gemma was very clear on all the details; she could list the various duties she performed every night for Millicent.

"It's obvious Millicent couldn't have left her room under an hour after she retired," Barnaby concluded, "and at eleven, she was going up the stairs with the rest of us."

Next they spoke with Treadle; expression bland, he confirmed that he and two maids had seen Jacqueline on her way to her room at close to seven o'clock that morning. He added, staring at the wall, that Jacqueline's maid could also confirm that Jacqueline's bed hadn't been slept in.

When Treadle departed, Barnaby glanced at Gerrard. "I didn't think to ask, but you are intending to marry her, aren't you?"

Gerrard stared at him as if he'd grown two heads. "Of course!" Then he waved. "No, no, I understand why you asked. Yes, I've asked her to marry me, but she wanted to put off any formal acceptance until after this matter was resolved, and she was free of suspicion and the murderer caught."

Barnaby nodded. "Entirely understandable. Now, let's take another look at those marks on the terrace."

They were hunkered down, studying the streaks where they ended by the balustrade, when Treadle escorted Sir Godfrey out.

The man looked thoroughly shaken. "What's this? *Millicent* pushed over the edge, too?" His color was high; he was almost gabbling. "Well, I—"

Rising, Barnaby held up a hand. "No, wait. Just listen to what we can prove so far." Concisely, Barnaby outlined Millicent's movements from the time she went upstairs until she was walking on the terrace. "Then, for some reason, she went down the steps and into the Garden of Night. How far in we don't know, but at least as far as the archway. That's where she got mud on her slippers.

"But then"—dramatically Barnaby pointed to the streaks— "some man grabbed her, and while keeping her from screaming, dragged her back up the steps, and flung her—not pushed, but *flung* her—down into the Garden of Night. There was a branch beneath her when we found her; the doctor confirmed it had broken off beneath her and saved her from death. If you go into the garden and look up, you can see where the branch broke off—it's plain as daylight Millicent wasn't pushed, but flung. *By some man.*"

Sir Godfrey had paled, but he'd followed all Barnaby had said. "Man?" he asked.

"Indubitably," Barnaby replied. "No woman could possibly have done it."

A t Gerrard's suggestion, they retired to Lord Tregonning's study and poured Sir Godfrey a brandy. He'd been deeply shocked, but now rallied.

Gerrard, watching him, picked his moment. "Sir Godfrey, you're a man of the world—I know we can rely on your discretion. Miss Tregonning and I intend to wed once this affair is settled. Consequently, she was with me throughout the night, from before Millicent's maid left her in her room, until seven o'clock this morning. Quite aside from my word on the matter, there are a number of staff who can verify that."

Sir Godfrey blinked at him, then waved his hand. "Complete discretion, I assure you. Anyway . . ." His tone hardened, his grip tightened on the brandy glass and he drained it. "This wasn't Jacqueline, but some man—some bounder, some blackguard who's been leading us a merry dance through murder after murder, and laughing up his sleeve because we've been afraid it was Jacqueline. That's not going to happen this time—*this time,* we're going to catch the devil."

"Indeed!" Barnaby sat forward. "We need to investigate what could possibly have drawn Millicent down into the garden. Her maid is certain she normally only strolled on the terrace, and it had rained."

"Millicent isn't all that fond of the gardens, y'know." Sir Godfrey nodded. "She must have heard or seen something."

Barnaby suddenly straightened; his gaze grew distant. "Ring for Treadle."

Gerrard did; when the butler appeared, Barnaby put one question.

"Indeed, sir," Treadle said. "Lady Tregonning often strolled on the terrace of a night. She had trouble sleeping."

"Just like the elder Miss Tregonning?"

Treadle bowed. "Their habits were well-known belowstairs, sir—and, of course, I always know when the terrace door has been opened after I've locked up."

Barnaby eyed him. "You don't, by any chance, recall if the door had been opened on the night before Lady Tregonning died?"

"I do recall, as it happens, sir. I distinctly remember thinking, when she appeared so haggard at the breakfast table the next morning—the morning of the day she died—that the poor lady must have walked all night. She certainly hadn't slept, and the terrace door had been opened."

Barnaby thanked Treadle, who bowed and withdrew.

Sir Godfrey looked at Barnaby, horrified comprehension dawning. "You think *Miribelle* heard something, too?"

Lips set, Barnaby nodded. "I think she heard or saw something, but went back into the house. . . . Whatever it was, she knew what it meant, but she thought whoever was involved—the murderer, let's say—hadn't seen her."

"But he had," Gerrard said.

"Possibly. Whoever it was knew he'd been seen by someone at least—later that day, probably because of something Miribelle said or did, perhaps simply because she looked so uncommonly haggard, he guessed it was she." Barnaby sat back. "So he killed her."

"Which means," Gerrard said, "that whatever Miribelle and presumably now Millicent saw or heard was dangerous, very dangerous, to the murderer."

Barnaby nodded. "So dangerous he killed without the slightest compunction to prevent them telling . . ."

"Why didn't Miribelle tell anyone, then?" Sir Godfrey asked. "If she knew what she'd seen enough to be so upset by it, why didn't she say?"

After a moment, Barnaby admitted, "I don't know. There'll be a reason, but until we know what it was they both saw, we won't be able to guess it."

"Regardless," Gerrard persisted, "everything hinges on what they saw. That's the critical thing. What could it have been?"

"*Who* could it have been?" Sir Godfrey put in. "Who the devil wanders the gardens at night?"

Gerrard knew. "Eleanor Fritham, for one." He met Sir Godfrey's eyes. "There's a telescope in my bedchamber—I've seen her on a number of nights, together with a gentleman I didn't see well enough to identify." Gerrard hesitated for a heartbeat, a remembered vision swimming before his eyes. "In addition to that, there's a lover's bower in the Garden of Night, well concealed, and someone is currently using it."

Sir Godfrey's brows rose high. "Is that so?" But then he frowned; after a moment he said, "Neither Miribelle nor Millicent would be likely to get hysterical over stumbling on a pair of lovers in the garden, so it won't be that per se. However"—his tone hardened; he looked at Gerrard and Barnaby—"I propose we ask Miss Fritham just who she's been meeting in the gardens at night, and see if either she or her beau can shed light on what Millicent saw."

At Barnaby's suggestion, Sir Godfrey sent to Tresdale Manor, requesting Eleanor's presence at the Hall. She arrived an hour later, with Lady Fritham, who led the way into the drawing room.

"I'm sure I don't know why you need Eleanor, Godfrey, but of course I brought her straightaway. All the ladies at my at-home are agog to know what's afoot." Lady Fritham smiled in pleasant query at Sir Godfrey.

The magistrate looked blank, then cleared his throat. "Ah—just a little matter I need to clear up, Maria. Perhaps . . ." He glanced at Barnaby. "If Mr. Adair and I could have a quiet word with Eleanor in the study, while you remain here with Marcus and Jacqueline and Mr. Debbington . . ."

Smiling easily at Eleanor, Barnaby offered his arm. She took it; she cast an uncertain glance at her mother, but Barnaby irresistibly led her from the room, with Sir Godfrey making haste in their wake.

"Well!" Lady Fritham looked nonplussed. "How strange."

Seated on the chaise, Jacqueline drew in a breath, strengthened her smile, and patted the cushions beside her. "Do sit down, ma'am. Whom did you leave at the manor? I know Aunt Millicent would love to know."

Frowning, Lady Fritham sank to the chaise. "Where is Millicent?"

"She's a trifle indisposed," Lord Tregonning said.

"Oh." Lady Fritham accepted that without a blink. "Well, let me see. There's Mrs. Elcott, of course . . ."

She ran through her guests; Jacqueline was racking her brains over how to spin out the conversation—but then Eleanor reappeared in the doorway.

An Eleanor transformed—her color was high, her eyes flashing. She gave every sign of being highly offended. "Come, Mama! It's time we left."

Lady Fritham blinked uncomprehendingly. "But my dear—"

"*Now*, Mama! I wish to leave immediately." Eleanor narrowed her eyes at Barnaby, who came to stand just back from the doorway. "I have nothing more to say to Sir Godfrey, *or* Mr. Adair. So if you please . . ."

Eleanor didn't wait for a reply, but swung on her heel and stalked off.

Lady Fritham looked stunned. "Good gracious! Well! I'm sure I don't know . . ." Her hand at her throat, she rose. "Do excuse us, Marcus—I have no idea what's got into her."

"Of course, Maria." Lord Tregonning and Gerrard rose, bowing as Lady Fritham, agitated, fluttered toward the door.

"Maria?" Lord Tregonning waited until Lady Fritham looked back. "Just one thing—I would appreciate it if you would inform your family and household that the Hellebore Hall gardens are to be considered out of bounds. It seems they've grown too dangerous."

"Dear me! Yes, of course I'll tell everyone, Marcus. Do tell Millicent I'll call later to see how she is." With a wave, Lady Fritham hurried out into the hall in the wake of her wayward daughter.

Barnaby walked in; an instant later Sir Godfrey joined them. They all waited for the front door to shut, then Gerrard asked, "What did you learn?"

"Very little." Barnaby dropped into a chair. "She flatly denied ever being in the gardens at night. She was lying through her teeth."

"Indeed." Sir Godfrey sank heavily into an armchair. "Never seen her like that before—all bold as brass and spit in your eye."

"She panicked," Barnaby said. "And took a high tone to conceal it."

Sir Godfrey humphed. "What I want to know is who she's lying to protect. Someone must know." He looked at Jacqueline. "Who's she interested in, heh? Anyone she's been seen with?"

Jacqueline opened her lips to say she had no idea, then paused. The four men all noticed her hesitation, and waited. She felt color rise to her cheeks; she briefly debated the question of loyalty to a friend, then remembered her aunt lying upstairs, silent and still. She drew in a deep breath. "Eleanor has a lover. I don't know who, but . . ." She gestured vaguely. "She's been seeing him for years."

Sir Godfrey's brows couldn't get any higher. "Same man for all those years?"

"As far as I know. And before you ask, I have absolutely no idea, no clue, as to who he might be."

"But he's someone who's always here?" Barnaby asked. "In the area?"

Jacqueline shrugged. "As far as I know."

Sir Godfrey frowned. "We'll have to find someone who knows more about Miss Fritham's secret lover."

They'd all heard footsteps in the hall, coming from the front door; all had assumed it was Treadle. But the footsteps abruptly stopped—just beyond the open door. As one, they looked up.

Mitchel Cunningham stood framed in the doorway, his face pale, his expression stunned. He stared at Sir Godfrey as if he couldn't believe his eyes, then he blinked, and frowned. He took a step nearer. "Is anything wrong?"

"Mitchel—do come in." Lord Tregonning beckoned. "You might be able to help us with this."

Swiftly, Lord Tregonning outlined what had happened; they all watched Mitchel's face—his shock was beyond question sincere.

"Good God! But she's all right?"

"Yes." Sir Godfrey took up the tale. "But . . ." He explained they were now searching for the gentleman Eleanor was in the habit of meeting in the gardens at night. "Do you have any idea who this blighter might be?"

Gerrard didn't know if it was his artist's perception, or if his connection with Jacqueline had made him more sensitive, but he had no difficulty reading the pained—nay, tortured—expression in Mitchel's eyes. For form's sake, he quietly asked, "It wasn't you, was it?"

His tone made it clear the words were more statement than question. Mitchel's dark eyes deflected to his face. Mitchel met his gaze, then slowly shook his head. "It wasn't me." The words were hollow, achingly empty.

None of them doubted he spoke the truth.

Lord Tregonning cleared his throat. "Thank you, Mitchel."

Mitchel nodded; he barely seemed to see them. "If you'll excuse me?"

They let him go.

When his footsteps had died away, Sir Godfrey asked, "Am I right in thinking . . ."

Gerrard nodded. "Mitchel has, I think, nurtured hopes, although I doubt it's gone beyond that."

"Hopes we've just dashed," Lord Tregonning said. "But better he learn now than later."

Briefly, they revisited all they'd learned; Sir Godfrey asked about protection for Millicent, and was reassured.

"When she wakes, she'll be able to point her finger at the villain." His gaze hard, Sir Godfrey sounded uncharacteristically bloodthirsty. "And heaven help him after that."

They determined to forge ahead with the ball. Gerrard, Barnaby and Lord Tregonning spent the afternoon writing and dispatching invitations, while Jacqueline attended to all the myriad arrangements.

After dinner, she retired to sit with Millicent, leaving the men discussing their plans. Later, Gerrard fetched her from Millicent's room, and followed her to hers.

Leading the way in, she crossed to the windows, and stood looking out at the black velvet sky. Closing the door, Gerrard paused, considering the line of her spine, head erect, the way she'd folded her arms. There were no candles burning; the room was washed with gray shadows. Slowly, he followed her, wondering.

Halting behind her, he reached for her, and drew her back against him. She leaned back, let her head settle against his shoulder. He glanced down at her face, at her stormy expression, and waited.

Eventually, she drew a long breath. "It's always, *always,* people who love me, who care for me, who get hurt. Who *die.*" Her next breath shook. "I don't want you to be in their number."

He bent his head, brushed his lips over her temple. "I won't be. And Millicent isn't dead—there's no change for the worse, no reason to think she'll die. Regardless, trust me, I'm not about to let this villain take me from you." With his gaze, he traced her face. "I'm not about to let him deny us this—what we have, what our future will be."

Commitment rang in his tone; Jacqueline heard it, and felt tears sting her eyes. What if she believed him, and then . . .

"It won't happen." Gerrard breathed the words across her ear; his grip firmed, holding her more securely. "All the times before, it was one person alone he had to deal with—this time, there's all of us. We're all ranged against him—you, me, Barnaby, your father, Lady Tannahay and the Entwhistles, Sir Godfrey. This time, he can't win."

Her champion, he'd gathered supporters to her cause; without him, she'd still be trapped in the nightmarish web her tormentor had spun.

Jacqueline closed her hands over his at her waist, felt the strength in his hard, warm body at her back. For the first time, she understood in her heart the nature of the fear that drove him to protect her, even over her protests. If she could lock him away somewhere safe until the villain had been caught, she would, in a blink.

It seemed his mind was following a similar tack. "I don't suppose you've changed your mind about announcing our betrothal."

Not, she noted, about agreeing to marry him, which she still hadn't done. "I told you—ask me once he's caught. Until then"—she

turned in his arms, lifting hers to circle his neck, meeting his gaze—
"we're just lovers."

His eyes, dark in the night, held hers. A long moment passed, then
he shook his head. "No. We're not."

He bent his head, covered her lips with his—and showed her.
Demonstrated, orchestrated a shattering display of how far beyond
mere lovers they were.

Impossible to deny, not just him, but the reality of what had come
to be, of the depth, the breadth, the overwhelming power of the connection that had grown between them. The heat, the searing need, the
possessiveness that flamed and raced through them both, cindering
any inhibitions, any residual reservations. It opened the door to passion unrestrained, to rampant desire and its assuagement. Infused
their minds and drove them, invested their touch, their bodies, their
souls.

Beyond physical intimacy, beyond desire and passion, beyond, it
seemed, the earthly realm, the power swelled, shone, and claimed
them.

Accepting their worship, their devotion—ultimately accepting
their surrender.

As night deepened and the shadows turned black, Jacqueline lay
in Gerrard's arms, listening to his heart beating steadily beneath her
ear while the strength and devotion carried in that connection surrounded and closed about them.

She wondered what the next fraught days would bring, knew he
was thinking the same.

Heard in her mind Timms's fateful words, suspected he did, too.

What will be will be.

There was nothing they could do but accept, and follow the
path on.

21

They gathered about the breakfast table late the next morning. Jacqueline had checked on Millicent; there'd been no change in her aunt's condition. Millicent lay straight and still under the covers, her eyes closed, gently breathing, looking far more fragile than she normally did.

Gerrard squeezed Jacqueline's hand when she slipped onto the chair beside him; she smiled weakly in return, then gave her attention to her father and the details of the ball.

Mitchel had breakfasted earlier and gone out about the estate, as he often did; breakfast was long finished, the trays cleared away, and they were discussing the best location for the portrait when he returned.

They all looked up when he strode in, alerted by the heavy deliberation in his stride.

Deathly pale, he halted at the end of the table. He looked at them all—Gerrard, Jacqueline and Barnaby—then his gaze settled on her father. "My lord, I have a confession to make."

The comment started hares in all their minds—confused hares; none of them saw Mitchel as the murderer. They exchanged glances, wondering.

"Ah . . ." Her father waved to a chair. "Why don't you sit down, my boy, and explain?"

Jaw set, Mitchel drew out a chair and dropped into it. Leaning on the table, he fixed her father with an unfaltering gaze. "I've betrayed you, and failed in my duty."

What followed was not a confession to murder; it was a disturbing tale nonetheless.

"I believed"—Mitchel's jaw clenched—"or rather was led to believe that my feelings for Eleanor Fritham were returned. More, I was encouraged by Jordan to think that I could win Eleanor's hand—I see now that they were both deceiving me, leading me on." Mitchel's gaze darkened; he met her father's eyes steadily. "They wanted information from me, and I gave it."

From his tone, that appeared to be the extent of Mitchel's crime.

"What information?" Gerrard asked.

"Details of Lord Tregonning's estate and business dealings." Mitchel spread his hands. "I didn't see all that much harm in it at the time." He glanced at Jacqueline. "I arrived here after your mother died. I believed everything Jordan told me about her death—that you were disturbed and needed to be kept at home, and that Jordan would eventually marry you and gain control of your fortune and Hellebore Hall—"

"*What?*" Jacqueline's stunned exclamation was drowned out by more violent expostulations from her father and Gerrard. She waved them to silence; dumbfounded, she stared at Mitchel. "*Jordan* intended marrying me?"

Mitchel frowned. "That's what he *said*. Whether it was true—"

The doorbell pealed. Not once, but continuously.

"What the *devil* . . . ?" Lord Tregonning glared, then the pealing ceased.

Treadle hurried past the open parlor door on his way to the front hall. A second later, a cacophony of voices spilled into the hall, too many voices to distinguish. Gerrard and Barnaby pushed back their chairs. They stood; Mitchel rose, too. They all looked out to the corridor.

Abruptly, Treadle appeared in the doorway, looking harassed and rather desperate. "My lord, they won't—"

He got no further; Mrs. Elcott thrust him aside and swept in. A veritable wave of neighbors poured after her, Lord and Lady Fritham, Matthew Brisenden, Lady Trewarren, Mrs. Myles, Mr. and Mrs. Hancock, and Sir Vincent Perry among them. Of the crowd, only Lady Tannahay and the Entwhistles, who looked frankly taken aback, had been invited.

Lady Trewarren headed for Lord Tregonning. "Marcus, we've just heard the sad, sad news! It's thoroughly *dreadful*! We didn't know what to think, but of course we're here to support you and Jacqueline through this latest ordeal."

Lord Tregonning had reached the end of his patience. "*What* ordeal?"

Lady Trewarren halted; she blinked at him. "Why, the ordeal of Millicent's death, of course. You can't possibly *not* call that an ordeal, surely. Why—"

The chatter rose again, threatening to drown out all else.

"*Millicent isn't dead!*"

Lord Tregonning's roar led to immediate silence.

Gerrard seized the reins. "From whom did you hear that Millicent had died?"

Mrs. Elcott stared at him as if she wasn't sure he was sane. "But she isn't dead—or is she?"

Gerrard hung on to his temper. "No, she isn't, but it's important we learn who told you she was."

Lady Trewarren exchanged a glance with Mrs. Elcott, then looked at Gerrard. "Why, I heard it from my staff, of course."

Others nodded.

"It's all over St. Just," Matthew volunteered. "My father had it from the innkeeper—Papa will be along shortly."

Lord Tregonning looked at Lady Tannahay. "Had you heard anything?"

Mystified, Lady Tannahay shook her head. Beside her, the Entwhistles did, too.

"But we're from further afield, Marcus," Lady Entwhistle pointed out. "This sounds like a rumor that's only just begun."

Lord Tregonning looked at Treadle.

So did Gerrard. "Any chance any of the staff spoke to anyone—or more likely, that someone visited here, and got the wrong idea?"

"No, sir, m'lord." Treadle drew himself up. "Mrs. Carpenter and I will take an oath on it—none of the staff have left the house nor talked to anyone at all, and no one has visited here. Not until"—with his head he indicated the crowd in the room—"just now."

Gerrard looked at Mitchel.

Equally puzzled, Mitchel shook his head. "I haven't spoken to anyone about Millicent."

Gerrard turned to Lord Tregonning. "The only person who would have thought Millicent was dead . . ."

Lord Tregonning nodded. "Indeed." He looked at the others. "We need to identify who started this rumor."

Matthew had been following the exchanges closely. "On my way out, I spoke to our gardener. He heard of it last night in the tavern—he said the head gardener from Tresdale Manor told him."

"My maid had it from her young man." Lady Trewarren glanced at Lady Fritham. "He's your junior stableman, Maria."

Lady Fritham looked confused. "My maid told me, too—I gathered all the staff knew."

"*I* had it from my maid Betsy this morning." The portentous note in Mrs. Elcott's voice had everyone turning to her. She nodded, acknowledging their attention. "Betsy lives with her parents and comes in every day. She heard the news from her sister, who's parlormaid at the manor—she, the sister, told Betsy that Cromwell, the butler at the manor, had overheard Master Jordan telling Miss Eleanor that Miss Tregonning was dead, and there was no more to be done."

All eyes swung back to Lady Fritham. She blinked, puzzled. "But Jordan didn't say anything to me. Hector?" She looked at Lord Fritham; nonplussed, he shook his head. Confused, Lady Fritham turned to Lord Tregonning. "Well, I'm sure I don't know what's going on."

"Damn!" Barnaby had stood quietly by, absorbing information; he suddenly leaned forward and spoke to Lord Tregonning. "My lord, I meant to ask earlier—has any man applied to you for Jacqueline's hand?"

Lord Tregonning frowned, started to shake his head, then stopped. His expression blanked, then he shifted and glanced at Jacqueline. "I'm sorry, my dear—I suppose I should have mentioned it, but indeed, it was such a . . . well, *insulting* offer, couched as it was. As a sacrifice, in fact—as he had no wish to marry any other young lady, he was willing to assist our family by marrying you and ensuring you stayed here, safely out of sight, kept close at home for the rest of your life."

"When was this?" Barnaby asked.

"About five months ago." Lord Tregonning's lip curled. "Even though at that time I wasn't sure . . . it was still a dashed stomach-curdling offer. I dismissed it, of course—told him I appreciated the thought, but it wouldn't be honorable to accept such a sacrifice on his part."

"He who?" Barnaby pressed.

Lord Tregonning blinked at him. "Why, Jordan, of course. Who else?"

"Who else, indeed," Barnaby muttered. Aloud, he asked, "And no other man applied for Jacqueline's hand?"

Lord Tregonning shook his head.

"Marcus?" Lady Trewarren had lifted her head; she was glancing up and around. "I hate to mention it, but I smell smoke."

Others started sniffing, turning around.

Treadle, eyes widening, met Gerrard's gaze, then stepped back and hurried out of the room.

"I'm really very sensitive when it comes to smoke," Lady Trewarren went on, "and I do believe it's getting stronger—"

"Fire!"

It was a maid who screeched from somewhere upstairs.

The crowd in the parlor tumbled out into the hall. The smell was more distinct, but there was no other evidence of flames. Everyone stared up at the gallery; with a thunder of feet, a group of footmen raced across, heading into the south wing.

"All the ladies into the drawing room." Barnaby started herding them in that direction. Some protested, wanting to see what was afire; Sir Vincent smothered an oath and went to help.

Treadle appeared at the head of the stairs. He came hurrying down. "It's the old nursery, sir." He glanced at Gerrard. "And your room, Mr. Debbington. The drapes have caught well and truly there. We're ferrying pails up the service stairs, but we'll need all hands possible."

"I'll help." Matthew Brisenden started up the stairs. The other men exchanged glances, then swiftly followed.

Jacqueline hung back. As Barnaby and Sir Vincent hurried back from the drawing room, she put a hand on her father's arm. "I'll check with Mrs. Carpenter, then return to the drawing room and make sure the ladies remain safely there."

Gerrard had dallied on the stairs to hear what she intended; he caught her eye, nodded, then turned and took the stairs three at a time.

Her father patted her hand. "Good girl. I'll go and see what's to do."

She watched him start slowly up the stairs. Confident Treadle would keep him from any harm, she headed for the kitchens.

As she'd expected, pandemonium reigned. She helped Mrs. Carpenter calm the maids, and organize them to help the stablemen lug pails from the well to the bottom of the south wing stairs. A chain of grooms and footmen hurried the pails up, some to the first floor, others to the attics.

Mrs. Carpenter looked grim. Once the maids were occupied, she drew Jacqueline aside. "Maizie found the fire in Mr. Debbington's room. She said it was arrows—arrows with flaming rags around them—that were tangled in the curtains. That's how the fire started. She was babbling on about how we shouldn't think it was coals dropping from the grate and her to blame—I told her no such thing, but thought you and his lordship should know."

Jacqueline nodded. Arrows. An arrow had been shot at Gerrard, and now there were more arrows. She hadn't heard the details of how Gerrard had been shot at, but the only way an arrow could have hit Gerrard's curtains was if it had been fired from the gardens, and she knew the gardens well. Knew there was no close, clear line to Gerrard's windows; the archer would have had to be a good way off, and skilled enough to allow for the cross breeze.

It was quiet living in the country; the local youth had plenty of time to perfect their archery skills, yet only a few were skilled enough to have made those shots, especially if, as seemed likely, they'd shot to the attics, as well. As she hurried back through the house, she considered the possible culprits.

Reaching the green baize door, she pushed through, into the back of the hall.

"Jacqueline!"

She whirled.

Eleanor, hair tumbling down, gown crumpled, frantically beckoned from the end of the north wing corridor. "Come quickly! There's another fire broken out along here! They said to fetch you.

We're struggling—we need every hand." She didn't wait, but plunged back down the corridor.

Jacqueline's heart stopped, then she picked up her skirts and raced after Eleanor.

Millicent's room was in the north wing.

She swung into the corridor just in time to see Eleanor dash into a small parlor nearly at the end of the wing—below the room in which Millicent lay. Jacqueline ran faster. She would have to call some of the stablemen from the kitchens—she'd look first, then she'd know—

She rushed into the parlor.

No flames. No smoke. No footmen beating out a fire.

She skidded to a halt. Behind her, the door closed.

She whirled.

Jordan stood two paces away, watching her, his gaze cold, contemptuous—calculating.

She stared. Was it *he* . . . ?

Her heart thudded; her breath clogged her throat. Looking into Jordan's eyes, she reminded herself that people who loved her were the ones at risk—*she'd* never been—still wouldn't be—in danger.

And her mother's murderer, Millicent's attacker, could be only one man—Eleanor's lover.

Eleanor moved away from the door, drawing her attention.

Dragging in a breath, Jacqueline took a step back.

Eleanor came to stand by Jordan's side, close, just behind his shoulder. Then she put a hand on his arm, sank closer still, and smiled—sweetly, yet patently—openly—insincerely.

The blood chilled in Jacqueline's veins. The hair at her nape lifted.

She stared into Eleanor's eyes; this was not the friend she'd known for years . . . She looked at Jordan. He appeared much as he always did, arrogant, superior, supercilious. Cold dread was creeping over her. Moistening her lips, she asked, "Where's the fire?"

Jordan held her gaze, then evenly replied, "What fire?"

Then he smiled.

Eyes wide, Jacqueline *knew*—suddenly saw what none of them had—knew what her mother must have stumbled on, why she'd looked so haggard, why she'd been killed, why Millicent had been flung over the balustrade, why Thomas had been coldbloodedly murdered all those years ago.

It came to her in a heartbeat.

She hauled in a breath and screamed.

"A aargh!"

With two footmen, Gerrard heaved the huge bundle of paint-spattered drop cloths out of the nursery window. They fell to the terrace below, out of reach of any embers.

Catching his breath, his back to the window, he paused, taking in the charred rafters and smoldering walls. They'd smothered the flames just in time, before they could take hold in the roof and spread.

A woman's scream, faint but distinct, abruptly cut off, wafted past the window, carried on an updraft from far below. For one fleeting instant, it sliced through the stamping and thumping, the oaths, the noisy chaos as footmen and gardeners used sacking to beat out the last flames.

Gerrard's senses pricked. He swung back to the window. He'd rushed to the attics, leaving Barnaby to see to his bedroom; he knew more about the dangers of paint-spattered wood and cloths, and the other deathtraps that lurked in artists' studios.

Dense smoke billowed out of his bedroom below, but it was thinning; the crackle of flames had subsided.

They'd saved the house.

It must have been a maid who'd screamed, but why now? Why from outside?

The premonition of wrongness intensified. He hesitated, staring unseeing down at the gardens, then he swore. "Wilcox!"

The head gardener looked up from where he was beating out glowing embers. "Yes, sir?"

"Round up your men and get down to the terrace. Something's happening down there."

Leaving the footmen to finish damping down the attics, Gerrard flung through the door and pelted down the stairs.

Behind, he heard Wilcox rallying his men. "C'mon, you lot—downstairs. Look sharpish!"

Gerrard hit the corridor and ran. His chest felt tight—from smoke, and nascent fear. He raced to his room, barreled through the open door, spared barely a glance for the charred mess, not as bad as in the nursery. Leaping over debris, he saw Barnaby and pointed to the balcony. The telescope stood where he'd left it, safe and untouched on its tripod in the corner; he grabbed it, swung it up and pushed past the milling figures onto the balcony.

"What?" Barnaby asked, reaching his side.

"Some woman screamed—from the gardens, I think." Working frantically, Gerrard set up the tripod, then readjusted the telescope and focused. "Send someone to check if Jacqueline's in the drawing room."

He felt Barnaby's start, but his friend didn't question him. A footman was dispatched, urgency stressed.

Gerrard swept the gardens. Even from this vantage point, not all the areas were visible; he scanned in arcs, hoping to pick up some movement—

"There!" He looked up, checked the direction, then looked through the telescope again. "There's someone rushing through Poseidon, heading into Apollo. Three people . . ." He refocused. "Jordan, Eleanor—and *Jacqueline*." He swore. "They're holding her between them."

He tensed to straighten; Barnaby's hand clapped down on his shoulder.

"No. Keep them in your sights—keep tracking them."

He did. "They're in Apollo now, hurrying further away. Where the devil are they taking her?"

Matthew Brisenden appeared beside him, gripping the rail, staring out.

Sir Vincent joined them. "Did I hear aright? The young Frithams are running off with Jacqueline?"

Gerrard nodded. "They're headed down the gardens—God knows why."

"They're kidnapping her!" Gripping the railing, Matthew turned his way. "They have to get to the stone viewing platform before they can take the path up through Diana, over the ridge to the manor."

Gerrard swore. "He's right. That's how they get back and forth without using the front door."

"Not this time." Barnaby leaned over the balustrade and called to Wilcox, now on the terrace with a bevy of gardeners. In a few short phrases, he explained; Wilcox and his men turned as one, and raced along the terrace, then poured down into the gardens, taking the most direct route through Athena into the garden of Diana to block the route to the manor.

"They'll see," Matthew said, "and go the other way. If they can reach the stables—"

"Or even the other cove," Sir Vincent put in. "There's a rowboat there."

Matthew was already turning. "I saw Richards below. I'll find him and get his men out on the paths along the northern ridge, so they won't be able to go that way, either."

"I'll help." Sir Vincent followed Matthew out.

Gerrard kept the telescope trained on the trio hurrying through the gardens. They were still in Apollo, crossing the bridge over the stream. Jacqueline was gagged; from the way Jordan and Eleanor were holding her between them, her hands were bound, too.

Behind him, he heard movement; Lord Fritham, Sir Harvey Entwhistle and Mr. Hancock appeared. They'd been assisting in putting out the flames. One glance at Lord Fritham's stunned expression told Gerrard he'd heard the latest developments.

So had the others. "Come on, old chap." Grim-faced, Sir Harvey dropped a hand on Lord Fritham's shoulder. "We'd best get down there and find out what that whelp of yours thinks he's about."

Lord Fritham nodded; he looked numb. The three older men turned and went out.

Barnaby returned to Gerrard's side. "Where are they now?"

"In Apollo, still some way from the second viewing stage." He paused, then added, "Jacqueline keeps stumbling. She's slowing them down." His voice flattened, grew quieter. "Jordan just hit her." A moment later, he went on, "That hasn't helped—she's slumped on the ground and refusing to get up."

Barnaby gripped his shoulder harder. "Stay with it a bit longer. We need to see where they go once they reach the viewing platform."

Gerrard slammed a door on his rising emotions, far beyond anger or simple protectiveness. Rage, fury, cold, deep and potent; Jacqueline was *his,* his to protect, but he could see the sense in Barnaby's tack. Gritting his teeth, he kept the telescope trained; in his head, he warned Jacqueline to take care, urged her to be careful. Cursed Jordan Fritham to hell and beyond.

Simultaneously prayed.

The older gentlemen came out on the terrace. Lord Tregonning was with them. They called up to Barnaby for directions, then headed off as fast as they could into the gardens.

Wide, long, densely planted, the gardens weren't designed for rushing through, for easy traversing. Quite the opposite. The action unfolded slowly; Gerrard took his eye briefly from Jacqueline to confirm that the gardeners had reached the higher reaches of the Garden of Diana—there'd be no escape for the Frithams that way. The stablemen, Matthew and Sir Vincent weren't as far advanced on the northern ridge, but they'd be in place before the Frithams could divert in that direction.

He swung the telescope back to Jacqueline—and watched Jordan and Eleanor hustle her toward the stone viewing platform at the end of the Garden of Apollo.

Jacqueline all but sobbed with relief when Jordan reached up and yanked his kerchief from her mouth.

"There!" His eyes were flat, hard and cold. "We're too far from the house. You can scream all you like—there's no one to hear." He glanced back at the house; a mocking smile curved his lips. "They're all too busy putting out the flames, and no doubt bemoaning the loss of that bloody portrait." His fingers tightened about her arm. "Now come on!"

He hauled her on. She dragged and stumbled as much as she dared, but she wouldn't put it past Jordan to knock her unconscious and carry her—it would be faster; she didn't want to provoke him to the point he realized that.

Eleanor, pale, tight-lipped, had hold of her other arm; she, too, pulled her on. They were both taller and stronger than she; together, they could almost lift her from her feet.

She knew the portrait was safe; it hadn't been in either Gerrard's room or the makeshift studio. Her father had taken possession; Compton and Treadle had carefully stowed the framed picture in her father's study.

Now didn't seem the time to mention that.

She'd almost managed to catch her breath, to shake off the effects of those terrible moments in the parlor, worse than any nightmare she'd ever dreamed. She'd never forget the sheer evil she'd sensed; the sun on her face assured her she was in the real world, yet . . . She dragged in a breath, fought to steady her voice. "Where are you taking me? What on earth do you hope to gain by this?"

"We're abducting you," Jordan coldly informed her. "Your sluttish behavior with that damned artist left us no choice." His tone suggested it was entirely her fault. "They're going to think we're on our way to Gretna, but in reality, I've a nice little inn down the coast in mind."

He glanced at her. "A few nights alone with me, and I'm sure your father will see the sense in agreeing to our betrothal."

She was certain she knew the answer, but still asked, "Why do you want to marry me? You don't even like me."

"Of course not. Innocents have never attracted me." He glanced at Eleanor, and smiled—a secret smile Jacqueline wished she hadn't seen—then he looked ahead, after a moment continued, "No doubt your artist has taught you a thing or two—it'll be interesting to find out how far he's taken your education. However, beyond the necessity of bringing about our marriage—no, I have little personal interest in you. All I want is Hellebore Hall."

"Why?"

He frowned, jaw tightening; he didn't look at her. "Because it should be mine. I need it more than you."

The stone viewing platform loomed before them; they forced her up the steps, Eleanor going ahead and tugging, Jordan pushing from behind. Once on the platform, they turned to the path leading to the Garden of Diana, their usual route between the Manor and the Hall.

Jordan thrust her before him; she stumbled into Eleanor and out onto the path. "We've horses saddled and waiting—we'll be away before they realize—"

"Jordan." Eleanor had halted. Staring up at the ridge, she pointed. "Look!"

Jacqueline lifted her head, and saw figures, still too far away to recognize but their number suggested they were gardeners or grooms, running along the higher paths out along the ridge. They were already pouring into the upper reaches of the Garden of Diana; there was no way Jordan and Eleanor, even alone and racing, could reach the path out.

Relief slid through her; she sagged, staggered back a few steps to lean against the side of the platform. "Untie me." She held out her hands, bound with laces. "There's no point going any further—you'll have to go back and explain—"

With a snarl, Jordan turned on her. "*No!* I won't let you go—won't let the Hall slip through my fingers." He seized her arm again, fingers biting. "We'll just go the other way." He jerked her upright. "Back inside."

He hauled her back up the steps, then out onto the path leading up the garden to the wooden pergola from which paths led on to the northern ridge and the stables. "We'll take horses from your stables."

They'd gone twenty yards, out into the open, when Jordan abruptly halted. Head up, scanning ahead, he swore. "They're up there, too."

Jaw clenched, he towed her around and propelled her before him, shoving her back to the stone platform. Once under the wooden roof, he halted; still gripping her arm, eyes wide, a touch wild, he looked first one way, then the other.

Eleanor was looking, too. Even paler than before, breathing rapidly, she turned to Jordan. "What now? We can't get out." Her gaze shifted to Jacqueline. "She's all we have to bargain with, but I haven't a knife or anything to threaten her with—have you?"

Jordan patted his pockets, then pulled out a penknife. He flicked it open; the blade was less than two inches long.

"That's no use!" Incipient hysteria rang in Eleanor's voice.

Jordan was silent, staring down at the blade, then he drew in a huge breath, lifted his head and looked down the gardens.

Jacqueline had no idea what he saw, but calmness enveloped him.

The wild look in his eyes faded, and he smiled. Coldly. "It'll do for what we need if combined with something else. Something more dramatic and final. And so very apt."

He tightened his grip on Jacqueline's arm, ruthlessly shook her. "Come on. I know just how to make your father and all the rest agree to everything I want."

Going down the steps, he hauled her after him, then set out, striding rapidly along the path into the Garden of Mars, heading toward the cove.

$\cdot$ $\cdot$ $\cdot$

Gerrard swore. Releasing the telescope, he swung around, ducked into the smoke-blackened room and headed for the door. "They've taken the path to the cove."

"The cove?" Barnaby followed. "But there's no escape that way."

"No escape," Gerrard ground out. "But something better. A gun to hold to our heads."

"Gun?" Barnaby kept pace as Gerrard ran down the corridor, then went quickly down the stairs. "What gun?"

Gerrard strode onto the terrace. "It's called Cyclops."

By the time Jordan dragged her up the steps of the last viewing platform, Jacqueline had solved his cryptic utterance; she knew where he was going.

She'd slowed them as much as she'd dared; she had a stitch in her side, her breathing was quite genuinely labored, and her legs wobbled alarmingly. She wanted nothing more than to collapse on the seat and recover. Jordan, who walked the gardens so often, appeared unaffected by their race down the valley. Eleanor, however, was flagging badly, as exhausted as she.

Seizing the moment when Jordan paused to note how close their pursuers were, Jacqueline dragged air into her lungs, straightened her shoulders, tried to ease the ache in her bound arms.

Jordan tightened his painful grip on her arm. "Come on." His tone was tight. "We've got to get there ahead of them."

He thrust her down the steps, following closely, jerking her upright when her ankle threatened to give way. He snarled, "Don't you *dare* slow us down." His eyes met hers, flat, cold—deadly.

How had she ever imagined him a friend, even a superior, aloof one? She was nothing to him, just a means to an end. As for Eleanor . . . Jacqueline looked at the woman whose nails bit into her other arm as she ruthlessly tugged her on. She'd never truly seen her before, but the Eleanor who'd stood beside Jordan in the parlor had dropped all pretense and contemptuously flaunted the truth. Recalling the lascivious details Eleanor had delighted in telling her over the years about her activities with her lover turned Jacqueline's stomach, but she now knew the truth.

She knew who Eleanor's lover was.

22

The last section of the path leading to the cove descended sharply through a wide curve. There were steps along the way, interrupting their headlong dash, forcing Jordan and Eleanor, despite their growing urgency, to slow.

Lungs burning, arms aching, Jacqueline stumbled on between them, searching for some means of delay. She could hear voices drawing nearer, lots of them. It was no part of Jordan's plan for her to die—not yet, at any rate—yet as she grappled with the enormity of all he'd done so far in his quest to own Hellebore Hall . . . she had no faith that if thwarted, he wouldn't sacrifice her out of revenge.

He couldn't be entirely sane.

She glanced sideways. On her right, Eleanor was nearing the end of her resources. Unlike Jordan, she looked frightened, increasingly panicky.

Jacqueline looked ahead; her gaze fell on the plantings bordering the path. They reached the next bend; three steps led down. Eleanor started down, her fingers locked about Jacqueline's arm, tugging her down, too. Jordan released Jacqueline to glance back up the path.

She let herself fall, dropping her shoulder, breaking Eleanor's grip, butting hard into Eleanor's side. Stepping down, already off balance, Eleanor lost her footing. She shrieked, flailed, then fell backward off the step into the bed alongside.

It was filled with large cacti.

Eyes wide, her mouth open, Eleanor froze, then she hauled in a breath and *screamed*. She thrashed; the cactus spines dug in, caught her skirts, caught everywhere.

Jordan stared, horrified—helpless to help her.

Then he rounded on Jacqueline.

She'd stumbled, but kept her feet. "She pulled me—I tripped."

His face contorted. She saw the blow coming, but couldn't duck in time; the back of his hand cracked across her cheek. She reeled, then fell to her knees, gasping, struggling to catch her breath.

Behind her, Jordan tried to calm Eleanor, tried to stop her from becoming more entangled. He grasped her hands and tried to pull her loose; Eleanor shrieked. The cacti had speared her in too many places, trapping her and her clothes securely.

"It's all right." Jordan let go. "It doesn't matter if you stay here—they won't hurt you. I have to get to Cyclops and make them agree to all we want. Once they've put it in writing, we'll be the victors here—we can have and do whatever we want."

Jacqueline staggered to her feet. She was too exhausted to run.

Jordan cast her a vicious, vindictive glance. "Later," he said quickly to Eleanor, "you can have your revenge on her—take a whip to her, do whatever you like. You can make her pay, again and again—tie her up and make her watch us. She'll be your slave. We'll be together and no one will be able to stop us. But I have to get her to Cyclops to win."

Eleanor's eyes widened; she reached out, grasping his hands. "No—don't leave me!"

Jordan's contemptuous exasperation returned. "I'll come back!" Glancing up the path, he shook off her hands. "I have to go—now!"

Eleanor howled. Jordan ignored her. He moved swiftly, ducking his shoulder, hefting Jacqueline up. Locking his arm about her legs, he headed as fast as he could for the cove. And Cyclops.

Jacqueline bounced on his shoulder. Unconsciousness threatened; she fought it off, managed to raise her arms and brace them against Jordan's back.

He was swearing continuously. As he bounded down the last section of path, she glimpsed figures above, some stopping by Eleanor, others streaming on. There were two paths that led to Cyclops, but the other, along the southern ridge, was longer.

Gauging the distance, Jacqueline accepted that Jordan, even carrying her, would reach Cyclops before any rescuers could reach them.

She'd done her best. Closing her eyes, she drew in a deep breath, smelled the salty tang of the sea—thought of Gerrard; she knew he'd come for her. Reaching deep, she marshaled her reserves. Whatever came next, she was going to need them.

G errard and Barnaby came to a precipitous halt on the path above the cove. Behind them, a group of gardeners was untangling a sobbing Eleanor Fritham from a bed of cacti.

Before them, high on top of Cyclops, Jordan Fritham stood, holding Jacqueline teetering on the edge of the blowhole.

Everyone else had gathered on the path, staying off the rock itself. In the center of the group, his neighbors supporting him, Lord Tregonning stood, leaning heavily on his cane; even from this distance his face was ashen.

Lord Fritham's pallor was even worse.

The bend in the path screened Gerrard and Barnaby from Jordan's sight. Through breaks in the foliage, they watched as he bargained with Jacqueline's life.

Higher up the garden, Mitchel Cunningham had passed them, racing back to the house for pen and paper. Sent back by Lord Tregonning in response to Jordan's demand, Mitchel had rapidly filled them in.

Jordan had threatened to disfigure Jacqueline, to put out her eyes then and there if they didn't meet his demands. If any rushed him, he'd drop her into Cyclops.

He'd asked for a deed to be written and signed by Lord Tregonning, and witnessed by everyone there, ceding Hellebore Hall and the estate to him outright, giving Jacqueline to him in marriage, and absolving him of all and any crimes they might think to lay at his door.

Gerrard was beyond swearing; Barnaby wasn't.

"Shush," Gerrard said. "Listen."

Lord Fritham was pleading with his son. "There's no need for any of this."

"Need?" Jordan's contempt-laden sneer reached them, carried on the sea breeze. "This can all be laid at your feet, old man—thanks to you, all I have is *need*. You and Mama have squandered what little inheritance I might have had, what with your entertainments, always trying to pretend you were as wealthy as your neighbors. The Manor is mortgaged to the hilt—don't you think I know? So what's left for me? I had to take steps to find myself a future. With Jacqueline's money, Eleanor and I will live in London—where we always should have stayed. No more being buried in the country. We'll live like kings in the capital, and leave you *damned* down here."

The last words rang with furious resentment.

Gulls wheeled; the swoosh of the waves on the rocky shore of the cove lent an eerie backdrop to the fraught scene.

The tide was coming in; Cyclops had yet to start gushing in earnest, but the hem of Jacqueline's gown was wet. The blowhole chamber emitted a low, steadily building grumble, more definite with every set of waves that rolled in.

"I wonder how much time we have before Cyclops really blows," Barnaby whispered.

"In about half an hour it'll start to gush."

It was Matthew who'd spoken; Gerrard turned as he and Sir Vincent joined them. The older man was panting heavily.

Matthew's eyes had locked on the unfolding drama. "It'll be an hour before Cyclops reaches full strength. Regardless, if he drops her in now, there's no way she'll escape. She'll either drown, or be battered to death."

On Cyclops, Jordan was speaking again. "As soon as that fool Cunningham brings paper and pen, all you have to do is write what I tell you, and sign it." A smile curved his lips. "I know you all—you're 'men of their word.' You'll do exactly as I ask so I won't be forced to let go." Jordan eased the arm about Jacqueline's waist—her feet immediately started to slip inward on the sloping side of Cyclop's funnel-like hole.

Everyone gasped, started forward, then stopped as Jordan laughed and hoisted her up again. "Just so." He brandished the knife close to her cheek. "Don't forget—stay back. I'm sure Cunningham will be here soon."

No one moved. No one said anything.

"Is Jordan insane?" Barnaby asked. "No one's going to feel obliged to honor a promise given under such duress."

"He's not insane." Sir Vincent looked grim. "Just think of the scandal fighting a written and fully witnessed deed will cause—for everyone."

"Oh, God!" Matthew grabbed Gerrard's arm; he pointed out to sea. "Look!"

A summer squall was sweeping in. A stormy, churning dark gray curtain, it steadily advanced, eating up the previously blue sky, the waves changing to slate before it, white crests rising, kicked up by the winds running before the front.

"It's coming this way." Matthew's voice was rising. "It'll drive the waves before it." He looked at the two figures on Cyclops, their backs to the approaching danger. "Jordan doesn't know. Cyclops will blow much sooner than he expects, and much harder. What if he loses his grip?"

Sir Vincent swore. "We'll have to tell him—"

"No." Barnaby was staring at Jordan. "If you force him to move away from Cyclops . . . It's his weapon. Without it, with just that little knife and a threat, he'll be vulnerable. He's liable to panic."

"He'll panic anyway," Matthew said. "I know what happens in storms. Cyclops erupts suddenly, without any gradual build—"

Gerrard clamped a hand on Matthew's arm, enjoining silence while his mind raced. "While Jordan holds Jacqueline over Cyclops, we can't do anything, so we're going to do something to change that—something Jordan won't expect."

"What?" Barnaby asked.

Gerrard met his eyes. "I need you and Sir Vincent to go out there and support Lord Tregonning, but not in silence. Jordan is vain—he thinks he's the victor here. Ask him about the previous deaths, get him to tell you how clever he's been—you know how to lead men like him to fill the time." Gerrard glanced at Sir Vincent. "Most importantly, between you, I need you to keep Jordan's eyes on *you*—on your faces. Don't let him look at the others."

Barnaby frowned. "Why?" Suspicion laced his tone.

Gerrard held up a hand. He looked back up the path, beckoned to one of the men surrounding Eleanor.

It was the senior undergardener. He came quickly. "Sir?"

"We need you to keep Miss Fritham there, and keep her *down*—we don't want her seeing what goes on out on Cyclops."

The man glanced at the rock, then saluted, and hurried back up the path.

Gerrard turned to Matthew. "Can we get from here to the cove without Jordan seeing us?"

Matthew frowned. He pointed to the right. "There's a gardener's track that swings around that way—it ends at the cove. Because of the dip where the stream runs down, there's cover all the way." He looked at Gerrard. "Why?"

His gaze fixing on the figures out on the rock, Gerrard drew a determined breath. "Because I'm going to do the last thing Jordan will expect. I'm going to climb Cyclops from the seaward side."

"No. You can't," Matthew said. "It's not possible."

Sir Vincent was shaking his head. "'Fraid he's right—it'd be suicide."

Gerrard turned his head and met Barnaby's eyes. "You often rib me about my county of origin—tell them."

Barnaby held his gaze, read his resolution, then sighed and glanced at the others. "Peak District. He's right. If anyone can climb the seaward side of Cyclops, it's him."

Like a giant awakening, the rumbling grumble of Cyclops rose beneath Jacqueline's feet. The blowhole gaped beside her; the powerful surge and swoosh of the waves steadily building within the rock cavern below filled her with terror.

Jordan's arm was her only link with life. If he let go, poised as she was, she wouldn't be able to save herself.

She was helpless, and one small step from certain death.

Panic threatened to engulf her. She fought it, but like the wetness seeping up her skirts, despair, cold and clammy, spread insidiously through her.

She had no idea what would happen, how the scene would play out, but the comber of tension running through Jordan's muscles told her he was nowhere near as in control of himself as he was striving to appear.

What if he fumbled and dropped her?

The rumble of men's voices was a counterpoint to that of Cyclops. She tried to make sense of the words, but couldn't seem to tear her gaze or mind from the yawning hole at her feet. It seemed to be waiting to suck her down . . .

Gerrard. If she slipped and died, losing him and their future would be her last and overwhelming regret; she was determined to fight for the chance to embrace both. That purpose, the certainty of knowing what she wanted, of knowing nothing else was more important in life, had allowed her to think, and delay, and remove Eleanor.

He'd given her a vision of her future to cling to.

Closing her eyes, she let that purpose once more infuse her, calm her.

A stir among those who were circling Cyclops had her raising her head, determinedly refocusing. Barnaby and Sir Vincent pushed through to join her father. Barnaby gripped her father's arm reassuringly. Her father, stone-faced, gave no sign he noticed, but she knew he had. Barnaby had a plan, but where was Gerrard?

Jordan was wondering the same thing; he searched the crowd, then asked.

Barnaby met his gaze. "He's injured. He had to stay at the house."

Her heart plummeted. Barnaby shifted his gaze and met her eyes.

And she knew it was a lie. Gerrard was here somewhere, doing something they didn't want Jordan to know about.

Her heart changed direction; her spirits soared. She listened, trying to get some idea of their plan. Trying to gauge what her part in it might be, steeling herself to do whatever was necessary.

Barnaby seemed resigned to Jordan getting his way; his conversation was clearly predicated on that. "You've planned this well," he told Jordan. "And over such a long time. But I'll admit I'm confused—*why* did you kill Thomas?"

Jordan hesitated, but couldn't resist the invitation to gloat before them all. "Obviously because he was about to offer for Jacqueline's hand, and she would have accepted him. He was about to poach what ought to be mine."

"Indeed." Barnaby nodded. "I quite see that. But why, once he was removed, didn't you ask for Jacqueline's hand and tie up the business then?"

"I would have." Jordan's voice took on an edge. "Except first she went into mourning for the idiot, and later, it became clear she wasn't likely to accept my suit."

"But you didn't give up?" Barnaby sounded intrigued. Jacqueline suspected he was, just not in the way Jordan thought.

"Of course not—I just hunted for another avenue to achieve the same end." When Barnaby waited, Jordan went on, "Miribelle was encouraging Jacqueline to go to London, but then Miribelle herself handed me the perfect solution. She poked her nose somewhere it shouldn't have been. When she tried to stop Jacqueline riding with us, we realized who'd seen us in the Garden of Night. So Miribelle had to be dealt with, quickly, before she drummed up the courage to tell anyone. And that, of course, was the key."

"You killed Miribelle," Sir Vincent cut in, his eyes and tone condemnatory, "and placed the blame on Jacqueline."

Jordan smiled. "Actually, no—I killed Miribelle, and *you all* placed the blame on Jacqueline. You *suspected*—and that was all Eleanor and I needed. All we had to do was blow gently here, then there, fanning your silly suspicions—it was so easy. You were all so gullible—it was the greatest game."

"One you played beautifully," Barnaby concurred.

Jordan inclined his head. "It gave me a scenario I could exploit to secure Jacqueline's hand, even against any resistance from her—in the circumstances, it was perfectly natural to propose a marriage of convenience to keep her quietly here in the country. It would have worked, too."

"But"—Barnaby looking confused—"I thought Lord Tregonning refused your suit?"

"He did." Exasperation and contempt laced Jordan's words. "He rambled about his honor and not accepting such a sacrifice—but he would have come around in the end. Once the rumors spread about Millicent's death, well, it was just a matter of time before the situation with Jacqueline became simply too pressing. Marrying her off to me would have been the only solution."

"Good God!" Sir Vincent was appalled, but then he swallowed and offered, "You really played us well."

Jordan smiled. "Thank you."

"One other thing," Barnaby continued, as if they were merely filling in the time until Mitchel returned. "How did you . . ."

· · ·

Standing on the rocks at the edge of the cove, hands on his hips, Gerrard looked up at the granite face of Cyclops. He could reach the narrow ledge circling it easily enough, but the climb up from there would be close to vertical for most of the way.

He eyed the wet rock, then walked across to its lower reaches, and leaned against it to tug off his boots. Leather soled, they'd be no help. In lieu of proper climbing boots, bare feet were the best alternative.

The waves were rolling in, angrily grasping more of the rock-strewn beach, feeding the roar, still muted, inside Cyclops's cavern. Without a word, Matthew took his boots. Gerrard stripped off his stockings and crammed them in, then methodically emptied his pockets. He would have preferred to remove his coat, but the material would give him some protection against the rough, encrusted rock. He was going to get cuts enough as it was.

Turning to Cyclops, he buttoned his coat.

Beside him, Matthew looked up at the granite monolith, black where the waves had wet it, and shivered. "You might not make it."

"I know." He had thought of it. "But if she dies, I'd never be able to live with myself if I hadn't tried."

He studied the face for an instant longer, then looked at Matthew. "Don't get seen until I reach the top."

Matthew nodded. "Good luck."

A crash of waves swallowed the words. Gerrard turned, reached for the narrow ledge and hoisted himself up.

The ledge was barely wider than his foot; clinging to the rockface with one hand, he quickly followed it along, circling the bulk of Cyclops until he reached the point he'd visually gauged as directly opposite where Barnaby and the others stood. As it happened, he would be climbing straight up one side and then over the top of the gaping maw where the sea rushed in, boiling and churning as it pushed into the cavern.

He didn't stop to consider. He climbed.

He'd been climbing since he could crawl. Despite all his years in London, he'd visited his home every year, and every year he'd climbed. He wasn't too rusty, too out of practice. Which was just as well. For someone of his experience, the rock itself was easy enough to conquer. What made the seaward ascent of Cyclops treacherous was the wet, and the constant but unpredictable crash and surge of the waves.

He didn't look down, but climbed steadily on. The moves were second nature—finding the next fingerhold, shifting his weight, searching for the next toehold, lifting up and on, over and over. There were a few strained moments, especially as he moved past the upper edge of the opening in the rock and footholds became scarce, but the tricks, the rhythm, and most especially the discipline, were there to see him through.

No rush. Never hurried. One small step at a time, steady and sure.

Behind him, the squall drew steadily nearer; the light started to dim.

He slipped on a patch of seaweedy slime he hadn't been able to see against the wet rock. He swung over the gaping hole—if he fell, he'd be swept into the chamber to a certain death. For an instant, he hung, fingers aching, muscles screaming, then he searched and found another toehold, and steadied.

He didn't think of anything but Jacqueline. Just her. Not what was going on above his head, but the feel of her in his arms, the scent of her in the night.

Spray and spume surrounded him; the roar in the blowhole chamber was gaining in intensity. He shut his ears to it, thought of Jacqueline's laugh—he hadn't heard it often enough yet for either of them to die.

What will be will be.

He clung to Timms's message like a promise, closed his mind to the pain in his wrists and grazed palms. Didn't think of the gashes on his feet, across his fingers.

Beneath him, the sea surged and crashed, demanding his attention, demanding he stop and look down. He ignored it and climbed.

The edges were more jagged the higher he went, less worn by the waves, sharpened by the wind. Clouds had blown in and now covered the sun; the wind freshened further, hurling froth and lashing the waves. He was soaked to his thighs, and was starting to lose sensation in his feet, but he was almost there.

Almost at the point where the vertical face ended and the rock curved toward its flattened summit. The first gradual slope would be the most crucial; he wouldn't be able to stand until he reached more level ground nearer to the blowhole, but throughout he'd be exposed, visible to those watching, and to Jordan if he turned around.

He was almost surprised to find himself lying prone, catching his breath on the top of the rock. He'd kept his head down; he hoped no one had yet sighted him. Drawing in a steadier breath, feeling his heart slow to a more normal rhythm, he focused on the discussion taking place mere yards away.

It had reached its culmination.

"Enough!" Jordan sounded harassed. "Just write a straightforward pledge, nothing fancy, stating you give Hellebore Hall and the entire estate to me, now, as of this date, that you promise that Jacqueline will marry me, and that you swear I'm not guilty of killing Thomas Entwhistle, Miribelle Tregonning or Millicent Tregonning." Jordan paused. "Just write it!"

No one moved; no one spoke.

Gerrard risked lifting his head.

Just as Jordan lost patience. He swung Jacqueline out over the edge—her feet left the rock and she shrieked. She clutched at Jordan's arm around her waist; he drew her back, but left her teetering on her toes, wholly dependent on his arm to keep her from sliding to her death.

"Now," Jordan snarled, "are you going to start writing?"

Gerrard rose into a crouch. All the men arrayed about the rock facing Jordan saw him. His eyes locked on Jordan, he crawled swiftly forward, until he was on sufficiently level ground to stand.

For one instant, he remained still, gathering every ounce of strength he had left, gauging what he needed to do.

Cyclops's eye was two yards wide, black and gaping. Jordan stood to one side with his back to him; he held Jacqueline balanced precariously over one sloping edge. She, too, was facing the other way. Even as Gerrard watched, there was a roar from beneath, then Cyclops spewed froth and water up and out over the rock, covering Jacqueline's ankles.

The salt water stung his cut feet. Her slippers were soaked—she'd have no purchase at all.

Any second Jordan was going to notice the direction of many of the men's shocked gazes.

Barnaby shifted, mouth opening, but Sir Vincent beat him to it. He tapped Mitchel on the shoulder. "Here—I'll kneel down. Rest the paper on my back and write what he wants."

"Just get on with it." Jordan spoke through clenched teeth.

"The deed first." Barnaby looked at Lord Tregonning. "What's the legal name of the estate?"

Jordan looked at Lord Tregonning, then looked further. His head moved as he scanned the faces.

He started to turn, to glance behind.

Gerrard exploded into a sprint, then launched himself in a flying tackle across the open hole.

Jordan saw him; stunned, he swung to face him—and let Jacqueline go.

She screamed, twisted as she started to slide.

Gerrard slammed into her.

He grabbed her about her waist, yanked her to him and let his momentum carry them on.

Jordan lunged for them, stabbing with the knife—missed.

Gerrard juggled Jacqueline as they fell, cushioning her against him as they landed heavily and skidded across the stone.

They were facing the hole when they landed. Both saw what happened next.

Jordan had assumed Gerrard would come for him. He'd braced, then, realizing his error, lunged forward to strike at them. Too late.

He overbalanced and toppled into the hole.

They saw his face as he went in, eyes wide, incredulous that any such fate would come to him.

His mouth opened in a scream, then he was gone.

The scream abruptly cut off, smothered beneath the cauldron of surging waves in the blowhole chamber.

For an instant, there was no sound beyond the crashing symphony of the sea and the eerily distant call of gulls.

Then exclamations exploded all around. Men rushed onto the rock, clustered around the hole. Someone called for rope, but they were a mile from the house.

Lying on their backs on the rock, catching their breaths, Gerrard and Jacqueline sensed the gathering roar before anyone else. They turned their heads, met each other's eyes, then Gerrard reached for her, wrapped her in his arms, kissed her temple.

She clung, wept, relief and joy, sorrow and loss intermingling.

He held her close, then slowly gathered himself and rose, lifting her with him as the roar built.

And broke.

Water gushed five feet above the hole as all the men leapt away.

"Good God!"

"Dear Lord in Heaven."

Numerous other horrified exclamations fell from shocked lips as everyone stared at the small fountain. At what it contained.

A high-pitched, unearthly scream rang out. Eleanor had fought free; she raced out onto the rock.

She flung herself at the hole.

They caught her, restrained her.

Jacqueline's last sight of her was Eleanor kneeling, keening as seawater stained with her brother's—her lover's—blood spread out on the rock about her.

T he squall hit, raged briefly, then swept on, leaving them and the gardens drenched, cleansed. The majority trudged back up the paths, shaking their heads, shocked but relieved.

Gerrard's feet were so badly cut, he couldn't put on his boots, much less walk back to the house. He sat on the rocks edging the rising bed bordering the path.

Jacqueline crouched before him, examining the damage. "I can't believe you did this."

She repeated the horrified comment three times, increasingly choked, before Sir Vincent, one of the gentlemen discussing Gerrard's predicament over his head, bethought himself of the rowboat in the next cove. Matthew volunteered to hie over and row it around; Gerrard decided he would have to appreciate Matthew and Sir Vincent as they deserved from now on. Richards left to saddle up a steed to carry him up to the house once they reached the cove.

Jacqueline, of course, took charge.

She'd been horrified by the state of his feet; when she saw his hands, when he winced as she turned his right wrist, the one he'd landed on, she was so upset she couldn't speak—not even to upbraid him.

Wise enough—experienced enough—in the ways of women to understand she felt she should, and that that in no way diminished her appreciation of his rescue, Gerrard kept his lips manfully shut and lapped up every ounce of her solicitous care.

By the time the boat arrived and they rowed around to the cove, and he rode slowly back to the house with Jacqueline, Matthew and Richards walking alongside, his feet had healed enough to hobble up the steps, across the porch and onto the blessedly cool tiles of the hall.

There, the ladies were waiting, to exclaim over them, roundly condemn Jordan and Eleanor, comment quietly, with real feeling, over the terrible legacy left to the elder Frithams, and to impart good news.

Millicent had awoken and was entirely herself, in full possession of her wits. In the same way burnt feathers brought some out of a faint, the smoke from the fires had revived her.

Jacqueline firmly cited his injuries as an excuse to cut the ladies' time short; she determinedly bore him upstairs.

At his suggestion, they looked in on Millicent, and found Sir Godfrey sitting beside the bed holding Millicent's hand.

Seeing them, Millicent quickly retrieved it, but her cheeks were pink, indeed, glowing; there seemed no doubt of her return to health.

"I stayed here," Sir Godfrey told them. "There are some things it's better for me not to see, if you take my meaning."

Gerrard did. But as it had transpired, he hadn't laid a finger on Jordan Fritham. Jordan had sowed the seeds of his own destruction, and reaped the bitter harvest.

Leaving Millicent and Sir Godfrey to learn the full story from the crowd milling downstairs, Jacqueline insisted Gerrard let her tend his wounds.

His room was wrecked; she took him to hers.

They didn't return downstairs that evening. Their own company was all they desired. All they needed.

But need they did.

Needed to reassure, to celebrate, to simply live.

To love. To take joy in each other, in what they'd found, to reaffirm all that had grown, so strong and vital, between them.

Jacqueline knew what he'd risked for her—not just his life but his ability to live. He was a painter; painting was his soul, yet he'd climbed Cyclops knowing that one too-deep cut, one slice in the wrong place, could have stopped him from gripping a brush or pencil again.

Her tears fell as she bathed the angry wounds, too choked to give voice to the emotions buffeting her; he leaned close, found her lips and gently kissed her, assured her his fingers still worked, that he could close them around hers.

She raised her head, returned the kiss—simply accepted. There was nothing else she could do.

Gerrard lay back and let her tend his cut hands, his lacerated feet. Let her tend to him as she wished. Let her restore him body and soul, let her lavish devotion, worship and love upon him.

Later, he returned the gift in full measure, let the power rise, take them and bind them forever.

In the depths of the night, he asked, and was granted his reward. For being her champion, for freeing her to live, all he asked for was her life, and she pledged it gladly. Joyously.

What will be will be.

As always, Timms was right.

EPILOGUE

~

April 1832
The Grange, Derbyshire

Summer waned, the year turned, and spring came again. Gerrard sat on the shaded terrace overlooking his gardens, and watched Jacqueline, his wife, stroll amid the flowers. She stopped here and there, admiring this bloom, then that. In his eyes, none could match her beauty.

He wasn't the only one who thought so. Her portrait, shown at his hugely successful winter exhibition, had garnered not just praise, but awe. He'd been credited with setting a new standard for portraiture; while the accolades had been sweet, the secret smiles they'd shared had been his nectar.

The true meaning of the portrait, the reason it had been painted, had been shared with few. There'd been no need, in the end, to make a point of it.

Jordan was dead, Eleanor locked away. Lord and Lady Fritham had disappeared, too shattered to remain in the area that had for so long welcomed them. Months later, Barnaby had traced them to a village outside Hull; they were settling in there. All sincerely pitied them and wished them well; they had known nothing of their offsprings' aspirations, let alone their perversions.

Marcus had emerged from his seclusion to give away both Jacqueline and, a month later, Millicent. Now he knew the truth of the deaths at Hellebore Hall, and all his neighbors did, too, the shadow of darkness, of lingering evil, had lifted from him, and from the house and the gardens, too. That little corner of Cornwall was emerging into sunshine once more.

There'd been considerable discussion over what to do about the Garden of Night. Jacqueline and their children would ultimately inherit the estate; she loved it and most of the gardens, but couldn't bear to go into the Garden of Night. Quite aside from having seen her dead mother and then Millicent there, like him, she'd guessed that Jordan and Eleanor had used the bower for their frequent trysts. Hardly surprising she couldn't stomach the garden as it was, yet it was an integral part of the whole.

Driven to slay every last dragon that plagued her, he'd unearthed the original plans for the gardens in the Hall library. He'd shown them to Wilcox, who'd agreed with his suggestions. Over the winter, the garden had been remodeled and replanted; he'd stuck with the original design, but by changing species, the new garden would be a celebration of love in the brightest and best sense, no longer steeped in the darker shades of passion.

Jacqueline's birthday was in May. She didn't yet know of the work on the garden; they were all planning it as a surprise gift when he and she traveled down to spend a week with her father.

And Millicent; she and Sir Godfrey had taken up residence at the Hall to keep Marcus company. The household was now relaxed, more easygoing and happy than any could have imagined it might be.

Gerrard watched as Jacqueline stooped to sniff a crimson rose. As she straightened, her hand drifted to her belly, to the slight, very slight mound there. Her face was that of a happy madonna, her expression one of wonder, of joyful anticipation.

The exact opposite of the expression he'd painted in the portrait to free her.

He stared, drank in the sight, his hand reaching for his sketch pad and pencil, as ever by his side.

Without taking his eyes from Jacqueline's face, he started to sketch.

Poured all he saw into the lines. Let his eyes see, acknowledge, let his fingers faithfully record.

In the months since they'd wed—by ducal command at Somersham Place during the Cynster summer gathering—the connection between them had developed and evolved, until it was more than tangible, until the link was so solid it would, they both knew, withstand any test on the physical plane.

They both counted themselves blessed.

And he'd finally fully understood what Timms had meant.

Love wasn't a happening one decided on—to indulge or not, to partake or not. To feel or not. When it came, when it struck, the only decision left to make was how to respond—whether you embraced it, took it in, and made it a part of you, or whether you turned your back and let it die.

Love was something humans experienced, not made happen. It wasn't in anyone's control.

Beneath his fingers, his sketch came to life. His next portrait, better, more revealing, than any he'd done before.

He already knew its title, what it would show, what he would paint into it.

The Truth About Love.

1

Early May
Avening Village, Gloucestershire

Apple blossoms in springtime.

Julius—Jack—Warnefleet, Baron Warnefleet of Minchinbury, reined in at the top of the rise above the valley of Avening and looked down on the pink and white clouds surrounding Avening Manor. His first sight of his home in more years than he cared to count couldn't, he felt, have been more apt.

Apple blossoms always reminded him of brides.

Regarding the sea of blossoms with a jaundiced eye, he twitched his reins and set his gray gelding, Challenger, ambling down the long hill.

Everything, it seemed, was conspiring to remind him of his failure—of the fact he hadn't found a bride.

Avening Manor had been without a lady for most of his life. His mother had died when he was six years old; his father had never remarried.

He'd spent the last thirteen years fighting for king and country, almost all of those years behind enemy lines in France. His father's death seven years ago had brought him briefly home, but only for two days, just long enough for the funeral and to formally place the running of Avening into the hands of old Griggs, his father's steward, before he'd had to slip back over the Channel, back to the varied roles he'd played in disrupting French shipping and commercial links, draining the life blood from the French state, weakening it.

Not the sort of battles most people imagined a major in the Guards engaged in.

Along with an elite group of fellow officers, he'd been seconded to work under a secretive individual known as Dalziel, who'd been responsible for all covert English operations on foreign soil. Neither Jack nor any of the six colleagues he'd recently met were sure how many operatives Dalziel had commanded, or how widespread their activities had been. What they did know was that those activities had been legion, and had directly contributed, indeed, been crucial, to the final, ultimate defeat of Napoleon.

But the wars were now over. Along with his colleagues, Jack had retired from the fray and finally turned his mind to picking up the reins of civilian life. The previous October, he and his six colleagues, all gentlemen blessed with title, wealth and the consequent responsibilities, and therefore all sorely in need of wives, had banded together to form the Bastion Club — their haven against the matchmakers of the ton, their castle from which they would sally forth, do battle with society's dragons, and secure the fair maid they required.

That, at least, had been their plan. Matters, however, had not fallen out quite that way.

Tristan Wemyss had stumbled across his bride while overseeing the refurbishment of the house that was now the Bastion Club. Shortly after, Tony Blake had, even more literally, stumbled across his bride along with a dead body. Charles St. Austell, fleeing the capital and his too-helpful female relatives, had found his bride inhabiting his ancestral home. And now Jack was fleeing the capital, too, but not because of female relatives.

The rattle of carriage wheels reached him. Through the screening drifts below, he glimpsed the black roof of a carriage smoothly bowling along the lane from Cherington. The carriage crossed the junction with the Tetbury lane down which Jack was descending, and continued west toward Nailsworth.

Jack idly wondered who the carriage belonged to, but he'd been away so long, he had no idea who might be visiting whom these days.

On returning permanently to England, he'd had to decide which of his responsibilities to attend to first. He was an only child; his father's death had set Avening in his lap with no one else to watch over it, but he knew the estate from the ground up—he'd been born and raised there, in this small green valley on the northwest slope of the Cotswolds. Avening had been in sound hands; he trusted Griggs as his father had. Much more pressing had been the need to come to grips with the varied investments and far-flung properties he'd entirely unexpectedly inherited from his great-aunt Sophia.

His mother had been the daughter of an earl and his father the grandson of a duke; an eccentric spinster, Great-aunt Sophia had been a twig somewhere on his paternal family tree. Her hobby had been amassing wealth; although Jack could only recall meeting her—briefly—twice, on her death two years ago Great-aunt Sophia had willed a sizable portion of her amassed wealth to him.

By the time he'd returned to England, various decisions associated with that inheritance had become urgent. Learning about his new holdings and investments had been imperative. He'd duly suppressed a deep-seated longing to return to Avening, to reassure himself it was all as he remembered—that after all his years away, after all he'd had to do, witness and endure, his home was still there, as he remembered it—and instead had devoted the last six months to coming to grips with his inheritance, welding the whole into one workable estate.

Although his estate now boasted numerous elegant country houses, to him, Avening was still the centerpiece, the place that held his heart.

That was why he was here, slowly ambling down the lane, letting his jaded senses absorb the achingly familiar sights and sounds, letting them soothe his abraded temper, his less than contented mood, and the dull but persistent ache in his head.

Temper and mood were due to his failure to find a suitable bride. He'd accepted he should and had bitten the bullet; while in London organizing his inheritance he'd applied himself to looking over the field. Once the Season had commenced, he'd assumed suitable ladies would be thick on the ground; wasn't that what the marriage mart was all about? Instead, he'd discovered that while sweet and not so sweet young ladies littered the pavements, the parks and the ballrooms, the sort of lady he could imagine marrying had been nowhere to be found.

He would have said he was too old, and too finicky, but he was only thirty-four, prime matrimonial age for a gentleman, and from experience he knew he had no physical preference in women. Short, tall, blond or brunette were all the same to him: it was the fact they were female that counted—soft perfumed skin, feminine curves and, once they were beneath him, those breathy little gasps falling from luscious, parted lips. He should have been easy to please.

Unfortunately, he'd discovered he couldn't bear the company of young ladies for longer than five minutes; he inevitably grew so bored he had difficulty remembering their names. For reasons he didn't comprehend, they had no power whatever to focus, let alone fix his attention. Inevitably, within five minutes of being introduced, he'd be looking for an avenue of escape.

He was good at escaping. Or so he'd thought.

Until he'd met Miss Lydia Cowley and her gorgon of an aunt.

Miss Cowley was the daughter of a wealthy industrialist, her aunt distantly connected to some Midlands peer. Jack had, as usual, found little in Miss Cowley to interest him. He, however, had been of great interest to Miss Cowley and her aunt.

They'd tried to entrap him. His mind elsewhere, he hadn't seen the danger until it was upon him. But the instant he did, his well-honed instincts sprang to life, the same instincts that had kept him alive and undetected through thirteen long years of living with the enemy. They'd thought they'd cornered him alone with Miss Cowley in a first-floor parlor, yet when her aunt swept in, with Lady Carmichael in the role of unwitting witness by her side, the parlor had been empty. Devoid of all life.

Put out, confused, the aunt had retreated, leaving to look elsewhere for her errant niece.

She hadn't looked out on the narrow ledge outside the parlor window, hadn't seen Jack holding Miss Cowley locked against him, her eyes starting above the hand he'd clapped over her lips.

He'd held her there, silent and deadly, precariously balanced two floors above the basement area, until the parlor door closed and the retreating footsteps died, then he'd eased the window open again and swung her inside. And released her.

One wide-eyed look into his face and she couldn't get out of the parlor fast enough. He hadn't tried to hide his understanding of what had happened, or his reaction to that, and her. She'd stumbled through a garbled excuse and fled.

He'd canceled all further social engagements and retreated to the club, there to brood over his situation. But then Dalziel had sent word that Charles had needed assistance down in Cornwall. The information had seemed godsent; he'd finished dealing with his inheritance, and, he'd decided, he was also finished with searching for a wife. With Gervase Tregarth, who had also been staying at the club, he'd ridden away from London, back to a world he understood.

While the action in Cornwall had ultimately ended in success, he'd suffered a crack on the head that had been worse than any he'd received before. Once the villain had been dispatched and Charles back in his own fort, he'd returned to London, head still aching, for Pringle to check him over. An experienced battlefield surgeon the members of the Bastion Club routinely consulted, Pringle had informed him that had his skull not been so thick, he wouldn't have survived the blow. That said, there was nothing seriously amiss, and no damage a few weeks of quiet rest wouldn't repair.

He'd stayed at the club for a few more days, finalizing his business, letting the club's majordomo, Gasthorpe, look after him, then he'd headed down to Cornwall for Charles's wedding.

That had been two days ago. Leaving the wedding breakfast, he'd ridden across Dartmoor to Exeter, then the next day had taken the road to Bristol, where he'd rested last night. Early this morning, he'd set out along the country lanes on the last leg of his journey home.

It had been seven years. Seven years since he'd set eyes on the limestone façade of the manor, and watched the westering sun paint it a honey gold. He knew just where to look to glimpse the manor's gables through the trees lining the lane and the intervening orchards. The scent of apple blossom wreathed about him; for all it meant bride, it also meant home. His heart lifted; his lips lifted, too, as he reached the junction of the Tetbury lane and the Nailsworth-Cherington road.

To his left lay the village proper. He turned Challenger to the right; head rising, he touched his heels to the big horse's flanks and cantered down the road.

He rounded the bend, heart lifting with anticipation.

A phaeton lay overturned by the side of the road.

The horse trapped in the traces, panicked and ungovernable, attempted to rear, paying no attention to the lady clinging to its bridle, trying to calm it.

Jack took in the scene in one glance. Face hardening, he dug his heels in, pushing Challenger into a gallop.

Any second the trapped horse would lash out—at the lady.

She heard the thunder of approaching hooves and glanced fleetingly over her shoulder.

Watching the trapped horse, Jack came out of his saddle at a run. With hip and shoulder, he shoved the lady aside and lunged for the reins—just as the horse lashed out.

"Oh!" The lady flew sideways, landing in the lush grass beyond the ditch.

Jack ducked, but the iron-shod hoof grazed his head—in exactly the same spot he'd been coshed.

He swore, then bit his lip, hard. Blinking against the pain, weaving to avoid being butted, he grabbed the horse's bridle above the bit, exerted enough pressure to let the animal know he was in the hands of someone who knew, and started talking. Crooning, assuring the animal that all danger had passed.

The horse, a young bay gelding, stamped its hooves and shook its head; Jack hung on and kept talking.

Gradually, the horse quieted.

Jack shot a glance at the lady. Riding up, all he'd seen was her back—that she had a wealth of dark mahogany hair worn in an elegantly plaited and coiled chignon, was wearing a plum-colored walking dress, and was uncommonly tall.

On her back on the bank beyond the ditch, she struggled onto her elbows. Across the ditch, their gazes locked.

Her face was classically beautiful.

Her dark gaze was a fulminating glare.

The Cynster Family Tree

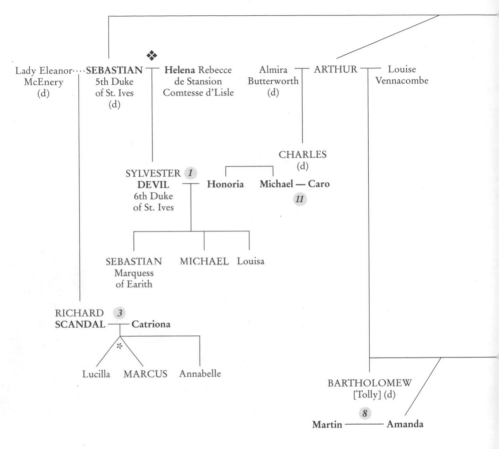

		❖						
Lady Eleanor····	**SEBASTIAN**	┬	**Helena** Rebecce		Almira	┬	ARTHUR ┬	Louise
McEnery	5th Duke		de Stansion		Butterworth			Vennacombe
(d)	of St. Ives		Comtesse d'Lisle		(d)			
	(d)							

CHARLES
(d)

SYLVESTER *1*
DEVIL ┬ Honoria   Michael — Caro
6th Duke   *11*
of St. Ives

SEBASTIAN   MICHAEL   Louisa
Marquess
of Earith

RICHARD *3*
SCANDAL ┬ **Catriona**

✻

Lucilla   MARCUS   Annabelle

BARTHOLOMEW
[Tolly] (d)

8

Martin ———— Amanda

THE CYNSTER NOVELS

1. *Devil's Bride*   *4.* *A Rogue's Proposal*   *7.* *All About Passion*
2. *A Rake's Vow*   *5.* *A Secret Love*   *8.* *On a Wild Night*
3. *Scandal's Bride*   *6.* *All About Love*   *9.* *On a Wicked Dawn*

❖ *Special—The Promise in a Kiss*